A Novel

THE GOLDEN CROSS

ANGELA ELWELL HUNT

WATERBROOK
PRESS

THE GOLDEN CROSS
PUBLISHED BY WATERBROOK PRESS
12265 Oracle Boulevard, Suite 200
Colorado Springs, Colorado 80921

The characters and events in this book are fictional, and any resemblance to actual persons or events is coincidental.

ISBN 978-0-307-45877-3
ISBN 978-0-307-45937-4 (electronic)

Published in the United States by WaterBrook Multnomah, an imprint of the Crown Publishing Group, a division of Random House Inc., New York.

WATERBROOK and its deer colophon are registered trademarks of Random House Inc.

Printed in the United States of America
2010

10 9 8 7 6 5 4 3 2

We shall not cease from exploration
And the end of all our exploring
Will be to arrive where we started
And know the place for the first time.

T. S. Eliot, *Little Gidding*

The Heirs of Cahira O'Connor

Contents

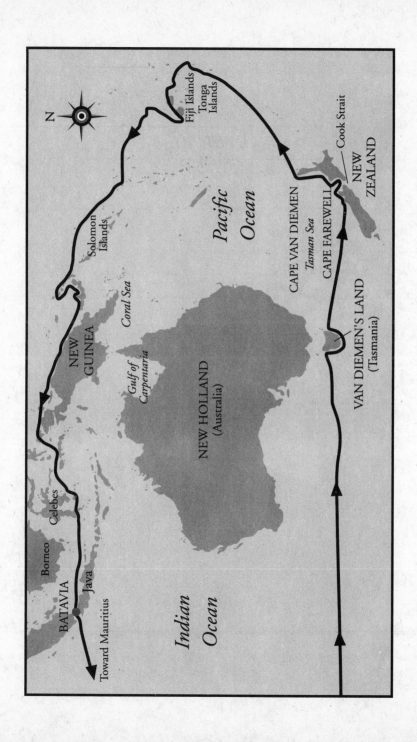

The
Heirs of Cahira O'Connor

Book 2

Prologue

The phone rang again, the fourth time. I skidded on the slippery tile as I rounded the corner, then nearly tripped over my mastiff, Barkly, who was cooling his two-hundred-pound carcass on the kitchen floor. Reaching over Barkly for the phone, I accidentally tipped over the chipped mug that held a collection of kitchen implements. Amid a clattering of spatulas and wooden spoons, I jerked up the receiver. "Hello?"

"Miss O'Connor?"

Grimacing, I lunged over Barkly and bent to pick up a wooden spoon before he decided to chew it. Only telephone solicitors call me "Miss O'Connor." I'd just destroyed my kitchen and nearly broken my neck for the chance to subscribe to *Southern Fly-Fishing* or prepay my funeral at cut-rate prices.

"Yes?" I frowned into the phone. "Listen, I'm really very busy—"

"I won't take much of your time, Miss O'Connor." The man sounded slightly apologetic. "But I've just finished reading your work, and I must say it surpasses anything I ever expected."

My breath caught in my throat as I finally identified the voice. "Professor Howard? You read *The Silver Sword?*"

"But of course, my dear." I could hear a smile in his voice. "And I was most impressed by your scholarship and attention to detail. Your work seemed very precise, quite well-documented."

1

I clutched the telephone cord and leaned back against the counter, momentarily forgetting about Barkly, about the book I'd been reading, about everything. Professor Henry Howard liked my work! What had begun last semester as a silly little research paper on piebaldism—the condition that had produced a distinctive streak of white hair above my left ear—had grown into a major undertaking.

"Thank you, sir," I stammered.

"I had no idea other such women had descended from Cahira O'Connor," he went on. "How on earth did you find them?"

"I just typed the words 'O'Connor' and 'piebaldism' into an Internet search engine," I muttered, stating the obvious. "And there they were, all four—Cahira, Anika, Aidan, and Flanna. Suddenly Cahira's deathbed prayer made sense. She had begged heaven that her descendants might break out of their courses and restore right in a murderous world of men."

"Incredible," he murmured. "I was very impressed. If you had been my student, I would have given you the highest possible mark. The manuscript read more like a novel than a research project."

"Well." Completely at a loss for words, I shifted my weight and leaned against the counter. "Thanks very much, Professor. Praise from you is high praise. I appreciate it."

Silence rolled over the phone line, and I could almost see the professor lifting his brow, tapping his pen on the desk, carefully choosing his words. "You mentioned in your cover letter that you plan to continue your research," he finally continued. "Might we meet for lunch one day this month to discuss what else you've discovered? I'm curious to understand how the past might affect your future."

"I don't know that it will," I countered. Ever since we met, I had been bothered by the professor's vision of me as some sort of twenty-first century Joan of Arc. "I know you think I'm one of Cahira's descendants, but I have nothing in common with either Anika of Prague or Aidan O'Connor."

The professor politely ignored my protests. "You also mentioned my assistant, Taylor Morgan." A teasing note had entered his voice. "He has read your work as well and would be happy to join us for lunch."

A blush burned my cheeks at the mention of Taylor Morgan, and I was glad the professor couldn't see me at that moment. Flush with the joy of completing a gigantic task, I'd been feeling a little bold when I wrote the cover letter and sent it with the manuscript of *The Silver Sword*. I had hinted—rather strongly—that Mr. Taylor Morgan was exactly my type. My type of research assistant, that is.

"Um, sure," I answered, wrapping the phone cord around my wrist. "I'm working part-time at the Tattered Leaves bookstore down on Sixth Street this summer. There's a little coffee shop next door."

"I know the place. Shall we say Friday, at one? I'd like to avoid the crowds if at all possible. And Mr. Morgan teaches until twelve-thirty."

"Friday." I felt a foolish grin spread over my face. "Fine. And in case you've forgotten what I look like, I'll be the redhead—"

"Miss O'Connor," he said, his voice crisp, "I could never forget what you look like. Your red hair led me to you in the first place."

They were waiting for me when I raced through the coffee shop doorway at five minutes after one. The professor rose and pulled out a chair for me, and Taylor Morgan stood, too, his blue eyes smiling at me from behind a pair of chic wire-rimmed glasses. He was wearing a cotton shirt and khakis, looking completely cool and elegant even in the city heat, and as I slid into my chair my mind stuttered and went blank. The sight of Taylor Morgan at close range could do that to any woman, I suspected, but he wasn't about to be impressed by my scholarship if I sat there and stammered like a starstruck schoolgirl.

So I looked at the professor instead. He was middle-aged,

soft, and infinitely respectable, and nothing about him gave me the tingles—except the fact that he liked my work.

We exchanged polite hellos; then the professor asked again how I'd found the other descendants of Cahira O'Connor. "The Internet search engine I used picked up four references to 'O'Connor' and 'piebaldism.'" I scanned the menu, decided on my usual tuna sandwich, and dropped the menu back on the table. "Each woman followed her predecessor by two hundred years, give or take a few. Cahira lived in the thirteenth century, Anika in the fifteenth, Aidan in the seventeenth, and Flanna in the nineteenth. All of them bore the O'Connor name, and all had red hair with a white streak above the left temple."

The professor's gaze darted toward the streak of white that marked my own hair. I sipped from my water glass, waiting for some kind of response.

"Do you plan to investigate these other women?" Taylor asked, his voice golden and as warm as the sun outside. "Will that work fit into your current studies?"

"I've already finished most of my research on Aidan O'Connor," I answered with a shrug. "I'm an English major, so I'll find a way to use everything I've learned. Or maybe I can talk to my adviser about setting up some sort of independent study."

"It would be a shame to let such scholarship and hard work go unrewarded." Taylor captured my gaze with his. "And I am eager to hear about the other women."

"What I want to know, Miss O'Connor—" The professor lowered his menu, then folded his arms on the table. "—is what you intend to do about your own involvement in the lineage. You are an O'Connor, and you have the same physical characteristic that marked the others."

"I have to admit that I've wondered about that." Uneasiness crept into my mood like a wisp of smoke. "I think I am supposed to be the chronicler, nothing more. If God did answer Cahira's prayer and her descendants are linked to me, then I am the only

one with the resources to tell their stories. I have access to the Internet, I have a computer—such technology was completely unimaginable until this century. So I'm the one entrusted with telling the stories, with weaving the threads of history together."

"For your sake, I hope you're right." Professor Howard's hazel eyes clouded in an expression of concern. "Because if you're not— well, I'd hate to think that armed conflict lies around the corner of the millennium. Didn't all of Cahira's descendants fight in a war or—"

I held up my hand, cutting him off. "That's not quite right, Professor. Cahira didn't say that her descendants would fight in wars, only that they would fight for right. Aidan O'Connor, for instance, didn't go to war. In 1642 she was living in Batavia, a Dutch colony on the island of Java in Indonesia, and the islands were at peace."

"How in the world did the descendant of an Irish princess end up in Indonesia?" Taylor's blue eyes flashed with curiosity.

I took a deep breath as my gaze moved into his. At that moment Mel Gibson could have walked into the coffee shop and I wouldn't have even glanced his way. "It's a long story. If you have to rush off to another appointment, I probably shouldn't even begin it."

Taylor leaned forward on the table and clasped his hands. "I cleared my calendar for you," he said, his voice low and smooth.

I vaguely heard Professor Howard say something about having a three o'clock dentist appointment, but his words barely registered. If Taylor Morgan was willing to sit and listen, I'd talk all day and into the night if he wanted me to. Such a sacrifice. Still, the man wanted to know...

"Okay." I smiled at him. "But first I'd like a Coke and a tuna sandwich. Let's order."

Taylor lifted his hand to signal the waitress, and I pulled my notebook from my purse. While he and the professor ordered sandwiches and soft drinks, I studied my outline.

"Okay, Miss O'Connor," Taylor said as the waitress moved away. "We're ready. Tell us how an O'Connor descendant ended up in the middle of the Pacific."

"Aidan O'Connor wasn't born in Indonesia," I answered, setting my notebook on the table. "Her parents, Cory and Lili O'Connor, were as Irish as shamrocks, but they were living in England when Aidan was born. In 1632, when Aidan turned fourteen, her parents risked everything to escape the plague that killed over twelve thousand Londoners that summer."

"The O'Connors emigrated?" Professor Howard asked.

I nodded. "Yes, to Batavia, capital of the Dutch colony in the Spice Islands. Many Englishmen fled London for the Caribbean, New England, and Virginia, but Aidan's father longed for something different."

"Wise move on his part." Taylor shifted in his chair.

"Not really," I answered, lifting my brow. "He died on the voyage. Upon their arrival in Batavia, Aidan and Lili found themselves with no patron, no resources, and no social welfare system in a colony that prided itself on industry and social order. Lili had to turn to the world's oldest profession just to survive."

"Prostitution?" The professor's face twisted in dismay.

"She guarded her daughter," I said. "But Lili became what the Dutch called a procuress—she procured whatever, ah, *entertainment* a visiting sailor might need in the port city."

"Wait a minute." Taylor held up his hand as the waitress placed a sweating soft drink in front of him. "You just said the Dutch were known for industry and social order. I can't imagine their tolerating such a practice."

"Batavia was like most other large cities: two very different worlds existed within it." I took my drink and nodded to the waitress. "There was the civilized world where respectable folk lived and worked, and a darker world they largely ignored. Oh, every once in a while they'd send the sheriff's constabulary to round up the beggars, cutpurses, and drunks, but for the most

part they enjoyed pretending that the notorious flophouses, musicos, and taverns did not exist."

"So our Aidan lived in the underworld?" Professor Howard frowned in concern.

"Yes, and she might have remained there unnoticed," I answered, "but everything changed one afternoon when Schuyler Van Dyck and his family went for a carriage ride along the waterfront."

Aidan O'Connor

*They are ill discoverers that think
there is no land when they see nothing but sea.*

Francis Bacon, *The Advancement of Learning*

One

July 22, 1642

Aidan O'Connor lifted her eyes to the green mountains in the distance and wished for a moment that she could lose herself in their velvet shadows. Surely she could find a cool breath beneath the gigantic trees that soared above the ridges. She knew the natives had built their thatched houses beneath the towering trees, secure in the cathedral-like stillness and shade.

But she was a child of Europe and therefore relegated to the "civilized" sections of Batavia—the squalid, crowded area near the wharf in general, and one crowded corner near the intersection of Market and Broad Streets in particular. Here the air smelled of ale and open sewers, occasionally punctuated by a particularly strong whiff of a prostitute's perfume. Crowds of sailors and merchants clogged the alleys; wagons and horses jammed the cobbled streets. Drunken seamen draped their arms about each other's necks and sang sea chanteys; women squealed in pretended protest as whiskey-logged lips pressed against theirs even in the revealing light of day.

Aidan glanced down the sloping length of Broad Street to the place where the cobbled road spilled into the bay. A tall, three-masted ship was sailing into the harbor, her sails fluttering as the eager seamen gathered them in. Soon the ship's crew would come ashore, thirsty, hungry, and eager to experience all they'd been denied in the strict discipline aboard ship.

Sinking to a stone bench outside the tavern, Aidan pressed the damp fabric of her bodice to her chest, wiping away the pearls of sweat that dotted her skin. Bram or Lili would come looking for her in a moment, demanding to know why she'd run out again. They didn't mind the noise, scents, and ribald atmosphere of the tavern, but Aidan did—terribly.

One of these days she would be done with the stale odors of frying oil, shag tobacco, and unwashed beer mugs. She'd get up and walk out forever. She wouldn't be welcome in the civilized part of Batavia, but she could stroll out to one of the native villages. And while the Javanese stared at her in wonder, she'd kneel in front of one of their sacred Banyan trees, close her eyes, and lift her hand in a solemn vow never to return to the tavern again.

God won't like it, some inner voice warned. The Almighty didn't approve of his children kneeling to pagan totems. But the God she had loved as a child had done nothing for her in recent years except take her father and blight her hopes. Perhaps he wouldn't even care if she ran away.

She lifted her skirt for an instant, tempted to forsake all modesty in exchange for the touch of fresh air upon her bare legs. But no lady exposed her feet in public, not even the brassy barmaids of the Broad Street Tavern.

A handsome coach-and-four pulled out of the traffic on Market Street and turned onto Broad, the horses' hooves clacking merrily upon the cobblestones as the coach moved toward her. Aidan paused, spellbound by the unusual sight. These were people of quality, that much was obvious from the uniformed driver who held the reins. So what were they doing on Broad Street?

The coach gleamed bright in the morning sun, and through the open windows Aidan could see three men and a young woman. The woman wore the contented, slightly superior look of a wealthy lady. Her gaze caught Aidan's as the carriage passed, and the superior look intensified as a small, smug smile quirked the corners of her mouth.

"Aidan—Lili's calling for you."

Orabel's familiar voice cut into Aidan's thoughts, and she looked toward her friend. "I'll be in soon, Orabel. Tell Lili I need a moment alone."

"You're an odd one, Aidan." Orabel sank to Aidan's side on the stone bench, then leaned forward to stare at the departing coach. "My goodness, did you see that woman's gown? Yellow satin! So pretty! I've always wanted a yellow dress. It's such a happy color, don't you think? The color of the sun, of morning, of flowers—"

"She didn't look like a happy woman," Aidan answered. Her gaze drifted down the road again. The carriage had moved away; only the bright brim of the woman's feathered hat was still visible. "I think red would be a better color for that one. Or maybe purple. She seemed a little high and mighty."

"Of course she did," Orabel answered, straightening. "Don't you know whose carriage that is?"

Aidan shook her head. "I can't say that I care."

"You should!" Orabel lifted her hand in a regal gesture and pointed toward the departing coach. "The gentleman who just passed was Schuyler Van Dyck, the cartographer. He's quite famous, you know, for his maps. The seamen all talk about him. They say he's employed by the Dutch East India Company."

"Who isn't?" Aidan looked at her hands, idly musing that all of Batavia might be said to be in the employ of the Verenigde Oost Indische Compagnie, more commonly referred to as the V.O.C. Even she and Orabel spent their lives serving whiskey and ale to seamen who sailed on the company's ships. Without the V.O.C. there would be no Batavia, no spice industry, no reason for the natives to resent the Europeans who had flooded this lovely island and defiled a natural paradise.

"He's an *artist*." Orabel emphasized the word. "Like you, Aidan. You ought to stop him one day and offer to draw for him."

"Of course." A cynical smile tugged at Aidan's lips. "And he will be so astounded at my talent he will be forced to take me

under his wing and teach me all he knows. He'll write the crowned heads of Europe to alert them to his grand discovery. And then I shall be famous! King Charles of England, or perhaps Louis of France, will invite me to become artist-in-residence at one of their grand palaces. And then I will send for you, dear Orabel, and together we shall sit in a gilded room and eat four meals a day, all the sweet cakes and pudding we like. We'll have clean slippers for our feet and all the yellow dresses we could ever wish for, of silk brighter than the sun!"

"You don't have to make fun of me." Orabel glared at her with burning, reproachful eyes. "I only thought you should meet him. You are a very good artist, Aidan. I only wanted to make you feel better."

"What is there to feel better about?" Aidan clasped her hands together and stared at them. "I'll never be an artist, Orabel, any more than you will be the governor's wife."

"I might be the governor's wife." Orabel spoke lightly, but pain flickered in her eyes and her voice trembled as she continued. "You never know what could happen in a day, Aidan. Things have to get better than this. If I thought this was the best we'll ever know—well, I couldn't bear it."

Stricken with sudden guilt, Aidan slipped an arm around Orabel's slender shoulders. "Of course things will be better. You're going to meet someone one day. Some nice man in the tavern will take a fancy to you and ask you to marry him."

"Just like Lili says," Orabel murmured, her hands rising to her cheeks.

"Just like Lili says," Aidan answered, stroking her friend's pale blond hair. Orabel was young, probably no older than sixteen, and more fragile than most of the others. Hope was all she had, and Aidan had been thoughtless to disparage her dreams.

"You see?" Orabel pulled away and looked at Aidan with suddenly bright eyes. "If I can find a husband, you can be an artist, just like you've always wanted to be. You could find this Heer Van

Dyck and draw a picture for him." A coaxing tone crept into her voice. "He will like it, I know he will."

Aidan opened her mouth to respond, then cringed as Lili's sharp voice cut through the muddled sounds of the morning. "Annie! Sweet Kate!" she called, using the girls' working nicknames. "What are you doing out here when there's work to be done inside?"

"Coming, Lili," Orabel sighed. She caught Aidan's eye and grinned as she stood up. "If we're going to catch rich husbands, I guess we'd better go back inside where the men are."

"I'm right behind you." Aidan stood to follow Orabel, then paused for a moment. She was no more likely to arouse Schuyler Van Dyck's interest than Orabel was to catch a decent husband in the tavern. But if Orabel wouldn't give up, why couldn't Aidan at least try to meet Heer Van Dyck?

The thought was so absurd that she laughed aloud.

❧

Struggling to conceal her anger, Lili swallowed hard as Orabel and Aidan sashayed back into the tavern and moved toward the bar. Bram thrust a tray of pewter mugs toward each of them and gestured at a group of rowdy seamen who sat in the far corner.

Lili pressed her hands against her apron and bit her lip, glad that this time, at least, the girls were of a mind to obey. Orabel had never been much trouble—the girl had a pliant spirit and a gentle one, as easily bendable as a young twig. But Aidan was twenty, well past youth, and as stubborn as a stuck door. She was more than old enough to be married, but she turned her pert little nose up at every lad Lili pushed her way.

"Honey, can I come see you later?" A slobbering sailor leered up at Lili and reached out to tug on her sleeve.

"Not today, laddie," Lili answered, smiling without humor. "I've got me hands full here, can't you see? But perhaps I can get one of the other lasses to bring you a drink. No sense in dyin' of thirst in a strange port, is there?"

The sodden fool nodded his head, blindly agreeing, and Lili gave him her brightest smile. "What's your pleasure, sir? Would you like to drink with the blond, or perhaps the redhead?"

His red-rimmed gaze cast about the room, and a smile ruffled his mouth as he focused on Aidan's flaming hair. "Faith, she'd do," he answered, his head wavering as he tried to follow her slender form moving through the room. "She'd do for later, too, if you can get her for me."

"Och, no sir!" Lili shivered in pretended horror. "Sure, don't I know she's a fair lass, but I wouldn't wish her on me own worst enemy. She's cursed, that one, and bad luck to any man who as much as touches her."

"Truly?" The sailor's eyes bulged in fear, and Lili felt a small fierce surge of satisfaction.

"Truly." She leaned forward, placing a hand upon the sailor's arm. "See that white streak of hair over her left ear?" She waited until the breathless sailor nodded, then went on in a broken whisper: "That's the sign. The white springs from her heart, only a few inches below her ear, don't you see? Any man who touches her will feel the white-cold hand of death upon him before morning dawns unless he's been properly married to her first."

"Blimey!" The sailor's voice faded into fearful silence.

Lili straightened. "I'll have her bring you a drink, sir, and you'll enjoy her company. But mind that you heed me warning. A terrible fate awaits the man who is overly familiar with our Irish Annie."

Leaving the man to ponder the dangers that awaited a roving hand, Lili snapped her fingers in Aidan's direction. The coppery head turned, and Aidan's eyes held Lili's for a moment before Lili gestured toward the man seated next to her.

A swift shadow of annoyance flitted across Aidan's face, then she resolutely tucked her empty tray under her arm and painted on a wide smile. "Come talk to this one, Annie, me girl." Lili forced a light note into her voice as her daughter approached. "Just in port from Ireland, he is. 'Twill do you good to hear a

bit of the brogue. Bring him a fresh pint, lass, and let the man talk."

Lili moved away, feeling the pressure of Aidan's hot eyes upon her. Aidan hated talking to the men, hated serving them, hated smiling and pretending to be interested in their ships and their mothers and their dreams of God, gold, and glory. But it was a decent life, the best a penniless girl could hope for, and Lili was grateful that she'd been able to offer it to her daughter—whether or not her daughter appreciated it.

Lili pushed past a pair of arguing men and another barmaid, then leaned against the wall, inhaling deeply of air that had been breathed far too many times. Shifting her weight, she folded her arms across her chest and lowered her head for a rare moment of silence.

"Well, Cory, 'tis not what you had in mind when you took us from England." She lifted her eyes long enough to see Aidan smother a yawn as she struggled to pay attention to the petrified sailor. "But I've kept her pure and reasonably virtuous. She'll make somebody a good wife, you mark me words."

Even now, after all these years, her eyes misted as she turned her thoughts toward the husband who lay somewhere at the bottom of the sea. "If you've an audience with the Almighty, put in a word for me and the girl, will you, laddie? We could use a bit of help now and again. Aidan's getting older, too old by many standards, and if I don't get her married soon, she'll spend all her days here at the tavern, just like me."

Lili paused to dash a tear from the corner of her eye. "Not that I mind, Cory, me love. But you left us with nothing. Bram offered this wee bit of help, and he's kept us out of the workhouse…most times." Her eyes focused on Aidan's gleaming red hair. "I've been left with nothing, Cory, and I wouldn't wish me lot upon another soul. So, if you'll beg the Almighty to overlook me sins, I won't hold your departing this life against you."

"Lili!"

Bram's roar shattered her momentary serenity. Lili pulled herself off the wall and began threading her way through the milling crowd. She was as much in control of her life and destiny, she supposed, as any woman had a right to be.

Two

Carrying a gunnysack containing all his earthly possessions—an extra change of clothes, a knife, a few packages of herbs, and that universal symbol of a physician, the urine flask—Sterling Thorne dropped heavily into the barge that would row him to the docks. Witt Dekker, first mate aboard the *Gloria Elizabeth*, followed, nearly upsetting the skittish craft with his massive weight. His yappy terrier, a brown mongrel the Dutchman loved with an unseemly passion, sprang from the deck into his master's arms.

Sterling moved silently toward the side of the boat, unwilling to risk an encounter with either the surly Dutchman or his dog. Dekker had been a hard taskmaster on the voyage, trying the patience of the predominantly English crew with his constant boasting about Dutch intelligence, foresight, and might. Well, now they were in Batavia, a Dutch colony, and Sterling intended to see for himself what the commercially minded Dutch had accomplished in this part of the globe.

Dekker settled on the bench with a self-satisfied sigh, drew the barking terrier into his lap, then nodded toward the oarsman. The barge set off, pulling through green water that sparkled in the afternoon sun. Around them, small barks and sculls paddled like curious ducks, skittering in and out among the larger ships at anchor in the harbor.

"So this is Batavia," Sterling remarked, clasping his hands as his eyes roamed over the horizon. Beyond the docks, a line of brown rooftops stood like a wall; behind the rooftops, majestic

green mountains rose like ancient warriors, determined to safe-guard the heart of the island against the encroaching Europeans.

"*Ja*, it is," Dekker answered, his broad hands holding the dog firmly in the boat. His deep voice rasped with excitement. "And what a time we shall have tonight, my friend. If you want to know where to find a drink, a bed, or a woman, you ask me, *ja?*"

"Thank you, Dekker." Sterling narrowed his eyes as he stud-ied the settlement that slowly came into view. "But I only want to find the home of my friend Dr. Lang Carstens. I hope to join him in his medical practice."

"Why would you want to stay on land when you've had a sweet taste of the sea?" Dekker asked, slapping Sterling on the back with more friendliness than he had shown in their entire journey. "Why not remain a ship's surgeon? The V.O.C. sends out a convoy or expedition nearly every month. And if you have a question about a particular captain's reputation, you come find me." One corner of his broad mouth twisted upward in a half-smile. "I know all the sea captains, and they all know me. And I can usually be found at the Broad Street Tavern, or thereabouts. That's a friendly place, and they don't mind if I bring Snuggerheid with me." He scratched the animal under its scruffy chin and chuckled.

"I'll keep that in mind," Sterling answered absently. He glanced for a moment at the obnoxious dog. Dekker had told Sterling—and anyone else who would listen—that he'd named the animal with the Dutch word for *intelligence* because his father had always insisted Dekker was as dull as a clod. The Dutchman obvi-ously hadn't known his son very well, for Witt Dekker was cun-ning, able to manipulate men in a ruthless manner that often sent a shiver down Sterling's spine.

Sterling leaned forward as the barge pulled up to the docks. A loader tossed down a rope and he caught it, tying the hawser with ease. Without lingering to say farewell to Dekker or the oarsmen, he leaped onto the dock and hurried to lose himself in the crowd.

He'd had enough of seamen. He yearned for the quiet atmosphere of a home, someplace where he could sit and converse with an intelligent man about something other than sailors' superstitions and seamen's complaints. He'd seen enough contusions, rope burns, and bleeding gums to last a lifetime. Though he didn't expect to find better conditions in this Dutch outpost, at least he'd be able to attend his patients in a room that didn't roll with every swell of the sea.

The long wharf curved nearly a half-mile around the edge of the harbor, with smaller docks protruding from it like stumpy teeth from an ill-tended mouth. Three-masted frigates and brigantines, schooners, and small sloops rode at anchor along the wharf, a full range of the ships that provisioned Batavia, a colony only twenty-three years old.

Sterling felt a shiver of anticipation ripple through him at the thought of working in a place not far removed from its frontier days. For this kind of experience he had left England and its traditional thinking. After spending seven years obtaining his Master of Arts at Oxford, he had acquired his M.D. degree at Montpellier, then had returned to London to be examined by the College of Physicians. Now, duly licensed and recommended by a letter from none other than King Charles's personal physician, he was eager to practice in a place where he would treat more than ague and the sweating sickness so common in England.

Sterling absently patted the parchment tucked between his shirt and his skin. The letter was from Dr. Beaton Norwell, Lang Carstens's English cousin and Sterling's friend. Beaton had never met his renowned Dutch cousin, but he was a good enough sport to give Sterling an excuse to leave the country. The renowned Dr. Carstens was bound to be advancing in age, Beaton told Sterling, and might be eager to acquire a younger partner to assist in his medical practice. "In any case, he is a gentleman," Beaton had assured him as he handed over the letter of recommendation. "Good manners, at least, will prevent him from tossing you out on the street without at least a meal and the offer of a night's hospitality."

The two men shook hands before Sterling departed, and even then his blood had run thick with guilt. He had told his weeping mother that he wanted to leave England to investigate prospects of opportunity for his brothers in Batavia, but everyone in the village knew better. The real catalyst for Sterling's abrupt departure was Ernestina Martin, a simpering country beauty who'd rather faint than fight. She had set her cap for Sterling long before he became a doctor, long before the crops failed and Sterling's father had to sell off most of the family acreage. Not even the threat of poverty could dissuade her from pursuing Sterling. Since his return from London she'd taken to sitting in his mother's kitchen, her eyes and ears attuned to anything that had to do with the Thorne's eldest son.

His mother wanted Sterling to marry her; his father had approved the match even before he died. But though Sterling could find no fault in Ernestina's beauty or her background, he did not think he would be able to abide her whining little sighs, her affected expressions, or her distracted feminine helplessness. How could a man lay down his burdens to sleep at night, knowing he would be driven batty all over again with the next sunrise?

As the eldest son, it should have been Sterling's place to inherit and maintain what little remained of the estate, but he had never felt called to be a farmer. And so, to escape Ernestina's earnest promise of a position in her father's house, he'd gathered a few belongings, cozened a letter of recommendation from Beaton, and signed as a surgeon on the first ship sailing from London to the Spice Islands. In the new colony he hoped to make a place for himself and one of his brothers—whoever did not end up marrying the simple-minded Ernestina. Neither Mayfield nor Newland would mind marrying the pretty girl, and Sterling would be happy to let them have the family estate as a wedding gift. But the other brother would have to find his own way in the world. Feeling responsible, Sterling wanted to do all he could to help.

Now he repressed a smile at the sound of his boots clumping

loudly over the docks. He walked stumpily, like a man unused to the solid feel of land beneath his feet. It had taken him three days to acquire "sea legs," and now it seemed as though it would take some time to acquire "land legs" as well.

The dock ended at a broad street jammed with carriages, horses, donkeys, and carts. He crinkled his nose at the sudden onslaught of scents, far different from those of the sea. The smell of grease and cooking meat drifted from an open window; the sharp stench of sweat and horse dung hovered above the street. He had heard the Dutch were famous for fastidious cleanliness, but there was no evidence of that quality here at the wharf.

Slinging his bag across his shoulder, Sterling stepped off the dock and into the sweaty, shoving mob, eager to find his place in the thriving colony of Batavia.

"Sterling Thorne?" Lang Carstens crinkled his nose as if he had caught a whiff of rotten potatoes. He was a plump little man with a curly gray beard that surrounded his face like a storm cloud, and from the bleariness of the old man's eyes, Sterling deduced that his visit had interrupted the doctor's afternoon nap. The housekeeper had led Sterling to the doctor's study, and after the space of several minutes, the elderly doctor had finally appeared in the doorway and tottered to his desk, his eyes intent upon the letter Sterling had delivered to the housekeeper.

"At your service, sir." Sterling bowed respectfully, then pointed to the crinkled parchment in the doctor's hands. "I believe the letter will explain all. Dr. Beaton Norwell, one of King Charles's personal physicians, is your cousin and my friend. Since I am rather in need of a position to practice the medical arts, Dr. Norwell thought you might be willing to take on an associate."

"An associate?" The doctor's frown deepened as he looked up.

"An assistant then." Sterling spread his hands and tried to smile. "At the risk of seeming immodest, I can assure you, sir, that I am quite capable. I served as ship's surgeon on the voyage from

England, and—" He managed a weak laugh. "—we didn't lose a single man."

"A ship's surgeon? Bah! Anyone could fill that post. Most ships just carry a carpenter on board; he can cut off a cracked leg as well as anyone."

Sterling folded his arms and took a deep breath. "I wouldn't think it advisable to cut off any man's leg, Dr. Carstens," he said, nodding formally, "but all the same, I was glad to fill that post and I believe I did my best. The captain of the *Gloria Elizabeth* will vouch for my skill with herbs and healing, if you would like to inquire further."

"I have no need of an assistant." The line of the doctor's mouth tightened a fraction more as he thumped his desk for emphasis, then waved the parchment in his hand. "But never let any man say I turned away another in need. You may stay with me a day or two, Sterling Thorne, but know this—I need no help from you or anyone else. I am as fit for service as I was when I arrived in Batavia."

Sterling shook his head slightly and gestured to the window behind the doctor. "The town I walked through was a busy place, Dr. Carstens," he said, smiling. "Surely there are more people who need a doctor than there are physicians to tend them. Why, the native population on this island alone must require a great deal of your time, and I saw a great many beggars and lame at the wharf."

"I don't tend savages or riffraff." The doctor dropped Sterling's letter to his desk. "If you wish to spend your time among that sort, that's your affair. My nature does not induce me to mingle with harlots and shysters." He looked across the desk with an expression of complete indifference. "I shall have my housekeeper show you to your room, then I suggest you look for a place of your own."

"I will." Sterling struggled to maintain an even, conciliatory tone. "And I am certain I will find patients enough no matter where I look. This is certainly a large enough place to support two doctors."

Carstens's lined lips puckered in annoyance. "The decent folk already have a physician, Dr. Thorne. As to the others—well, Batavia is not like Europe. For one thing, the warm climate makes common people take leave of their senses. Tempers are short, and morality is in small supply, particularly among the idlers and beggars. You should stay away from the docks and the wharf; the people who live there practice immorality that is not tolerated among decent and respectable people. If you fancy yourself a gentleman, you might as well take yourself back to a more gentle country."

"I don't fancy myself much of anything," Sterling answered, irritated by the doctor's mocking tone. "But I am a good physician, and I believe God himself commands us to look after those who are weak."

He retrieved his letter from the desk, glanced pointedly at the empty chair he had not been asked to take, then pressed his hat to his chest. "If your housekeeper could show me to a basin, I'll wash up and take myself to the streets. I would like to be as little trouble as possible, and am reasonably certain that a willing man of my skills can find a suitable position without too much trouble."

"But not among the respectable folk of Batavia," the doctor snapped, wagging a finger in Sterling's direction. "I'm their physician, and I intend to remain so until the Almighty himself prevents me."

"Then I give you good day," Sterling said with another bow. "Until the Almighty prevents you, sir, I suppose I'll have to look after folk who aren't respectable."

He spun on his heel and moved through the doorway before the old man could protest further.

Three

Moving through gauzy veils of evening, Aidan danced upon the beach in her bare feet. Her partner, a stranger whose face remained shadowed by a cloud shrouding the moon, moved with her, his graceful steps matching her own. A starry sky swirled above her, the diamond pinpoints of light reflected in the bright satin of her dress. The glorious burgundy gown moved like a whisper in the darkness, its shimmering softness a delight to her senses. The wet sand was firm beneath her feet, the steady crash and roar of the sea a wonderful accompaniment to the song of the stars.

Her companion smiled in appreciation of her beauty, his teeth gleaming through the mask of shadow, and Aidan's heart surged upward as her hands gripped his.

This is but a dream, but it is yours to enjoy.

Sonorous music reverberated from some celestial place, filling the night with warmth and emotion and feeling. Aidan danced without thinking, feeling the music, the warmth of the sea breeze, the pleasure of her companion. This was no sailor who'd spent too much time in his cups; this was a man who admired her, who appreciated her, who thought her special and worth seeking. She knew without asking that he had not come from the tavern; she must have found him as her heart wended its way to the sea.

A sudden flash of light seared the back of her eyelids, dispelling the ocean, the man, and the music in one bright slash.

"Ow!" she yowled crossly, bringing her arm over her eyes as she squirmed on her pallet. "Shut the door!"

"Get up, Aidan, the merchants are already stirring. Orabel, comb your hair and wash your face. Is that mud on your hands?"

Lili's voice. Always Lili's. She was a mother hen to all of them, though Aidan was the only one to have been carried in that expansive womb.

Aidan lifted one eyelid enough to see her mother's stalwart form moving through the small chamber that served as home to Lili and six other women. In exchange for one meal a day and a roof over their heads, the girls contributed 50 percent of their earnings to Lili, who passed the money on to Bram. Bram asked no questions about where the money came from; he only insisted that the girls bathe at least once a week and not pick any pockets while they were inside the tavern.

All the women but Orabel and Aidan had already rolled up their pallets and stashed them in the corner; they were undoubtedly outside by the rain barrel, trying to tidy their faces and knot their hair. Bram wanted his barmaids to look approachable.

Aidan sat up, stung by a sudden bitterness. Why did morning have to come so soon? Why did it have to come at all? Life had become a series of endless mornings on this seasonless island. One day was much like the next, bringing the same chores, the same inane flirtations, the same prayers that some sailor would pass out in the alley with enough money in his purse for the girls to buy a decent meal or a badly needed pair of shoes. Only in her sleep had Aidan found any sort of peace or pleasure, and morning came all too soon when she'd been forced to stay up half the night listening to some young seaman blubber about the friend he'd lost off the coast of Spain.

She leaned forward and hugged her knees, knowing that at any moment Lili would appear at her side and issue her usual dire warnings. If Aidan didn't get up and clean her face, she wouldn't draw any man's attention. And if the men wouldn't look at her, how was she supposed to gain their trust? Without their trust and interest, how was she supposed to catch a husband?

"I'm about as likely to catch a husband in Bram's tavern as I am to find gold in the sewer," Aidan murmured. She squinted her eyelids tightly, trying to conjure up the image of the mysterious stranger who had danced with her by the sea, but the noise and distractions of the street outside were too great. Bram had already thrown open his doors, and the first wave of thirsty seamen would soon flood the tavern. Anxious for whiskey, wine, and women, the men had little else on their minds.

She'd leave it all if she could. Cory O'Connor had never intended for his daughter to become a barmaid. She had been well educated in London; her father had employed a governess to teach Aidan how to read, write, and sew. But when the Black Plague swept London in the summer of Aidan's fourteenth year, Cory had decided that he and his family would flee to Batavia, a more settled and less dangerous colony than the wilds of Virginia. Loyalty to the Crown had lured many Londoners to Virginia, but Cory and Lili were Irish, and felt no particular affection for King Charles.

And so they had boarded a ship...and her father had died a month after they left England behind. With only a trunk and the clothes upon their bodies, Aidan and her mother had been set ashore at Batavia, left to find their own way in the world.

Well, Lili had found hers, Aidan mused. She turned and leaned her head against the cold wall, where the rough planking prickled her cheek. Despite her protestations, Lili seemed to actually find fulfillment in her role as guardian of the young women who came to Batavia and found themselves in a desperate situation. The tavern was a sort of life raft for women who were uprooted, displaced, or evicted from their former places in society. With no other means of survival, they assumed working nicknames and entered the peculiar wharf-world, where outcasts catered to the needs of seamen far away from home. As brutal and degrading as life in the tavern was, it was far better than starving in the streets.

And life was not completely hard. Aidan knew her mother

held a certain fondness for Bram. She also took pride in her reputation as the tavern hostess, especially when sailors first arrived in port and walked into the tavern demanding to meet the famous Lady Lili.

But Aidan was not like her mother. Not much like her father, either, though the passage of six years had clouded her memories of him. He had been an outgoing sort, quick with a joke and of a ready wit, with an Irishman's love of poetry and song. But though he had no ties to English aristocracy, Cory O'Connor was a gentleman descended from the ruling O'Connors of Ireland, a man who would have been readily accepted into almost any house in London. Even an artist like Schuyler Van Dyck would have touched the brim of his hat in respect as he passed by Cory O'Connor, for he was respectable, a decent man with a fine reputation.

"Respectable," Aidan murmured, raking her sleep-touseled hair from her forehead. Respectability was the thing she missed most. No one had looked at her in pity or aversion in London. No one had crossed to the other side of the street as she approached. The fine ladies of Batavia, however, scattered like rats on those rare occasions she happened to leave the immediate area of the wharf and venture into the city beyond.

Once, at sixteen, she'd left the wharf and encountered the most terrifying nightmare of her life. She was arrested by one of the sheriff's constables and ordered to serve in the workhouse— and all because Aidan had picked up a child's fallen purse and tried to give it back. The child's mother had taken one look at Aidan's worn dress and flowing hair, then clutched her child to her and screamed for the *baljuwen*. The constable who answered her cry was not one of those assigned to the wharf, and therefore paid to ignore the petty crimes that only injured outsiders. He grasped Aidan by the arm and took her to the workhouse, where she was assigned a mandatory six-week sentence for thieving.

The workhouse, designed to turn idlers, beggars, and other assorted ne'er-do-wells into industrious members of society, only

served to humiliate Aidan. For fourteen hours each day she performed whatever menial labor was assigned her—mostly cutting and binding sheaves of straw which would become brooms for industrious Dutch housewives—while the *ziekentrooster,* or curate of souls, recited daily prayers, catechisms, and instruction in the rudiments of the faith from a lectern in the front of the workroom. For this mindless, grueling work she earned eight and a half stuivers a day, a meager wage that might buy her a loaf of white bread when it was offered on Saturday. But by far the worst aspect of the workhouse occurred on Sunday. After the inmates listened to an obligatory sermon, the general public, for the price of a copper coin, was admitted to gawk at the inmates busy at their labors.

After her release from the workhouse, Aidan resolved that she would never again venture into the "civilized" part of Batavia unless her life depended upon it. She could not deny that life was low and immoral down at the docks, but was life with the "respectable" people so much better? To all outward appearances, the leaders of Batavian society were clean, thrifty, and industrious, but Aidan recognized several of the gawkers in the Sunday workhouse crowd as men who regularly visited the tavern in search of whatever "entertainment" Lili could provide.

Since her fifteenth year, Aidan had quietly despised her life. She hated the crime, drunkenness, and coarseness of the wharf, yet she also despised the hypocrisy of that other world. A permanent sorrow seemed to weigh her down, and she could find no way to escape it.

She doubted that she would ever be respectable again, even if she followed Lili's advice and found a husband among the seamen. Only those who had accomplished great things or won great fortunes found true respectability. Though hard work and virtue were expected from the gentry, the gentry seldom recognized or rewarded those qualities in people who lived near the wharf. As proof of this notion, Aidan had only to look at the native villages.

The Javanese, who had been conquered by the Dutch when they arrived more than twenty years before, were simple folk who planted rice and flowers and kept to their own villages, yet they were held in contempt by the newcomers.

"Aidan, are you going to sit there all day?" Lili stood in the doorway, her hands planted firmly on her wide hips. "Bram sent me to fetch you—there's a new sailor at the first game table, and Bram thinks he'll take a liking to you. Brush your hair, dear, and take him a pint or two. Today could be the day you find a husband!"

"Didn't you tell him about the curse that leaves men cold?" Aidan asked, her tongue heavy with sarcasm. "Or perhaps he's heard it from Bram. No one will want to marry me, Lili, if you keep spreading that story."

"Och, love, don't be so hard on your wee mother." Lili's expression grew serious. "I only tell that story when I'm worried for you. And anyone who is fool enough to believe it doesn't deserve you, don't you see? There's no harm in it, and I know my little tale has saved you from many an unwanted attention."

"But not nearly enough." Feeling restless and irritable, Aidan knotted her hair at the back of her neck. She rose from her pallet, smoothed her skirt, and ran her hands over her stained bodice. This poor sailor would have to take her as he found her, though he probably wouldn't mind her bedraggled appearance if he'd been at sea for a month or two.

"Who knows?" she murmured, ignoring Lili's approving look as she stepped out into the sunlight and made her way to the tavern. "If he's rich, he might have money enough for me to buy a sheet of parchment. And I'll paint a picture for that artist. And then he'll write the crowned heads of Europe about me, and Orabel and I will be living in a palace before the next rainy season."

Aidan slipped into the bustling tavern, then saw the sailor sitting at the first table. The boy looked up as she approached, and she caught her breath, noting the beardless face, the youthful features,

the slender frame. This boy was no more than sixteen—Bram and Lili must be more desperate to marry her off than Aidan had realized.

Forcing a smile, Aidan leaned her elbow onto the table and looked him in the eye so steadily that he squirmed under her gaze. "Hello. They call me Irish Annie," she said. "What can I bring you, sailor?"

⤜⤛⤛

Two hours later, buoyed by an inexplicable resolve, Aidan walked toward the stationer's shop, fully aware of the hard glances that turned her way as she made her way through the streets of the "good" part of town. A huge, foul-smelling blotch adorned the front of her skirt—a remnant of the young sailor's inability to retain Bram's foul-tasting spirits in his gut. He'd been richly embarrassed that he couldn't hold his ale, and when Aidan had helped him out of the tavern and led him to the rain barrel to wash, he had offered her ten stuivers for her help. At first she'd been too embarrassed to accept—after all, she'd been hoping to get him drunk so she could rifle his pockets herself. But then, in a spirit of humility, she had accepted his gift.

Found money. Her own money. Ten stuivers that Lili wouldn't know about, that wouldn't be accounted for under Bram's watchful eye. Coins that wouldn't have to provide the roof over their heads or flour for the bin. Ten stuivers, righteously earned, that just might buy her way out of the wharf and pave the road to respectability.

A bell jangled as she opened the small door to the shop that advertised "writing sundries" in the window. The proprietor, a short, stout man with a balding head and immense dignity, frowned as she entered.

"Good morning," she said, lifting her chin. She moved toward him with all the determination she could muster. "I'd like to buy some parchment please."

One bushy brow shot up in a question. "What kind?"

32

She hesitated, not certain how to answer. Paper was uncommon in the tavern—Bram usually did his calculations on the tabletop, scratching his figures and lists with a sharpened stick or a piece of coal.

"What do you want to use it for?" the man asked.

"Oh." She smiled. "It's for a picture." As a sudden inspiration seized her, she asked, "Do you know Schuyler Van Dyck?"

"Of course." The man's expression softened a bit. "A fine artist and map-maker."

"Well, I want to do the kind of work he does."

"Very well, then. What is your medium?" His brows lifted the question when she didn't answer. "Do you draw with pen, pencil, or chalk?"

Pens, pencils, or chalk? She'd had no idea she'd be faced with such choices. If she used a pen, she'd have to use ink, and in the tavern a bottle of ink was likely to be spilt while the quills would be damaged or lost. But a pencil—what was a pencil? Aidan wasn't sure she'd ever seen one. She was familiar, however, with the small stones of white chalk, but white chalk would not show up on white paper.

She squinted and peered around the room for some clue. "Um—does Heer Van Dyck use a pencil?"

"Of course," the man answered, the corner of his mouth dipping low. "Every artist begins his work with a pencil sketch."

"Then I want a pencil," she said slowly, not quite certain what she was asking for. "To go with the parchment."

To her amazement, the storekeeper moved to a desk where he brought out a small cylinder of wood, then he proceeded to pull out a knife and shave the end in a diagonal slant. "When the point wears down, you cut away more of the wood," he said matter-of-factly, letting her watch as he sharpened the instrument. "But be careful not to break the stem. 'Tis formed in two pieces, and it will snap if you are careless."

Aidan nodded wordlessly, watching as he laid the sharpened

pencil down on his desk. "Now, vellum might do nicely for the pencil." He moved toward a curtained alcove at the back of the room. "It would pick up any shading you might wish to do and it is far stronger than parchment. How many sheets would you like?"

Suddenly it occurred to Aidan that she might not be able to afford this unbelievable luxury. "I only have ten stuivers," she called after him. She glanced around the shop. She was alone; the owner was in the back. It would be so easy to grab the pencil and a few sheets of paper and run out the door with her ten stuivers still in her pocket. Maybe she was a fool for not doing so. The other barmaids wouldn't hesitate to take whatever they needed, and maybe even Lili would understand—

No. She thrust her hand into her pocket and felt the coolness of the coins upon her skin. If she was going to be respectable, she was going to behave as a respectable lady from this point forward. Heer Van Dyck certainly didn't steal his supplies, and neither would she.

The man returned with two sheets of large vellum in his hands and a broader smile on his face. "Ten stuivers," he said, smoothing the heavy material.

In a surge of relief Aidan spilled the coins from her palm, took the vellum and pencil, and hurried away, consumed by the irrational fear that at any moment the constable would appear and arrest her for pretending to be a lady.

⌘

Aidan knew Lili would be looking for her if she didn't return within an hour or so, but Lili would never understand this. She followed Broad Street until the buildings thinned and the road narrowed to a footpath, then crept under the spreading fronds of a banana tree. None of the respectable residents of Batavia would venture out in the midday heat, and Lili would never look for Aidan this far away from the wharf.

With one piece of vellum rolled up and reserved for safekeeping, Aidan spread the other on a spot of hard ground and knelt

before it. Almost reverently, she ran her fingers over the large expanse, feeling every bump and lump and grain of sand that pressed through the paper to meet her questing fingertips. A very expressive surface, this vellum. Perhaps it would be able to capture the feelings and emotions that stirred in her heart.

The pencil was another oddity, quite unlike the pens she'd learned to use in England. Carefully she pulled it from her pocket, then touched the point to her fingertip. It was softer than she expected. She brought it to her tongue and tasted it—no taste, no smell. Only a faint whiff of wood from the casing.

A bird flew overhead and fluttered to rest on a nearby shrub, and Aidan studied it, committing its form to memory. Carefully she lowered the pencil to the parchment and made a bold stroke, marveling as the dark point left its mark across the ivory expanse.

Within seconds she was transported, her eyes filled with the image of the bird, the tilt of his head, the darkness of his eyes, the curve of his wing. Knowledge of the creature flowed like a tangible sensation through her brain and down to her fingertips, and her hand moved over the paper, recording her impressions. Time stood still as she worked, and not until the silhouettes of the palm trees stood black and slender against the glory of a golden sunset did she realize that she had finished.

She glanced down, truly seeing her work for the first time. The pencil, now dull and blunt, had brought the bird to life on the page. His bold black eyes watched her, his soft body fairly trembled with life.

Shaken to the core, Aidan lifted the vellum closer to her face till the image blurred, then pressed it to her bosom as tears flowed down her cheeks. Her first picture. Perhaps Orabel was right. Perhaps she was an artist after all.

⁂

Three days later, Aidan woke with the sun, smoothed her hair, and tiptoed toward the large trunk where the women kept an assortment of skirts, bodices, sleeves, and shirts. From the tangled pile

of clothing she selected a plain skirt of blue watchet, a white underbodice, and a pair of light blue sleeves. She drew the skirt down over her nightshirt, then carefully pinned the underbodice to the skirt and the sleeves to the bodice. The combination wasn't elegant, but the resulting garment was clean, at least.

She looked toward her pallet, where she'd hidden the remaining sheet of vellum and her pencil, and saw Lili watching from her bed. Aidan lifted her chin as she stepped out onto the street, resisting her mother's unspoken approval. Lili thought she had risen early to accost some young sailor down on the docks and invite him back to the tavern for a sociable morning. She would throw a royal tantrum if she knew what really pulled Aidan from her bed at such an early hour.

Over the last few days Aidan had made quiet inquiries among the seamen and other visitors to the tavern. Schuyler Van Dyck, she learned, was a wealthy and well-known artist, though valued by the Dutch East India Company for his skills as a cartographer. Rumor held that he was scheduled to depart soon on a voyage with the V.O.C.'s adventurous Captain Tasman. If so, Aidan realized, the renowned artist might soon make his way to the Company's office.

On Friday and again on Saturday Aidan had placed herself directly in front of the V.O.C.'s dockside offices in the hope that the rumors were correct. If she could have just five minutes of Heer Van Dyck's time, she felt certain she could convince him that she had some sort of talent—something worth cultivating, in any case. Perhaps he could advise her or recommend an art teacher. Even a single word of encouragement would give her hope. She planned to show him her sketch of the bird. If he didn't believe her hand had drawn the portrait, she had kept the other piece of vellum and was prepared to sketch anything he might ask to see.

There had been no sign of Heer Van Dyck yet, but Aidan resolutely told herself that each passing day only brought her a day closer to his coming. If he did plan to sail on a V.O.C. ship,

he would have to venture down to the docks eventually. And if Aidan had to wait on the street until his day of departure, she would. If the situation required it, she'd throw herself at his feet as he boarded. She had lived too long in the dismal swamp of hopelessness, too long in a mold that would never suit her.

Aidan paused at the water barrel to splash her face, then jerked in surprise when Orabel's voice surprised her: "*Goede morgen.*" As Aidan wiped her wet face on her apron, Orabel lowered her voice to a secretive whisper. "Are you going to the docks again today?"

"Yes." Aidan glanced around to be certain Lili was not close enough to overhear. "And not a word to my mother, do you understand? She would say I was wasting my time."

Orabel nodded, and a faint flush rose on her cheeks. "Can I come with you? I looked; there aren't any new ships in the harbor this morning. Yesterday's new arrivals are still asleep, and Bram isn't likely to miss me if I'm gone."

Aidan considered a moment, then nodded. "All right, let's go."

With a quick glance to be certain no one followed, the two girls slipped away from the tavern and blended into the streaming Monday morning traffic of buggies, donkeys, and wagons. Aidan curled her nose at the sour odor of day-old fish at the fisherman's market, and the girls quickened their steps until they were upwind of the smelly place.

"Wait, Aidan." Orabel stopped suddenly in her tracks, her eyes moving to a cross hanging above the silk importer's door. "Let's say a prayer. Perhaps you will meet your famous artist today."

"Do what you like, but I'm not praying." Aidan gritted her teeth. "I haven't prayed in years, and I'm not about to start now."

"Why not?" Orabel's eyes widened in genuine surprise. "God loves everybody. Don't you listen when the minister comes around?"

"Why should I listen to a man who does nothing but criticize us?" Despite her resolve, Aidan's eyes drifted up to the cross that

had caught Orabel's attention. It was simple and smooth, of plain wood without ornamentation of any kind. The pious merchant had boldly tacked it right above his door, an obvious advertisement that he was a God-fearing man with whom one could safely do business.

"But you wear a cross," Orabel protested, pointing toward Aidan's ruffled neckline. "I've seen it beneath your shirt. I thought it meant that you—"

"It was a gift," Aidan interrupted. "It means nothing, not anymore. You can pray if you want to, but God stopped answering my prayers years ago. I have no reason to think he would start answering them now."

Orabel lowered her head, her lips moving soundlessly as she pressed her hands together, and Aidan glanced down the street to be certain no one paid them any particular attention. She wasn't about to end up in the workhouse for this—she'd run into the sea before she'd willingly go with the constable again.

An oxcart passed on the street, loaded with heavy stalks of green bananas, and at the sight of the fruit Aidan felt an odd hunger gnawing at her heart. Her father had often spoken of the glories of tropical Batavia, of the fruit and flowers that grew like weeds in the densest part of the jungles. "God never created a prettier paradise," he had told her, his wide blue eyes sparkling with love and enthusiasm. "He will take us safely there, little one, and you will love the place."

Aidan turned away from the sight of the oxcart, her heart twisting in pain. Her love for God and her love for her father had been intertwined, and when one left, the other vanished too. All that remained of either love was heaviness and an occasional yearning to return to the simpler, more trusting days of her childhood.

Orabel finally looked up and gave Aidan a wide smile. "I prayed you would meet him today," she said simply. "Your artist friend. And he will like you and will want to help you."

The sound of her dream being verbalized in words so simple and forthright made Aidan's heart fall. This was a waste of time; she had thrown away ten stuivers on a useless pencil and vellum and had probably been cheated in the process. Orabel might as well have prayed that they would all be invited to Amsterdam to study with the great artist Rembrandt, for Aidan was about as likely to impress him as she was to meet this gentleman Van Dyck.

"I feel a little sick," she muttered. "I think we should go back."

"No, we won't." Orabel linked her arm through Aidan's, pulling her toward the offices of the Dutch East India Company. "You've come this far; I won't let you turn away."

"But this is crazy, Orabel. I don't care how many prayers you chant, this isn't going to work. No gentleman would even stop to talk to me, much less watch me scratch with a pencil." She took a shallow breath and heard her pulse roaring in her ears. "Stop, Orabel, I think I'm going to be sick."

"I won't let you stop now," Orabel repeated. "Now come along, you can sit once we reach the place. Once we're there you can rest and wait. I'll pray again if I have to, but I won't let you turn around!"

Too weak to resist, Aidan followed her friend.

Four

*W*ill you be coming back, sir?" A tremor of apprehension echoed in the housekeeper's voice. "I mean...will you be back in time for supper?"

"As always, Gusta," Schuyler Van Dyck answered, stepping out onto the front porch of his house. "I expect my children, too, so there will be four of us for dinner." He tempered his voice as he looked down at the woman's quivering chin. "I've not gone yet, so don't worry yourself. And it's not as if I'm planning to sail off the end of the world."

Gusta nodded, her broad face stiffening beneath the tidy cap she wore. She took a deep breath, about to say something else, then apparently thought better of it and clamped her mouth shut.

Smothering a smile, Schuyler turned away. He stood on the veranda for a moment, admiring the spangled green foliage that surrounded the house, and waited until he heard the housekeeper close and bolt the door behind him. Gusta was a good servant. She'd keep a wary eye on things until he returned...no matter how long he stayed away.

As Schuyler descended the stairs, the subject of his recent conversation with the housekeeper flooded his mind. Last night he'd received word that Abel Tasman had been given command of two ships and official permission to sail from Batavia in search of silver, gold, and a sea route to Chile. He was to serve as the expedition's official cartographer, to sail with Tasman to map any lands they might discover. At long last the journey of a lifetime lay within his

reach, and though Schuyler had told his servants, he had no idea how he would break the news to his children.

A light morning rain had swept away the suffocating haze that had blanketed the settlement for the last few days, and now the cobblestones of the street steamed in the rising heat. Van Dyck vainly smoothed his doublet. The linen fabric would be hopelessly wrinkled within the hour; it was the price a gentleman paid for living near the equator. Heat and humidity were part and parcel of life in Batavia.

Frowning, he stepped onto the scrubbed stone path that led to the road. He had errands to run, letters to deliver, and an appointment with his lawyer. Everything must be in order before he departed Batavia, every eventuality prepared for. Sea travel was a great deal safer than it had been in years past, but the whims of the ocean still could not be predicted. Although Magellan had proved that the earth could be circumnavigated, the Portuguese explorer had left port with five ships and 250 men. His crew, 18 skeletal survivors, later returned in one ship—without their captain. Magellan had given his life in the quest.

No, Mistress Ocean did not take kindly to men traversing her bosom, and Schuyler's grown children, Henrick and Rozamond, would not hesitate to remind him of the danger.

Van Dyck gripped his walking stick and kept his eyes on the uneven stones of the road. Just ahead of him, Broad Street was intersected by Market Street, the unofficial boundary between the "good" area of Batavia and the "bad." The east side of Market Street was fronted by a ramshackle row of shops and taverns; behind those rooftops rose the tall masts of ships anchored in the harbor.

The sight of those masts now quickened Schuyler's steps. He wouldn't have believed that the prospect of adventure could still thrill him, but with every year that passed he became more desperate to leave his mark on the world before he passed out of it. He was now sixty-two, well past his prime. This voyage might be

his last chance to publish his work, to leave a piece of himself behind.

Hessel Gerritz's famous map of the Pacific, now twenty years old, had commemorated the voyage in which Willem Schouten and Jacob LeMaire discovered and named Cape Horn. But the center and southern edge of that map was a void, filled in with useless pictures of swelling seas and three-masted ships, disguising an abominable lack of knowledge. Schuyler longed to create a map that would reveal the unknown and illustrate the mysteries of *Mar Pacifico*.

He could do it on this voyage with Tasman. Unlike Gerritz, who had drawn his map from Schouten's and LeMaire's journals and charts, Schuyler wanted to work on the actual journey, to create a sea chart that would be at once useful and breathtakingly beautiful, a combination of art and accuracy, truth and revelation. Like the European map-makers who painted gilded sultan's tents upon the deserts of northern Africa, he would illustrate his map with realistic depictions of flora and fauna never before seen in Europe. His map would illustrate both beauty and science; the original might hang in the Amsterdam offices of the V.O.C. while copies would be distributed throughout the modern world...

A sharp female screech interrupted his musings, and he looked up, pausing on the road with a firm grip on his walking stick. Lost in thought, he had scarcely noticed when he approached the wharf area, a run-down section inhabited by itinerant seamen and women of questionable morals. A group representing both sorts of individuals loitered outside a tavern at the corner of Market and Broad Streets. The scents of whiskey and Jamaican rum floated out to him from inside the darkened building, mingled with the sounds of women's laughter and men's raucous voices. The screech had come from a plump brunette who struggled in a sailor's grasp.

"Excuse me." Schuyler advanced and used his walking stick to tap the seaman on the shoulder. "But I don't think the lady wants to go with you."

"What?" The seaman turned around, his face blank with stupidity.

The woman showed her teeth in an expression that was not a smile, and her eyes glowered at him above a bodice designed to attract unsuitable attention. "Is it any of your business what we're doing here? He means me no harm." She glanced back at the staggering sailor. "Do you, love?"

"Not a bit," the seaman answered, hiccuping. "I just wanted a wee bit o' fun."

"Indeed." Schuyler stiffened. "Judging by the sound of your protest, I surmised that you were in distress."

"Here's the kind of distress I'm in, love." Winking broadly at Schuyler, the woman reached out, clasped her hand behind the swaggering sailor's neck, then drew his head forward until he sagged against her generous frame. "A girl's got to earn a living, don't she, sir? Now if you'll leave us, I was just going to take this fellow inside."

The seaman's eyes closed in a drunken stupor, and the woman took advantage of his lapse to smile at Schuyler. "I could find entertainment for you later, if you like, sir. Just ask for Lady Lili."

The corner of Schuyler's mouth twisted with exasperation, and he leaned heavily upon his cane. "That won't be necessary. I give you good day, madam."

He exhaled a frustrated sigh and turned toward an alley that would take him around the most awful flophouses and taverns. Batavia was no worse than many other port cities, he supposed. Still, his steadfastly Christian soul recoiled from the open excesses of sin even as his heart broke for the wayward people who seemed to wash up on the island like starfish after a storm.

Down here, at the wharf, clapboard warehouses of two, three, and four stories crowded together, shuttered against the steaming heat of midday. The salty sea air mingled with the rank stench of open sewers, and Schuyler fumbled at his belt for a handkerchief to cover his nose. A sea journey might be a welcome relief to seamen

who spent all their time in this part of Batavia. And any other civilizations they might discover upon the lands of Mar Pacifico could not possibly be as distasteful as the life that existed here along the wharf.

He turned another corner and sighed in relief when he recognized his location. The building that housed the offices of the V.O.C. was just ahead, only a few yards from the docks.

Schuyler halted abruptly at the sight of movement in the shadows of an alley next to the building he sought. His son had warned him that the area was not safe. Even in daylight, Henrick insisted, cutpurses and robbers lingered in every alley and doorway.

He clutched his cane, reassured by the solid feel of the brass handle against his palm, then relaxed when he saw that two young women stood in the shade of the alley. They were simple-looking, both dressed in patched dresses and dingy bodices, but certainly not thieves.

The first girl, a blond, fragile-looking child, leaned against a barrel and held up her hand, her curled index finger serving as a perch for a bright butterfly. The second, a slender young woman, faced the building, her eyes frequently glancing toward the butterfly, her hands almost independently chalking its image upon the wall. Her flaming red hair curled nearly down to the small of her back, its molten coppery shades marked by a brazen white strand that seemed to flow like quicksilver from the girl's left temple. The mere sight of that tide of hair was unnerving, for all modest women braided their hair and hid it beneath neat little caps.

Stunned, Schuyler stepped back into the shadows, bracing his back against the building as he watched. The redhead was a capable sketch artist; in just a few deft strokes she had caught the essence of form and movement. She drew with a simple white rock, one like thousands of others that littered the interior of the island, and shaded her drawing with a skill that surprised Schuyler. He watched, entranced, as the butterfly flapped slowly, elegantly pirouetting on the other girl's outstretched finger.

"Hurry now, Aidan, he's about to fly," the blond called in English. "The honey's not going to hold him much longer!"

"It's okay, you can let him go. I've got him—" The artist absently tapped the side of her head. "— in here. I won't forget."

The younger girl gently blew upon the butterfly, coaxing the creature into flight. The insect lazily drifted off, flapping for a moment above the red-haired girl before rising on a current of air and drifting away.

Schuyler rubbed his chin, thinking. 'Twas a pity he was leaving the colony in less than a month. Ability like hers ought to be encouraged. But the girl would undoubtedly think him a fool if he dared to suggest that she had talent. By her dress and attitude he suspected she was one of the unfortunate ne'er-do-wells who dwelt in this area, and if he encouraged her attention, she'd probably pick his pockets bare before he'd even finished wishing her a good morning.

Regretfully pushing his noble intentions aside, he straightened himself and strode forward to cross the alley.

"Aidan, look! It's him!"

Aidan glanced up, and felt her mouth suddenly go dry as the gentleman she sought appeared as if from nowhere. He walked purposefully toward the V.O.C. office, his cane tapping steadily on the street, his eyes fixed to the cobblestones. He moved with surprising speed for a man so advanced in years, and if she tarried one more instant, her days of waiting would all have been for nothing.

She dropped the stone in her hand. "One moment please, sir!" Her voice was louder than she'd intended, and he jerked at the sound of her greeting as if she'd threatened him with bodily harm. His eyes were wary under the brim of his hat; his mouth pursed with suspicion. And why not?

Alstublieft, Heer Van Dyck," she called in Dutch. Dusting her grimy palms on her skirt, she rushed forward to stop his progress.

She managed a tremulous smile before speaking again. "If you would be so kind, sir, I'd like to sketch your portrait."

The man stopped abruptly, and his pursed mouth opened slightly in surprise as Aidan fumbled beneath the edge of her bodice and pulled out her remaining sheet of vellum, damp now with perspiration.

"If you please, sir," she said again, her fingers trembling as she unfolded the crinkled paper, "I have a pencil. I'd like to sketch your picture or any picture you like."

His eyes, when she looked up, were dark brown and soft with kindness. "And I suppose you'll charge me a stuiver for the pleasure." He spoke in careful, clipped English, but there was no trace of annoyance in his deep voice. "Is this some new trick you girls have connived to waylay hapless passersby?"

"No sir." Aidan rose to her full height, her courage like a rock inside her. "I won't charge you anything. I only want you to see me draw." She felt an unwelcome blush creep onto her cheeks. "I have heard, sir, that you are an artist."

His eyes left her face and drifted to the building beyond. "I should go, I have an important meeting. Other responsibilities call me forward, my dear. Perhaps at some more opportune time."

"There is no more opportune time." Startled at her own boldness, Aidan lifted her chin. "I have waited here three days to see you, Heer Van Dyck. I ask only that you watch me draw something—anything you like."

He pulled away slightly, his eyes roving over her, taking in her ragged hem, her patched skirt, the too-small bodice, the wrinkled sleeves. Then those brown eyes searched her face, and Aidan flushed hotly beneath the pressure of his gaze. Finally, he nodded and clasped his hands behind his back.

"All right," he said simply, his handsome face reserved in its expression. "Draw whatever you like. You have piqued my interest."

"No," she insisted, pulling her precious pencil from her

pocket. "You tell me what to draw. And whatever it is, I shall do my best."

"A true artist draws what is in his heart," he answered, a trace of a smile lighting his eyes. "But perhaps you are not accustomed to peering inside your soul. So look yonder, dear child, and tell me what you see."

Aidan followed his glance, and saw the open sea and the ships that rode upon it. "I see the harbor."

He jerked his head in a brief nod, sending a shock of white hair spilling into his eyes. "Draw the harbor, then. Let me see what you see."

Aidan's mind raced as she lifted the vellum and braced it against the nearest wall. Orabel stepped forward to hold the paper securely against the rough bricks of the Company building, and Aidan ran her hands over the parchment for a long moment, thinking.

What did the man mean by "draw the harbor"? Did he expect to see the ships, the sea, the men upon the docks, or all three elements? She'd heard he was a cartographer—did he want a map of the place? Aidan had no idea of the harbor's shape or size in relation to the entire island of Java, for she had not been outside Batavia since landing here six years before.

She heard his cane tapping against the cobblestones and knew he was impatient to be under way. In that instant she decided to sketch a ship, for it represented all the elements of a harbor. Its hull was made of deeply rooted island trees, its power came from the men who sailed within it, and its transport was the ocean itself.

In three bold lines she drew the mainmast, mizzen, and foremast; in a series of swooping lines she created the sharp line of the bow and the sensuous curves of the stern. A ship, she told herself, her pencil busily crossing over the vellum, symbolized travel and adventure, a means of escape, and the promise of returning home.

Within a moment she had forgotten about the tall man standing behind her, and with only two more cursory glances over her shoulder she had captured the image and projected it onto the parchment. The wind, full of movement and bluster, filled her ship's sails; round-cheeked, bright-eyed sailors crowded the decks and peered into a swirling sea where something mysterious and beautiful shimmered beneath the surface. On and on she drew, until Orabel's discreet cough reminded her that she had an impatient audience.

When she turned around, Heer Van Dyck stood motionless in the middle of the alley. His mouth had taken on a curious twist, and his eyes were fixed upon the vellum in her hand.

"For you," she said simply, offering with the page her dreams, her future, the only hopes she had dared to conjure in all her years on Batavia. He put out his hand to take the paper, but a sudden gust of salt-scented wind snatched it from her hand. She watched in stunned amazement as the breeze caught the sketch and sent it careening toward the sea, taking her hopes and dreams with it.

"I'm so sorry, my dear," Van Dyck murmured, his eyes following the fluttering paper as it rose like a rebellious bird and moved away on the wind. "I would like to have kept that sketch."

"It was all the paper I had," she answered, fighting to speak over the lump that rose in her throat. "I had hoped you would be able to look at it and give me some instruction. But I still have this." From a pocket inside her skirt she pulled out another square, this one folded many times and smudged with grime. She gave it to him, then waited while he took it and slowly unfolded it.

The bird sketch. She had hoped she wouldn't be required to surrender it, for it was her first attempt at working with a pencil and proper paper, and the scrawny image on the page seemed a sad substitute for the charming winged fellow she had met that afternoon in the brush.

Van Dyck lifted his gaze from the page to meet hers, and his

dark brown eyes grew somewhat smaller and darker, the black pupils training on her like gun barrels.

"How do you do it?" he asked, cocking one silver eyebrow toward her.

"Do what, sir?"

"How do you make the image come to life?" The beginning of a smile tugged at the corners of his mouth. "The bird is looking at me, I can almost hear him chirping. And when you sketched the boat, I knew the seamen were eager to be away, happy to be making the journey. So how do you do it?"

How? she silently quizzed herself. "I haven't the faintest idea," she whispered, scarcely aware of her own voice. "I just look and draw. That's all."

Clothes hanging from a line stretched across the alley made soft snapping sounds in the breeze as Heer Van Dyck stood in silence for a moment. "I believe, my child," he finally said, speaking slowly, "that I should give you more than a few instructions." He glanced toward the street. "Is there some quiet spot we can sit and talk? Does some place near here have a proper table?" His eyes narrowed as he glanced toward the doors of the Dutch East India Company, then his gaze returned to her face. "Some place where we would be welcomed?"

Aidan understood the subtle question. A woman of her type would never be allowed through the doors of the prosperous V.O.C. Well, if the downtrodden could not rise up, members of the upper class were welcome to descend.

"There's a tavern near here." She pointed toward Broad Street. "On the corner. Do you know it?"

"I believe I have seen it." Heer Van Dyck stroked his beard. "Yes, I know the place. All right, then. You go there and wait for me, and I will join you shortly."

"Truly?"

"*Ja,*" he answered absently. "I will have to get some supplies— pencils, I think, and parchments. It may take awhile."

"But what about your meeting?" Aidan's mind raced. "You said you had an important meeting. I wouldn't want you to miss it on my account."

"The meeting will wait," the older man answered. "But you, I fear, will not. So go ahead, while I gather the things I need. Then you shall draw for me again, and I shall have an answer for you."

Aidan watched him move away, noticing that he walked with a firmer, more resolute step. Orabel reached over and squeezed her hand. "He said he'll have an answer for you," she said. "What does that mean, Aidan?"

"I'm not sure." Aidan shook her head. "I don't remember asking a question."

The two girls began to walk slowly back to the tavern, and Aidan took a deep breath, resisting the wave of doubt that threatened to rise from somewhere deep within her. Could she trust this man? She had thought she had seen a gleam of interest in his eye, but perhaps he was merely eager to rid himself of an annoying pest. Perhaps even now he intended only to walk around the block and return to the V.O.C. offices when he was certain she and Orabel had left. He would go about his business without another thought for her.

But he had been surprised at her picture of the ship—of that she was certain. Whether he supported her or despised her, he had at least been surprised that a lowly wharf rat could hold a pencil and draw.

⤖⤙

His face burning in hot agony, Schuyler shouldered his way through the rowdy mob gathered outside the Broad Street Tavern, wondering why in the world he had agreed to meet the young woman here. Why had he agreed to meet her at all? He had no desire to take on a student, no time in which to train a protégée. He didn't even want to recommend another teacher in town, for by the look of the girl's dress she wouldn't have the money for private

instruction, and he doubted that any of the girls' schools would take her. She was too old for school, too poor for a private tutor.

So why was he here with his arms loaded with parchments and pens?

"Excuseert u mij," he murmured again and again as he moved through the crowd. Half the faces around him were bleary with drink; at least a dozen men seemed moments away from passing out. How could they be totally inebriated before the sun had reached midday?

But these were not the kind of people he was accustomed to. These were men at liberty after a long voyage, eager for wine, women, and a bit of merriment. Perhaps he would understand them better after he had been at sea for several months.

He paused just inside the doorway and took a deep breath, his eyes searching the gloom, half-hoping that he'd see no sign of the red-haired woman. If he couldn't find her, he could leave with a clear conscience, satisfied that he'd at least obeyed his impulse to help the ragamuffin. He had come to believe that the merest encounter on the street could be a divine appointment, and the girl's talent and sincerity had convinced him that she should not be brushed aside. But other than giving her a few art supplies and a dozen encouraging words, he had no idea what else he could do for her.

All too quickly he ran out of distractions. He saw her sitting alone at a table in the center of the room, her fair skin stretched over high cheekbones, her eyes fixed upon the card game at the next table.

He wouldn't even be able to slip in and cower in a corner, he realized, groaning under the burden of his parcels as well as the imminent blight upon his good name. *If anyone tells my children that I've been frequenting taverns even before dinnertime...*

He glanced around and smiled grimly. Not much chance of that rumor spreading. None of his children's associates would so much as venture into this part of town without some extremely compelling reason.

She looked up and caught his eye as he made his way through the boisterous crowd, and he gave her a smile, holding the bulky packages to his chest lest they be knocked from his arms. She blushed as he approached, and he wondered if perhaps his attentions embarrassed her. Or maybe she thought he was mocking her.

"I am glad, my dear, that you waited for me." Schuyler dropped his parcels to the table where she sat. He placed his hand on the back of an empty chair, then lifted a brow. "May I sit?"

"Please do." She straightened in her chair, her thin fingers tensing on the tabletop. After a moment, a flicker of a smile crossed her face. "I was beginning to wonder if you'd come at all."

"Of course I came." He unwrapped the largest package, a stack of parchments and assorted papers. "I promised I would help you, and I want to see you draw again. You show remarkable promise, my dear, and it would be a shame if you neglect the gifts God has given you." He gave her a brief smile. "I particularly liked the butterfly sketch."

"You saw that?" A pensive shimmer flickered in the shadow of her eyes. "I don't usually go around drawing on buildings, sir. I only wanted to practice until you arrived."

"Your drawings would greatly improve most of the buildings in this part of town," he answered simply, smoothing the parchments. He slid the stack toward her, then produced a freshly sharpened pencil from a pouch at his belt. "Here, my dear. Draw for me."

She took the pencil and frowned at him. "Draw what?"

"Whatever your heart tells you." He folded his hands across his belly as he leaned back in his chair. "Forget I am here, forget everyone in this room. Just draw. Let your inner eye see what it will, and record that image on the paper."

She paused, touched the tip of the pencil to her tongue in a strangely quaint gesture, then ran her left hand down the parchment, seeming to evaluate its texture, sight, and scent. Her eyes closed for a long moment, and when she opened them again they

burned with a faraway look. The pencil began to move over the page, and within five strokes Schuyler saw that she had sketched a man—a craggy-looking fellow of exceptional height, callous hands, and massive oarsman's shoulders. She sketched the docks under and around the man, lending an air of isolation to the tall figure.

Schuyler said nothing, but he felt his breath catch in his throat as she slowly brought the image to life. The skin of his palms grew damp as he realized he was watching a talent unlike any he had ever seen before. He had trained with the learned painter Joachim de Heem, had traveled to Amsterdam, London, Paris, Nuremberg, and Italy to perfect his art and technique. He was skilled and relatively well known in the art world, but in the space of five minutes this girl had demonstrated more natural ability than Schuyler would ever possess.

She turned the pencil now to shade in the telling details and shadows, and Schuyler thought he could almost see the man's chest rise and fall, that at any moment those full lips would curl into a laughing smile. He had noticed a similar quality to her picture of the butterfly; he had wondered if the creature might mount the warm breeze and simply fly away.

A crowd had gathered, a quiet knot of men and women who stood behind the young woman and murmured in appreciation as her pencil flew over the paper. But the artist seemed not to hear them. Her entire being was concentrated upon her work; her spine curled toward the page, her fingers willing the pencil to create the image her mind held.

Schuyler gripped the arms of his chair as a sense of inadequacy swept over him. The Almighty had been gracious to give him a measure of talent, but God had obviously given a far greater measure to this girl. Why?

After a few more strokes, the young woman dropped the pencil and slid the sketch away, knowing without being told that her rendering was perfect and complete. How long had it taken him to

recognize completion? For years he had struggled with the temptation to add, to tweak, to erase, to disguise. Even now he often had to put his pens and paints aside and conduct a mental debate over whether or not a work was complete. Yet this young woman—barely more than a girl—seemed to know instinctively.

She sat silently, her head bowed, waiting for his inspection, his help, his approval. What could he say? She had more talent than he; she lacked only what he could not give. With training and time, she might be the greatest artist Batavia had ever known, quite possibly a sensation even in Europe. But he was scheduled to depart within the month. Besides, he was too old to take on an apprentice—

She needs you.

The Voice came from within, and Schuyler instantly acknowledged it.

Ja, Lord, she does, Schuyler responded. *But what should I do with her? She is a waif, a young woman of questionable repute. And I am leaving in a few weeks. I will not be here to tutor her.*

You need her.

Schuyler swallowed hard, then gripped the arms of his chair again. He was not one who heard the voice of God in every slight whisper of the wind, but he had heard it often enough to recognize it. And when God spoke, Schuyler knew he had to obey.

He summoned all the courage he could muster to acknowledge the call. *"Dank you, goed Vader,"* he whispered under his breath. "Give me wisdom now."

He cleared his throat, searching for words. "Young woman—what, if I may be so bold, is your name?"

The eyes that lifted to his were filled with a curious deep longing. "The people here call me Irish Annie," she answered, "but my true name is Aidan O'Connor."

Five

"Joffer O'Connor, you have a great gift. There is something about your work...something that shows great promise."

If Heer Van Dyck's assessment of her ability startled Aidan, she was equally shocked by the fact that he'd addressed her using the respectful Dutch title "Joffer," meaning "Miss." His announcement brought cheers and applause from the onlookers, and Aidan tensed at the noise, ready to leap out of her chair and flee. Whatever had possessed her to invite him here, where everyone could see her? And why had she kept this rendezvous with the old gentleman? He was a respected artist, she was nothing.

He said she had a gift...but when she looked up again, she saw that his eyes were fixed upon her picture. He was not smiling.

"Did I—did I do something wrong?" She lowered her voice as the crowd of onlookers moved on to find other amusements.

"No, my young friend," Van Dyck said quietly. "You did nothing wrong. You did everything right." He reached out and turned the picture so he could study it more closely. "You have a remarkable talent. Have you studied under a drawing teacher here?"

Aidan felt the corner of her mouth twist. This man wouldn't want to know about the kind of teachers she'd had in Batavia. Betje had taught her how to pick a man's pocket; Francisca had taught her how to cut a man's purse string while dancing....

"No, sir," she answered, leaning back. "I haven't had any

drawing teachers. But if you could give me some instruction or a few ideas that might be useful, I'll be very grateful. I know you have other important things to do."

"Nothing that can't wait." Leaning his chin on his hand, he looked across the table at her, his eyes gleaming with speculation. He might have been planning to offer her a bag of golden guilders or employ her as a maid. Aidan couldn't tell what he was thinking, but his expression encouraged her. His was a gentle smile, not at all like the leering grins of the seamen who swaggered up to her in the tavern.

"You have a remarkable gift, young woman," Van Dyck repeated. "Now we should begin to improve it. I'm not quite certain how I can help you, for I will be leaving Batavia in a few weeks, but I am certain God wants me to lend you my attention. And while my artistic eye pales in comparison to yours, I am skilled with the tools of the craft. I am a cartographer by trade, an artist only by avocation, but I think I may be able to offer some assistance as you begin your artistic endeavors."

Aidan shifted her weight in the chair and glanced at her picture again. "I don't have the faintest idea how to begin an artistic endeavor," she murmured. Suddenly her picture looked very poor. "Perhaps this is not a good idea."

By his own admission, Van Dyck would soon leave Batavia, and what good would a few art lessons do her? Perhaps it was better not to hope, not to whet an appetite that could never be satisfied. A serious study of art would require months—perhaps years—of instruction, time to learn and practice and paint. She would also need a patron, for neither Lili nor Bram would willingly spend good money on a frippery like art.

"My dear." Van Dyck leaned forward eagerly. "Please listen. I am willing to help you all I can. I am leaving Batavia soon, but I'd like you to come live in my house until I have to depart. I will teach you all I can in whatever time we have, and I give you my word that you will be treated with respect and honor."

Stunned speechless, Aidan snapped her head back. She'd heard such propositions before, usually from drunken seamen or young gentlemen who wandered through the wharf looking for a night of naughty fun and devilment.

"Sure, and don't I know what that means?" She blinked in consternation, unable to believe a gentleman could issue such a brazen invitation. "No matter what you may think, sir, I'm a decent girl. I've never lived with any man, and I'm not about to begin now, no matter how many lessons you offer."

"Oh, my." A flush of color rose up from his collar. "My dear, what you're thinking—I mean, I never intended what you're thinking. I can assure you, there is nothing untoward or indecent in my offer. You would be completely chaperoned at all times. My housekeeper will attend to your personal needs, and while you reside with us I will teach you about art."

He paused, waiting for her reaction, and Aidan pressed her lips together, thinking. He was truly shocked—and that was a good thing. Surely this man was a true gentleman. He had a gentle manner, and his refined features fairly exuded intelligence and good breeding. If he kept his word, perhaps she could learn a thing or two. And often ships were delayed out of port, so an expedition scheduled to depart in a few weeks might be delayed for even a few months.

Yes, this might be a very good thing.

Van Dyck was smiling now, his expression distracted, as though he listened to something only he could hear. After a moment his eyes widened as if he'd just received a revelation.

"You seem to have a skill for the things of nature—that butterfly was really quite remarkable," he said, running his hand through his white hair. "I'm afraid I am more attuned to lines and geography, images and shapes which do not move or breathe." He shot her a twisted smile. "Perhaps you could teach me a thing or two, if I am not too old to learn. I have a great need for someone who can teach me to accurately draw the flora and fauna of—"

His voice faded slightly as his eyes turned toward the open doorway. "—of our world."

Aidan bit her lip. "I wouldn't know how to teach you anything, sir." She twisted her hands in her lap. "I don't even know how I do what I do. It just comes out of me."

"That is very obvious, my dear, and as I said, it is a gift." Heer Van Dyck fished in his doublet pocket for a moment, then produced a little card scrawled with an elegant handwriting. "This has my name written upon it. Can you read?"

Aidan felt her cheeks flush as she nodded. "Of course. I was educated in England."

"I should have known." Featherlike laugh lines crinkled around his eyes as he smiled at her. "But there's a bit of the Irish in you too. I can hear it in your voice."

"My parents were Irish," Aidan answered, smiling back at him. Aping her mother's brogue, she tilted her head at a jaunty angle. "Sure, and there's a wee bit of the blarney in me, but 'tis not such a bad thing to be Irish."

The artist grimaced in good humor. "Of course not. The Irish are a charming lot." Van Dyck clapped his hands together, then looked around the room. "Have you someone—a guardian, perhaps—that I should speak to on your behalf? I'd like to assure them that I mean you no harm. I believe you can be a great artist someday, and I'd like to help you begin."

Aidan frowned, thinking of Lili. Faith, Lili would wet her skirts if she knew her daughter had encountered an honest-to-goodness kind and generous Rich Gentleman. She would stop at nothing in her effort to marry him to Aidan, herself, or one of the other girls....

"I have no one; I speak for myself," Aidan answered, "but I might be inclined to visit your house before I agree to this arrangement. Where do you live?"

"Follow Broad Street west of this place," Van Dyck answered, pointing toward the doorway. "It's a white house, surrounded by a wide porch. The door is painted blue, like the sea."

He lived on the Other Side of Batavia—the place where good-wives and housekeepers scrubbed their faces and their floors and condemned to the workhouse anyone who didn't meet their high standards of physical and moral neatness.

Aidan pressed her damp hands to her skirt, wiping away sudden drops of perspiration. "Perhaps I'll come." She lifted her chin and forced her lips to part in a curved, still smile. "But I don't need a nursemaid. If you agree to teach me, I'll work hard. I want to learn."

"Indeed." His eyes flashed with something that might have been admiration or humor, then his eyes fell upon the drawing on the table. "Do you mind if I keep this?" he asked.

"No, please do," Aidan answered, amazed that he would want anything she had done.

He took the sketch, rolled it up, then stood and bowed as formally as if she were the Queen of England. A group of barmaids watching from a nearby table tittered with laughter at his dignified gesture, but Heer Van Dyck seemed oblivious of them. After saluting her, the gentleman moved through the doorway and left Aidan alone at her table.

"Got a new gentleman friend, Irish Annie?" A sailor yelled over the noise of the tavern. "I could show you a better time than that old goat."

"You'll not show me any kind of time, haven't I said so before?" Aidan called back, rising from her chair. "And if you can't tell an honest gentleman when you see one, then you, sir, don't have both oars in the water."

Undiluted laughter rang through the room as she walked back to the bar.

❧

"Schuyler Van Dyck," Orabel mused, fingering the damp little card. She and Aidan were sitting in the small chamber Bram leased behind the tavern, the only place where Aidan and the other women felt they were not on public display.

"Van Dyck," Aidan repeated. She leaned back upon one of the loosely stuffed pallets that served as a mattress. "Sort of a stuffy-sounding name, isn't it? I imagine he's right up there with the Vanderveers and the Van Diemens—"

"He seemed like a nice man." Orabel pushed a pile of soiled garments out of the way, lay back, and gazed dreamily at the ceiling. "I think you should accept his offer. Even if he can only teach you for a few days, it wouldn't hurt you to go to his house and enjoy a bit of the good life." She turned on her side and smiled at Aidan. "Can you imagine what they serve in his house? Real tea with sugar, Aidan, and sweet biscuits. Doesn't that sound a sight better than the gruel and ale Bram gives us?"

"I don't know." Aidan rolled over and propped her head on her hand. "What good will only a few lessons do? He'll have to leave, and I'll know a wee bit more about painting—but what good will that do me here in the tavern? I'll still be nothing but a barmaid, Orabel."

"Being a barmaid's not the worst thing in the world." Orabel's voice was soft with hurt. "And you're luckier than most of us."

Aidan bit her lip, shamed into silence by her own thoughtlessness. Bram couldn't afford to put all the girls to work in the tavern; as a favor to Lili he usually kept Aidan pouring at the bar. But Orabel, Sofie, Brigit, and several of the others had to pick pockets and beg for money enough to eat. Though they rarely spoke of it, Aidan knew they sometimes found other ways to earn their keep.

"I'm sorry, Orabel." Aidan shrank from her friend's wounded expression. "I'm truly sorry. I'd give anything if I had enough money to get us both out of here. I'd buy us a little house on the other side of town where we could live in peace, and we'd be genteel ladies. No drunken seamen around, no bossy Bram. No fights, no one cursing in our ears all the livelong day, no threats of the workhouse…"

Aidan's voice trailed away as a deep, painful blush washed up from Orabel's throat and lit her face. "That would be nice, Aidan.

But I'm not expecting anything from you or anybody else. I'm fine. I'm really fine."

Aidan closed her eyes for a moment, regretting her words. Two years before, frightened, fragile, and slightly daft from her experience on an ocean-going ship, Orabel had disembarked in Batavia. Her parents had sailed with her from England, but both had succumbed to a mysterious ague that plagued the passengers. With no protector aboard ship, thirteen-year-old Orabel had been attacked by drunken seamen and abandoned on the wharf—forlorn, orphaned, and pregnant.

Lili and the others had taken the child in. Sofie tried to teach Orabel the finer points of picking a sailor's pocket, but the girl was too shy and hesitant to be much good at filching a man's money belt. Orabel found herself working with Aidan in the tavern, and as the girl's pregnancy progressed, Lili assigned Aidan to the task of caring for her.

One hot day in May, the baby came much too soon. The infant, blue and frail, spilled into Aidan's waiting hands and died without uttering a single cry. Weeping silently, Aidan wrapped the baby in an old shawl and left it on the church doorstep, knowing the minister would give the baby a proper burial in the pauper's graveyard.

Throughout the ordeal of childbirth, Orabel never uttered a word or shed a tear. After a week of silent mourning, she rose from her bed, dressed, and went out to the corner as if she'd been born to the role of streetwalker. With her wan complexion, petite frame, and cornflower blue eyes, "Sweet Kate" brought Bram and Lili a great deal of money.

But Aidan knew Orabel hated her life. She had not been born to play the guttersnipe; some twist of fate had simply placed her in a role for which she was disastrously well-suited.

"Well, girls, fancy finding you here when there's work to be done." Lili's voice, breathless and mocking, broke into Aidan's thoughts as the woman came into the room. "A bit soon, isn't it,

to be resting on your laurels? Last time I checked, there was a room of thirsty men waiting in the tavern, or could I have been seeing things?"

Aidan frowned as her mother loomed over her and continued her diatribe: "How much did you earn this morning, dearies? A gold florin? A guilder? Surely a king's fortune rests in your pockets, or you'd not be here lollygagging about when there is work to be done."

Wordlessly, Orabel held the small rectangular card under Lili's nose.

"What's this?" Lili eyed the card suspiciously.

"An elderly gentleman's calling card," Orabel answered. "He watched Aidan draw, and he's offered to give her lessons."

"Lessons?" Lili cocked an eyebrow at the girl. "Aidan knows how to read and write, for all the good those lessons did her. And it's too late for either of you to be learning anything new, haven't I said so? You can't teach an old dog new tricks." Her painted mouth spread into a thin-lipped smile. "It's nearly too late for you to be marrying, and you'll never find a husband if you're laying about in this room whilst the men are out in the tavern!"

"I don't want a husband!" Aidan snapped, jerking upright. Resentment struggled with affection as she stared across the empty space between them. "Heer Van Dyck is an artist, a respectable gentleman, and he has agreed to teach me a few things about art. Perhaps it will not amount to anything, but I will never know if I don't take the chance!"

"Teach you? About *art?*" Lili's shook her head contemptuously. "Aidan, lassie, that's the silliest thing I've ever heard. What kind of food will art put on the table? How are you supposed to clothe yourself with pictures? In faith, will paintings buy shoes for your feet? No! Only rich folk have time and money to fiddle with such things."

"He's willing to teach me," Aidan repeated, plunging on carelessly. "And I trust him. He's a good man, a real gentleman."

"'Tis a bit strange, don't you think, that a gentleman of wealth

and position should be taking such an interest in you?" Lili paused, her tobacco-stained teeth shining faintly in the dim light of the room. "Have you stopped to think that maybe he's got immodest designs on you? You're a pretty lass, in case you've forgotten, and I'll not have my daughter being some gentleman's mistress when she could win an honest husband."

"He doesn't want me like that." Aidan spoke slowly, straining to hold her temper. She sat up and pushed a wayward curl from her eyes, watching as two deep lines of worry appeared between Lili's brows. Lili loved her, to be sure, but that love was sufficient to drive Aidan to distraction. Lili loved her enough to allow Aidan to work in the tavern instead of joining the girls on the street; she loved her enough to criticize her appearance, her way of walking, her way of speech, even her way of thinking. But Lili didn't understand her daughter. She had no idea of the passions and thoughts that burned in Aidan's heart, of Aidan's heartfelt conviction that she was not meant to live this life.

"I approached *him,* Mother," Aidan said again, tucking the renegade strand of white hair behind her ear. The other girls said the singular white streak, which grew like a weed from Aidan's left temple, was proof that Aidan had been set apart for some special destiny. Lili didn't understand *that* either. Her own hair was still full and brown, even at her advanced age. She was always harping on Aidan, telling her to cut the white streak out, to color it with wine, to hide it beneath a cap, but Aidan steadfastly refused. The brazen mark that set her apart, that would have made her extremely identifiable if she were ever caught snitching a gentleman's purse, only reinforced her conviction that she was different.

"Heer Van Dyck would not have spoken to me if I had not approached him," she told her mother now. "I heard about his art, and I wanted to know more. And so I waited for him, and I spoke to him before he could slip by. And I hoped that he would listen, and would see my art. Though he can't help me for long, he has promised to help me while he can."

"He's an old man, you say? Old men tend to be daft," Lili countered stubbornly. "You are being foolish as well, lassie. You'll be sorry when you come to harm in his house. All I have done to keep you safe and pure will be for nothing!"

Aidan's eyes fell upon Orabel. "Then I'll take Orabel with me when I visit his house." She winked at her friend. "And while I'm talking to Heer Van Dyck, Orabel can look around. Who knows, maybe she'll spy a bag of Dutch florins within reach at the front door."

"Or a handsome son in the parlor!" Orabel added, joining in the joke.

But Lili just stared at her daughter, and Aidan could find no answering trace of humor in her mother's eyes.

Six
❦❦

"Heer Van Dyck." Standing in the doorway of the library, the housekeeper spoke hesitantly, as if about to say something she knew she would regret.

Schuyler looked up from his letter and saw that a warning cloud had settled upon the woman's features. "What is it, Gusta?"

"There are two young women—slatterns, really—at the door. They say they are Aidan O'Connor and Orabel." The housekeeper's thin mouth drew downward in distaste. "The other woman gave no surname, of course."

Schuyler pushed himself back from his desk, surprised beyond speech. The girl had come! He had been right to invite her; God knew she would respond.

"*Ja*, bring them in at once." Hurriedly he sprinkled sand over the wet ink that glistened on his parchment. As Gusta moved away, Schuyler shook his head and slid the letter to a corner of his desk. In spite of himself, he chuckled at the thought of his housekeeper's dour disapproval. He would love to have seen Aidan O'Connor's encounter with Gusta at the door. He had the distinct impression that the fiercely opinionated housekeeper might have met her match in the young artist.

The wide door creaked open, and the two young women walked in, followed by Gusta's stalwart form. Aidan led the way, moving with the hard grace of a woman who has total control of herself, her manner as regal as any highborn woman in Amsterdam.

He rested his chin on his hand, welcoming the opportunity to

examine her under the more genteel circumstances of his library. She had said she was twenty and she looked her age, though her countenance still maintained a youthful flush of innocence. She was slender, of medium height and delicate features, and from her left temple that remarkable white streak coursed through her riotous red hair like lightning through a fiery sunset sky.

Her pale green eyes fastened tenaciously upon him. "Heer Van Dyck," she said, as formally as if she paid social calls every afternoon. But beyond that greeting she apparently had no gift for social conversation; she came immediately and directly to the point. "You said you might give me art lessons. I think I should know why you would be willing to do this, knowing that I cannot repay you." Even wide open, her eyes had a faint catlike slant to them. Those eyes narrowed slightly as she added, "And what sort of things could you teach me?"

These two might not know how the proprieties were observed, but Schuyler would not take advantage of their naiveté. He smiled and stood, bowing first to Aidan, then to the younger girl.

"A pleasure to see you ladies again," he said, noticing the blush that rose in Aidan's face as he observed the proper social ritual. "Won't you have a seat?" He spread his hand, indicating two carved chairs that sat before his desk. The two young women hesitated, and Schuyler nodded to his housekeeper.

"I think our guests might like a cup of tea," he suggested, giving Gusta a knowing look. "And those sweetbread cookies might be nice, as well as the little sandwiches you served for dinner last night."

At the mention of refreshments, both girls sank into the chairs, Orabel sighing in satisfaction. Schuyler smiled at the success of his little distraction and moved out from behind his work area. Perching on the edge of his desk, he folded his hands and regarded the young artist with somber curiosity.

"Aidan O'Connor," he murmured. He spoke slowly, feeling his way through his thoughts and her apprehensions. "A lovely

name for a lovely young woman. As I told you before, Joffer O'Connor, you have been given a great gift. As to why I want to help you—" He paused, lifting a brow. "—I seem to recall that you asked for my assistance."

"I know that." Her flush deepened to crimson. "But nobody's ever given me whatever I asked for just because I asked. So why are you willing to help me? I can't pay you anything. It took a blessed miracle for me to buy two sheets of vellum and a pencil. And I know this can't be a good time for you, not if you're planning a journey."

"Death, childbirth, and travel," he said, smiling. "Never a convenient time for any of them, I'm afraid."

Neither girl laughed at his joke. The younger girl smiled blandly, while Aidan's pretty mouth dipped into an even deeper frown. Schuyler weakly slapped his leg and looked toward the door, fervently hoping that Gusta's insatiable curiosity would bring her back soon.

"Why are you willing to help me?" Aidan persisted. She gave him a bright-eyed glance, full of shrewdness. "You don't know me. For all you know, I could be the worst thief in Batavia, and yet you would allow me to live in your house."

Schuyler gazed at her in amused wonder. Did she truly have no idea how gifted she was? "If you robbed me blind while I taught you," he answered, easing into a smile, "I believe I'd consider the loss a worthwhile investment in your talent."

She did not respond but still stared at him with confusion in her eyes. He gentled his tone. "My dear, I did not invite you here to bully or mistreat you, if that's why you're worried. I invited you because God urged me to. And I see that you have the artist's eye."

"I beg your pardon?"

"The artist's eye." How could he explain it so she would understand? "The artist's eye, you see, is a rare way of seeing the world and other people. It's a unique gift. Some people are born with it. Most are not, but those who have it must create or die

unfulfilled. Tell me—why did you draw that butterfly on the building? Surely you had other things to do. Certainly you knew the rain would wash the picture away. So why did you bother drawing it at all?"

She kept her features carefully composed. "I was only practicing—to meet you."

"Then tell me about the man you drew in the tavern? Who was he? A special friend? Someone you've met and admired?"

"No." Her expression darkened with unreadable emotions, and she looked away. "He was just someone I saw on the street—a gentleman from one of the ships. I never met him. He would never talk to…someone like me."

He had struck a nerve, yet the flame of defiance still burned strong in her eyes. Schuyler waited in silence for her to collect her thoughts, marveling at the persistence of the creative spirit within her. From the looks of her patched skirt and faded bodice he surmised that she had spoken truly when she said she had no money for art supplies. Yet she had found a way to create with a blank building and a chalky island rock.

"There is more to it than you realize," he murmured when she looked up and her gaze met his again. "Art and insight come from the creative Spirit. Almighty God has given you a gift, and I have seen the depth of the gift within you. I would be neglecting my responsibilities to God himself if I did not help you as much as I am able."

The girl met his gaze evenly. "I don't care much about God these days," she answered, "but I know a lot about life. I've lived six years in that tavern, Heer Van Dyck, and I've seen things that would make a gentleman like you shudder. But I want to be an artist. If being a good artist can take me away from the tavern, I'll do anything to learn."

Schuyler crossed his arms, impressed by the depth of determination in her voice. "There is much to learn, my dear. Though you have an incredible eye and a sure touch, you must learn how to

apply that eye and that touch to canvas. I can teach you to work in oil and watercolors, to outline skillfully and to blend color. If you want to take your art to the world, if you want it to be enjoyed," he lowered his voice and smiled, "you must trust me. We will not have time to waste. Your will is formidable. I can see it in your eyes, and I do not have time to break or tame it. I am sailing from Batavia in less than a month, and may be gone for a very long time."

An almost imperceptible expression of pleading filled her face. "When might I begin—that is, if you agree to teach me?"

Schuyler smiled in approval. The apple was overripe and ready to fall from the tree. He would never have a more eager pupil. If only he had discovered her a year ago!

"Come again tomorrow," he said, standing. "Bring whatever you like, and I will supply whatever you lack. You will have my daughter's upstairs room."

"Your daughter?" Aidan's green eyes flashed like jewels. "Won't she mind having company in her room? I don't suppose she's used to sharing her chamber with…a woman like me."

Schuyler folded his hands. "Rozamond is married now, with a home of her own. Her room is vacant, and I have no doubt she would be pleased to know someone is using it again. My son, Henrick, lives here, too, but spends most of his time at his place of employment."

Aidan fell silent for a moment, and he could feel the strength of her desire. She was tempted; she wanted to learn, yet something held her back. Was it fear? Uncertainty?

"How do we know," the blond girl suddenly blurted out, her blue eyes peering out from sockets like caves of bone, "that this isn't a trick? Aidan is a proper young woman, you know. She's not a hussy; the most wrong she's ever done is filch a purse or two when a sailor's too drunk to walk—"

"Orabel!" Aidan gasped.

Schuyler looked down at his hands and tried to ignore Aidan's

sudden embarrassment. "I'm certain Joffer O'Connor will have no need to filch anything while she is here with us," he said easily. "I will provide everything she needs. My housekeeper, Gusta, will serve as chaperone and teacher."

Aidan gave a grimace of distaste. "What does that old crone know about art?"

A violent rattling of teacups and saucers brought Schuyler's heart to his throat. The "old crone" had appeared in the doorway at an extremely inopportune moment, and obviously had heard Aidan's comment. Gusta scowled furiously at her master, her brows knitting together over eyes that burned hot with resentment.

"Gusta will teach you about life, Joffer O'Connor," Schuyler sighed. "If you are to move and live in the art world, you'll have to know more than how to hold a paintbrush. I will teach you about art; Gusta will teach you how to live in, ah, refined society."

In acknowledgment of her name, Gusta strode into the room, huffing her disapproval as she lowered the tea tray to Schuyler's desk.

"I'm not certain I understand why I have to live here." Aidan's brows pulled together into a frown as pronounced as the house-keeper's. "I could stay where I'm living now."

"If I am to give you a complete course in the short time I have available, I will not be able to spend precious hours escorting you to and fro or searching for you in that tavern."

A blush began to creep up her cheeks again, and Schuyler moved his gaze to the tea tray. Considering where the girl had come from, she had an uncommon amount of pride. Quite unusual for a barmaid.

From the corner of his eye he saw her swallow hard and lift her chin. "How do you expect to be repaid for this kindness, Heer Van Dyck? I've been on the street long enough to know that no one does something for nothing. Even the minister down at the church makes the natives give up their idols and such before he'll give them a decent meal and a clean shirt."

"How will I be repaid?" Schuyler took a moment to ponder

the question, then stood and moved to the shelves behind his desk. He ran his fingers lightly over the leather spines of several volumes, then pulled out a thick collection of copperplate engravings done by Sibylla Marion.

"Joffer Sibylla Marion," he said, placing the book on his desk and opening it to an especially lustrous engraving of insects upon plant life, "is a Dutch woman who specializes in painting butterflies and other assorted insects. She has published this book and others like it. The sale of such books provides a steady income for her family."

He slid the book toward her, noticing with approval that Aidan leaned forward in anticipation. Her hand trembled as she reached out to leaf through the heavy vellum pages, and he let her peruse it at her leisure, watching as her green eyes began to sparkle with pleasure and an undeniable look of awe overtook her face.

"She is paid for painting things like this?" she whispered, a catch in her voice. "These pictures are beautiful. They're so real!"

"Positively yummy," Orabel agreed, nibbling on one of the sweetbread cookies from the tea tray. She gestured toward the teapot and lifted a brow.

"Help yourself please," Schuyler said, moving so the girl could have better access to the refreshments. Slowly he came round to stand behind Aidan and looked at the Marion book over her shoulder.

"You could create a collection just like this one," he said, lightly tapping her arm. "You have the gift, the artist's eye. You only need the training—and the opportunity." He smiled when she looked up at him. "And if you cannot believe that I would help you from the goodness of a godly impulse, then perhaps you could be convinced to believe that I would appreciate a share of your future earnings."

He had no intention of ever taking a single penny this young woman might earn, of course, but the idea seemed to make sense to her, and she nodded. Her world was much more primitive and

harsh than his, he reminded himself, and she was obviously un-acquainted with selfless generosity.

Moving toward his worktable at the window, he pulled a sheet of heavy vellum from the drawer, then attached it to the clips upon his cloth-covered easel. "Have you ever worked in water-colors?" he asked, glancing over his shoulder. All traces of concern and false pride had vanished from Aidan's eyes; she watched him now with undisguised curiosity and eagerness.

"No." With self-conscious dignity she moved to stand behind him and reached out to touch the easel.

"Paper is important." He gestured toward the vellum. "Feel this—notice how smooth it is? This is Not paper, my particular favorite."

"It's not paper?" She crinkled her nose. "It *feels* like paper—"

"That's merely the name, Not paper," he answered, smiling at her. "There are smooth papers, medium papers, and rough papers. Most artists prefer Not, a medium paper, because it has enough texture to hold the paint but not enough to interfere with color and detail."

Her eyes clouded. "Is it terribly rare? I could never afford an expensive paper."

"Another reason you will be better off living in my house." Schuyler removed the sponge from its tray. "I can supply all the materials you will need. I may be wrong, but I imagine you would have difficulty even storing the necessary equipment at your home—er, where you live."

He unclamped the paper, turned it, and wiped the damp sponge over the back of the sheet. She moved closer. "What are you doing now?"

"Thinner papers must be stretched so they don't buckle when you apply paint," he explained, wetting the paper in broad, smooth strokes. "The piece of fabric upon the easel will absorb any residual water, but the paper is now flexible, ready to catch the ideas you will put on it."

"Me?" Surprise siphoned the blood from her face, and she took a hasty half-step back. "Oh, I could never use your paints and papers, sir. I don't know anything about paint, I've only worked with chalk and a pencil."

"Don't fret about paints and papers; they can be easily replaced." Schuyler turned and leaned upon his worktable. "I'll be giving you my time, and at my advanced age, time is infinitely more valuable than parchments and paints. I am willing to give, dear girl, so what keeps you from accepting? Come to my house; be my apprentice. I will train you until I have to sail."

Beneath the smooth surface of her face there was a suggestion of movement, as though a hidden desire were trying to break through a layer of ice.

"Why should you draw on sidewalks and buildings?" Schuyler went on. "God has gifted you with the tools to be a great artist, Aidan, but you must not be afraid to begin."

She took a quick, sharp breath and stepped back, nearly colliding with the girl at the tea tray. "I'll—I'll have to think about it." Her face was firmly set in deep thought, her eyes fastened to the blank page upon the easel.

"There is not much time," Schuyler answered, praying he would not betray his impatience. "Come tomorrow if you will come at all. Go home, think about my offer, consult with anyone you must. And I pray you will join me in learning." He smiled as he remembered her eagerness to accost him in the street. "I am sure I would find the experience of teaching you quite…memorable."

"I'll let you know tomorrow." She tugged on her friend's sleeve. Orabel snatched up a handful of cookies, bobbed toward Schuyler in a quick curtsy, and followed Aidan O'Connor out the door.

꧁꧂

Sitting in the corner of the women's room, Lili watched her daughter pace back and forth like a dog on a chain. Aidan's green eyes snapped with impatience and indecision, her body tense as a

bowstring. In the hour since she and Orabel had returned from Heer Van Dyck's house, Aidan had only grown more upset, more confused, and more indecisive.

"I only asked him for a suggestion or two." Aidan's words were directed as much to the other women in the room as to her mother. "I thought maybe he'd give me a moment of his time. I never dreamed that he'd offer more—or that he'd want me to live in his house. I want to draw, I want to learn—but he'll be leaving soon, and then what will I do?"

She had explained Heer Van Dyck's offer in simple terms and spent the better part of the last hour half-listening to the other women's suggestions. Sofie and Orabel urged Aidan to take the old gentleman at his word, for such generous offers didn't come along every day. "Who knows what treasures you'll find in that house?" Sofie remarked, giving Aidan a sly wink. "If it doesn't work out, take whatever suits your fancy and slip out in the middle of the night. The old fool will be too proud to report you to the authorities. The constable would only say he got what he deserved for taking a ragamuffin in."

Aidan stiffened at Sofie's remark, and Lili pursed her lips, at once proud and ashamed. Proud that her daughter still retained enough conscience to consider stealing an embarrassment, ashamed that she had ever been forced to steal in order to survive.

When Lili married the handsome, copper-haired Cory O'Connor, she never dreamed that he would lead her to the wharf of a sweltering Dutch colony near the equator. As always, life had surprised her. To escape hard times in Ireland, she and Cory had fled to England, where just outside London Aidan was born an English subject of King James. Cory found an honest job working for a prosperous cooper, but when the Black Plague struck London in 1636, killing the cooper, Cory signed on with the Dutch East India Company to move his family out of reach of the disease. Aidan was but thirteen when they sailed, and observed her

fourteenth birthday aboard ship on the very day her father died, a late victim of the plague he had tried to flee.

Lili and Aidan landed in Batavia with no protector, no home, no means of employment. Lili had spent several frustrating weeks ashore seeking employment as a lady's maid, but none of the Dutch housewives wanted a maid with a honey-thick Irish brogue and a comely fourteen-year-old daughter.

And so Lili had survived in the only way she could. She cut her first purse from a drunken sailor's belt in an act of sheer desperation, and in time the act of pilfering hurt her conscience less and less. Soon she had developed an entire routine: Incoming sailors, eager for a little feminine company and alcoholic spirits, smiled at her, bought her drinks, and fell happily and drunkenly asleep upon her bosom. 'Twas a simple matter to empty their purses and rifle their money belts, and Lili took pains to always leave the men a stuiver or two. She left no man penniless; in fact, she wondered if any of them ever sobered up enough to realize that she'd whittled away at their earthly lucre.

Within six months of landing in Batavia she met Bram, who agreed to lease a room for her and Aidan if she would serve as his procuress. As the months passed, Lili drew other defenseless and desperate women under the umbrella of her protection. To the naive and unskilled she taught certain tricks of her trade—how to be safe from pregnancy, how to escape if a seaman became violent, where to hide from the constables when the townsfolk occasionally decided to purge the wharf of evil and unrighteousness. She did not hesitate to speak the bald truth as she saw it, and once laughed in the face of a minister who dared to upbraid her for poverty and scandalous behavior.

"Well, naturally, you blame us poor and derelict for needing the charity of the rich," she told the clergyman, shooting him the coldest look she could muster. "But you forget, Reverend, that the rich need us poor folks for the quiet of their souls. How can they

lie down to sleep unless they've tossed a beggar a stuiver or two to ease their guilt over the twenty guilders they spent on some useless frippery?" Leaving the minister speechless in the street, Lili wrapped the rags of her dignity around her like a fine lady's cape, turned her back on the preacher, and stalked away.

Now Lady Lili was a legend of sorts in the Dutch city, and she took quiet pride in her accomplishments. She'd saved at least twenty women from outright starvation and had actually seen half a dozen married to seamen and happily transported back to Europe. The others she'd taught were survivors at any cost—all except Aidan, whom Lili had sheltered as much as she dared.

Her own daughter, Lili realized more clearly with every passing day, was unique. The girl's artistic gift had first manifested itself when she was only four or five. While other children splashed in the muddy streets of London and painted themselves brown and gray, Aidan decorated the side of the building with whatever materials she could find in the street. Once Lili had to literally haul her screaming child away from a particularly putrid puddle—someone had emptied the chamber pots from the house above onto the street, and Aidan had wanted to investigate the colors of the stinking mess.

Aidan constantly rebelled against her mother's boundaries. Even though Lili *thought* Aidan appreciated the fact that she didn't have to work the streets because Bram employed her as a regular barmaid, she nevertheless disliked being singled out from the other girls. Still Aidan worked hard—sloshing drinks for thirsty seamen, dodging their drunken caresses, and earning enough in the process to keep the other girls from complaining that she didn't pull her fair share.

Having saved her daughter from life on the streets, Lili had been quietly content with Aidan's progress, hopeful that she would someday find a husband among the visitors to the tavern. Years ago in England, Lili would never have imagined the life she'd come to lead, but at least Aidan had been spared the worst of it.

Lili still had courage enough to hope that her daughter would find a husband...and a better life.

The trouble was—Lili glanced at Aidan now as the girl sat near the doorway, lost in thought—Aidan exhibited a young woman's typical independence. The pulling away that began at age twelve had evolved into a genuine stubbornness. Now the fastest way to get Aidan to do something was for Lili to beg her not to do it.

Sighing, Lili pulled her handkerchief from her bosom and absently blotted perspiration from her skin. Aidan ought to go with this Heer Van Dyck. She would find a better life in his house than she would ever find here at the wharf. But if Lili suggested that such a move might be wise, Aidan would undoubtedly stiffen her neck and dig in her heels. She'd plead loyalty to Orabel, or proclaim Heer Van Dyck a snob, or cry that she feared being sent to the workhouse if she didn't meet her master's expectations.

Maybe she should be afraid. The world on the opposite side of Market Street was completely alien. The Van Dycks and Van Diemens and Vander Hagens preached purity and cleanliness, scrubbing themselves, their houses, and their souls with equal fervor. Aidan had not grown up in that climate, and she might not know how to cope with such ruthless single-mindedness. Lili had heard too many cutting comments to think that she could ever live in that world.

But if anyone could adjust, Aidan could. Aidan had not despoiled herself; she was still chaste, still honorable. And there was something special about her, some elusive quality born of sorrow or blood. Lili felt the distinction, as if some spirit had stolen the child from her womb and replaced it with a changeling.

But Aidan *was* her daughter—of that there could be no doubt. One had only to look at those green eyes, that stubborn chin. She and Lili were cut out of the same cloth.

Lili hugged her arms to her and looked away, trying to decide how to respond to Aidan's dilemma. Why was motherhood so

difficult? You brought a little girl into the world and hoped she'd be everything you were not, knowing that one day she would look at you with wide eyes that see all that you are. And that seeing, that *understanding* of your frailties and faults, would tear her from your grasp and keep her forever at arm's length…

Aidan had to go with Heer Van Dyck. This was her chance, and Lili would have to make her take it.

Her heart squeezing in anguish, Lili wiped her brow with the sticky handkerchief and straightened her back. "There's only one thing to be done, of course," she said brusquely. "You simply can't go with the man, lass. I'm thinking there's some folly going on in his house, for what kind of man would ask a girl young enough to be his granddaughter to live with him?"

"I'm twenty, Mama," Aidan answered, her eyes like emeralds, cold and sharp, as she looked up. "And Heer Van Dyck is not my grandfather."

"All the same, I wouldn't do it." Lili sighed heavily and blew a wayward curl from her forehead. "Bram will have to find a new girl to work behind the bar, and Orabel hasn't the strength to haul trays all day. Sofie might serve to take your place, but she'd steal Bram blind, and he won't have it." Her voice was firm and final. "No, you can't leave Bram, nor all the young men who come in for a drink just because they fancy Irish Annie."

"What?" Aidan countered.

Icy fear twisted around Lili's heart, and she shifted her gaze to meet her daughter, trying to maintain her fragile control. "How will you ever catch a husband if you're painting all day in some old man's house? The tavern is where you'll find the solid men. You're not a young lass any more, Aidan, and if you don't find a husband—" Shrugging, she let her voice fade away, implying that all hope was lost if Aidan didn't marry soon.

Aidan's face sharpened in a scowl. "Am I to be drawing ale for the rest of my life then?" she demanded, rising to her feet. "Is that

all you think I can do? I could do more, Mama. Heer Van Dyck says I have the eye of a great artist."

"Hrumph." Lili picked up a stiff fan and waved it to cool her face. "I don't know how you got such an eye, for your father couldn't draw a straight line. And I'm as likely to wake up with King Charlie of England on the morrow as to produce a babe who can paint an honest picture."

"I can!" A swift shadow of anger swept across Aidan's face, and Lili braced herself for the explosion that was sure to follow. But when she looked up at Aidan again, the girl's eyes welled with hurt.

"I can paint, Mama, and I think I can be good," she answered thickly. "Not great, perhaps, but very good. And this is my chance...to be respectable."

Aidan looked away, a glazed look of despair beginning to spread over her face, and Lili felt a vague shudder of humiliation pass through her. Aidan hadn't actually come out and said that they weren't respectable now, but there was no denying the truth that underlined her words.

Lili *wasn't* respectable, not anymore. She was no longer a good mother, a moral Christian, or a virtuous lady. Life—harsh, rough, and unrelenting—had chiseled all the fine edges and useless vanities out of her soul. And though she had no doubt that Aidan loved her, her daughter was also deeply ashamed of what they had become.

She looked away, hardening her heart against the tears that rose in her throat. If she showed her true feelings or exposed any sign of weakness, Aidan might surrender to sentimentality and refuse to take this unheard-of opportunity. One sign of affection now might ruin her daughter's life forever.

At last Lili threw her head back and pulled herself up from the pallet she'd been sitting on. "Go be respectable then," she snapped. Her voice came out cold and hard, and she could feel the

other women's looks of surprise and alarm. "Be gone from here, you ungrateful girl. I dare you to make something of yourself! But don't you come back if you quit, or the girls and I will never let you forget it."

Aidan's mouth clamped tight for a moment, and her slender throat bobbed once as she swallowed. "Mama—"

Turning away, Lili moved through the doorway in a flash of skirts, one soft sob escaping from her as she pushed her way through the crowd outside the tavern.

"Go with God, lass," Lili murmured, reaching out to steady herself against a streetlamp as she rigidly held her tears in check. "I will pray for your every happiness and joy."

Back in the women's room, Aidan drew a long, quivering breath, struggling to master the passion that shook her. Her mother had just cast her off in front of Orabel and the others, and all because Aidan wanted to be something more than a harlot or barmaid or street beggar.

She turned her back to hide her tears and stormed toward the chest that served as a bureau for all Lili's women. Hoisting the heavy lid, she looked down into the jumble of skirts, bodices, and sleeves. Anything in this trunk would only look worn and out of place in Heer Van Dyck's fine house. Besides, the other girls would sorely miss anything she might take.

"Aidan?" Orabel's gentle hand fell upon her sleeve. "She didn't mean it. She loves you so much."

"It doesn't matter." Aidan let the lid fall with a heavy slam and turned, leaning upon the trunk as she took one final look around the room. Heer Van Dyck had told her to bring whatever she wanted, but there was nothing in this room—in her entire life— that she wanted to take with her.

Except maybe Orabel. "Don't worry about me." She gave Orabel a fleeting smile and patted her friend's hand. "I should have known that Lili would not want me to go. By some quirk of

fate she brought me into this world, but we haven't agreed on anything in years. And now it is time we were parting."

"I'll miss you." Orabel's mouth twisted into something that was not quite a smile.

"I'll miss you too." Girding herself with resolve, Aidan lifted her chin, smoothed her skirt, and walked out into the noisy street, determined not to look back.

Seven

Schuyler lowered his crystal glass and studied his daughter over the rim. Marriage certainly seemed to agree with Rozamond. Her dark eyes glowed behind her spectacles, and she had taken to wearing her hair in a trim, matronly bun at the top of her head. Tiny side ringlets of dark hair fringed her pale face, and her smile flitted easily between her brother, Henrick, and her husband of less than a year, Dempsey Jasper.

"If you'll allow me, sir," Dempsey was saying with a frown, "I believe the V.O.C. should devote as much attention to its current colonies as to the proposed explorations. The natives here are not as dull-witted as we think. With a solid effort, I believe they could be enlightened and put to service as manual laborers. Just because a man has brown skin does not mean his brain and heart are deformed as well."

"Enlighten the natives?" Henrick shifted in his chair, then rested his chin in his hand. "My dear brother-in-law, surely you jest. We have barely managed to convince them that a wise man really ought to come out of the rain during a deluge."

"Excuse me, Heer Van Dyck." Gusta's worried face appeared in the doorway, and all conversation ceased. "You have a guest. That *person*—that woman—has come."

"Really?" Schuyler lowered his glass to the table. The young artist was proving to be an ever-changing mystery. When she left he wasn't certain he would ever see her again, and yet here she was, an entire day early.

He clasped his hands and smiled at his children. "Henrick, Rozamond, you must meet Aidan O'Connor. A most extraordinary young woman."

"A young woman?" Rozamond's smile flattened. "Father, what have you done? I thought we decided it would be foolish to hire another servant when you are preparing to leave."

"She's not a servant."

Schuyler ignored the confused expressions on his children's faces, pushed himself out of his chair, and went toward the hall. A moment later Aidan O'Connor appeared in the doorway, her jaw set with determination, a glimmer of apprehension in her eyes.

"Miss O'Connor," he said in English, bowing stiffly. "I pray you have not eaten. We would have waited dinner for you, but I did not expect you this evening."

"I saw no reason to wait," she murmured, her voice soft and uncertain as he led her into the dining room.

"Henrick, Rozamond, Dempsey," Schuyler said, glancing at each of them in turn. "May I present Miss Aidan O'Connor, from—ah, from London."

The trio sat, blank, amazed, and stupefied. Then, as if he had suddenly remembered his manners, Henrick rose from his chair. "Miss O'Connor," he said, nearly stumbling over his seat as he hastened to the young lady's side. The smile he gave her was genuine and openly admiring. "A pleasure to meet you."

Dempsey was slower to rise, but he finally stood and bowed. "Delighted," he muttered as his sharp eyes took in every inch of the girl's impoverished appearance. "And charmed."

Rozamond was not so quick to offer her hospitality. "Miss O'Connor," she murmured, her lids slipping down over her eyes. "Welcome to our—to my father's house. Won't you join us for dinner?"

Aidan's gaze fluttered over the table set for four, the men's elaborate garb, Rozamond's silk and lace gown.

"I couldn't, for I've eaten already," she murmured, twin stains

of scarlet blossoming upon her cheeks. "If I might be excused, sir, I'll go to my room until you call for me."

"Are you quite certain?" Schuyler asked. "It is no trouble for Gusta to set another place."

"I couldn't eat another bite." But her eyes betrayed her as they fixed on the leg of lamb, the steaming bread, and the heaping mound of spiced fruit in the center of the table. "Thank you, sir, but I'll go to my room, if that is all right."

"Very well then." Schuyler understood—as well as he could, at any rate, without ever having been hungry himself. The poor thing was probably starving, but she felt terribly out of place in this formal atmosphere. He inclined his head in a gesture of agreement and extended his hand toward the hallway. "Make yourself at home, Miss O'Connor. You'll find Gusta in my library, and she will show you to the upstairs room. I'll have her send up a tray...just in case you grow hungry later." He stopped and gave her a heartfelt smile. "I am very glad you decided to come, Miss O'Connor. God usually takes longer to answer my prayers."

She turned and hurried away toward the library, where Gusta appeared in the doorway like a vengeful guardian spirit. Schuyler thrust his hands behind his back and rocked on his heels for a moment. He wanted to make certain Aidan wouldn't change her mind and bolt for the door at the last moment.

"Gusta, would you please show our guest to the upstairs chamber?" He kept his voice civil and ignored the storm of displeasure in the housekeeper's eyes. "And make her a tray for supper, will you? She might be hungry...later."

When Gusta had silently led the girl toward the stairs, he turned at last to confront the incredulous faces awaiting him in the dining room.

"*Upstairs?*" Rozamond squealed. "You're keeping that woman upstairs in my room?"

"Father, this is truly unconventional. What will the neighbors think?"

"Heer Van Dyck, far be it from me to question your judgment, but what purpose could this girl possibly serve? Surely you don't need another housekeeper—"

"That girl," Schuyler interrupted, "just may make my name great." He jauntily cocked his head to one side and looked at his daughter. "And what I do under my roof is really none of your concern, Rozamond; you should look to the affairs of your own household." He turned to his son. "This is only for a short time. The neighbors will have no cause to gossip; we are fully chaperoned with Gusta here." Finally he looked at his gaping son-in-law. "Dempsey, that young woman is the most talented artist I have ever had the honor of meeting. She is untrained, but I have a strong feeling the scope and glory of her work will one day far surpass mine."

That said, he resumed his seat, picked up his knife and spoon, and sliced off a healthy portion of the lamb. "If none of you has any further objection, I would like to finish my dinner in peace."

They finished the meal in stunned silence. Henrick could not help but notice that his father gulped his food, bolted his drink, and excused himself before the others could gather the courage to launch another series of questions. The old man forfeited his usual cigar at the dinner table and moved immediately to his library.

"Look at him!" Rozamond hissed when their father was safely out of earshot. "What in the world could have possessed him? Where did he find this woman? Do you think—" Her face twisted in a grimace. "—she has somehow bewitched him? I've heard of older gentlemen being seduced by young women, but never thought my own father could fall for such foolishness."

"She's a comely lass, for certain," Dempsey inserted, obviously unaware of the scathing look Rozamond shot him. "I could see why any man would admire her, but she seems a bit bedraggled for Heer Van Dyck's taste. If he wanted female companionship, surely he would have gone a-courting among the eligible and noble women of this town."

"I've seen her before." Henrick squinted across the room, trying to conjure up the memory. "Down at the docks, I'm sure. I've seen her among the women who frequent the tavern at Broad Street. Do you not remember the group that loiters on the street corner? There's a girl who sings for pennies, and a pair who dance. And this one, I'm certain, is a barmaid at the tavern." His eyes narrowed as he considered the events of the evening. "If Father says she is an artist, he is undoubtedly right. He has always recognized others…with his gift."

Which neither Rozamond nor I have. He wanted us to be artists, and we aren't like him at all.

"Be reasonable, Henrick. Great artists don't wait tables in a tavern! This girl is nothing but a tramp, one of those brazen dockside hussies the minister is always threatening to arrest." Flushing, Rozamond pushed back her chair and stood. "And I will simply not allow Father to put her in my room. She'll rob us blind! By this time tomorrow our father will be dead in his bed while a tribe of those wastrels ravage the house—"

"You cannot discount Gusta," Henrick interrupted. "If this woman is up to mischief, Gusta will have her back out on the street before the woman knows what's hit her. I don't think we need to fear for Father's safety."

"Still—" Dempsey lifted his glass and swirled the liquid inside. "I'd feel more at ease if I knew where the woman came from and what her intentions are. Everyone has a past, and everyone has a purpose. I'd just like to know what Aidan O'Connor's plans are."

"All right then." Henrick rubbed his hands on his trousers and inclined his head. "I will see what I can discover about her."

❧

"If you need anything—" The housekeeper spoke slowly, as if forcing unwilling words from her tongue. "—bring it to my attention." The woman's dark eyes drifted pointedly over Aidan's slender form. "Though since I can see that you have brought nothing, you shall probably need everything."

"I don't require much." Aidan met Gusta's accusing eyes without flinching. "This gown has always been quite fine enough for me, and your master said he'd furnish the art supplies and such."

The housekeeper's left eyebrow rose in indignation. "That gown must be washed at once. And you must take a bath. I cannot allow you to sleep on Miss Rozamond's clean sheets with a layer of grime upon your neck and only God knows what filth on the skin I cannot see." The right brow rose to match the left. "Good gracious, I hadn't thought—I suppose you have lice."

The woman's caustic tone made Aidan flush. "No more than anyone else!" she snapped. "I'll have you know we aired out the chest at least once a month, and beat the buggers off our clothes. I'm not a wallowing seaman, no matter what you're thinking. I'm a woman, same as you, and as decent as you, too."

The housekeeper marched to the tall bed and snatched the quilt from it. "Take this." She tossed the quilt toward Aidan. "Take off your skirt, bodice, and shirt—every stitch of fabric you have on. Wrap yourself in the quilt while I have the laundress bring up the tub and hot water."

"Hot water?" Aidan gasped in honest horror. "Sweet sky above, surely you're not planning to boil me alive?"

Gusta nodded with enthusiasm. "Boil you, scrape you, parch you, and iron you if need be. But when you go to bed tonight you'll be clean, by heaven, or—" She paused and narrowed her eyes. "Or I'll tell the master I'm afraid you're planning to steal the silver in the kitchen."

Aidan's mouth dropped open. "You'd tell such a lie? I haven't done a thing!"

"But you might." The grim line of the woman's mouth relaxed slightly. "I know your type, sloven, and I know what's going through your mind. You're thinking you'll stay here a night or two, and if you find the work too hard you'll be on your way with a pretty bauble or two for your trouble."

Aidan clamped her mouth shut, stunned by the woman's

bluntness. 'Twas almost as if the housekeeper had overheard her conversation with the other women this afternoon. Sofie had advised Aidan to do exactly as Gusta said.

The frown of concentration deepened above Gusta's brows. "Tell me this, girl—why are you here? Are you here only to steal? If you are, why don't I give you a trinket and let you be on your way?"

The question caught Aidan off guard, and she shifted through her own thoughts. What *had* brought her to this place? Had she come only to spite her mother? No, her reasons went deeper than that. Heer Van Dyck had promised that art could make her respectable, could make her a great lady.

"I'm here to learn." Aidan stiffened, momentarily abashed, then looked up and gave the housekeeper a twisted smile. "You may not believe me, but I'm here to learn about art. That's all. And I don't know how long I'll be staying."

The woman lifted her head, like a dog scenting the breeze, and crossed her arms. "Well," she said, "I'm going to see that you don't take advantage of my master. There's more going on in this house than you know, and if Heer Van Dyck asks you to work hard, you'll work hard. You're here, and I can't help that, but if you stay you'll do all he asks with a willing heart." She gave a snort of warning. "Because if you don't, I have the power to make your life miserable. And I will, mark my words."

Aidan clutched the quilt in front of her like a shield against the woman's aggressive devotion. "I'm not a slave," she whispered. "You can't beat me or force me to do anything against my will."

"Of course not, none of us would. But you're not quality folk, either, and you mustn't be forgetting your place. The Van Dycks were a first family of the Netherlands, fine people, important people. And if you want to live in this house, if even for a short time, you must clean yourself up."

"*Live* in this house?" Aidan glanced pointedly at the tall, narrow bed, the neat dresser, the polished chamber floor. "This isn't a house, it's a museum! How can anyone live here? The bed is so high I'm

liable to break my neck if I stumble in the dark while getting up to answer the call of nature—"

"Be that as it may," Gusta answered, a heavy dose of sarcasm in her voice, "at least you will have the comfort of knowing you have died in clean linen." She held out an imperious hand. "Now give me those clothes. You'll find a clean shirt in the wardrobe, but don't you dare put it on until after your bath. I'll send up some lye soap to take care of the lice."

Still holding the quilt to her chest with one hand, Aidan struggled to untie the strings holding her sleeve to her bodice. "All right," she murmured. If one had to bathe and scrub in order to be respectable, she might as well begin.

Eight

Schuyler struggled to contain a gasp of pleased surprise when Gusta announced Aidan's presence the next morning. After walking past the housekeeper, his young guest turned in the doorway and managed to complete a most graceful curtsy. "Good morning, sir," she whispered, her voice softer than he had imagined it could be.

He gazed at her wordlessly. Pretty enough even in the tattered gown she had worn yesterday, the girl positively glowed with radiance in her new attire.

The housekeeper's broad face wore an expression of mingled pride and disapproval. "My compliments, Gusta," he murmured. "You have done well."

Gusta had outfitted the young woman in one of Rozamond's old gowns. A full skirt fell in gracious wide pleats from a high, narrow waistline, and the young woman's slender, freshly scrubbed arms hung gracefully at her side beneath short, puffy sleeves. A double linen collar framed Aidan's pink face, and her rebellious mane of red hair had been neatly corralled into a sizeable topknot at the crown of her head.

All in all, the young woman appeared tidy, neat, and nearly civilized, but the green eyes were still flashing—a sure sign that the housekeeper had managed to tame and polish only the exterior.

"Good morning." Schuyler found his voice and pushed back his chair. "I trust you slept well."

"Tolerably enough." Aidan's mouth pulled into a slightly sour

smile as she clasped her hands at her waist. "It was too quiet in that room. I kept dreaming—an old dream, a pleasant one where I'm dancing on the beach—and then I'd suddenly wake up, realizing that there was no music, no sound at all. I feared that something terrible had happened."

"Ahem, well." Schuyler looked down at his desk, not wanting to ask what sort of sounds usually kept the girl awake. Given where he had found her, a typical evening could have contained all sorts of nefarious activities.

"I've been busy," he looked up, "preparing a schedule for our next several days together. I plan to teach you a lesson each morning and set you to a task, then I must be about the business of preparing for my upcoming expedition. I do hope you understand." He gave her a proud smile. "You may have heard the rumor that I am to sail on Abel Tasman's next voyage. If the weather holds and the arrangements are finalized, we shall sail sometime in mid-August."

She did not answer, but twisted her hands slightly. Was she nervous?

Better to keep her busy; tomorrow would take care of itself. "I've been gathering the equipment you will need to get started," he said, moving toward the easel he had set up near the window. "You have the gift and the artist's eye, I could see that straightaway, but I suspect that you have not been exposed to the different mediums."

"The what?" Uncertainty crept into her expression.

"Watercolors, oils, pen and ink, pencils." Schuyler gestured toward his worktable. "I think I would like to tutor you most particularly in watercolors. Of course, you can learn other techniques later, but I've a particular project in mind where watercolor will be most appropriate."

She walked slowly toward the worktable, her expression softening as her eyes took in the collection of paints, brushes, and papers. "Do you work in watercolor, sir?"

"Sometimes." He pulled a portfolio of his own work from a shelf. "I'm a cartographer, and I usually paint maps." Interest gleamed in her eyes as he lifted the cover and pointed to some of his previous work. "Cartography is a science and an art, you see, a necessary meeting of the two. I take the charts compiled by ships' captains and then translate their readings and notations onto the page."

He turned the page and picked out one of his favorite pieces, a map of the Indonesian archipelago. "See this?" He ran his finger over the fine lines. "This is Indonesia, and this island is Java, where we live. This small dot," he pointed to a spot on the northwestern shoreline, "is Batavia, our own city."

He heard her breathing, quick and light, as her own hand gently traced the island. Those observant eyes absorbed every detail. "This space," she whispered, "is the sea?"

He nodded. "The Pacific Ocean. And these shapes are other islands which surround us—New Guinea and New Holland." He paused, then lowered his head in order to look up into her eyes. "Have you never seen a map, Miss O'Connor?"

One of her shoulders rose in a shrug, then he saw a blush run over her cheeks. They would make slow progress if she insisted on becoming embarrassed or defensive every time he asked a simple question.

"My dear Joffer O'Connor," he said, "you need not fear ridicule from me. A student learns best when she realizes that she has much to learn, and you need not be embarrassed by your lack of knowledge. Question freely; speak your thoughts, for I will not castigate you, nor will I be astounded at anything you say." He offered her a small smile. "Indeed, I shall only be amazed at your talent, which gives you every right to be here."

She looked fully into his eyes, and in that silent moment he felt something—a transfer, however brief, of her trust. "I am not afraid of you, sir. It is only that—" She hesitated and bit her lip. "You cannot know how much I have longed for an opportunity like this. But I was certain it was never meant to be."

"God works in mysterious ways, my dear." He turned and walked toward the glass-paned door that opened into the garden. With one gesture he turned the doorknob and flung the door open, then smiled as Aidan gasped in delight at the sight of the summer garden beyond.

"You drew a butterfly, so I guessed that you have an affinity for nature." He silently congratulated himself upon his first success with her. "I believe we will start with a lesson on how to paint flora in watercolor. So please, come with me into the garden, and let us find some flower you'd like to paint today. I'll have one of the servants set up your easel in a suitable spot."

They walked together, silently, through flaming beds of winding bougainvillea, bright hibiscus, and flowering frangipani, the sweet flowers the natives used to create wreaths and circlets of fragrant blossoms. After a few moments, she paused beside a pool in which lotus lilies grew in abundance.

"Here," she said. Her eyes fastened upon a single elegant blossom that lifted its head far above the others. "I would like to paint this."

Schuyler nodded to his steward, who had quietly followed with the easel. A sheet of prepared parchment and a small tray of watercolors arrived a moment later, and he saw Aidan's eyes fill with appreciation and delight to find such treasures at her fingertips.

"You might wish to sketch it first," he suggested, indicating the pencil in the tray. " I shall leave you to your work." He took the small stool from the steward and positioned it for her. "When you have finished, I shall answer any questions and provide a helpful critique." He bowed slightly. "But only if needed."

She sank onto the stool, her eyes moving again to the jewel-bright flowers, and Schuyler backed away. She was very much like him, this young woman. Already he could see the creative spirit of the artist within her, a spirit he had not found in either of his children. But such things came from God, and the Almighty had

gifted Rozamond with charm and wit, while Henrick had obtained a steadfast heart and the will to work.

He left her alone and walked slowly back to his library. Strange, how God worked. The Lord had given him two wonderful children, but the offspring of his body did not share in the artistic depths of his soul. And now, after all these years, the Almighty had sent him this girl—not his own blood, but someone to whom he could pass on his knowledge and his love for art, beauty, and creativity.

"*Ja,*" he murmured to himself, moving slowly back to his worktable. "God is good."

Nine

❦

Feeling irritable and out of sorts, Sterling Thorne moved swiftly down the street, his jaw tight and his hands locked behind his back. He had been in Batavia for six days, and in that time he had come to the conclusion that the Dutch were the most stubborn people on God's green earth. Lang Carstens had not softened his stance one whit, even in the face of Sterling's dedication to winning the old doctor's approval. The physician had proved an able—if grudging—host, but he was no more willing to share his medical practice than a two-year-old child was to share a toy.

Sterling looked back over his shoulder at the terraced rice fields that rose in the distance. After fruitlessly trying to win Carstens's approval, he had gone to the nearest native village, reasoning that all people needed a doctor. But after encircling his neck with fragrant flowers and leading him to the chief's hut, the smiling Javanese assured him that they preferred their own form of medicine. The chief, an affable fellow with piercing dark eyes and long brown hair, pointed to the Banyan tree that grew in the center of the village. "The spirits of health and life live dere," he said, his English as weak as Sterling's Dutch. "We have no need of white man's medicine."

Sterling sipped from the aromatic punch someone had given him and pondered whether life in Batavia was worth trying to win the chief over. Undoubtedly it would take time before the natives could be convinced to trust Europeans, but time was something he did not have. He had arrived nearly penniless in this foreign

place with only his wits, brains, and strength to sustain him. Winning the confidence of the Javanese might take years. He needed a position *now*.

He had smiled his thanks to the chief, bowed, and distributed a few cookies—courtesy of Dr. Carstens's housekeeper, who seemed to fancy Sterling a bit too much for his comfort—among some children playing in the sand.

Sterling walked slowly back to the city, mulling over his limited options. Dr. Carstens wasn't about to share his practice among the Dutch settlers with anyone. The natives clearly didn't want a European physician. Only one other group in Batavia might benefit from his services—the sailors, barmaids, and drunks down at the wharf. They needed a doctor, probably more urgently than most of the folks who lived in the neat houses west of Market Street. But his chances of earning a living among them were about as remote as his odds with the natives.

Pensively, Sterling gazed out across a land studded with coconut palms and palmettos. Myths and glorious legends about the riches of these islands had reached every country in Europe, and men had flocked to the ports to try their hand at establishing their own wealth. Sterling's teachers had warned him that the Spice Islands were a virtual cesspool of humanity, and according to all he had seen thus far, the description seemed to aptly describe the wharf district. But why not treat those people? Lang Carstens wasn't eager to offer his services to those folk. They were uprooted people, with no homes of their own, no sense of permanence—just like Sterling.

Then the undeniable and dreadful fact struck him. He had no home, no office, no means of support. How could he treat anyone? Unless he stood on the corner like the strumpets of Broad Street, he had no way to even advertise his willingness to serve them.

He paused beside a rice field and leaned against a palm tree. Two worlds—one high, one low—converged here: the prosperous

and tidy merchants west of Market Street, the misfits of humanity on the east side. And Sterling, born into one group and thrust into the other, could think of no way to bridge the gap.

His thoughts drifted back to the day he had arrived here. He'd been so eager to explore new horizons, to make a place of his own. In England, a single letter of recommendation from a friend's friend might have opened the door to a lifelong association, but apparently such conventions were unknown, or at least unobserved, here in Batavia. So what was he to do?

"You could sit down in a tavern and drink yourself senseless," he muttered, watching a pair of sea gulls quarrel over some bit of food they'd plucked from the ground. "Or you could take yourself to a merchantman and give yourself over to a life of rope and sails."

A dark voice rippled through his memory—Witt Dekker bragging about his contacts. *I know all the sea captains, and they all know me. And I can usually be found at the Broad Street Tavern or thereabouts.*

Sterling chewed on the inside of his lip and considered it. Why not go back to sea as a surgeon? Surely some captain would appreciate a man with the ability to do more than amputate limbs whenever the need arose. The Dutch East India Company was a vast enterprise, sending out merchant ships and expeditions nearly every month.

Sterling allowed the idea to germinate within him. If he returned to the sea, he would have to steel himself against men like Witt Dekker. Unscrupulous and coarse they might be, but they would be his future patients. And unless he found a position as a doctor, he might very well be forced to become a common sailor, surrendering his scalpel for a needle and a pack of canvas thread.

He sighed, then straightened his shoulders and pressed his hat more firmly upon his head. The Almighty had brought him this far. Wherever Sterling was to go, God would lead.

"Like you always said, Papa," he murmured, fixing his eyes on

the rooftops of the city ahead, "what lies behind us and before us are insignificant matters compared to what lies within us. I believe there's a lot in me—but we shall see, shan't we?"

The only answer from the quiet jungle around him was the continuous omnipresent buzz of the island mosquitoes.

⁂

"Will you have a drink, lovey?" Lili asked, pulling a jug from behind the bar. The young sailor before her was already three sheets to the wind; he would not notice that this time his twenty stuivers bought more water than ale. "Shall I pour us both a drink?"

Cocking his head to one side, the inebriated customer woodenly thrust his mug toward her, then gave her a sodden smile. "You're beautiful, do you know that?"

"Faith, and you're a sweet lad for saying so," Lili replied smoothly, sloshing liquid into two pewter mugs. She slid one toward the young sailor, then lifted the other and winked at him. "To you and me, love. To the joy of living." As the peach-cheeked sailor lifted his mug and guzzled, Lili's mind drifted to her daughter. There had been no word from Aidan since she left for Van Dyck's house, and Lili feared that at any moment her daughter would come dragging back through the doorway, her exuberant hopes dashed forever.

The drunken boy extended a hand toward the ruffle at Lili's neck, his head falling down upon his arm as if it were suddenly too heavy for him to hold upright. "Can we go somewhere...together?" he croaked in a hoarse whisper. Lili smiled down at him and shook her head. The poor dear was scarcely a day over sixteen; what on earth had driven him to sea at such a tender age?

Whatever his reasons, he would not have to fear her tonight. He was moments away from passing out. As soon as he closed his eyes Lili would have Bram carry the boy to the women's room where he could sleep off his ale in peace. She'd make certain his

pockets remained unmolested too. He could pay for his liquor; that was enough.

"My wee love," Lili murmured, running her hand through his sandy hair. At her touch his eyes rolled back in his head; he sighed as his head lolled blissfully, dully to the wooden bar. Lili looked up and waved for Bram's attention, then pointed toward the unconscious boy. Bram grinned and came toward her, wiping his hands on the apron at his waist.

Lili moved away from the bar, pressing her hands to the small of her back as she stretched and looked around for a new mark. She didn't like being a procuress, but she had come to terms with her situation years ago. It was a degrading existence, and often brutal, but her life at the Broad Street Tavern was a far sight better than that of many women who worked for less understanding men than Bram.

At least Bram's establishment had a reputation for fair gaming, pretty women, and fine liquor. Bram had engaged the services of a group of Polish Jewish fiddlers who played from four in the afternoon to eleven at night. Pausing only to take an occasional drink, the musicians were kept busy by the seamen who demanded to hear "The East Indies Rose Tree," "A Parsley Posey," and the foot-stomping "Cabbage Salad" dance. On Fridays and Saturdays, when the Jews observed the Sabbath, a small harmonium kept the music flowing and the atmosphere cheerful.

The door swung open, spilling a horde of seamen into the tavern on a tide of chatter and shouting. Lili turned to examine the newcomers. Most were Dutch sailors, tall, robust, and stout, dressed in white shirts and navy trousers, with the whiff of sea salt upon them and the mark of the sun upon their reddish-brown faces and forearms. They flowed through the room toward the bar, one or two pausing on the way to finger Orabel's silky hair or catch a fleeting glimpse of her smile.

Lili pressed her fingers to her own hair, checking to be sure her

curls remained in place, then froze as a tall, elegant male figure filled the doorway.

Now this was a man—and as luck would have it, Aidan was not here to meet him. The man standing on the threshold was dressed in a fine embroidered doublet and breeches, worn but of good quality. Still, his manner caught Lili's eye even more than his fine clothing. His well-groomed appearance was incongruous with his suntanned skin, for gentlemen did not sun themselves...unless they had just come over aboard a ship. Like a moth to a flame, Lili found herself drawn to him. But Orabel was faster.

Orabel had already slipped her hand through the stranger's arm by the time Lili reached him. "Can Sweet Kate be helping you at all, sir?" the girl asked, her voice sweet and high above the noise of the tavern. *"Spreekt u Engels?"*

"Yes, I speak English," the man answered, a wave of blond hair falling casually across his forehead as he removed his hat. Good looks and manners too! Lili reached out for the man's other arm just as Orabel opened her mouth to speak again.

"Good evening, sir," Lili said firmly, with a warning look in Orabel's direction. "I am Lady Lili, mistress of the Broad Street Tavern. What is your pleasure this fine night? Bram has music, food, and gaming to offer, if you're of a mind to play and have a few pennies to wager." She looked up into his dark blue eyes and smiled. "And if you're new in town and lonely, there are girls aplenty who'd keep you company for a drink or two. You have only to tell me what sort of girl you like."

The man looked down, and Lili saw that the tops of his ears had begun to redden. "Actually, I am looking for a man called Witt Dekker. We sailed together aboard the *Gloria Elizabeth*."

"I know Witt," Orabel chimed in, tightening her grip upon the man's arm. "He's playing cards in yonder corner. Let me take you to him."

She caught Lili's eye with a questioning glance. Lili nodded slightly and released the handsome stranger. She might as well let

Orabel have him. Though he was handsome and well bred, any man who blushed to find himself in the company of women like Orabel and Lili wouldn't want to marry one.

Sighing, Lili patted her hair, checking her curls again, then smoothed the bodice of her gown and looked about for another easy mark.

Ten

⸙

"Y̲ou are a surgeon."

Abel Tasman, the man behind the desk, folded his hands across his stomach and looked at Sterling through a small pair of spectacles. The sea captain was still a young man, not yet forty. He was a small-sized fellow, but solid through the torso and shoulder, and the sea captain's uniform became him. He wore his brown hair in a simple style, parted in the center and falling without curl or ribbons to brush the top of his wide collar. Wide brown eyes dominated his face, balanced by a thin brown moustache that rode his upper lip like an afterthought.

"Yes, I am." Sterling lowered his hat to his lap and tapped it, trying to make his point. "I came here to set up a medical practice, but Dr. Carstens will not—well, he does not think it practical for two physicians to work in Batavia. He believes there is not enough sickness to keep two men occupied."

A flash of humor crossed Tasman's face. "Well, you have sailed once, so you know there is plenty aboard ship to keep a physician busy." Leaning forward in his chair, the sea captain glanced at Dekker, who sat beside Sterling, and inclined his head in a small gesture of acknowledgment. "Dekker says you worked very well aboard the *Gloria Elizabeth*. And I have read the letter of recommendation from King Charles's personal physician." He turned back to Sterling, regarding him with a speculative gaze. "Dekker is not a man easily impressed, nor am I. But I must admit, Dr. Thorne, that I am inclined to believe you a good surgeon and an honest gentleman."

Sterling smiled tentatively and tried to summon up a feeling of gratitude as Dekker stood up and took his leave of the captain. He hated being indebted to a man like Witt Dekker, but at the moment he had no other options. Returning to sea was a logical choice. He would have honest work that paid well, particularly if they discovered gold or took a prize on the journey, and he would be gone for some time, perhaps as long as a year.

"I would, ah—relish the opportunity to return to sea." He forced the stubborn half-truth from his tongue, then added, quite truthfully, "Batavia has proved to be a difficult place in which to make a new start. And while Dr. Carstens has been most hospitable, he is not willing to take on an associate. Perhaps if I go to sea, I might find him more inclined to accept me upon my return."

Tasman lifted an eyebrow at this, but he let the remark about Carstens pass. "Well then," he said, idly scratching his neck as he shifted his gaze toward the window, "we are planning to sail sometime in mid-August. I trust you will have accommodations until then?"

Sterling hesitated. He might as well be honest, for he had no other options. "Actually, sir," he said after a pause, "I fear I may have outworn my welcome in the good doctor's house. If there is a barracks, or some place where you allow the seamen to sleep—"

"The sailors sleep on their ships or in the flophouses at the wharf," Tasman answered, "but something tells me you would not be comfortable in a flophouse." He lowered his hands, folded them, and looked at Sterling with a curious, self-satisfied gleam in his eye. "How old are you, Dr. Thorne?"

Sterling blinked at the unexpected question. "Thirty, sir. I've had experience, if that's what you're wondering."

"Married?"

"Um, no." What sort of interview was this?

"And you're English. Well, we can't hold that against you, can we?" The captain's expression grew suddenly animated. "Since you

have an honest face and King Charles's physician to recommend you, sir, we will be pleased to take you aboard as ship's surgeon and doctor. And you shall not have to worry about finding a place to sleep until we depart. I shall have my own dear wife make up the guest room, and you shall stay at my house."

"Your house, sir?" Sterling looked up, surprised.

"Indeed, yes." The captain stood, his hands jerking downward on his doublet to smooth the fabric. "We'll expect you for dinner tonight. Six o'clock, please. You'll meet my wife and my daughter, Lina."

Sterling stood and bowed, wondering what he had done to deserve such generosity. "I thank you, sir. I will be prompt."

"The honor, Doctor," Tasman answered, a dark light sparkling in his brown eyes, "is all mine."

❧

Abel Tasman's home, Sterling discovered, was located three blocks from Dr. Carstens's house, secure within the prosperous area of town. After knocking and being greeted by the housekeeper, Sterling found himself in a square room, the *voorhuis,* or receiving lobby. Maps of the East Indian Dutch possessions hung on the east and west walls, advertising Tasman's connection and illustrious position within the V.O.C. A large landscape and at least a dozen other paintings hung in the same small room, a density of visual decoration that indicated more art was to be found in the rest of the house.

The Dutch, Sterling had noticed, were fond of ornamentation, and paintings in particular. Every wall was apportioned to display as much artwork as possible, and a man of Tasman's stature obviously felt compelled to display—in gilt frames—as many paintings as he could afford.

After leaving him alone for a few moments—the better for him to appreciate the vast collection of artwork, Sterling supposed—a serving maid led him into a room off to the right of the front lobby. Rich tapestries hung on two walls of this room, and in the center

twelve chairs stood around a massive ebony table. Just as Sterling caught sight of his own startled reflection in a gilt-framed mirror large enough to encompass the entire room, Abel Tasman entered from another doorway, his eyes alight with expectation, his hands raised in welcome. "Dr. Thorne! I am so glad you have come."

With the grace of a man completely at ease in his own home, Tasman pulled out the chair at the head of the table and indicated that Sterling should take the chair at his right. "I hope you don't mind the informality, but we are dining *en famille* tonight." He gave Sterling a broad grin. "My wife and daughter are the only guests. Since I am literally placing my life and health in your hands on this upcoming voyage, I thought it only right that my loved ones should meet you."

"I assure you, sir, this is quite formal enough to suit me." His eyes drifted over the table, laid with silver tableware and fine porcelain. "After dining on hardtack and dried beef for so many weeks, I will find anything your cook prepares to be quite sumptuous."

"Of course. But on the *Heemskerk,* you must dine with me in my cabin. And while I would never wish to disparage the English, I think I am safe in saying that we Dutch provide a great deal more for our sailors in the way of victuals. I am certain you will find the food aboard the *Heemskerk* much more enjoyable than hardtack and dried beef."

"That would be a blessing," Sterling admitted.

The rustle of silk and satins broke through the thread of their conversation, and Sterling looked up to see two women at the threshold of the room. The first woman, a tall, thin lady with her dark hair pulled tightly under her cap, looked out at him with the directness of a hawk.

"Ah!" Tasman jumped to his feet. "Dr. Thorne, meet my wife, Jannetje." While Sterling murmured pleasantries, the woman stared at him like a cat sizing up a mouse for dinner. Without answering, she moved quickly to the seat at her husband's left hand.

A bit bewildered, Sterling hesitated, wondering whether or

not he was truly welcome, but the reason for the lady's stern appraisal became clear a moment later. The second lady, who was nearly obscured by the older woman's formidable presence, approached the table and dipped in a formal curtsy. Abel Tasman introduced his daughter, Lina.

The young Miss Tasman was about twenty, Sterling supposed, with dark hair and darker eyes. She had dainty features and small wrists—a petite and flowerlike creature with a touch-me-not look about her. This girl, Sterling realized with a shock as he returned a bow for her curtsy, was the perfect age for marriage. And apparently the captain's wife thought he had been invited to dinner as a possible suitor.

"Joffer Tasman, I am honored," Sterling murmured as the girl approached the empty chair at his side. He pulled out the chair and held it for her, and she blushed prettily as she spread her dark skirts and sat down. He seated her and returned to his own seat, aware that Jannetje Tasman's appraising eyes gauged his every move.

"Well, then," Captain Tasman said, rubbing his hands together. "Shall we ring for dinner and give thanks?"

⌘

"So my dear," Abel whispered to his wife as they lay in the darkness of their bedchamber, "what did you think of him?"

"Him who?" Jannetje murmured, feigning ignorance.

Abel rose up on one elbow and frowned at the barely discernible silhouette of his wife. "The good doctor, who else? Is he not a fine young man? Handsome, well-suited, and bright? He is ever so much more than that dullard our Lina moons for. He will make a far more suitable husband."

"Abel!" Jannetje's voice was dry and sharp. "When will you learn not to meddle? Our daughter loves Jan Van Oorschot."

"Our daughter is a fool," Abel snapped, lowering himself to the mattress again. He folded his arms across his chest and breathed heavily. "A foolish girl, but an obedient one. She will marry Sterling Thorne, and she will be happy with him."

"What of the doctor?" Jannetje asked, her voice now unnaturally smooth. "How will you mold *him* to your will? He is not your son; he will not feel compelled to obey your wishes."

"He will obey." Abel twisted the end of his moustache. "He will be aboard my ship, and under my command. He will obey, and he will make our daughter happy—or he will rue the day he ever came to Batavia."

Eleven

"H eer Van Dyck?"

Schuyler looked up. Gusta stood in the doorway, her brow set in an unconscious furrow. "Captain Tasman and Meester Visscher are here to see you."

"Of course, Gusta, show them in." Quickly he shuffled his correspondence from his desk, then stood and smoothed his doublet. Within a moment the two men entered the library. Schuyler bowed deeply as they approached. "Captain Tasman! And Meester Visscher. You honor my home with your presence."

"You honor us with your time," Tasman answered. The captain waved his hat. "May we sit and discuss the upcoming voyage? We thought to settle a few things with you before our meeting with Governor Van Diemen."

"But of course!" Schuyler gestured toward two chairs near the window. "Have a seat gentlemen, and take your ease." He looked up at Gusta, who hovered in the doorway, and lowered his voice. "Gusta, some tea and biscuits, if you please. I'm sure our guests could use some refreshment."

"Cool water, for me, if you have any," Visscher said, glancing over his shoulder as he sat beside Tasman. He sent Schuyler an apologetic smile. "This heat is stifling. I don't know how the natives stand it in those huts." The heavyset Visscher was perspiring profusely, a line of sweat across his brow and upper lip. Schuyler rubbed his finger over his mouth, suppressing a smile. Obviously the man had not lived in Batavia very long.

In time, a body became accustomed to the heat.

Schuyler pulled over the small stool that stood beside his easel. "Perhaps the natives don't suffer because they've known nothing but warm weather."

"I suppose you realize our plans are well under way," Tasman rubbed his hands over his trousers as he assumed control of the conversation. "We are planning to sail before the month is out. The ships are now fully manned. We've been given two excellent ships, the *jacht de Heemskerk* and the *flute de Zeehaen*. Yde T'jercksen Holman will skipper the *Heemskerk,* and Gerrit Janszoon will serve as skipper of the smaller *Zeehaen*. You, of course, my friend, will sail upon the *Heemskerk* with me. I will command the voyage from that ship."

"And you?" Schuyler lifted a brow in Visscher's direction. "Surely you will sail with us?"

"*Ja.*" Visscher's serious face split into a wide grin. "I am first mate of the *Heemskerk*. You'll see a great deal of me, Heer Van Dyck. We are to share a cabin."

Schuyler's smile broadened in approval. "Already, gentlemen, my heart beats in anticipation. Being chosen for this opportunity is perhaps the greatest honor of my life."

"Word of your skill precedes you, or Heer Van Diemen would not have chosen you as official cartographer." Tasman nodded in respect. "The governor general, a great admirer of your art, is quite determined that we map out this area while we have predominance in this part of the world."

"We know there is a great south land somewhere out there," Visscher inserted, reaching under his spectacles to pinch the bridge of his nose. "But two previous expeditions have been unable to find it. Pool died before he could thoroughly explore the area, and Tasman's last voyage was cut short by disease—"

"Scurvy," Schuyler interrupted, looking at the captain. "I heard you lost nearly half your men."

The corners of Tasman's mouth tightened. "It couldn't be

helped. Matthijs Quast was the commander, I was only a skipper of one ship."

Schuyler instantly regretted his words. "I'm not blaming you, my friend," he added softly. He couldn't help overhearing rumors that Tasman often mistreated his crew and lacked the stomach for true adventure, but he couldn't afford to offend the man who held the reins of his own future.

He took a deep breath and adjusted his smile. "God often works in ways we cannot understand."

"Indeed." Cold dignity masked Tasman's features. "Well, Heer Van Dyck, we trust that our upcoming voyage will meet with more success. I have engaged the services of a doctor, an English gentleman who comes highly recommended by no less a personage than King Charles's physician."

"Truly?" Schuyler's brows rose in amazement. "How did you come by such a man?"

"As you said," Tasman answered, a look of satisfaction creeping over his features, "God works in mysterious ways."

Visscher shifted heavily in his chair. "We wanted to discuss the voyage with you so you will be prepared with the sea charts."

"Of course." Schuyler reached over his desk for a pencil and paper, ready to take notes.

Tasman folded his hands on his knee. "We are to sail first to Mauritius, then south into fifty-two or fifty-four degrees south latitude, searching for the southern continent." His words, flat and uninflected, ran together in a monotone. "You, of course, will map our progress, our depth soundings, and our landfalls. We hope your work will be a valuable addition to the charts in the archives of the V.O.C."

"It will be my privilege and honor to assist the Compagnie," Schuyler answered, placing his notes back on his desk, "but I must confess that I look forward to the work with a different motivation. The thrill of discovery drives me, gentlemen—the desire to leave a mark upon the world before I depart for a more heavenly

clime. You, sirs, are explorers and seamen, while I am an artist, a soul in search of expression."

He avoided their eyes, certain they would not understand, but determined that they should know why he wanted to sail with them. "My gift to the world," he said with quiet emphasis, "will be a map unlike any other in existence. It will reveal not only the geographical layout and such knowledge as one might expect to find on a sea chart, but will also illustrate the flora and fauna and the peoples we may discover...out there."

Schuyler paused, smiling as he thought of his secret weapon. Last night he had sat in this very chair and reexamined Aidan's sketch of the bird, wondering how he could ever replicate it, and the answer had come to him like a voice on the wind. *Why not take the girl on the voyage?* He could not ask her yet, of course; he'd had difficulty enough persuading her to join him at his house. But if he gained her trust and her agreement, she could sail on the Tasman voyage and embellish his map with the finest, most lifelike renderings he had ever seen—better by far than the works of Sibylla Marion.

"So of course, gentlemen," he said to his guests, "though I hope we find gold and lands and honor, I care far more for the lasting benefit of the chart we shall produce."

"Your commitment to excellence is noted and appreciated." Tasman's brown eyes had glazed slightly during Schuyler's speech, and he turned restlessly toward the window. Schuyler frowned as he followed the captain's gaze. Tasman had focused on Aidan's slender figure at her easel in the garden. "By heaven, Schuyler, I thought your daughter had married."

"She has," Schuyler answered, folding his arms. "That young lady is my...ward, a most talented artist in her own right." He cleared his throat as the light of inspiration dawned. "Indeed, Captain, you might find her useful aboard the *Heemskerk*. She is a wonderful illustrator of animals and flowers."

Visscher rose from his chair for a look. "A pity there are no

women allowed aboard ship," he murmured, crossing his hands behind his back as his eyes studied Aidan's fair form through the window. "Just the sight of her would be art enough to satisfy."

"No women?" Schuyler lifted a brow. "But I thought women were perfectly welcome. You, Captain, sailed with your wife when you commanded the *Engel*."

"Wives are not women, sir, if you catch my meaning," Tasman answered, giving Schuyler a knowing smile. "The men will respect another man's wife, knowing that he has vowed to guard her with his life. But unattached women are a plague upon any ship. They distract the men, they sow strife at every turn. And two women together—" He closed his eyes, and waved his hand, a clear signal that two women aboard ship would transgress the boundaries of any man's patience.

"No woman will ever sail aboard my ship unless she is married." Tasman drew his lips into a tight smile. "And I'd prefer never to take along a wife. I've convinced my own Jannetje to remain in Batavia with our daughter while I am gone."

"And how is your lovely daughter?" Schuyler smiled at the memory of the pale young woman he had met on several social occasions. Lina Tasman had been Rozamond's chief rival for the affections of Dempsey Jasper, and many a night Schuyler had been kept awake by Rozamond's sharp criticism of the captain's daughter.

"Lina is well, thank you." Tasman's face betrayed no knowledge of their daughters' rivalry. "She is engaged to be married as soon as God grants us a safe return."

"You had best keep a sharp eye on her," Schuyler answered, rising as Gusta entered with a tray of drinks and sweet cakes. "My daughter was so determined to be wed that I found it hard to restrain her enthusiasm. If we are detained on the voyage, your little Lina might slip away and marry with only her mother's blessing."

"She would never do that, sir." Tasman's stern expression cracked in a smile. "I will have her intended groom on board my

ship. He is Sterling Thorne, my ship's surgeon and a most excellent physician."

"Sterling Thorne?" Schuyler tilted his head. "I do not know the name. It is not Dutch."

"He is recently arrived from England. Witt Dekker, who will serve as first mate aboard the *Zeehaen*, brought him to me, and I was impressed when I interviewed the man. Lina was likewise pleased by his manner and intelligence, and I am only days away from finalizing the arrangements of their betrothal."

"Ah, very good then." Schuyler clapped his hands together and regarded his guests. "Shall we drink to their health and happiness?"

"And to profit," Visscher answered, standing. He lifted his glass of water from the tray. "There is certain to be gold in the undiscovered continent, my friends."

"To discovery." Tasman lifted a china teacup.

"To God's blessing." Schuyler took the final cup from the tray. "And to posterity, for those who come after us will review what we have done and know that it was accomplished by the grace and will of God."

"Amen," the other men echoed.

Schuyler lifted his cup and sipped his tea while his mind raced with a new and perplexing question. He knew he wanted Aidan to sail aboard the *Heemskerk,* but how could his plan be accomplished now that Tasman had forbidden women aboard ship?

His mind burned with the memory of their first meeting. The Spirit of God had clearly said, **She needs you. You need her.**

Sighing in frustration, Schuyler replaced his cup on the tray and walked with his guests to the door. Visscher and Tasman offered their farewells, then turned and left, their figures gradually disappearing down the cobbled walkway.

Schuyler closed the front door and leaned against it, lifting his eyes to the ceiling. If Aidan could not sail with him and help with his grand map, then for what possible reason had God urged him to invite the girl into his home?

"No, no!" Gusta shook her head. "A thousand times no! A lady does not gobble her food. She nibbles it with the utmost delicacy."

Aidan let her knife fall to the table with a resounding clatter, then folded her hands in her lap and fought to restrain the temper that bubbled under the surface. She had passed a wonderful morning in the garden, another in a glorious succession of hours where she was learning to paint and create under Heer Van Dyck's patient tutelage. But her new master had declared that Aidan's afternoons would be devoted to Gusta and lessons in ladylike deportment.

"You will never make a lady," Gusta was saying now, her face wrinkling in a dour expression of disapproval. "Not in a thousand years."

"I hope," Aidan answered, gritting her teeth, "that I won't live that long. Especially here! I cannot abide another hour of this, much less another week!"

The housekeeper drew herself up to her full height, her bosom jutting forward like the prow of a ship. "You ought to be grateful that Heer Van Dyck sees something of promise in you. And you should thank God above for such a gift, for there is certainly no other reason why the master should have glanced twice at you!"

"I didn't ask God to give me anything." Aidan cast a withering stare in the woman's direction. "And I only asked your master for a wee bit of instruction, not lessons in dining and etiquette."

Aidan heard a soft hiss as Gusta drew in her breath through her teeth. "You didn't *have* to come."

Unable to answer, Aidan strangled on the words that rose to her lips. *Yes I did. If I am ever going to be respectable, if I am ever going to be more than a guttersnipe, I have to learn how to be a great artist.*

But Gusta would not understand the motives that drove Aidan. The housekeeper was not a great lady, but she was genteel and respectable. She had never fallen to the bottom of humanity's

barrel, never watched her friends suffer with disease and starvation and fear.

Neither could she understand the yearnings and frustrations that rose in Aidan's breast every time she saw the sun falling at a certain angle upon a rose in the garden. Her heart stirred in the same mysterious way when she saw a butterfly lighting on a hibiscus blossom, and she knew she could paint that picture. If she were only given the materials and instruction, she could make that butterfly live forever; she could preserve that sunset-gilded rose for all time.

Once, long ago, Aidan imagined that all people were plagued by those frustrated feelings and visions, but over the past few years she had come to realize that she was decidedly odd. Orabel could look at a sunset and feel nothing but relief that the day would soon cool; her mother looked out upon the sea and saw only the miles and miles of ocean that separated her from Ireland. But Aidan saw textures, shapes, and colors of a million hues. A sunset could make her delirious with joy; some dark aspect of the sea could cause her to weep. But these things did not seem to affect anyone else.

Except Heer Van Dyck. Yesterday she had discovered a small caterpillar in the garden—a wondrous creature colored with orange and green, with a perfect brown circle on his back, like a saddle. Long, tufted hairs adorned his head and tail, and she had stared at the animal in simple fascination for what felt like only a few seconds.

But when she let the leaf fall and stepped back to her easel, she found Heer Van Dyck watching her, a gentle and bemused smile on his lips. "I was wondering what caught your attention," he said softly. She gestured toward the bush, thinking that he would want to see the unusual creature for himself, but his eyes never left her face.

"A caterpillar," she answered simply, pointing toward the hibiscus. "I've never seen anything like him."

"You stared at him for nearly a quarter of an hour." Van Dyck tilted his head slightly and studied her in a way that made her feel a bit like a wee bug herself.

"Really?" Aidan felt a slow blush burn her cheek. "I had no idea."

"You were caught in the Creator's time." Van Dyck sank to the small stone bench in the garden and gestured for her to resume her seat by her easel. *"Chronos* time, everyday time, seems to stand still when creativity is present. Just now, my dear, you were watching the caterpillar in *kairos* time, God's time. When we are lost in contemplation of God's creation, when our inner artist is at work, we are living in *kairos* time. *Chronos* time passes without our noticing it. We accomplish more—we *are* more—than we are when we live by a timepiece."

Watching Gusta's face now, Aidan suddenly wished she might abandon *chronos* time forever. These hours with the determined housekeeper were pure torment, for Aidan wanted to be painting, she wanted to lose herself in her work. Under Heer Van Dyck's forbearing instruction she could almost believe again in a patient and loving God...but every paradise had its resident serpent to contend with.

A scullery maid thrust her head through the door. "Beggin' your pardon, Gusta, but the master wants to see the young lady in his study."

"But we're not finished!" Gusta snapped.

Aidan stood and cast the older woman a triumphant grin. "Yes, we are," she said, pushing back her chair with far more noise than grace. "Thank you, Gusta, for your instruction. But as I shall never make a lady, I don't see how it will benefit me."

Leaving the housekeeper speechless, Aidan turned in a whirl of skirts and flounced down the hall.

❧

Heer Van Dyck stood at the window, his back straight, his hands folded behind him as if he were lost in contemplation. Aidan

slipped quietly into the room, recognizing that he was deep in thought, perhaps even experiencing a bit of the creative fog she had lately begun to enjoy. What a relief it was to discover that she was not a complete eccentric.

As she moved quietly toward a chair, she noticed that his work-in-progress, a beautiful illustration of Java and the surrounding Indonesian islands, lay spread on the worktable. She thought she made no sound, but he knew she was there, for after a moment he spoke without turning around. "Do you see the map on the desk, Aidan?"

Startled by his use of her familiar name, she stammered in reply. "Y-yes."

He nodded slightly, his gaze intently focused on the garden and the ripple of blue sea in the distance. "As you know, Captain Abel Tasman will leave very soon on a voyage during which I intend to complete that map. As you can plainly see, there is a void at the right margin. Governor Anthony Van Diemen has commissioned me to travel upon the flagship as the official cartographer."

Aidan caught her breath. He was trying to tell her that the time of her departure had come, and far sooner than she expected. He would soon leave, and Gusta would send Aidan back to the tavern, back to waiting tables and hauling ale and rifling through drunks' pockets to find money enough for food.

"You are leaving soon?" Her voice sounded weak and strangled to her own ears.

"*Ja.*" He turned slightly, his strong profile barely visible above that glorious beard. "Perhaps I should have mentioned this sooner, but I wanted you to fall in love with the work. I wanted to be certain you were passionate about the art. Because what I am about to ask is very difficult indeed."

He turned slowly, and Aidan saw that the customary expression of good humor was absent from the curve of his mouth, the depths of his eyes.

"It is a time of confession, I suppose," he said, sinking into his

chair and gesturing that she be seated across from him. "Of course you knew my departure was fast approaching. When I invited you here, I obeyed the impulse of God without completely thinking through the consequences. I didn't consider what I should do with you once the time came for my sailing."

"Please, sir." She lowered her eyes, dreading the dismissal to come. "Speak plainly. If you want me to go, say so. I'll go at once."

"All right, I'll speak plainly." He rubbed his hand lightly over his knee, then lifted his gaze to meet hers. "Aidan O'Connor, when I watched you draw in the tavern I knew I needed you—as an artist. Your gift for depicting nature, for instilling life into drawings of insects and birds and flowers, is like nothing I have ever seen here or in Europe. Together you and I could create a great work, the most beautiful chart humanity has ever seen."

She stared at him in total incredulity. " But how? I know nothing about maps or charts or sailing—"

"That's the beauty of it. You don't have to understand cartography. That is my area of expertise." His face creased into a sudden smile. "Haven't you noticed how my maps are adorned with pictures? I drew a sultan's camels upon the African desert, ships upon the sea, natives upon the islands. Art is what sets one chart apart from another, Aidan, the beauty of the art!"

He leaned forward, expecting something of her, but Aidan lowered her gaze in confusion. "The art?" she whispered. "I don't understand."

He smiled benignly, as if dealing with a slightly thickheaded child. "Abel Tasman has been charged with discovering new lands, Aidan. Therefore we shall doubtless encounter new flowers, new wildlife, and new creatures—living things no European has ever seen before! The map we create on this voyage will be unlike any other in existence!"

"We?" She drew back, puzzled and more than a little frightened of the change in his demeanor.

"Our map shall feature complete and careful renderings of

those new flora and fauna, and there will be nothing like it in the world! But I can only create it...*if you sail with me.*"

She sat motionless as the shock hit her full force. He didn't want to cast her off! He wanted to take her on a voyage into the unknown!

"Sail with you?" The muscles of her throat moved in a convulsive swallow. "But I hate the sea! I could never board a ship!"

"Yes, you could. Sea travel is as safe as it can be, given the dangerous times in which we live. The Dutch East India Company regularly sends ships to Europe and back; sailing is not nearly as risky as it was years ago." His eyes squinted with excited amusement. "I don't know what you've heard about the ocean, but—"

"I didn't have to hear—I have traveled the sea myself!" Aidan's heart began to thump painfully in her chest. Memories of her voyage from London came crowding back, noisy and obnoxious, like unwelcome guests. With a shiver of vivid recollection, she saw again her father's pale face, heard his dying gasps and the horrifying sound of his body splashing into the sea. Memories of that sea voyage, her first and last, made her shudder like the touch of a ghost.

"My parents and I sailed from London together six years ago," she said, her voice shakier than she would have liked. "My father died on that voyage. And they—the seamen—threw him overboard, into the sea."

"I didn't know," Van Dyck answered softly. "Forgive me, but you never speak of your parents."

"I am a grown woman; you need not concern yourself with my past," Aidan answered, folding her arms across her chest.

"I don't mean to pry." Van Dyck coughed softly into his clenched fist, then a thoughtful smile curved his mouth. "Think of the art, dear girl. Of the *kairos* time. You and I will be painting things no civilized person has ever seen before. You will be the first woman to dip your brush into the colors of an unknown bird, to depict the rush of a strange insect's wing." His left eyebrow, snowy

white, rose a fraction as he watched his words take hold. "You can learn nothing, child, without moving from the known to the unknown. If you want to broaden your horizons, take this step. Life will shrink or expand in direct proportion to the measure of your courage."

I want to succeed. She dredged the admission from a place beyond logic and reason. She wanted to be respectable, but could she risk her life on the sea in order to achieve her dreams?

"After our masterpiece is done, your sketches and that marvelous memory of yours will serve you well," Van Dyck went on. "You could publish a book of engravings, and thousands of cultured, appreciative people throughout Europe and the civilized world will marvel at your talent. Though they are miles away, they will see with your eyes and many of them will *understand.*"

Aidan tilted her head, listening. As always, Heer Van Dyck had managed to put his finger upon the heart of the matter. Though something in her resisted the thought of disappearing again into the dark bowels of a seagoing vessel, the end result might be worth the fear and trepidation.

If she did as he suggested, she might finally find respectability. Lili would be proud. Perhaps Aidan could actually earn enough to provide a decent place for all the girls at the wharf, a safe place where Orabel, Stella, Sofie, and the others could live and sleep in peace.

"I'll consider it." She gripped the arm of her chair. "If I may be excused, I'd like to go into the garden and think about it."

"There is one more thing." Van Dyck paused for a moment, then rose with fluid grace and stood straight and tall before her. "Joffer O'Connor, I would never have voluntarily considered the action I am about to suggest, but necessity compels it." He took a deep breath, swelling the front of his doublet. "You are an artist. You will want to go on this voyage—you *should* go on this voyage. Unfortunately, Captain Tasman will not allow any woman aboard ship unless she is married to one of the officers."

He lifted a white brow and waited as the significance of his words struck her. "But if I cannot go—" she began.

He held up a hand and cut her off. "Joffer O'Connor—Aidan—because I truly believe God would have you travel with me, I do most humbly ask for your hand in order that we may be wed. Working together, we shall produce the most glorious sea chart the world has ever seen."

She had thought he could not surprise her further, but as his words fell upon her ears, ripples of shock began to spread from a point somewhere at her center, moving through her stomach and flowing outward to her fingertips.

"It will be a marriage in name only, of course," he went on rapidly, anxiously. "I would not dream of attaching my advanced age to your youth and beauty. But it is the only way, you see." Gracefully, he folded his hands and glanced down at his feet. "When my time on earth is done, I can promise that you will be well-compensated for your sacrifice. I am an old man, and considerably wealthy. As my wife, you will share in all I possess. After my death, if the idea pleases you, you will be free to marry for love."

"*Marry*...you, sir?" The words, a full moment too late, broke from her lips. She clung to the armrests of her chair as a tide of confused emotions crashed over her—bewilderment, compassion, affection, gratitude, horror, fear. Part of her, touched by his tender compassion, wanted to weep; another part wanted to recoil from the inappropriateness of his suggestion. She was a ragamuffin, the daughter of a procuress, and he was an esteemed Dutch gentleman, the father of two respectable grown children.

"Sir—" She tried to keep the stunned disbelief out of her voice, but failed miserably. "This suggestion is not well made! If I cannot go to sea unwed, then I shall not go! The idea is sheer folly!"

Heer Van Dyck held up a restraining hand. "Please consider the idea overnight." His eyes kept moving away, as though afraid to rest very long on her countenance. "And I will seek the will of

our Heavenly Father. Perhaps there is another way. Perhaps I was wrong to suggest such an idea to you. I assure you, my dear, that while I have grown quite fond of your nature and am in awe of your talent, I have no wish to force my affections upon you."

"Sir, I—" Aidan stopped, not knowing what to say. She could not imagine marrying a man older than her father, but neither could she insult or hurt him. Schuyler Van Dyck had been the personification of kindness and honor from the very moment she met him.

"Good night, sir," she murmured, feeling heat flood her face as she stood and moved toward the door. "I will consider your offer."

Her master did not answer. His artistic hands, motionless as empty gloves, rested on the desk as she left him alone in the library.

Twelve

H eer Van Dyck was not in the library when Aidan ventured downstairs the next morning, nor did he appear in the dining room at lunch. She suspected he was avoiding her out of embarrassment or even shame, and her heart contracted in compassion as she thought of his generosity. He certainly did not love her as a husband ought to love a wife, yet Aidan did not doubt that he would treat her with gentleness, kindness, and understanding.

Her own feelings for him were terribly confused. In the past few days she had come to esteem his wisdom, talent, and gentle nature. Certainly his name was renowned, and she would achieve respectability in one moment if she married him. Lili would faint from sheer joy to know that her daughter had married a landed and wealthy gentleman.

But though he was handsome, honorable, and gallant, she found it difficult to think of Schuyler Van Dyck as anything other than a benevolent father figure. The thought of his lips pressing to hers sent prickles of cold dread crawling along her back, and the notion of spending a sea voyage crowded with him into a small, confined ship's berth—the doors of her imagination slammed shut. She refused to consider it. Yet as his wife, that is where she'd have to be, consistently at his side amid a crowd of raucous sailors who'd leer and elbow each other and make jokes about the old man and his girl bride.

After lunch she returned to her easel, breathing deeply of the

humid, hot air in the garden. She was just about to make a bold stroke with her paintbrush when Gusta's hoarse shout shattered the garden's quiet. "The children are coming to dinner," the housekeeper called to the scullery maid, her voice booming through the open windows like a clap of thunder. "Make haste!"

Aidan felt her stomach lurch with the first stroke of the brush. The children were invited for dinner? Surely Heer Van Dyck did not plan to use the occasion for some sort of announcement! She was quite confident that Schuyler's children would not approve of their father taking a barmaid to wife.

She had scarcely formed the thought when her master himself appeared, a strange and livid hue overspreading his face. "Joffer O'Connor," he said, nervously fussing with a kerchief at his neck, "I am glad you are here. I have decided to withdraw my offer of marriage. Apparently we were both discomfited by the idea, and I fear the suggestion was made in haste." A faint glint of humor lit his eyes when he finally met her gaze. "I trust you will believe that the withdrawal is strictly due to my own weakness?" he asked, smiling gently.

"Completely, sir," she murmured, wiping her paint-splashed fingertips upon her apron. "It was a generous gesture, but one which would not bring you honor. I am sure you would not want someone like me for a wife."

"Hrumph." Abruptly he folded his hands behind him and cleared his throat. "You are too harsh in your own judgment, Miss O'Connor. But we shall not speak of this again. There is, however, one thing I must know—are you still willing to consider the voyage? If I can find a way to get you aboard the *Heemskerk,* will you agree to go?"

Aidan turned and studied the smeared painting on her easel. All morning her inner eye had dwelt upon possibilities of the voyage; her brush had transposed the blue, green, and aqua hues of the sea's heaving surface to the canvas. Her uncertainty was represented there, as well as her fear and her dark memories. But the

sapphire sky was lit by a single beam of radiant sunlight, the hope that would call her out of the past and into a new life.

Heer Van Dyck came up behind her and studied the painting with a keenly appraising eye.

"Well." Thick emotion clotted his voice. "You have caught it very well, my dear. The deep, unknowable mystery of the sea."

"Would that we could know it," she murmured, dipping her brush into one of the jars of water on her easel. "Yes, Heer Van Dyck. If you can find a way, I want to go. I want to work with you." A small smile tugged at the corners of her lips. "I might even pray for the opportunity to work with you."

"Very well." He turned aside, but not before she caught the glimmer of wetness upon his lashes. Which had affected him, her work or her answer?

"Please join us at dinner," he said simply, moving toward the doorway. "I must tell the children of my plans."

Schuyler took his place at the head of the table and noted with approval that Aidan had never looked more lovely. While he doubted that Gusta's lessons had done anything to smooth the girl's sprightly and unconventional temperament, at least a veneer of grace covered over her rough edges. She wore a new gown the dressmaker had just provided, a cream-colored concoction of brocade woven with red roses and trimmed at the bodice and cuffs with lace. For the first time in their acquaintance she had taken the time to arrange her boisterous curls into tiny ringlets to frame the sides of her face, and her glowing hair served to emphasize the creamy expanse of her throat and neck.

Even the children noticed the transformation. When Aidan entered the dining room, Rozamond gazed at the girl with outright horror, doubtless born of jealousy, and Dempsey regarded her with a sort of fascination. Henrick, whom Schuyler watched with particular attention, seemed struck speechless by the girl's metamorphosis into a presentable young lady.

The evening began with little fanfare. After pronouncing a blessing upon their gathering and the meal, Schuyler waited until his silent children served themselves and began to eat. "I have asked you here today," he said in English, for Aidan's benefit, "to discuss something that concerns us all."

"Speak whatever is on your heart, Father," Dempsey said. As always, the word *Father* sounded unnatural and forced on his tongue. "You know we are always pleased to visit you."

"I intend to speak freely," Schuyler went on, ignoring his son-in-law. "I have no time to play games. You should know that Captain Tasman plans to sail within a few days—before the end of August, if the winds are favorable."

"Father, that's wonderful!" Henrick dropped his knife and grinned. "That is sooner than you expected, is it not?"

"How lovely, Papa." Rozamond couldn't help sneaking a victorious glance toward Aidan. "I suppose you will want to close up the house while you are gone. Henrick and the servants can come to stay with us, of course, unless you'd rather Dempsey and I moved in here to keep an eye on things."

"Henrick is a grown man; he can manage the house." Schuyler sliced into the plump chicken breast on his plate. "I am not worried about what I leave behind. I am more concerned about what I must take with me. I have a difficult situation to solve and am counting on you to help me resolve it."

"Anything, Father Van Dyck." Dempsey cupped his glass in his hand and gave Schuyler a broad smile. "Name your service, and we shall be pleased to perform it."

"Very well." Schuyler lowered his utensils and folded his hands above his plate. Intensely aware of Aidan's presence at the end of the table, he swiveled his gaze toward each child in turn. "My problem is this: I wish to take Joffer O'Connor with me on the voyage, but Tasman will not allow an unattached woman on the ship. All women must be family members."

He paused, but the faces before him—including Aidan's—

were frozen in expectant silence. When Rozamond recovered enough to lift a brow, he turned and stared at his son with earnest concentration. "It is my hope, Henrick, that you might consider taking Aidan to be your wife. She is a wonderful girl, strong, spirited, utterly charming. And talented! She would make a great name for you and honor this family."

"Father!" A rich rose color suffused Henrick's face from chin to hairline.

"Heer Van Dyck!" Aidan gasped. There was a flash, like light caught in water, when her gaze met his. "This is not the plan I hoped for."

"Why not?" Surprised by the tumult, he glanced around the table. Rozamond was openly glaring at Henrick, while Henrick's gaze was fastened to his plate, his face a study in humiliation. Schuyler glanced at his son curiously—he had never seen quite so many shades of red upon one man's countenance. This scene would make an interesting painting, if one could only capture the right hues of burgundy, cerise, crimson, garnet, and vermilion.

"Father Van Dyck!" Dempsey protested, his own face an interesting example of repressed contempt. "Surely your son has a right to choose a bride from his own rank and station."

"He has the right to agree or refuse, of course, Dempsey." Schuyler picked up his knife and spoon again. "But I seem to recall partaking in the arrangement of your own marriage. It is a father's right to make suggestions. If, however, marriage is not agreeable to either Aidan or Henrick, there is always the option of adoption." He took a bite of chicken and paused to chew it, smiling benignly at Rozamond's horrified expression. "I will adopt the girl," he said, swallowing. "She will be my daughter, and thus she will remain under my protection. Tasman plans to leave his daughter at home, but there is no reason I should not bring mine on the voyage—"

"You would adopt this *harlot?*" Rozamond shrieked.

Dempsey gasped in delighted horror, then an unnatural

silence descended over the dinner table. The empty air between them vibrated, the silence filled with anger, shock, and dismay.

Rozamond was the first to recover. The veins in her slender throat stood out like ropes as she stared at Schuyler from across the table. "Father, are you insane? Have you lost all sense? This girl is—"

"I know what I am," Aidan snapped. Taking a deep, unsteady breath, she stood, pushing back her chair. She pressed her hands to the dining room table, her eyes blazing as she looked from Rozamond to Dempsey to Henrick. When she spoke she made no effort to hide the rough Irish brogue of her heritage: "I am Aidan O'Connor, daughter of England and Ireland, and proud of it. I'd not marry any one of you, not if the state of my eternal soul depended upon it!"

Her glittering green eyes found Schuyler's and held them. "Thank you, sir, but this is the most foolish idea you've had yet. If you'll excuse me, I believe I have lost my appetite."

In a flurry of silk she whirled away from the table and left the room, leaving Schuyler and his three stunned children to stare at each other. Jagged and painful thoughts pressed against Schuyler's forehead, and he rubbed his temples with his hands, sensing the beginning of a monstrous headache.

"Mama will be turning in her grave," Rozamond finally hissed, turning the full fury of her eyes upon Schuyler. "Her lovely things! How could you even think to share them with a woman like that? She's a tavern tramp, one of those hussies—"

"I don't think so." Schuyler rested his aching head against his hand. "At worst, I believe she was a barmaid, and probably not above picking a pocket or two if the need arose."

"The need?" Rozamond frowned with cold fury. "Why would anyone ever feel the need to steal?"

"I believe it's called hunger." Schuyler's head began to throb in earnest. "Often akin to starvation, it affects people at the wharf more often than you might think."

"Father, you can't be serious!" Henrick straightened in his chair. "I can't believe you would suggest that I marry her! Have you no higher regard for me? She is not qualified to be my wife."

"I have the highest regard for you, Henrick," Schuyler answered, blinking slowly at his son. "And I think Aidan may be *overqualified* to be your wife. You have no need of property, since you and Rozamond will inherit all I possess. You will want a wife of charm and of beauty, and Aidan possesses those traits in full abundance. Why shouldn't you also seek a woman with skill and the rare gift of artistry?"

"Father, I don't understand artists."

"No," Schuyler answered softly, smoothing his brow with both hands. "You do not."

Silence filled the room, giving emphasis to his words. His children had never understood him, and yet he had loved them anyway. The time had come for them to put aside their petty concerns and learn to respect the gift that had brought honor to the family.

"Father, you can't do this." An escaping curl tumbled over Rozamond's forehead as she shook her head. "You are tired from your preparations, and you are not thinking clearly. Have you consulted with Captain Tasman? Perhaps you need to seek advice from the minister. I know he would tell you that it is folly to take a viper into your home, to hold a snake to your bosom."

"I have spoken to a counselor," Schuyler sighed. He might as well tell them everything, they'd find out in due time if anything happened to him on the voyage.

"A counselor?" Henrick sent a wide smile winging toward his sister. "Well, then, surely you were advised to disavow this ridiculous notion of yours."

"I spoke to my lawyer this morning," Schuyler went on, "and he has made provision for Aidan in my last will and testament. If something happens to me on the journey, she will inherit one hundred twenty thousand florins—enough that she will not have to worry about living expenses while she pursues her art."

"Why—that's nearly twenty thousand English pounds!" Dempsey Jasper slapped his hand on the table. "Surely, sir, you could have put that money to better use!"

Schuyler ignored Dempsey and glanced up at his son. "Henrick will inherit my art pieces, my estate, and my house." He turned his gaze toward his dumbfounded daughter. "And you, dear Rozamond, have already received your dowry and your husband. My endowment to Aidan will have little effect upon you."

"Little effect?" Her voice, hoarse with shock, held a note halfway between pleading and disbelief. "Father, by your gift, you are elevating that—that *tramp*—to a social level equal to my own!" Her dark brows slanted downward in a frown. "How am I supposed to attend balls and parties knowing she might be there?" She flung up her hands in disgust and sent him a fiery glare. "People will talk, Father! They will know her money came from you, of course. They will speculate that you had some sort of immoral relationship with her."

"Rozamond!" Henrick's face went pale.

"Well, they will!" She turned on her brother with the fury of a determined tigress. "You don't listen to the women talk, Henrick. You have no idea how cruel they can be. And though I am Mejoffer Dempsey Jasper, I will still be associated with this harlot, this hussy—"

"That is quite enough, Rozamond." Schuyler lowered his glass to the table, suddenly irritated with the conversation. True to form, his children were thinking more of themselves than of him, and they had not caught even a glimpse of the purpose underlying his intentions.

"Stay, enjoy your dinner," he said, abruptly pushing back his chair. "I am tired. I bid you all good night."

❧

Henrick could think of nothing to say as his father stood and left the table. He waited until the sliding door to the dining room had safely closed, then he lowered his gaze and caught Rozamond's eye.

"Could he really want me to marry that woman?" he asked, his mind still reeling at the thought. He could not have been more surprised if his father had suggested that he marry Gusta. A wife would be nice, and marriage ought to be in Henrick's near future, but he had always planned to seek his wife among the leading merchant families of Batavia. Never would he have considered marrying someone from the wharf.

"He is fatigued," Dempsey answered calmly. "Preparations for this voyage have exhausted his faculties. Do not forget—and I say this with due respect—your father has always been charmingly eccentric. The artist in him, I suppose? But this time his eccentricity has gone too far." He took a sip, then lowered his glass and casually stroked his upper lip. "Should we find a doctor? Perhaps he is not mentally competent to participate in this voyage…or to change his will."

Rozamond uttered a soft murmur of disagreement. "Father is too beloved and well-known to be portrayed as a lunatic. He and his lawyer are old friends. Father could show up in the town square eating daisies, and his lawyer would never admit that Schuyler Van Dyck was mentally incompetent."

"There is so little time," Henrick pointed out, drumming his fingertips on the linen tablecloth. "The ship sails very soon, and the captain will command all hands to board at least a week before they weigh anchor. We would have to find a doctor, and arrange for Father to see him—which he would not be willing to do. Besides, the V.O.C. is counting on Father. It is to our advantage that Father sails with Tasman, for this voyage will make him famous. He has not exaggerated the importance of this upcoming expedition."

Dempsey's eyes narrowed in thought. "Well, if you won't marry that woman, Henrick, she won't be going. Tasman will not allow women on ship, true? So when your father sails, you will be master of this house." He raised one eyebrow. "If she persists in her association with this family, if she troubles you at all, you would be

perfectly within your rights to ask the constable to arrest her. That is why we have a workhouse." He shrugged. "But she may simply disappear among the riffraff at the docks. Perhaps she will marry a sailor." He reached out and tenderly wrapped a finger in one of Rozamond's curls. "She might even vanish, never to be seen again."

Rozamond fairly purred under her husband's attentions. "Wouldn't it be lovely if she sailed back to Europe? When the time comes for Papa's will to be settled, if she cannot be found—"

"The money will remain with the estate, where it belongs," Dempsey finished. He smiled at his wife and returned his gaze to Henrick. "I think we have nothing to fear. After your father departs, you can take matters into your own hands. The voyage will last many months, and any number of things could happen to a young woman down at the docks."

Henrick stared at his plate, conscious of a small stirring of guilt, but he valiantly fought it down. Dempsey was right, as always. This young woman was no kin to him; she had no part in this family's fortune or in any of their lives. This time his father's eccentricity had gone beyond the boundaries of duty and common sense. His responsibility, as the eldest son, was to make certain that the Van Dyck name and fortune were safeguarded for legitimate generations.

But still…the young woman had worn a hurt, haunted look as she rose from the table and fled the room. And Henrick, who had never willingly hurt a living thing, could not bear the thought that he had unwittingly caused her to suffer.

"Here," Dempsey said, lifting his glass. "Let us drink to the future, to the voyage to come. We will pray a safe and prosperous journey for our father, and he will find the southern continent filled with gold and treasure."

"To the voyage!" Rozamond twined her fingers around her glass.

"The voyage," Henrick repeated. But as he lifted his glass to drink, he could not stop himself from pondering what would become of the girl who had clearly touched his father's life.

Early the next morning, Aidan pulled the simplest gown she could find from the trunk in her chamber. Gusta had burned the skirt, bodice, and sleeves she had worn when she arrived at this house, and she had no choice but to leave in a gown provided by Heer Van Dyck's generosity. Still, she could not be beholden to Schuyler Van Dyck any longer. Though he was a benevolent and honorable man, 'twas clear enough that his children hated her. Sooner or later his affection for her would turn to contempt, for every father wished to please his children…even as hers once had.

She slipped into the skirt, fastened it at the back, then began the painstaking process of pinning the sleeves to the bodice. When she was dressed, she smoothed her unruly hair with her hands, tied it quickly in a knot atop her head, absently pulling a few wisps down to frame her face. She didn't look at all proper and neat today, but it didn't matter. Gusta would no longer have to bother with her; Van Dyck's children would no longer stare as if she were nothing more than an annoying bug on the carpet. She would say farewell, give her thanks to the master of the house, and she would return home—a failure.

Aidan paused at the door, impatiently pulling her drifting thoughts together. The harder she tried to ignore the truth, the more it persisted. Lili was right. Aidan would have been better off remaining at the tavern, flirting outrageously with sunburned seamen until one of them was fool enough to ask her to marry him. Well then. Perhaps today would be her lucky day. If any sailor on Broad Street was sober enough to smile at her this afternoon, she just might ask him to marry her, thus putting an end to all Lili's harping and cajoling. She'd forget about art, forget about respectability. She'd settle for being poor and rough and two meals shy of starvation.

She smoothed her bodice, adjusted her skirt, and paused for a moment to study her reflection in the small looking glass on the dressing table. Her eyes were still a bit red-rimmed from the tears

she'd shed during the night, and her lips seemed as pale as her countenance. She pressed her lips together and pinched her cheeks, trying to instill a little color into her wan complexion. She wanted to leave this house with her head high. Van Dyck must think she had changed her mind about going to sea, and his children must never know they had defeated her.

Going home, she thought, returning the mirror to the table, would be hard enough. Lili would lead the other women in a chorus of "I told you so's," and Orabel would weep silently, sorrowing for Aidan's missed opportunity. But even they would never know that something far deeper in Aidan had died.

She could not be an artist. If God had gifted her, he had made a mistake. If he had meant for her to make something of her gift, he should have provided her with the proper tools and opportunities. She couldn't even manage a spoon and knife to Gusta's satisfaction—so how was she ever supposed to become a great artist and respectable lady? She had almost begun to believe in Heer Van Dyck's loving God, but the gentleman's children had refocused her eyes upon reality.

Leaving her regrets in the small chamber, she stepped through the doorway, then descended the stairs. Gusta's sharp voice echoed from the dining room where she was probably serving breakfast, so Aidan slipped through the dark-paneled hallway until she came to the master's library.

Something in her had hoped he would be out—she could have left a note and slipped away without having to confront him one final time. But Schuyler Van Dyck sat at his worktable, his chin resting in his hand, his eyes fastened to the window and the garden beyond. He was thinking—and she knew instinctively that he was thinking about her.

"*Goede morgen,* sir," she whispered. As he turned, she folded her hands and gave him a calm smile. "I trust you slept well. I would not disturb you this morning, but must speak to you before I—"

"I did not sleep at all," he interrupted. A trace of unguarded tenderness shone in his eyes as he looked at her. "I stayed awake all night, first burdened by the intolerable rudeness of my children and their actions toward you, then tormented by my own guilt. I should never have sprung my ideas upon you and Henrick without consulting you first. I embarrassed you, and I must apologize."

With renewed humiliation, Aidan looked away. "Think nothing of it, sir."

"But I must think of it, because our problem is not yet solved. Before the night was half-spent, I began to wrestle with the problem of getting you aboard my ship."

"That is what I have come to tell you." Aidan lowered her eyes, finding it difficult to meet his eager gaze. "Sir, I have decided to remain here. I cannot go with you."

"You're right, you can't."

Stunned by his rapid agreement, she looked up in surprise.

"Tasman won't allow unattached women, and there's naught we can do about that, right?" A broad smile lifted his cheeks as he looked at her. "You can't marry me, and you shouldn't marry Henrick—the boy is a fool for not seeing your true worth. I can't even adopt you and take you as my daughter, for my children are bent on their own selfish ways. All right, then. You can't go with me as wife, daughter, or daughter-in-law. But there is yet another way."

She stared wordlessly at him, her heart pounding. Dreams she had resolutely buried in the night rose up again, bringing unexpected hope.

"What way, sir?" she whispered.

Heer Van Dyck rose from his place and crossed to the door, then closed it.

"You shall come with me," he said, a blush of pleasure brightening his face as he turned to face her and leaned against the door, "as my ward."

Aidan frowned. "Your ward? But Captain Tasman will not allow—"

"He will not allow a *woman*," Van Dyck answered. "You shall join me on this voyage as a young *man*."

Aidan stared at her master in a paralysis of astonishment. How in the world could she pretend to be a boy? She was tall, true, and unfashionably slender, but she'd heard enough jokes at the tavern to know that she did possess a womanly face and figure.

Still, the suggestion intrigued her. A *boy?* Her eyes drifted toward the flower beds outside, where the gardener's son worked in an oversized shirt and cap. Perhaps, garbed like that, she could pull off such a ruse. If she wore an oversized shirt and kept her hair twisted up in a cap or braided like the seamen; if she smeared her face with grime and kept her eyes lowered; if she grunted in monosyllables like the midshipmen who regularly mooned at her from behind the tavern bar—perhaps such a charade would work.

Aidan looked up at her master. "Gusta has always said that I would never make a lady."

Heer Van Dyck chuckled so irrepressibly that she couldn't help laughing herself.

Thirteen

T his is how we shall accomplish it," Van Dyck began, delighted by the surprise and pleasure in his protégée's eyes. "No one shall know except Gusta. For your own sake, we shall have to tell someone of your whereabouts. Since we don't know where we'll go or when we'll return, someone has to be able to account for us if we don't return after an appropriate interval."

He studied Aidan's face as she sank into the nearest chair. Her eyes were narrowed in speculation, her attention focused on him. "Why must Gusta be the one to know?" Her brow crinkled in thought. "Truth to tell, sir, I don't think she has much regard for me. She might tell your children what we are doing before the ship sails, and they would lodge a complaint with the captain. They certainly would not support this plan."

"Gusta loves my children, but she is wholly devoted to me." Schuyler lowered his voice and sank into the tufted chair by his desk. "She will keep our secret and carry it to her grave if I ask her to. We will continue here as if nothing is amiss, but on the night before we are to report to the ship, Aidan O'Connor shall pack her bag and leave my house. We'll even arrange an audience—my children shall come to dinner, and they shall see you depart."

She quirked an eyebrow in a question. "Isn't this a bit deceitful, sir? 'Tis not like you to deceive your children."

"They can't handle the truth." Schuyler lifted his chin. "And I'll not tell them a lie. But if they make certain assumptions, are we to blame if they presume wrongly?"

She tilted her brow, unconvinced.

"I know you have no use for Scripture," he went on, "but you may recall the story of the harlot Rahab, who deceived her kinsmen and saved the Israelite spies at Jericho." He watched as a series of emotions played across her lovely face. "Do you think she had any qualms about hiding those godly men from the evil folk of her city? I think not, my dear. She did what seemed right, and she did it bravely. And so we shall accomplish this small diversion in order to keep my selfish children from thwarting our plans."

"I don't suppose it matters if they know the truth once the ship has sailed," she said, regarding him with somber curiosity. "But if they discover our plan beforehand, they will send word to the captain."

Schuyler frowned and leaned back in his chair. "I wish Henrick and Rozamond were more understanding and considerate, but after a certain time the twig will grow as it is bent, and there's not much a gardener can do."

He smiled, realizing from the expression on her face that she didn't understand. How could she? A young woman, barely twenty, could no more understand the pangs and regrets of parenthood than an ignorant native could fathom the wonders of civilization.

"Anyway," he said with a dismissive gesture, "you needn't worry about my children. They will complain and groan and carry on because they resent your talent, but don't let them concern you, my dear. They simply do not understand all the things I've been trying to teach you. Rozamond cares more for her place in society and her position upon guest lists than she does about art, and Henrick's mind has been filled with nothing but ledgers and bills of lading since he assumed his position in the Oriental Spice Company."

"I know they don't like me—because of what I am." Aidan looked at him with a bland half-smile. "I don't blame them. If I were from a fine family, I wouldn't want someone like me in the house, either."

"Aidan O'Connor!" he interrupted vehemently. "You are speaking foolishness. Don't you know what you are? You are a person created by God, the same as any of us were created, and loved just as much. And you, my dear, have such a special gift, a wondrous capacity for understanding the things of God."

Words hung in his throat as he gazed at her, wondering how in the world he could ever convince her that she was incredibly talented, immeasurably more intuitive and gifted than himself. "My dear girl," he murmured, his voice dropping in volume, "the position of the artist is both a humbling and an ennobling one. We are called by God, gifted by the Holy Spirit, a partner in the creative process. We are blessed because we have been entrusted with this gift, and you must never think of yourself as less than anyone else. You only need to be disappointed if you neglect the gift God has given you, or deliberately do shoddy work, or cheat your fellowman. Work hard, be true to your calling, and God will direct your path."

Aidan did not answer. She stared down at her hands, a betraying flush brightening her face. "I do not think of God very often," she finally answered. At last she looked up at him, her eyes soft with pain. "I don't know how, Heer Van Dyck. I've never felt God's presence. I wouldn't know how to begin."

Her misery was so overwhelming, so palpable, it was like a shadow upon her face, a dark, ominous presence. How could he hope to break through that darkness?

"My dear young lady!" A pain squeezed Schuyler's heart as he thought of the sorrows in her past. "The Scriptures say that in order for God to draw near to us, we have only to draw near to him." He paused, searching for words to frame his thoughts. "It is like when you begin a painting. At the beginning, when you have chosen your subject, the painting is somewhat outside you. But as you begin to work and immerse yourself in the colors, the subject, and the idea, you find that you have moved inside the painting."

"Yes." She gave him a brief, distracted glance and tried to

smile. "I think I know what you mean. And I shall try...to find God, if that will help me paint."

"You will learn." He cleared his throat, anxious to get to work. "Well, we are to report to the ship in one week, so we have much to do and not much time. But before we begin, I must know—are you truly committed to this endeavor? This is a masquerade you cannot desert when and if you grow tired of the disguise. Captain Tasman is not known for toleration or leniency, and he has strictly informed me that he will not allow women aboard either of his ships. We are risking a great deal, both you and I."

She looked down and pressed her lips together, and for a moment he thought he saw the shimmer of tears in her eyes. But then she lifted her eyes to his and spoke with quiet, desperate firmness. "Heer Van Dyck, I want to be a respectable artist. And if I could only accomplish this goal in a native disguise, I would wear a grass skirt and pierce my nose."

Schuyler's mouth twitched with amusement as he read the determination in her eyes. By heaven above, this girl just might make his name great. His map would set a high standard for posterity, but without a doubt his greatest gift to humanity would be the discovery of Aidan O'Connor.

"It is settled then," he said, clapping with satisfaction. "Let us call Gusta and explain our plan. The masquerade will be accomplished much more easily with her help."

⁂

Gusta hesitated, blinking with bafflement, as her master explained that Aidan O'Connor would sail with him upon the sea voyage as a boy.

"Excuse me, sir," she whispered, her mind spinning with bewilderment, "but did you say this person would travel with you?" She pressed her hand to her throat. "Dressed as a young man?"

"Exactly! Precisely!" Heer Van Dyck slapped his leg in approval. "I knew we could count on you, Gusta. We will need

your help, of course. We will need two sets of boys clothes, a bag of the type that a young man might take to sea, and whatever naval supplies a young man would need—a length of rope, a kerchief, a hat, a knife, that sort of thing. Of course I will pack all the parchments, paints, and canvases, but I can't send Aidan out to shop for breeches and a doublet."

"A boy?" Gusta asked again. She looked up at her master, completely confused. "Why, sir, would you want to do such a thing? 'Tis impossible." She lifted her hand and pointed to the interloper. "With one look anyone could see that this woman is no boy. Her features are fair, her hair long, and what about—" She paused delicately and lifted her brow. "How do you intend to conceal her womanly endowments?"

"I'll be a chubby boy." Aidan grinned in that cocksure and common way of hers. "I'll wear baggy trousers and blousy shirts. With my hair in a braid, what's to notice? Besides, I know sailors. I know how they walk and talk and joke, and most of them have hair as long as mine, they just wear it tied back in pigtails or braids. Why couldn't you give me a wee trim and plait it for me? I could wrap the braids up in my cap when I'm out and about."

Gusta felt her heart pounding heavily. The mistress must be throwing a tantrum in heaven! No wonder the children were furious with this copper-haired hussy.

"Gusta," her master spoke now in an oddly gentle tone, "I don't like resorting to deception, but in this case, it has become necessary to keep the truth from all others. We have exhausted all other options."

"How so?" She heard the chill in her own voice, but she couldn't help it.

"Well, for one, Captain Tasman has decreed that no unattached women are allowed on the journey. So unless you would have me marry this girl—"

"*Goejehelp!*" Her eyes flew open as she took a wincing breath. "No sir, I wouldn't want you to even consider such a thing."

Grief, black and cold, welled up in Gusta's heart. For months she had been dreading the thought that her beloved master was about to undertake a journey that would part them for months, but now he had set this sprite between them, this brazen barmaid with more beauty than was decent and more talent than was just.

Now he wanted to marry the girl! No. Far better to let them travel as master and student than husband and wife. Gusta would not be able to sincerely pray for his safety on the voyage if she thought for one moment that her master loved this wanton woman.

"The truth, Gusta—" Heer Van Dyck's voice came as if from far away. "—is that I need this girl. If my map is to be all I hope it can be, it needs Aidan's artistic touch. No one can draw flowers the way she can; have you noticed how nature comes to life under her hand? Surely you've recognized her gift."

Slowly, Gusta nodded. She'd noticed many things, but it wasn't her place to set the master straight.

Taking a sharp breath, she offered an option that might not have occurred to him: "The woman could remain here and draw the flowers after you return."

"No." A note of patient tolerance filled his voice. "She has to see them for herself. How could I describe a flower no man has ever seen? Or a unique butterfly? Or any of God's creatures we have not yet met? No, Gusta, I need her eyes with me. And so we must deceive Captain Tasman, and we must conceal the truth from Henrick and Rozamond. I would not want them to make trouble before we sail."

At the mention of the children, Gusta lifted her chin again. "They won't like this. Is it fair, sir, to deceive your own family? I cannot think that God would smile on this endeavor."

"My children do not understand, nor are they fond of Aidan." A muscle clenched along her master's jaw. "No, for their own good, they must not know. This deception will not hurt them, so my plan is really none of their concern. And you, Gusta, must keep this confidence until I return."

Gusta envisioned Rozamond's dark eyes. "I cannot lie to the children," she whispered. Even as wee ones, Rozamond and Henrick had always been able to wheedle her into anything, so great was her love for them.

"You will not have to lie to them," Heer Van Dyck answered. "You will simply remain silent. I plan to invite the children for dinner the night before my departure, and we will all bid farewell to Aidan publicly. After that, you need not say anything until I return."

Gusta closed her eyes as the heavy burden of secrecy descended upon her. "*Ja,* master," she whispered, clenching her fist. "Though it pains me greatly, I will keep my word."

They passed the next morning in the garden. Heer Van Dyck showed Aidan the neat trick of using day-old bread as an eraser and he taught her how to take advantage of the whiteness of her parchment.

"The brightness of watercolors comes from the reflection of light back through the paint," he said, studying the rosebuds she had been painting for the past hour. "Think of the paper as an extra color on your palette, my dear. You do not have to cover every inch of the page, nor do you have to make the paint work so hard. Remember—the paper has given you a dose of white, or ivory, perchance, and you can let it work for you."

"Thank you, Heer Van Dyck." For days Aidan had been struggling with the bright light on rose blossoms. Rather than attempting to paint white spots, she should have just left the page blank—to let the inner white shine through.

"You have taught me so much," she murmured. Sinking onto her stool, she rested her hand under her chin and studied the painting on the easel. It was so much better than anything she had ever dreamed she could create. She owed everything to the gentleman beside her. Perhaps he was right. In time, she might become the great artist he dreamed of and the great lady she wanted to be.

But though Heer Van Dyck had taught her many things, she knew she still had much to learn. Always, he smiled at her work and complimented her by saying that she held "great promise," but what did he mean? What sort of promise did he see in her? The promise of greatness? Of excellence?

And how would she know when she had fulfilled his expectations?

"Alas, there is something else I must teach you," he answered, shifting his cane from one hand to the other. His bearded cheeks fell in worried folds over his collar. "Come with me to the barn. If you're to sail with me as a young man, you must know what every young man should know."

Curiosity reared its head as she stood and followed her mentor. "What every young man should know?"

"Ja." A wide grin split Van Dyck's face as he opened the garden gate and waited for her to precede him. "'Twill be my pleasure to teach you."

⁓⁂⁓

The wide doors of the barn yawned open, and Aidan was pleased to see that the stable boy and groom were nowhere in sight. Van Dyck's horses, a quartet of handsome sorrel geldings, stood in their stalls, munching contentedly on their oats. With his distinctive lumbering gait, Van Dyck moved to the center of the barn where a thick layer of hay lay upon the floor.

"If you are to be a boy—a young man, really," he said, propping both hands on his cane, "there are some things you should know." His lids came swiftly down over his eyes. "Men are not like girls, Joffer O'Connor."

"I hate to disappoint you," Aidan answered dryly, crossing her arms as she leaned against the open barn door, "but I've noticed."

The color in Van Dyck's cheeks deepened, and he gave her a quick smile before looking down at his hands again. "No, there are subtle differences. And though I have not spent too much time

144

aboard ship, I did notice a few things on my voyage to Batavia." He rubbed a hand over his face as if to assist his thoughts. "For one thing, men are quick—women take far more time. You must be quick if you are to pass as a boy."

"Quick—about what?" Aidan frowned, not understanding.

"In the head," he answered, blushing furiously. "When you go to relieve yourself. On a ship filled with men only, many will doubtless relieve themselves standing up, perhaps off the bow itself, so you may occasionally have to resort to a bit of pantomime. But when you do find it necessary to visit the head, make sure you are quick about it."

Aidan bit her tongue in an effort to keep from laughing aloud. Without doubt, if women took longer than men in that very private function, it had more to do with the voluminous skirts they wore than any biological difference. But if Heer Van Dyck wanted to believe that dawdling over a chamber pot was a particular feminine quality, then so be it.

"Thank you, sir, I will remember," she said simply, lifting her face to look at him. "What other advice have you?"

"Women," he said, moving to a low stool just inside the doorway, "are always touching one another. Gusta is quick to embrace Rozamond, and even as a child, Rozamond was always patting Henrick, much like a beloved pet." He looked toward the horizon for a moment, and his eyes softened. "My wife was fond of patting my arm or my shoulder. In any case, I've noticed that women are more tactile—and so you must be careful not to pat a man, or pull a friend into your embrace. Such a move might reveal more than you want others to know."

Aida nodded, mentally filing this recommendation away. It was an astute observation, and something she'd not thought of. And he was right—the women down at the Broad Street Tavern were a very tactile bunch, and if she wasn't careful she might find herself tugging on some sailor's arm just from the force of habit.

"Another thing," Schuyler added, apparently gaining courage

with each suggestion. "Women always want to know how some-one *feels*. Men don't care about feelings, they care much more about another man's *actions*. Men want to *do* exploits, not *feel* emotions. If something happens aboard ship, remember—no one will want to talk about his feelings. Men don't like to talk as much as women, in any case. They would rather take action than discuss a matter."

That revelation was certainly no surprise. "I'll remember," Aidan promised.

"One more thing," Schuyler said.

Aidan sighed. Thus far she had promised not to touch, talk, or take too long in the privy—what else could he possibly have in mind? "Yes sir?"

"A man must know how to defend himself. There is a sort of pecking order aboard ship—and since you've not sailed before, you'll be at the bottom, though I will ask Captain Tasman that you be allowed to serve me. As I said, young men do not debate matters of dispute, they usually take action. And as part of estab-lishing that pecking order, I'm afraid some of the others may want to take a punch at you—"

"A punch?" Aidan burst out, shocked. She straightened and lifted her chin. "Whatever for? I've never hit anyone in my life!"

"Women don't generally fight." Van Dyck rubbed his bearded chin. "Though I've heard that some of those poor souls down at the workhouse get into it now and again. But you most certainly will have to prove yourself. And though it will be over quickly, the important thing is that you do not run away. Stand there like a man, take the punch or two that's thrown, and throw one back if you can. I thought I could show you a thing or two, that's why I brought you out to the barn. The hay is soft; it will cushion your fall."

As Aidan watched in amazement, Van Dyck dropped his cane and lifted his fists, holding them in front of his face like a back-alley brawler. When she did not move, he jerked his head abruptly and shook his fists at her. "Come now, dear, I won't hurt you. But

this is important. Please consider it just another lesson." He circled slowly in the barn, raring to go. "Please. Come."

The artist Van Dyck was an ever-changing mystery. Shaking her head, Aidan slowly left the wall and moved to the open space before her master.

"Bend your knees a little," he said, frowning at her skirt. He bobbed his head in satisfaction when she bent her knees and the material creased. "That's good. Now—drat those skirts, I can't see a thing—spread your feet apart enough that you have a wide base. Think of yourself as a statue, a solid sculpture. You must have a good base upon which to balance yourself."

"All right." Aidan spread her feet shoulder-width apart, then moved in tiny, shifting steps, mirroring her master.

"That's good." His voice rang with approval as she bobbed and shuffled in the hay. "Of course it will be easier when you're wearing trousers. You'll feel as light as a bird then, and you'll likely be quicker than any sailor. The heavy ones tend to be slow and clumsy—remember that." With a distracted nod, he returned her smile. "Now. Put your hands up like mine."

Laughing, she did as he ordered, mimicking his positions exactly, even as he moved over the straw in a hopping motion. She'd seen lots of fights in the bar between drunks, but those sloshing fools did little but smash each other over the head with chairs and clubs. This light footwork was quick and lively, almost like a dance. This she could learn to enjoy!

"Drat these skirts!" she mumbled. "You'll forgive me, sir, if I can't keep up with you—"

"Don't mind your feet now, look at my hands," he instructed. "Use your feet to sidestep your opponent, to keep him off his guard. But when you intend to land a blow, plant your feet firmly on the floor and keep your eyes locked upon your opponent's. Anything is legal, my dear—stomping kicks to the feet, a straight punch to the nose—the bigger the nose, the better the target— and, if you're really in danger, remember to poke a finger in your

foe's eye. But to quickly rid yourself of a noisome pest—" He paused and lowered his voice to a secretive whisper. "Nothing defeats a swift kick to the groin."

Aidan stopped suddenly, resisting the urge to throw her head back in a great peal of laughter. He had just told her what every tavern maid knew by instinct.

"All right now, no time for dallying." Van Dyck lifted his fists again. "Use one hand to punch, keep the other high to protect your lovely little face. There—that's good. Now let's pretend. I'll take a jab at you, slowly, and you bring your arm up to block it. There—no, too slow. Try again. You see, I'm coming in with my right hand, so you must lift your left arm to block me."

Biting her lip, Aidan whirled slowly and played along. After a moment or two she discovered that she had a gift for this sort of thing. "You know, sir," she called, dodging his blow with her arm, then playfully tapping the end of his nose with her fist, "I think I've got it!"

"Right," he answered, tossing another blow and checking it just as it landed short of her ear. "You'll have no problem if you face a sixty-two-year-old tormentor who fights in slow motion."

He ducked suddenly as her arm came from out of nowhere, but his reflexes were not what they had been in younger days. Her fist struck his cheek, and her squeal of dismay filled the air as the blow sent him reeling in the straw.

Fourteen

~⌘~

Sterling walked slowly over the cobblestones, his thoughts wrapped around the difficult situation into which he had blundered. He hadn't meant to propose to Lina Tasman; in retrospect he seemed to recall that the idea had been suggested, approved, and voted on before he could even voice his opinion of it. Abel Tasman, of course, had been the one to broach the topic of a union between his daughter and his new surgeon, and Jannetje Tasman, to Sterling's complete surprise, had enthusiastically endorsed the idea. She and Lina would plan the wedding while the men were at sea, the lady said, and as soon as the *Heemskerk* returned, Lina and Sterling would be married and establish a household in Batavia.

Tasman's suggestion had swiftly progressed from idea to confirmed betrothal, but Sterling had not objected. Lina Tasman was not a great beauty, but she was certainly quiet and pleasant. She did not speak unless spoken to, and her answers were well-formulated and voiced in a pleasant tone. She was slender, with brown hair that sparkled in the lamplight and large brown eyes like a doe's. She would undoubtedly bear him many children with eyes as dark as hers, and they would have a pleasant life as Doctor and Mistress Thorne in Batavia.

The marriage certainly seemed to answer his current problems. With Tasman's sponsorship and his new bride's dowry, he would have the means to establish a practice in Batavia, Dr. Carstens be hanged. Within a year he'd be able to send for one of

his brothers—whichever one had managed to elude the matrimonial plotting of Ernestina Martin. His grand plans, doomed to failure only a few days ago, vibrated now with new life and hope.

The cost? Several months of his life on a voyage and marriage to this shy girl. At least Lina Tasman was not the simpering fool that Ernestina Martin had been; he was certain he could endure and perhaps even enjoy marriage to the captain's daughter. Of all the girls in Batavia he could consider for a wife, surely there were dozens less pleasing than Miss Tasman.

And he would enter this marriage with his eyes open. Immediately after dismissing his wife and daughter after dinner on the night of their first meeting, Abel Tasman had made it clear why he wanted Sterling for a son-in-law. "You may think it strange that I should offer you my daughter's hand on such short notice," he said, swirling his goblet as he regarded Sterling over the dining table. "After all, though Witt Dekker spoke well of you, I scarcely know you. But I know you are no simpleton; you are too well-spoken. You are obviously ambitious, else you would not have journeyed across the ocean to establish a place in this colony."

"The question did occur to me," Sterling answered, running his hands over the fine damask tablecloth. "You should know, sir, that I am not a man of great means. I have come here to make my fortune, not to transport it."

"I like you primarily because you are not Jan Van Oorschot," Tasman answered abruptly, slamming his hand upon the table. "That youth has been calling upon my daughter for many months now, and I will not allow that union. If you are betrothed to my Lina while we are at sea, honor will keep her safely inside the house, and decency will keep young Jan away. I can leave safely, knowing that rascal will not steal my daughter from beneath my nose."

"Does she love this man?" Sterling frowned, confused.

"She is a child; she knows nothing of love." Tasman smiled, but his smile held only a shadow of its former warmth. "She will

marry whomever her mother and I tell her to marry. And you, Doctor, are a fine and ambitious young man. Someday—" He spread his hands to indicate the room in which they sat. "—all this will be yours and Lina's. But I could never rest in my eternal peace thinking of that worthless youth sitting in this house."

Sterling shrugged to hide his confusion. "I think I understand, sir."

Tasman lifted his glass as if to make a toast. "So—to you and Lina, who will make a fine couple."

And then he had tilted back his glass and drunk deeply, while Sterling sipped from his goblet, weighing this new development.

A week ago he had nothing but hope and experience; now he had prospects, a betrothed bride, and a future. *God, give me the courage to face whatever lies ahead.* Thrusting his hands behind his back, he lifted his eyes from the cobblestone road to the mountainous beauty beyond the rooftops of the tidy town. This place was like heaven; he could think of nothing like it in all of Europe. Gauzy clouds drifted before the face of the mountains while birds sang in the trees and insects hummed. If all went according to Tasman's plan, this tropical paradise would soon be his permanent home.

But was the price too dear? Could he marry this young girl, suspecting that she had feelings for another? Love took time to grow, his mother had once told him, and you could love anyone if you committed your will to it. Jesus, after all, had loved us, while we were the most unlovely sinners....

But love, he argued with himself, lowering his eyes to the cobbled road again, shouldn't have to be forced. Surely affection could grow into love, just as liking grew into affection, but he wasn't certain that he even *liked* Lina Tasman. Still, one day he would take her hand and lead her into a bridal chamber where they would become one for the rest of their earthly lives.

At least Lina had a brain and the will to use it, he reminded himself. Though quiet, she was nothing at all like Ernestina, who prattled endlessly about nothing. Lina was thoughtful, at least.

He stopped again, shocked by a sudden elusive thought he could not quite catch. Something moved at the corner of his eye, and ringing shouts filled the silence of the afternoon. Turning slightly, he looked across a well-kept garden to a barn, where an old man and young woman grappled in the sunlight, the man repeatedly reaching out as if to strike the young woman in the face.

"You there! Stop at once!" Without thinking, Sterling vaulted the low stone fence and sprinted across the expanse of garden grass, lowering his shoulder until he hit the old man squarely in the gut. Amid a great screaming and screeching the old man went down, then the tussling began in earnest as some sort of harridan landed upon his back, small fists pummeling his neck in a frantic sort of rhythm.

"Get off him! Stop it!" the woman shouted, and Sterling pulled himself upright long enough to see an expression of absolute horror upon the old man's bearded face. Sterling turned sideways to see what sort of witch rode his shoulders, but a stern command from the older gentleman halted the girl's tirade.

"Stop! At once!" the old man wheezed. "Get away and leave this to me!"

From behind his ear, Sterling heard the girl gasp, then she flew off his shoulders as swiftly as a bird. Sterling would have followed her, but the older man firmly grasped his doublet and hung on with the tenacity of a terrier.

"Leave her be!" the old man demanded. Streams of sweat ran from his forehead. "And let me up, will you? Hand me my cane; it lies on the ground behind you."

Stunned, Sterling rose and extended his hand, helping the old man to his feet, then retrieved the man's cane. From the quality of the man's clothing and manner Sterling knew immediately that this was not a fight between a groom and a maid, as he had first thought. This man wore the clothing and dignity of a gentleman, while the woman—where had she gone?

Sterling turned and looked around, but the sprite had vanished.

All he had managed to see in the midst of the brouhaha was a slender figure and a flash of red hair beneath a cap.

"I apologize, sir, if I have injured you," Sterling forced a note of iron into his voice, "but you must understand that I felt it my duty to come to the aid of a young woman. Although 'tis obvious she was not much hurt—"

"She is not hurt at all; I am the one with a bruised cheek and a swollen nose," the old man croaked, tenderly brushing his red nose with trembling fingers. He looked up, then gripped his cane and gave Sterling a forced smile and a tense nod of dismissal. "We thank you for your attention, sir, and wish you good day."

"Sir—" Sterling paused. What eccentric old men did to while away their afternoons was really none of his business, but engaging in fisticuffs with a young woman, no matter how adept she was, was not a fitting entertainment for any gentleman. "Sir, if you would pardon my curiosity, what just happened here?" Sterling crossed his arms and widened his stance, making it clear that he would not leave without a word of explanation.

The older gentleman frowned, then pursed his lips. "What happened here?" He brought his hand to his neat white beard, then lifted his eyes to the sky, as if the answer might appear there. "That's a good question," he murmured in Dutch, probably assuming that Sterling did not speak the language. He mumbled softly, as if speaking to himself. "How *do* I explain it? The truth won't do, and a lie would seem false no matter carefully stated."

After a moment he lowered his gaze, gave Sterling a broad smile, and responded in English: "There is no explanation, sir, that I can give." He shifted his heels together and bowed with formal grace. "I thank you for your noble intentions, but you can be certain I never intended to hurt the young lady."

"Then pray have a care for yourself, sir," Sterling answered, not moving. "I seem to recall the young lady punching at *you*."

"Did you now?" The old man tilted his head and chuckled slightly, wheezing as he drew a deep breath. "That's good," he

mumbled in Dutch. "Oh, that's very good. Very credible, I must say, and after only one lesson. Of course one never knows how a situation will go in the heat of the moment, but still, that's very good."

Ignoring Sterling, the old man turned to walk toward the house.

"Sir!" Sterling called, more bewildered than ever. "I must have your word that you will not engage in this sort of thing again! I cannot leave the young lady if she will be in danger here."

"She's in no danger, sir." The old gentleman rocked slowly on his hips as if they were stiff. "No more than I am, at least. Now good day."

Sterling waited without moving until the old man disappeared into the house, then scratched his head and looked into the open barn. Nothing moved inside but four horses, their tails moving in rhythm, swatting horseflies away. He could see nothing of the young woman.

With a heavy sigh Sterling turned and moved back toward the garden wall. He'd stumbled onto a pair of eccentrics, maybe even lunatics. Perhaps the heat of this place got to everyone eventually.

He stepped over the garden wall and thought of supper waiting at Tasman's house, where his silent bride-to-be would watch him eat and drink and say nothing. Lately her watchful dark eyes made him as nervous as a cat.

Perhaps it was good that he'd soon be sailing away on an extended voyage.

⌘

From her hiding place behind the hibiscus hedge, Aidan watched the stranger move away. When he had climbed back over the garden wall and moved down the street, she stood and crept back toward the barn. Her heart stirred with emotions she had thought long dead, and she needed a moment of quiet to sort through them all.

She recognized him almost instantly. He was the handsome man she'd spotted walking along the wharf weeks ago with his gunnysack over his shoulder, the one who walked with the peculiar heavy gait

of one who'd just come ashore. His striking face had remained in her mind, and this was the stranger she'd sketched for Heer Van Dyck that day in the tavern. He was still a stranger, but what a man!

How heroic he was! Supposing her in danger, he had leaped the wall and come to her rescue without a moment's thought, nearly imperiling Schuyler's plan. Of course her master could have truthfully explained their situation, but the upper crust of Batavia was a close-knit community. If even one person learned of Aidan's intended disguise, it was a sure bet the entire colony would buzz of it before the expedition set sail.

Who was he? Aidan was quite sure she'd never seen him at the tavern. He'd seemed quite gallant, really, the way he hurled himself at Heer Van Dyck and forced the older man to the ground. He was an Englishman, judging by his voice, and educated, for his manners and speech hinted at a genteel background. He was too down-to-earth for an aristocrat, but he was no ruffian either.

One of the horses whinnied softly, and Aidan reached into a bin for a handful of oats and lifted her cupped hand to the horse's soft mouth. As the gelding's lips tickled her palm, she smiled at the thought of her handsome rescuer. How Lili would love this story! She'd have the stranger pegged as a possible husband for Aidan within five minutes of meeting him, but Aidan had never needed a husband less than she did at this moment.

The horse ran his velvety mouth over Aidan's arm, searching for more oats, and she scolded him gently as she wiped her hand on her skirt. From this point forward, she would have to put away all thoughts of Lili, the other girls, and the tavern. She was about to become a boy in order that she might become a lady, and she couldn't afford to be distracted by romantic notions of heroes who leaped over garden walls. She had a plan, and she would have to see it through no matter what happened.

"If you are ever going to become respectable," she told herself, leaning against the stall as blue-veiled twilight began to creep into the barn, "you can't think of anything else."

Schuyler Van Dyck

What is there that confers the noblest delight?
What is that which swells a man's breast with pride above that which
any other experience can bring to him?
Discovery!
To know that you are walking where none others have walked;
That you are beholding what human eye has not seen before;
That you are breathing a virgin atmosphere…
To be the first—that is the idea.

Mark Twain, *The Innocents Abroad*

Fifteen

"A re you ready then?" Gusta's round face was seamed with disapproval, but Aidan nodded in contentment. They stood on the threshold of the greatest game Aidan had ever dreamed of playing, and the grandness of her ambitions still staggered her. In less than one hour Heer Van Dyck's children would gather for dinner and Aidan would leave the house to return to the tavern, ostensibly saying farewell to the Van Dycks forever.

Henrick and Rozamond would be happy to see her go, of course. Though they would undoubtedly be a little anxious to send their father on a voyage of exploration, Aidan knew they would be relieved that the "interloper" was out of his house.

"Is your bag packed with the things I found?" Gusta's gaze drifted toward the small satchel containing the clothes that would transform Aidan into a boy. The housekeeper had proved remarkably clever in the matter of creating a disguise. She'd procured two pairs of loose-fitting trousers, three oversized cotton shirts, and a cap that could be pulled down to cover Aidan's hair.

The housekeeper had flatly refused to cut Aidan's tresses. "Does not the Scripture say that hair is given to a woman for her covering?" she had asked earlier that morning, a flame of righteous indignation in her eyes. "You can braid it like the seamen do. It will hang down your back, out of your way."

"But the color is unusual, and someone may remember it," Aidan protested. She feared that her plans might come undone

due to the woman's stubbornness, but apparently the housekeeper had thought of everything.

Gusta produced a bottle of olive oil from her pocket. "Swipe this through your hair," she said, dropping the container into Aidan's satchel. "Red turns to ruddy brown when it's wet with oil. Keep your cap on, and no one will be the wiser."

Aidan tucked the last of her traitorous red hair up into a lady-like lace cap, then smoothed her gown. The sumptuous dress was new, supposedly a farewell gift from a teacher to his prized student, and Aidan actually felt pretty as she twirled in the golden silk and held up her looking glass. When she had published her first book of engravings, she would buy another dress just like this one. Perhaps she'd wear it to the governor general's ball, or to the opening ceremonies of the school she intended to establish for orphans and wayward girls. For when she was respectable and a veritable fountain of virtue, she would stretch forth her hand to the less fortunate. No one should have to suffer as she and the others had.

Henrick's voice drifted up the stairs, and Gusta thrust her head through Aidan's chamber doorway. "Rozamond and Dempsey have arrived, and Henrick is home from work," the housekeeper called, just before moving down the hallway. As Aidan stepped out to follow, Gusta turned. "Wait for the space of ten minutes, then come down to join us. I suspect you know what to do."

"I do." Aidan folded her hands. "And I want to thank you, Gusta, for all you have done. I—we—couldn't do this without you."

The housekeeper uttered a soft grunt of disagreement, then moved down the stairs and out of sight.

⌀

Dempsey Jasper ran a finger around the tight collar at his neck, then forced a smile as his father-in-law stepped into the dining room. "Heer Van Dyck, how well you are looking!" He bowed slightly. "You are as calm as a man sitting for a portrait. I would never think that on the morrow you will leave to join your ship."

"The morrow will take care of itself," Schuyler answered easily. He stepped forward to give Rozamond a light kiss on the cheek, greeted Henrick, then gestured toward the table. "Shall we sit? Gusta has been detained for a moment, but I have no doubt our dinner will be served soon."

Despite his comment about Schuyler's calm, Dempsey thought their host seemed a bit on edge as he took his place at the head of the table. A glow suffused his face, as though he contained a candle that burned brightly, and his eyes were alight with mischief and inspiration. Dempsey wondered if the upcoming journey could account for the man's changed demeanor. Or was there more to it? And did the little guttersnipe have anything to do with Schuyler's air of expectancy?

Dempsey seated Rozamond, then took his own chair across from Henrick. Rozamond asked some silly and pointless question about Captain Tasman's daughter, but Schuyler barely responded. His gaze moved instead toward the hall as the sound of a silken rustle reached the dining room. Dempsey turned, too, and stared at the young woman who stood in the doorway.

It was the wastrel, no doubt, but all traces of depravity—the clinging, dingy dress and the hungry, brazen look—had vanished from her face and figure. She wore a golden gown that must have cost a working man's monthly wages, and that unrestrained red hair had been tucked neatly into a modest lady's cap. A double linen collar of fine white contrasted pleasingly with the pale ivory of her skin, and her hands were encased in a pair of long gloves. A striking gold cross of Celtic design hung from her neck and shone against the linen collar, advertising a piety Dempsey was certain she could not possess.

Ignoring the others at the table, the girl lifted her eyes to meet Schuyler's gaze. "I must thank you, Heer Van Dyck," she said simply, dipping into a small curtsy as she spoke. "You have been most kind to offer me shelter and instruction. But now, as you prepare to go on your journey, I must leave you. I will always remember

what you have taught me, and to do justice to your kindness and hospitality I shall strive to improve my lot." She gave him a brief, fleeting smile, then stooped to pick up a small satchel that lay on the floor in the hallway.

"Go with God, my child," Schuyler answered formally. "I shall expect to hear great things about you when I return."

And then, while Rozamond frowned and Henrick gaped openly, the exquisite changeling turned and disappeared into the hallway. The Van Dycks sat silently, listening as the front door clicked shut and the sound of her light footsteps faded from their hearing.

"I shall miss her," Schuyler said. An undisguised tenderness lingered in his eyes as he turned to his children. "She was an interesting student, but of course I could not leave her here with Henrick while I am gone."

"She will return to the wharf?" Henrick asked, disbelief in his voice. "It is such a terrible place. The gaming houses, the taverns, the musicos…"

"It is where she belongs," Rozamond snapped. "It is only right that she return. She could not stay here, after all, with you in town and only Gusta to guard the house."

"Miss O'Connor understands, and she will go wherever she wants to go." Schuyler picked up his spoon, tapped it against his glass, and looked expectantly toward the hallway. "Gusta! What is keeping you?"

Dempsey lifted his hand to his chin and stroked it for a moment, thinking. Rozamond and Henrick had accepted this little act at face value, but the words were spoken too smoothly, with too little fuss or emotion, for Dempsey to believe this touching little farewell scene. If he had been housed, fed, and entertained for several days by a great gentleman like Schuyler Van Dyck, he would not have willingly returned to the hovel from which he had sprung. The price of a golden dress would not have been enough to induce him to quietly disappear.

"Perhaps," Dempsey drawled, his voice so dry that Rozamond cast him a sharp, questioning glance, "Gusta is overcome with grief at the prospect of losing her young friend. Perhaps you should send a messenger to that saloon where you found the hussy, Heer Van Dyck, and make certain she has safely returned to her place."

Schuyler frowned, then rose from his chair and stepped into the hallway. "Gusta!" they heard him call, then he moved away toward the kitchen.

"I am so glad she is gone," Rozamond confessed in a low whisper, shaking her head as she looked at her brother. "Perhaps a few weeks at sea will clear Father's mind. I don't know how a man of his dignity and position could allow himself to be taken in by a trollop."

"I am a little alarmed that she was still here when I arrived," Henrick confessed. "And more alarmed at the look of her when she left. Did you notice the change? She could easily pass for a lady. I fear she will not know how to go back to her old life after living here—"

"Gentility is not dirt, Henrick; it does not rub off on those who rub up against it," Dempsey interrupted. He tugged irritably at his sleeve, then glanced quickly from his wife to his brother-in-law. "The woman was gutter mud and she still is gutter mud, no matter how carefully she is dressed or how graciously she speaks. And more important, she still stands to inherit a considerable portion of this estate—unless your father has visited his solicitor again." He looked evenly at Henrick. "Do you want that, brother? When your father's will is published, do you want the world to know that a barmaid and harlot bought your father's favor?"

A furious blush glowed on Henrick's high cheekbones. "By all that's holy, no." His voice was a suffocated whisper. "What would people think?"

"They will think nothing." Dempsey leaned back in his chair. "Trust me to take care of everything. We may not be able to

change your father's opinion or his will before he sails, but we can make certain the girl will not make trouble for us. I'll visit the wharf on the morrow."

"What will you do?" Rozamond's eyes brightened with speculation.

Dempsey reached out and squeezed his wife's round cheek. "Whatever has to be done, my sweet."

⁂

Walking eastward on Broad Street, Aidan clutched the handle of her satchel and resisted the urge to swing it in the sheer exuberance of joy. That had not been difficult at all! Van Dyck's children had been surprised to see her, but their relief at her departure had been evident in their faces.

A young man leaned out of a passing carriage to look at her, his eyes alight with interest. In a gesture of goodwill, she inclined her head toward him. In this dress, such a gesture would be regarded as merely friendly. If she had nodded at him dressed in her tavern rags, he probably would have insulted her with words too vile to be repeated.

Amazing, how society excused the eccentricities of a lady while it condemned the mere existence of the tavern maids. Aidan swung her satchel high into the air. At this moment, she didn't care what anyone thought of her behavior. Let them stare! For the first time in her life she felt pretty and confident, for such was the magic of this golden gown. Heer Van Dyck had given her more than a mere garment. The woman who wore this gown would be taken seriously and treated with respect.

She smiled to herself. Perhaps he had planned to send her back to the wharf in an altered frame of mind as well as a new garment. It would be like him to think of such an idea, for he was always seeing things in her that Aidan could not believe.

Another carriage passed, and this time two women craned their necks to see her, doubtless spurred by curious jealousy. She lifted her chin, absently smoothing the silk of her skirt, allowing

her palm to caress the shimmering richness of the fabric. She would hate leaving this garment behind, but she could give it to Orabel, who just might find her long-awaited husband once she tasted the gown's power. Anyone would look like a queen in this regal softness.

Aidan reached the intersection of Broad and Market Streets and paused for a moment, letting her eyes rove over buildings and faces she had not seen in more than a week. Strange, how the taverns and flophouses seemed dirty and decrepit to her eye. No one scrubbed the doorsteps here, no one swept the cobblestones to keep the area free from filth and decay. A deep, pungent smell assailed her almost immediately—the mingled scents of cheap tobacco, wet wood, day-old fish, unwashed bodies, and the constant warm breath of the sea.

The gusting, steady wind shrilled from the harbor, flapping her skirt and sleeves. Aidan lowered her head and used her free hand to hold her cap firmly to her head. Moving slowly, she crossed the crowded street, attuning her ears to the sounds of the wharf—loud voices like a deep, angry buzz, punctuated by the faint sound of distant shouts and underscored by the howling wind. For a moment she felt as though she had entered a riptide eager to pull her under. Then she shook her head. She had friends who lived along this street. This was not a hostile civilization; it was a tavern, and the people here were just like her.

"This is home," she muttered, pausing in the center of the road before Bram's tavern. The torches had already been lit. Their golden light pushed at the darkness and gleamed in the harlots' hair, a welcoming beacon for any who wanted to leave the neat and ordered world behind.

Stepping nimbly over a mud puddle and the drunk that lay sprawled beside it, Aidan lifted her head and moved resolutely forward. "Heaven above, who is that?" a drunken sailor called, turning from the harlot in his arms to watch Aidan move through the milling mob outside the doors.

"A bit haughty, aren't we, lady?" A hussy called. Then a moment later Aidan heard, "*Niet te Geloven,* that's Irish Annie!"

Aidan lifted her skirts and pressed her lips together, threading her way through the crowd until she reached the threshold of the tavern doorway. She paused before the door, drew a deep breath, and forbade herself to tremble. Her mind whirled with confusing emotions; past and present and future tugged at her, sending her heart downward in a sickening lurch. This was home; these were her people. Why then did she feel like an alien?

She pushed the door open and blinked, waiting for her eyes to grow accustomed to the smoky interior. Music and voices and shouting blended together in a busy chorus, but the sounds faded and died away as Aidan stepped into the room.

"Holy heaven, what have we here?" She heard the deep rumble of Bram's voice and turned toward it. He stood behind his bar, a pair of pewter mugs in one burly fist. "I'm sorry, Madame, but you should not be here without—"

"Bram." She gave him a wavering smile. "It's me, Aidan. Where is my mother?"

His broad face went absolutely blank with shock.

"Aidan?" Orabel stepped forward from a group around one of the gaming tables. "*Goejehelp,* it is you! Look at you! You look every inch a lady!"

"Shhh," Aidan teased, stepping forward to draw her friend into a warm embrace. Orabel laughed and Aidan lifted her head to gaze at the dumbstruck gawkers. Lapsing back into her thickest brogue, she frowned and said, "Faith, are you all a pack of amadons and eejits? Get back to your gossipin'. 'Tis only me, Irish Annie. Have you never seen a girl cleaned up before?"

The room erupted in laughter, and within a moment life went on. "Look at you!" Orabel whispered, her eyes roving from the cap on Aidan's head to the dainty slippers peeking from beneath her hem. "You're quite the beautiful lady! Have you found that rich husband after all?"

"No, and I'm not likely to." Aidan pulled Orabel toward the door. "Come, let us find a quiet place where we can talk. I've a secret to tell you."

"A secret?" Orabel's eyes lit with pleasure. "There's nothing I'd like better to hear. Can it be that you're getting married at last? Or have you sold a painting to some fine gentleman who will make your name great throughout Europe?"

"Nothing like that." Aidan pulled Orabel down the street to the narrow door of the women's quarters. She flung it open and smiled in relief to find the room empty. "The others are all out?" she asked, moving to the box where Lili kept a candle and a flint.

"*Ja,*" Orabel answered as she followed Aidan into the room. "They are working, of course."

Aidan fumbled with the flint for a moment, then lit the candle. As the pinpoint of light flickered and brightened the room, Aidan looked around her home with new eyes. Strange, how cluttered this place seemed compared to the spare, elegant furnishings of her chamber at Van Dyck's house.

Aidan peered around to make sure Lili had not left any drunks behind to sleep off their ale, but she and Orabel were quite alone. She sighed in relief and sank to one of the sleeping mats on the floor. Her gown pooled around her, a molten mass of golden silk.

"Such a pretty thing you are," Orabel whispered. Awe filled her voice, and she settled a respectful distance away. "Such a lovely gown! I should have known you'd make a fine lady, Aidan."

"I haven't become a lady at all," Aidan hissed, rapidly growing impatient with the deferential attitude that had greeted her at every turn. She tugged at the lace cap and pulled it off, then yanked on the neat bun that held her hair. "And on the morrow I shall not even be a woman." She looked at her friend. "Orabel, I need your help. I need you to keep a secret. And in return for your help I want to give you this gown."

Orabel's eyes flew open wide. "That gown? *Sakerloot,* Aidan, that would never do. How could I beg a stuiver wearing something

like *that?* No one would give me a penny if I was dressed like the richest lady in Batavia. I would starve in a dress like that."

"In a dress like this," Aidan answered, already fumbling at the ties that held the sleeves to her bodice, "you might find a husband. You'd look like a very genteel lady, Orabel, and who knows what sea captain might look at you and feel his heart stirred? This is not a begging dress, but perhaps it is a *courting* dress." She caught Orabel's eyes, which were filled with infinite distress and uncertainty. "I had all manner of gentlemen's curious glances bestowed upon me as I wended my way to this place, Orabel. And so may you, for you are much prettier than I." She gave her friend a knowing smile. "Besides, you always said you wanted a yellow dress."

Orabel's eyes softened as she reached out and tentatively touched the silk skirt. "Why would you want to give me something like this, Aidan? You're the one that deserves a husband. Not me. No man will want me after—"

Aidan pulled her sleeve from the bodice with a firm yank. "I'll not be needing this dress, nor any other where I'm going." She tossed the sleeve into Orabel's lap. "So you take it. I want you to have it."

A tremor touched the younger girl's lips. "Where are you going? What do you mean?"

"I'm going to sea," Aidan answered, pulling the other sleeve free of its fastenings. "In breeches, a shirt, and cap. And no one must know where I've gone, or how, at least until the boat sails. Heer Van Dyck thinks we'll be aboard for at least a week until the captain is ready to cast off."

Orabel's face emptied of expression. "You are going to sea? As a *man?* Have you lost your mind? The captain will flog you or clap you in stocks if he finds out! I've heard what they do to those who disobey orders, but I've never heard such a hare-brained scheme!"

"Heer Van Dyck will be my protector." Aidan untied the laces that held her bodice to the full skirts of the gown. She stood and turned her back for Orabel's help. "So help me now, and you'll

have yourself a fine dress. Perhaps you could go into town and find a position as a lady's maid."

Orabel kept up a stream of steady protest as her fingers tugged on the fastenings at Aidan's side. "Aidan, think of yourself! You have managed to keep yourself chaste and virtuous, but how do you intend to preserve your honor if you're discovered on a ship filled with seamen?"

"I can take care of myself." A smile flitted across Aidan's face as she recalled Van Dyck's rudimentary lessons in self-defense. "I imagine I will handle myself very well. Haven't I had to dodge the lecherous embrace of every drunk around Bram's gaming tables?"

"But why?" The skirt fell to the ground, billowing slightly as it settled. Orabel's eyes widened further as she took in the sight of Aidan's fine embroidered undershirt.

"So I can become a respectable lady on my own terms." Aidan shrugged out of the bodice and shirt and tossed those garments into Orabel's arms. Then she reached into her satchel for the plain sailor's shirt she would wear night and day for the next several weeks. As Orabel covered her mouth and gaped in horrified amazement, Aidan thrust her arms through the long sleeves and pulled the rough shirt over her head. After untying her silk stockings and flinging them toward Orabel, she pulled the thick men's stockings from her bag, slipped them on, and tied them above the knee with a garter. Finally came the pants, baggy trousers that came up and over the long shirt and tied at the waist with a length of rope Gusta had thoughtfully provided.

"That should do," Aidan murmured when she was fully dressed. "I suppose I'm young enough no one will think it strange that I don't have a beard or a deep voice."

Her fingers groped at the bottom of the bag, and she pulled out a rod dagger, one essential piece of equipment every man carried. Gusta had been reluctant to pack one for Aidan, but Heer Van Dyck had insisted. Aidan grinned at the blade, then tucked it into her belt at the center of her back.

"Aidan!" Orabel's fine, silky brows rose nearly to her forehead. "If you don't explain, I'm going to sit on you and keep you here. I'm afraid you've lost your mind."

"I'm going to participate in a project of Heer Van Dyck's," Aidan explained, tucking the excess length of the shirt into her breeches, then adjusting the rope knot. "He will make the map of our journey and the new worlds we explore, and I will draw pictures of the flora and fauna we discover. We will be published, and my name will be recognized. Heer Van Dyck says I may later complete a book of copperplate engravings, and my name will be renowned not only here, but at home in England. Then I shall return to Europe and find a nice gentleman to wed. I shall be respectable, don't you see?"

She sank to the floor and looked into Orabel's wide blue eyes. "I'll no longer be a wharf rat, a pickpocket, a barmaid, or a drudge. Never again will a drunken sailor paw at me, nor will I have to smile and listen to them spout nonsense while beery breath blows in my face."

"Is that all?" Orabel spoke in a slightly strangled voice, and her eyes glistened with unshed tears. "Is that all you're running from? I think perhaps you're running from Lady Lili, the best-known procuress in Batavia, and your best friend, the harlot called Sweet Kate."

A tear tangled in Orabel's lashes and fell, smearing the heavy rouge on her cheek. Smitten by a sudden rush of guilt, Aidan reached out and put her hand on Orabel's shoulder. "Don't ever feel that way," she whispered. "I love you, Orabel, just as I love Lili. But each of us is responsible for our own lives. I have to try to do something. Heer Van Dyck has offered me a way out of the wharf, and I have to take it."

"And if you die trying?" Orabel clutched the silken bodice and sleeves as Aidan reached into the bag for the bottle of olive oil.

"It will be worth it," she answered, uncorking the oil. "Now help me do this, will you? Gusta said I must comb the oil through

my hair, then braid it into one long braid. The oil will make the color less noticeable."

Orabel set the gown aside and waited for Aidan to settle down in front of her. Aidan handed Orabel the bottle, then sat still as Orabel sprinkled the oil on Aidan's tresses and finger-combed her hair.

"I think we may be able to hide the white streak in a braid," she said, a note of deep regret in her voice, as though Aidan had already gone. "Anyone who had remarked upon it here would not see it and guess your secret."

"No one will recognize me anyway. I'll wear a cap and darken my face with dirt, if I have to," Aidan answered, resting her wrists atop her bent knees. She had to admit, a woman had far more freedom of movement in breeches than in a bodice and skirt. She closed her eyes, enjoying the sensation of Orabel's fingers in her hair. Lili used to play with Aidan's hair in just this way, when they lived in England. Before the summer of plague…and her father's death.

The memory of her father's gaunt face came back to her. "Here, me darlin'," he had said only days before he died on the ship en route to Batavia. Choking back tears, she had watched as he removed his necklace, a solid gold Celtic cross, and pressed it into her palm.

"I had it engraved before we left London," he whispered, his voice fainter than air. "I wanted it to be a wee birthday present for you."

Aidan had tried to control her feelings, but her lip quivered and her eyes filled in spite of herself. Blinking back tears, she turned the cross over and read the inscription on the back: *"My love is yours forever, Aidan."*

"Da," she had whispered through her tears. "Da, this is gold. You ought to keep it; we might need it later—"

"Some things are worth holding on to, darlin'," he answered, patting her hand. His own eyes were bordered with tears. "Gold

might buy a loaf of bread, but on the morrow you'd be without bread or gold. You keep that, until you reach a place where you can't go back. Like I can't go back now."

The memory sent a hot tear trickling down Aidan's cheek. Orabel squeezed her shoulder. "Put on your cap, Aidan, and let's see what you look like."

Sniffing, Aidan wiped her eyes on her sleeve. She had reached that place of no return—she couldn't go back, ever. She would have to cut all ties, move out into the great unknown. What had Heer Van Dyck once told her? *To live a fulfilled and creative life, you must lose your fear of being wrong. Just proceed. Believe. And place your faith in God.*

She wasn't going to live in the shadow of yesterday for one more hour. She clamped her lips, imprisoning a sob, and pulled the chain with its golden cross over her head. "I want you to have this, Orabel." She turned and pressed it into her friend's hand.

Orabel's smile vanished. "Oh, Aidan, I couldn't! This is yours!"

"No, it's yours now. I want you to have it. You have a new golden dress—a proper lady should have a necklace to match."

"Aidan!" A dim flush raced across Orabel's beautiful face as she stared at the chain and cross in her hand.

"Tomorrow is a new day for both of us, Orabel." Aidan shifted her weight and turned to sit cross-legged on the floor facing her friend. Orabel seemed too stunned to move, so Aidan gently took the necklace and dropped it over Orabel's gleaming blond hair. For a moment the two girls sat silently, then Aidan leaned forward until her forehead touched her friend's.

"My da told me never to look back. And Heer Van Dyck told me that I should shoot for the moon, because even if I missed it, I would still land among the stars."

"The stars?" Orabel spoke in a weak and tremulous whisper.

"*Ja,*" Aidan answered. "By this time tomorrow night, we should both be on our way."

Sixteen

～ఎలాగ～

Stepping from his coach at the intersection of Broad and Market Streets, Dempsey Jasper automatically pressed his handkerchief to his nose against the sharp smells that rose to invade his nostrils. Though the Broad Street Tavern was too rough even for his tastes, he often visited other establishments in this area under the cover of darkness. Then the scents and sights of the wharf did not seem nearly so disagreeable as in the bright and unforgiving morning light. This place belonged to the darkness.

A brief ray of sunlight broke through the cloud cover that promised a respite from Batavia's insufferable heat. Dempsey slowly sauntered toward the Broad Street Tavern, looking for a man who fit the description of one called Witt Dekker. This Dekker, Dempsey's streetwise groom had assured him, was rough, dependable, and completely at ease with whatever action might be required of him. The groom had sworn that Dekker could be found within or near the Broad Street Tavern, and so was certain to know the girl who had lately left Heer Van Dyck's house.

Dempsey strode into the tavern and paused for a moment to peruse his surroundings. The cavernous room was quiet, for the real business of the place would not begin until after dark. Only four people were on the premises: a dour-faced woman sat before a table counting a stack of guilders; in a far corner a musician blew forlornly upon a horn for a sleepy boy, and behind the bar stood a burly man with arms as big as a bull's thigh. An empty stool stood near the big man, so Dempsey made his way toward the bartender.

"*Goede middag,*" he murmured, taking a seat on the wooden stool.

The burly bartender lifted his gaze, then frowned. "If you're from the reverend or the constable, I can assure you that nothing untoward happened here last night. I'll give you a drink, but nothing more, for we already pay the constables enough to keep a horde of elephants away."

"I can assure you, sir, that I represent no one but myself," Dempsey answered, glancing behind him. A group of sailors noisily came in and moved to a table; the old crone lifted her eyes, then continued her counting. Dempsey turned back to the bartender, fished a guilder out of his pocket, and dropped it to the bar. As the coin spun in a wobbly circle, Dempsey lifted his brows and looked up at the barkeeper again. "I'm looking for a man who is a regular customer. I mean him no harm; I only mean to employ him."

"Who would that be?" The bartender's busy brow rose in mock surprise. "We have few regular customers, for the ships are in and out again—"

"Witt Dekker." Dempsey suppressed a smile as a mask of indifference fell over the barkeeper's face. "And don't try telling me you don't know him. I know he stays here when he's in port, and I know he's in port now. I could probably identify which harlot kept him company last night, but if you'll tell me where I might find this man, I'll give you this guilder and another besides."

Greed and conscience wrestled briefly in the man's dark eyes. "Leave the gold on the table," he whispered gruffly. "Go out of the tavern, walking toward the harbor. Turn into the first alley, and knock on the first door you come to. That's the women's room, and Dekker's inside, still asleep." An odd mingling of wariness and amusement shone in the man's eyes. "I'd be careful about waking him if I were you."

Dempsey dropped another guilder on the table and moved outside, his resolve strengthening with every step. He had been

half-afraid he would actually run into Aidan in the tavern, but apparently the girl had more sense than to return to her old haunts. And despite what he had said last night, Dempsey did not think Schuyler Van Dyck would return his prized pupil to the rough streets. He had undoubtedly found a safe place for her to live while he was away, but Dempsey did not have the time or the freedom to search all of Batavia for one lousy wharf rat.

He found the door the bartender had indicated, then pushed it open without knocking. "Witt Dekker?"

In the semi-gloom of the windowless harlot's den Dempsey could see two forms—a blond girl in a glimmering gown, and a bulky masculine shape sprawled across a pallet on the floor. The girl rose from a low stool as Dempsey closed the door behind him. Her wide blue eyes flickered toward him only for an instant as she moved away from the man on the mattress.

Dempsey began to move forward, then reconsidered his bold intrusion. Remaining in the doorway so that he blocked the girl's exit, he tilted his head and studied her for a moment. Too bad this one had fallen; she bore signs of real beauty. Cornflower blue eyes dominated her delicate features, but already her face bore the hard lines of grief and sorrow. Soon that ivory skin would develop the disfiguring pockmarks of venereal disease. She would not live to be thirty, if she lived that long.

"Girl," he called, his eyes piercing the short distance between them, "know you a wench called Aidan? She is often in this vicinity, I hear. A lovely creature, with red hair and a fiery temper to match."

"There is no one by that name here, sir." The girl fixed her gaze on the floor. "She is not in Bram's employ."

"I only want to know where she is." Dempsey tempered his tone and gave her his most charming smile. Still blocking her escape, he stepped forward and wrapped his arm around the girl's waist. As he nuzzled her lovely neck, he whispered into her ear, "I mean her no harm, love."

The figure on the mattress groaned and stirred. Dempsey abruptly released the blond and took a quick step toward the man. He stopped abruptly when he heard a low growl from the shadows. A mongrel terrier rose to its feet, its hackles raised, its brown eyes fixed on Dempsey.

"Kate?" The man looked up and peered at Dempsey through bleary, red eyes. "Who dares disturb my sleep?"

"I don't know him," the girl answered, lowering her eyes again. Her hands fluttered nervously over the front of her bodice, pale butterflies against golden silk. She dropped her voice and whispered intensely: "Please, sir, let me pass."

"Of course, my dear." Dempsey lowered his head in a stiff bow as the girl grabbed up her skirts and ran out of the room. The man on the mattress sat up and sleepily ran a hand through his wiry hair, but his eyes, when they fastened upon Dempsey, flickered with wariness.

"Witt Dekker, I presume." Dempsey stepped into the room. "I hear that you are a good man to make problems disappear."

The dog released a warning bark, but Dekker silenced the animal: "Down, Snuggerheid!" The terrier obediently dropped to its belly on the floor, and Dekker's gaze moved back to Dempsey. "When a man is properly motivated, almost anything can be made to disappear. It all depends upon what sort of problem a man is facing."

"My problem is a simple one—a woman."

Dekker released a scornful laugh. "I have never had a *simple* problem with a woman."

Dempsey drew a deep breath. "My problem is a wench called Aidan, who used to work as a barmaid in this tavern. A certain gentleman has taken a fancy to her, a fancy that will cost his family thousands of English pounds."

Dekker's brows rose in surprise, then he let out a long, low whistle. "That's some fancy. But I don't know the girl; perhaps she's worth the price."

Dempsey shook his head. "No woman alive is worth that amount. And the gentleman is not fond of her as you or I might be fond of a wench. She has convinced him that she is better than she is, and he has written her into his will. When the old man dies, she will share in his estate, and I'm certain you can understand why his children would rather that she not appear to stake her claim."

Dekker pinned him with a long silent scrutiny, then smiled. "So who are you, and what is your interest in this matter? I know no Aidan, and you are a stranger to me. Why should I help you?"

Dempsey wasn't certain how one introduced oneself to a hired killer, but he bowed as if this were a formal introduction and inclined his head in a deep gesture. "I am Dempsey Jasper, formerly of London, presently of Batavia. My wife is daughter to the gentleman I mentioned. We are not thinking of the financial profit, of course, but of the scandal that would ruin my wife's happiness."

Dekker closed his eyes while a wide smile slowly spread across his face. "Ah, I see. Well. What is your wife's happiness worth to you then? This will have to be a quick job, for I am due to sail within a fortnight. If I cannot find this wench—"

"She left my father-in-law's house last night," Dempsey answered, his patience growing thin. "Heer Van Dyck has probably arranged for her to stay in some safe house, but she is a woman of the streets, and I am certain she will be returning to her old haunts. We hoped to have this settled as soon as possible, for Heer Van Dyck is scheduled to depart soon, as well. He is sailing with Abel Tasman and one cannot know what might happen on the uncharted sea."

"Sailing with Tasman?" The man's watery eyes held absolutely no expression. "I shall meet him then, for I, too, am sailing with Tasman. I will serve as first mate upon the *Zeehaen*."

Dempsey felt a sudden lurch of his stomach. This ruthless killer would be leaving with Heer Van Dyck. He closed his eyes, considering. What would a certain accident upon the high seas cost?

He opened one eye, scarcely daring to breathe his thoughts. "If you find the girl and can guarantee that she will not step forward to claim her inheritance," he said slowly, forcing the words out, "I will pay you five thousand pounds. And if, by some chance, Tasman returns to Batavia and announces that my wife is now fatherless, I will pay you double."

"Ten thousand pounds to kill two people?" Dekker propped his arms upon his bent knees. "It is a decent wage."

"Are we agreed?"

Dekker nodded with a taut jerk of his head. "Consider it done. I shall begin with Sweet Kate, for she knows everyone in these parts. If the wench is to be found at the wharf, Kate will know where she is."

Dempsey drew in his breath as the image of the blond girl flickered across his mind. Of course! He should have seen it sooner, but had been so intent on finding this red-haired temptress—

"By all means, find the blond harlot," he said, smiling grimly. "She knows. She is wearing the gown Aidan wore from Van Dyck's house last night."

❦

Sitting at a table in a quiet corner of the tavern, Aidan pulled her sailor's cap down over her head and chewed the tip of her thumbnail. Orabel moved through the growing crowd like a graceful sylph, a vision of loveliness in the golden gown. Aidan resisted the urge to smile at her, then turned her thoughts toward a more pressing worry. For the past two hours she had mentally debated whether or not she should share her plans with her mother. Lili would not want Aidan to embark on this journey. She would think it a foolish, reckless, mindless act, and everything in Aidan warned her to forego the farewell to her mother and walk straight to the ship.

But Lili was her *mother*. And if, God forbid, something happened on the high seas and Tasman's ships did not return, Lili deserved to know what had happened. She shouldn't have to

spend her life waiting for a daughter who would never come home. Orabel had urged her to visit Lili, of course, but Aidan knew if she didn't go, Orabel would still keep her secret.

Aidan closed her eyes and dropped her head on her folded arms. She'd spent the morning in the bar, but had passed the night outside, curled into a small corner at the intersection of two buildings. Anyone who saw her would have thought her just another young sailor without money enough to buy anything but a bowl of morning gruel.

Her eyes flitted to the place where Orabel stood at the bar, a gaggle of eager, bug-eyed seamen around her. Aidan smiled slowly, then reluctantly rose from her chair and tugged again on her cap. Street grime streaked her cheeks, mud marked her shirt and breeches. She knew she looked like a typical street urchin, but she could not help feeling nervous as she stepped out of the tavern and walked toward the chamber where Lili and the others rested during the day.

She pressed on the door and entered without knocking. Sofie and Frederica lay sprawled upon mattresses, their mouths slack with sleep. Lili herself sat against the back wall, a drunken sailor snoring in her lap. Her eyes were closed, her hair disheveled and askew, her bodice marked with stains and the drunken drool of last night's guest.

Lili looked up and squinted toward the widening beam of sunlight as Aidan entered. Frowning, she sheltered her eyes with her hand. "What do you want here, boy?" she demanded. "There's no one here for you now. Come back tonight." She chuckled hoarsely. "Faith, why don't you wait and come back when you grow a beard?"

Steeling herself for this last difficult task, Aidan closed the door and leaned against it. "Mama," she said simply. "I've come to say good-bye."

❧

Lili blinked at the sound of Aidan's voice, convinced that the sunlight, the ale, and her tired eyes had conspired to play a devilish

trick on her. The slender youth moved forward in a thin stream of light from a crack in the door, his face backlit and indiscernible in the chamber's dimness.

"Aidan?" Lili whispered, her hand going to her throat. Her palm was slick with sweat, but her mind had gone cold and sharp, focused to a dagger's point. Surely Aidan had met with some mischief and this was a ghost, some spirit come to accuse her of corrupting her daughter, of allowing a pure and virtuous girl to be reared in a den of thieves and harlots.

"Mama." The youth spoke again, and squatted a few feet beyond the spread of Lili's skirts. "I'm sailing soon. I wanted to say good-bye before I left." The youth reached up and rubbed her nose, a gesture so Aidan-like that Lili gasped. If this was a phantom or sprite, surely it possessed Aidan's very soul—

"*You* are not my daughter!" Lili shrank back against the wall as a bead of perspiration traced a cold path from her armpit to her rib.

"Yes, it is me, Mama." The apparition spoke again, calmly, and in one smooth gesture pulled the cap from her head. Lili stared, blinked, stared again. Aidan's hair shone like dull copper in the faint light. She had darkened it somehow, but traces of brilliance remained. The feminine form was hidden beneath the oversized man's clothes, and the voice was unfamiliar only because it came from a form Lili found incomprehensible.

"Faith, child, what's happened to you?" Lili pushed the sleeping drunk away and allowed him to roll, still in a stupor, onto the floor. She sat up and smoothed her hair, suddenly embarrassed. Her daughter had been away among fine people; what must she think, finding Lili like this? On the other hand, what was Aidan doing in that unbelievable outfit?

"I told you, Mama." Aidan's voice was calm and still, with a note of deadly determination. "I'm going to sea, and must do it in disguise, since no women are allowed aboard Captain Tasman's ship. But Heer Van Dyck will protect me, and we will work together. When I return—" She looked down at the cap she was

spinning in her hands. "—I will publish my work. It is the only way to achieve my dreams."

"Going to sea?" Slowly Lili's mind fitted the puzzle pieces into place. "Aidan, you can't be serious! I've heard about sea captains, and about Tasman in particular. There have been complaints lodged against him, you know. And you'd be nothing but a ship's boy, the brunt of every command."

"I'm going, Mama." Aidan laughed softly and glanced for a moment at the women sprawled upon the mattress. "Could life aboard ship be worse than this?" Her eyes met Lili's, and Lili felt her blood chill at the determination in them. "Nothing you can say will change my mind."

Love fought with reason as Lili stared at her daughter. The more she protested, the stronger Aidan would resist. Only by remaining silent could she hope to win this argument.

The ship wouldn't sail right away. If God was merciful, Aidan might be discovered and put ashore before Tasman gave the order to weigh anchor.

Lili drew a deep breath to still the panic rioting within her chest. "Go then," she said simply, placing her hand over the damp skin at her throat. "Go and ignore those of us who will do nothing but fret for you until you return. Go, and think nothing of the mother who gave you life, who worked in the meanest possible ways just to put food in your mouth. Go, and—"

"All right, I'm going." Aidan stood, cutting her off. Before Lili could gather her senses, her daughter was gone. The drunken seaman stirred and muttered in his sleep, and his hand fell limply upon Lili's skirt.

Lili balled her hands into hard fists, fighting back the sobs that boiled and burned in her chest. What had she done? She hadn't remained silent at all. Once again she had made poor choices, but she had been driven to them!

Just as she had driven Aidan away. Her eyes filled with tears of frustration as she recalled her harsh tone and nagging taunts.

These feelings were only the tip of a long seam of guilt that snaked its way back through the years.

But what could she do? The harder she tried to understand Aidan, the further the girl slipped away. Lili's noble admonitions came out as harsh retorts that only insulted her daughter; her love and concern only evoked Aidan's resentment.

Would God hear the prayers of a procuress who had taught her daughter to steal and lie and cheat and fend for herself no matter what?

Desperate enough to try anything, Lili rose and stumbled toward the wardrobe chest, hoping to find an outfit presentable enough to wear to church.

⌘

Witt Dekker tossed back a glassful of Bram's finest liquor, then wiped his mouth with the back of his hand and turned to survey the tavern before him. Ten thousand pounds was no paltry amount, and getting rid of the old man would be easy once they were at sea. But finding and killing the girl might be tricky, for he had responsibilities aboard the *Zeehaen* and would be expected to report there soon. He would have to find this wench within a few hours.

Dempsey had said that Sweet Kate knew her. Dekker tilted his head and studied the blond girl loitering near a table of card players. She had one hand on a gentleman's shoulder and the other near the pocket hidden under a slit in her skirt. Undoubtedly she was slipping the man cards. A most dexterous, clever, and pleasing girl, that one.

Witt dropped his glass back on the bar behind him, then straightened and made his way toward the gaming tables. Kate's blue eyes flew open wide at his approach, but she lowered her gaze to her gentleman friend's cards as if immersed in the game.

Witt moved closer and pressed his hand against the creamy whiteness of her neck. "Kate, my love," he whispered loud enough for her companion to hear, "I need a word with you outside."

"I'm sorry, sir." She kept her eyes fixed on the game. "But I am with this gentleman now."

"Why do you interrupt?" The card player lifted his gaze to meet Witt's. "Sir, the lady is engaged."

"She is no lady," Witt answered, tightening his grip around Kate's thin arm, "and she is going with me."

His words hung in the air, like flags of battle, and the sounds of gaming, chatter, and music stopped abruptly as the man at the table rose to his feet. For an instant he seemed to swell, sizing Witt up as if in some primal territorial dispute. "Sir," he said, tension fairly crackling between them, "this wench is mine, bought and paid for. Find another to please you—"

His last word was cut off in a gurgle as Witt's hand closed on his throat. For an instant defiance sparked in his eyes, then his countenance withered like an empty balloon. Witt released him, then waited until the player sank back into his seat. With his other hand still tight around Kate's arm, he lifted a brow and asked, "Have I your permission to go then?"

"By your leave, sir," the card player croaked, fumbling with his cards.

Witt dragged the unwilling girl through a sea of somber spectators, then pulled her out of the tavern and toward an alley that jutted toward the sea. A jumble of barrels and discarded packing crates were piled at the side of one building. Witt led the hussy toward them, then turned and lifted her like a rag doll, setting her atop a barrel. She had made no sound as he pulled her from the tavern, but when he lowered his hands to her arms and gripped her tightly, a little squeak escaped her lips.

"Sweet Kate, my love," he trained his eyes upon her with deadly concentration, "you're looking fair today. I meant to tell you last night what a lovely dress that is. Is it new?"

"N-n-no—I mean yes," she stammered. "It's new to me."

"And how could you be affording such a fine frock? It's pure silk, is it not?"

"It is a castoff." Her blue eyes were like dark holes in her pale face. "A lady gave it to me."

"Ah." Witt lifted one hand and gently traced her cheek. "This fine lady friend of yours—how would I find her?"

He felt her shudder in his grasp. "I wouldn't know." She lifted one shoulder in an attempt to shrug. "She—she doesn't usually come down to the wharf."

"Then how did she give it to you, my sweet?" Witt tilted his head toward her and gave her his most charming smile. "Did she come and offer it in a bag? Or perhaps she took one of your old dresses in exchange?"

"I'm not certain what she did." Her words came out hoarse. Witt lowered his hand to the slender column of her throat, enjoying the feel of her spine, her breath, beneath his hands. A golden cross hung about her neck, rising and falling now upon her heaving chest. He tilted his head to stare at it, amazed that she should own such a precious trinket.

"What's this?" he asked softly, using his other hand to grasp the cross. "'It's gold, Kate—not the sort of thing I'd expect a cheap hussy to be wearing. Can you tell me where you got it?"

She shook her head, then swallowed hard. A vein in her neck pulsed erratically against the skin of her dainty throat.

"Well, let's see." Witt flipped the cross over, then saw the inscription. He couldn't read the fancy script, but one look into the girl's terror-filled eyes convinced him that he'd stumbled onto something important.

"What does it say?" he snarled, moving his hand around her jaw. "Tell me!"

"My love," she whispered, her breath coming in short gasps, "is yours forever, Aidan."

The shadow of a cloud blew away, leaving them in stark, hot afternoon sunlight. Witt had only a few hours to find the girl. "Listen, Kate." He slipped his hand to her throat and moved closer. "I know about this Aidan O'Connor, and I know she gave

you that gown and this necklace. Now you will tell me where to find her, for I am growing weary of these games."

"I can't tell you anything—" she began. In a burst of anger his hands tightened around her throat. He felt a gentle snap and frowned, pulling his hand away. The harlot's head lolled forward, broken away from the spine he had caressed only a moment earlier.

Witt muttered a curse, released the girl, and stepped back. He hadn't meant to kill her—at least not until he got the information he needed. And although no one would mourn the passing of another wharf harlot, several men would rejoice to see Witt Dekker safely locked away in jail. Worst of all, he was no closer to finding this Aidan O'Connor.

He eyed the girl's body. Sitting on the cask like that, her head slumped slightly forward, she could almost be asleep. Dekker moved toward her and arranged her arms so that she appeared to lean on a box piled atop the debris. He lowered her head until it was pillowed on her arms. Then as a final gesture, he extended two fingers and closed the girl's sightless blue eyes.

There. Any passerby would assume the girl had sought a quiet moment to escape from the tavern. Anyone might logically assume that she came here often to watch arriving ships and catch a breath of unsullied air. He took a final step back, about to depart, but her golden necklace winked at him in the sunlight. Why not take it? After claiming her life, he deserved a trophy.

Besides, the cross had clearly belonged to Aidan O'Connor. Dekker's time was running out—it was clear he probably wouldn't be able to find the girl and do away with her before Tasman set sail. That part of the job would have to wait until his ship returned to Batavia. If she had completely disappeared by then, he would have the cross to show to Dempsey Jasper. It shouldn't be difficult to convince the man that the girl was gone forever.

Witt stepped forward, picked up the cross from Sweet Kate's still-warm skin, then lifted the delicate chain from her throat. Whistling a sea chantey, he dropped the chain around his neck,

tucked the cross inside his shirt, and sauntered back to the tavern for one last round before boarding the *Zeehaen*. Aidan O'Connor was still out there somewhere, but pigeons did always come home to roost. Maybe he'd get lucky and the girl would turn up before he had to set sail.

Seventeen

~⚬⚬⚬~

A band of storm clouds swept in from the sea, and from the road where he walked, Sterling Thorne could see a dark curtain of rain hanging beneath them like a veil. He would spend his first day aboard ship in wet clothes, no doubt, and there was no help for it. Just as there was no help for the ticklish situation he now found himself in.

The dark clouds above reminded him of Lina Tasman's melancholy face as she told him good-bye. For one who had recently been betrothed with her parents' blessing, the girl was the personification of somber formality. "I wish you Godspeed on your journey," she had said, primly pressing her hand to his as he extended it in farewell. "But you should know that my heart, though pledged to you, will forever belong to another."

Sterling had accepted her hand and her words with a grace that would have made her father happy. He was doing a noble thing, honoring a father who wished to make a good match for his daughter, and he was determined to be a good husband for the girl. Lina Tasman was nothing like Ernestina Martin, whose simpering and foolish affection had sent him running half a world away. In Lina's eyes he saw a modicum of intelligence and sobriety, and if he couldn't love her, he could certainly *respect* her. He had no desire to bully her, or force her love against her will, but it might have been nice to see at least a soft glance of affection in those dark eyes.

No matter. He would be gone a long time, perhaps even a

year, and the old folks did say that absence made the heart grow fonder. His mouth tipped in a wry smile as he wondered if time would work its magic on his heart as well.

Market Street lay just ahead of him, the boundary of the town's wharf distract, and he unconsciously moved toward the center of the road, avoiding the crowds that milled outside taverns and flophouses even at this late afternoon hour. He had only to reach the docks, then find his ship. He'd settle into his quarters, inventory his supplies, and familiarize himself with the ship's design. He'd already stocked his medicine box with such herbs as he could find at the physic's shop, and he sincerely hoped that the good captain had thought to arrange for a roomy cabin or some other private space where his surgeon could work and think in peace.

A crowd of singing Dutchmen staggered out of an open doorway. Sterling dodged their boisterous approach, ducking into a narrow alley cluttered with the discarded casks and crates of various taverns and flophouses. He leaned against the wall for a moment, annoyed at the impediment to his progress, then caught a whiff of salt-scented air. He turned, feeling the breath of the wind on his cheek, and followed the alley. Perhaps he could find a shorter route to his destination.

He started in surprise when he saw a slender female form perched upon one of the discarded barrels. Clad in a fine golden gown of exquisite quality and design, the girl seemed strangely out of place. Her blond head rested upon her folded arms, her eyes were closed. A lady's maid, perhaps, catching up on the sleep she had missed while her mistress cavorted in the night.

"Excuse me, mistress," he whispered, reluctant to disturb the sleeping maiden, "but can you tell me if this alley leads to the docks?"

She did not respond or stir. Sterling stepped closer, his curiosity growing, and his practiced eye noted that her bodice did not rise and fall with the movement of breathing. He looked at her face, then dropped his bag with a startled cry when he saw that her full

lips were blue. He rushed forward and lifted her hand, fumbling to find the steady pulse of blood that usually ran through the wrist.

Nothing. The girl was stone cold dead.

❧

Wanting to say a final farewell to Orabel, Aidan walked up to the bar and grinned with pleasure when Bram did not recognize the grime-streaked "boy" who asked for Sweet Kate. In response to Aidan's question, Sofie lifted her head from the table where she dutifully watched a card game. "Kate has gone out already," the older woman muttered, looked at Aidan through eyes smudged with exhaustion. Strands of hair had escaped from the knot at her neck and pasted themselves to her painted cheeks. "She should be free by now, so check the street. She left more than an hour ago."

Aidan went out into the streets, peering down alleyways and calling her friend's name. "Orabel! Where are you hiding?"

Then she saw her friend, pretty and relaxed, perched upon a barrel at the end of an alley. A clean-shaven gentleman in a feathered hat held her face and patted her cheeks.

"Excuseert u mij," Aidan called hesitantly. She knew she ought to leave, but she was desperate to say a final good-bye to her friend. She moved slowly down the alley, her hands tucked into her rope belt, trying her best to approximate a boy's swaggering gait. "I'd like to speak to Kate for a moment, if you please."

The man turned his head, and Aidan had to bite her lip in order to suppress a gasp of recognition. This was the man who had leaped into Heer Van Dyck's garden to stop their exercise in fighting! Why was Orabel with him? Quickly she donned a blank expression and backed away. "I—I'm sorry."

"Boy!" The man's voice was rough and abrupt. "Do you know this unfortunate girl? I have just now found her dead!"

Dead? Orabel? She couldn't be dead! Perhaps she was asleep. She might have been beaten—such things happened occasionally to Lili's girls.

Aidan moved closer, her eyes fixed on the gray flesh, the bluish

lips, the purplish black marks on the girl's throat and neck. "She *can't* be dead!"

"I'm a doctor," the man answered, gently placing one of Orabel's hands upon the other. "I'm afraid I know death when I have the misfortune to see it." He stood back and cleared his throat. "Do you know her? Did she have family we should contact?"

Unable to face the awful truth, Aidan stepped back. Wave after wave of shock slapped at her, and she drew herself up and swallowed to bring her heart down from her throat. "Not dead," she repeated, but the finality had left her voice. "She *can't* be dead. She never hurt anyone."

"Listen to me, young man." Her ears filled with a strange buzzing, and Aidan heard the gentleman's words as if from a great distance. He was saying something about how even a lady's maid deserved a decent burial. Aidan clapped her hands over her ears and retreated further down the alley. Who was this man? And how could he talk about Orabel? He didn't even *know* her!

"Don't run, boy!" The man called. "If you knew her, you must help me make the arrangements. Where did she live? Who were her parents? Who is responsible?"

Aidan stopped and lowered her hands, her mood veering sharply to anger. She turned and took an abrupt step toward him. "How do I know *you* weren't responsible for this murder?" she yelled, hearing her voice echo among the buildings of the alley.

"Don't be a fool, boy." The man's blue eyes, narrow with fury, bored into Aidan's. "If I were capable of this girl's murder, do you think I'd be standing here chatting with you now? No. I'd snap your skinny neck like hers, and I'd be off to sea, forgetting about the lot of you Batavian brats."

Aidan swallowed hard and gave him a hostile glare. Though she wasn't certain she could trust him, he *seemed* to be a gentleman. But what would an English doctor know of life on Batavia's streets?

She leaned against the building and closed her eyes. "No one

cared for this girl," she said, spitting out the words in contempt. "She lived here by the taverns; her parents are dead and rotting in the sea, and there is no one to take responsibility for her."

"Then I shall." The doctor turned back to Orabel's body. "Run and fetch the constable, will you? We'll make a full report of this, but it must be done quickly, for I'm due at the docks by nightfall."

Aidan trembled at his words. *She* couldn't find a constable! The constable and his men knew the women of the wharf district nearly as well as they knew their wives. The chances were great she'd be detained…and questioned. But this man was willing to take care of Orabel, and surely any gentleman who would leap a garden fence to defend a lady's honor could be trusted.

The man moved to lift Orabel, but Aidan interceded. "Wait!" She stepped up to her friend's body. "Good-bye, dear Orabel," Aidan whispered. She brushed her fingers across the silk folds of the golden gown. Why had she ever given that dress to Orabel? What sort of madman had it attracted?

Suddenly her mind blew open, and her eyes moved to Orabel's bruised neck. The necklace was gone! This wasn't murder alone, it was robbery!

"No!" she groaned, guilt washing over her. If she hadn't given the golden cross to Orabel, she wouldn't have been accosted, she wouldn't be dead. Aidan had always tucked the necklace inside her bodice, hiding it from prying eyes, but Orabel had been so proud of her new dress. She had worn the cross at her neckline for all the world to see. And now she was dead.

Orabel's head lolled onto the doctor's shoulder as he lifted her. Aidan stepped back, pressing her hand over her mouth to stifle a sob, and fled the alley before the man could see her retreat and command her again.

⁂

Watching from across the street, Witt Dekker saw a boy fly out of the alley, his face as pale as paper and his eyes glittering like a mad

cat's. Witt pursed his lips, then lifted his tankard to his lips and drew a deep draught. The boy had undoubtedly seen the body and was either running out of fear or rushing to get help. Or—another thought rose to goad him—perhaps the street urchin had been hiding in the alley and had seen everything.

Prodded by an unfailing sense of self-preservation, Witt pulled himself off the wall where he'd been leaning and whistled for his dog, then followed in the direction the boy had fled. The slender figure was still ahead of him, darting like a scared rabbit through the milling crowd of seamen and loaders, heading steadily toward the docks.

Suddenly a horse and wagon moved into the road, blocking the path, and Witt smiled. He'd catch the wharf rat now for sure. But to his surprise, the scamp darted under the wagon, losing his cap in the process. Just when Witt was sure the boy was gone, he reappeared long enough to snatch his cap out of the dust and dirt. Witt caught a glimpse of wet coppery hair, a long braid, and features almost too delicate for a boy.

The wagon moved away, and Witt followed, his eyes fixed upon the advancing figure as the boy's hurried strides led to the docks. The urchin paused for a moment at the harbor master's desk, then turned toward the dock where the *Heemskerk* and *Zeehaen* were berthed.

With Snuggerheid at his heels, Witt approached the harbor master's desk. "A moment ago, sir," he said, pushing his own cap up at a jaunty angle, "a boy came by here and asked for directions. About so tall—" He held his hand out at nose level. "—and pale skinned. Remember him?"

The harbor master shrugged. "*Ja.* I remember."

"Well, do you know who he is?"

"*Ja*, I know."

Witt stifled the urge to strangle the man. "What's his name?"

The harbor master shook his head. "He's nobody. A *ketel-binkie.*"

"A ship's boy?" Witt's patience began to unravel. "On what ship?"

"The *Heemskerk*."

Witt smiled. Whoever the lad was, he had run straight into Dekker's hands. "Did the ship's boy give his name?"

The man shrugged again. "Just a ketelbinkie," he repeated.

Witt scratched his chin. If this lad was traveling as a ship's boy aboard the *Heemskerk,* there would be plenty of time to find out who he was and what, if anything, he knew about Sweet Kate's murder. Dekker was in no rush. They would be on a long journey, one that would offer a thousand opportunities for unfortunate mishaps.

"Well, Snuggerheid," he murmured as he scooped the dog up into his arms, "it seems as if we will have two people to keep an eye on now." He turned toward the sea, thinking. Though he'd have to deal with the old man eventually, the ketelbinkie probably knew nothing. And if he did, two could be washed overboard or cracked on the skull by a flying spar as easily as one. Accidents happened nearly every day at sea. Aidan O'Connor could wait until after the ship returned to port, for Dempsey Jasper couldn't inherit a guilder until he had official word of the old man's death.

He turned back to the close-lipped harbor master. "Have you a pen and paper?"

"You know I have," the master answered.

"Then take this down, and send the message straightaway to Heer Dempsey Jasper. Tell him that the old mouse is already in the trap and will not be returning to Batavia. I'll expect his debt to be paid when I return."

The man scratched the message over the parchment, then dipped his pen into the ink and offered it to Dekker. "Shall you sign it?"

Witt backed away, unwilling to advertise the fact that reading and writing were not among his many skills. "No," he answered, patting the dog so the harbor master could see that Witt could not

be troubled with pens and paper at the moment. "Just send it right away, will you? I'm expected aboard my ship."

With a grunt and a nod, the harbor master sprinkled blotting sand on the wet ink, then shook it off and neatly folded the parchment.

Witt smiled. His orders would be carried out. Dempsey Jasper would know that he was on the job. And both Van Dyck and the ketelbinkie would be well within his reach once they set sail.

Whistling, he moved toward the dock, where the *Zeehaen* bobbed at anchor. They might not discover gold on this voyage, but it nevertheless promised to be a trip that would make Witt Dekker a very wealthy man.

Eighteen

T he sinking sun had not yet reached the tops of the masts when Sterling wearily made his way to the *Heemskerk*. Tasman would undoubtedly be angry that his surgeon and future son-in-law had disappeared for half a day, but tending to the girl's burial had taken longer than Sterling had anticipated. At first the constable had glared at him with outright suspicion. Then once the man recognized the poor girl's face, he had waved Sterling away as if he'd discovered a dead housefly. "Have no fear, we'll bury her in the pauper's grave." The constable shrugged and moved away from the corpse, barely even glancing at the girl's sweet face. "If nobody pays for the burial, that's what she gets."

"Surely she deserves more," Sterling had answered. "Look at this gown! This is a fine lady, someone of consequence! You can't just ignore her!"

"Look," the constable said, running his hands over the paunch at his belly, "this is a port city. All kinds of people mingle down there at the wharf—pirates and their women, foreigners, and people who are running from trouble in Europe. Not every lady who wears a fine dress is rich, and not all of them matter, if you take my meaning." He looked up and gave Sterling a conspiratorial wink. "Trust me, sir, if no one comes for her within a day or two, no one is missing her. But to please you, I'll keep her in the dead house until sundown tomorrow. Then she goes to the pauper's field."

Frustrated at the constable's impertinence, Sterling produced a gold florin from his own purse, and, lest it disappear into the

constable's pocket, waited until the man grudgingly called the carpenter and commissioned a teakwood casket for the girl's final resting place. Satisfied at last that the carpenter was an honorable man who would do his duty, Sterling left the girl's body in the constable's office and made his way to the docks.

The *Zeehaen* lay at anchor in a berth beside the *Heemskerk,* and Sterling caught sight of Witt Dekker on the deck of the smaller ship as he passed by. Instinctively he lowered his head, not wanting to enter into conversation with that man unless absolutely necessary. In that respect, at least, his acquaintance and new affiliation with Tasman was a blessing. He would sail on the commander's flagship, the *Heemskerk,* under commander Tasman and skipper T'jercksen Holman while Dekker served as first mate on the *Zeehaen* under skipper Gerrit Janszoon.

He passed the *Zeehaen* and came upon the *Heemskerk,* a proud ship that heaved elegantly upon the swell of the tide, straining at her hawsers as if already eager to be under way. A horde of sea gulls dived and shrieked among her masts and rigging, their voices as raucous as the shouting of the seamen.

Sterling paused before a heavy man standing watch at the gangplank. *"Goedenavond,"* he murmured, offering the man a casual smile. "I am to report aboard."

The man's eyes raked over Sterling's form, taking in his boots, his breeches, his worn shirt and frayed doublet. "Are you English?" His voice dripped with suspicion. "This is a Dutch ship, sir, commissioned by the V.O.C.—"

"I know," Sterling interrupted. He drew a deep breath and shifted his bag from one hand to the other. "I am Sterling Thorne, lately employed by Commander Tasman to serve as surgeon on this ship."

"Ah." The man threw his head back, though a decidedly unpleasant look remained on his face. "You are the doctor."

Sterling straightened and attempted to bow, not an easy feat when one stood at the end of a shifting plank.

"I am Francois Jacobsz Visscher, pilot major of the expedition as well as first mate of the *Heemskerk*."

Sterling pushed down his increasing irritation. "I'm honored, sir. Now, if I might pass, I believe the commander is expecting me. I was detained at the wharf this afternoon by a bit of unpleasant business."

Visscher eased away from the plank and allowed Sterling room to pass. He hefted his bag and moved ahead, one hand clinging to the insubstantial rope that served as a railing, and prayed that they would soon be under way. Cuts, bruises, broken bones, and weak bowels he could handle, but he had neither the patience nor the skill for shipboard politics.

Organized chaos reigned on the deck. Bodies darted to and fro, popping up through hatchways and dropping suddenly out of the rigging like hanged men. The sails that would send them to parts unknown lay in ivory stacks upon the deck, their upper folds billowing in the breeze. At other points a steady stream of native loaders sidestepped sailors as they carried livestock, barrels, crates, and trunks of supplies for the voyage.

Sterling moved forward until he came to the mainmast at the center of the ship. There he paused, trying to stand out of the way until he could catch sight of Abel Tasman. He was astonished, however, when the first familiar face he saw was that of a distinguished older man who stepped out of a small cabin beneath the forecastle. Sterling paused, trying to fix the face in his memory. This man hadn't been aboard the *Gloria Elizabeth,* this memory was fresher...

The man looked up and caught Sterling's eye. For a moment confusion clouded his eyes as well, then a smile twitched into existence within the neat thicket of his beard. "My friend the defender!" he cried in careful English, opening his arms as if Sterling were a long-lost relative. "Are you sailing with us?"

"Yes." The pieces fell into place, and the memory of their meeting brought a wry, twisted smile to Sterling's face. "I am the ship's surgeon. But you—"

"I am the voyage cartographer," the old man supplied. "Francois Visscher is the pilot major and keeper of the charts, of course, but the Company has hired me to produce a map of the lands we will discover and explore."

"Of course." Sterling tipped his head back and looked at him. "Since we will be traveling together, we certainly should be properly introduced. I am Sterling Thorne, and I am pleased to be at your service."

"I am very honored to meet you, sir," the man chuckled, "and now I understand why you were so eager to preserve life and limb when you came to my ward's defense. I am Schuyler Van Dyck, and I am most pleased that we shall be friends."

"Your ward, sir?" Sterling tilted his head. "The young lady was your ward? I was not certain of the association between you, but it did appear odd that you should be teaching her to duel with fisticuffs."

The older gentleman coughed and blushed crimson. "Ah, well, yes. The girl is most unusual, there's no disputing that fact. And I must apologize for the way she, er, attacked you." He gave Sterling a bemused glance. "I did not expect her to jump on your back. I hope you were not hurt."

"Not at all." Sterling shifted his shoulders, slightly embarrassed by the memory. "I can only assume that you were teaching her to fend for herself since you were going away. Though it is unconventional, still, it seems that there was no harm done." He smiled at a distant memory. "I have two sisters who used to regularly pummel me and my brothers."

"You are quite right; that is exactly what I was doing." Van Dyck nodded in emphasis. "Teaching her to take care of herself. And she took to my teaching like a duck to water, I believe." He cocked his head and looked at Sterling, his eyes glowing with pleasure. "She is a right pretty thing. Did you get a look at her?"

"No, I'm afraid I did not." Sterling smiled and wondered if Heer Van Dyck was as eager to marry off his ward as Abel Tasman

was to betroth his daughter. "But I've discovered that the Dutch are great judges of beauty. If you say she is one, I will not doubt your word."

"Beauty and morality," Van Dyck answered, nodding. "You cannot have one without the other, though both are too often counterfeited. As a painter, I value beauty wherever I see it, and as a Christian man, I cherish morality and virtue. My late wife possessed both beauty and a pure heart...and I miss her dreadfully." His eyes glazed as he stared out to sea. "Are you married, sir?"

"Not yet." Sterling shifted his weight as the conversation grew burdensome. "Though I plan to be as soon as we return to Batavia."

Van Dyck made a soft sound of agreement, though his eyes did not leave the watery horizon. "Marriage is a wonderful thing."

"Heer Van Dyck!"

A youthful voice broke into the conversation, and Sterling and the old man turned together as a slender boy in breeches and a billowing shirt emerged from the cabin beneath the forecastle. He carried a painter's palette in one hand and a brush in the other, and with a smile Sterling noted that a definite smear of blue paint adorned the tip of the boy's pert chin.

"I can't get the color right," the boy said, not glancing up as he neared the older man. "The sky seems more azure than turquoise today, and yet I can't get the colors to blend properly. What element am I missing?"

"Mind your manners, Aidan," the gentleman remonstrated, clasping his hands at his waist. "We have a guest. I'd like you to meet Sterling Thorne, the ship's surgeon."

The boy looked up then, and the shock of recognition hit them both at the same instant. Sterling recognized the slender form, the delicate features, the wide green eyes—this was the boy from the alley!

"You!" he murmured, aware that the skittish boy might flee if he reacted too strongly.

The boy took a hasty half-step back, tipping the painter's palette so that it fell forward onto his shirt.

"You know my assistant?" Van Dyck's glance moved from the boy to Sterling and back to the boy again. His smile faded. "You recognize him?"

Sterling frowned in exasperation. "Well. I certainly never expected to see you again. I asked you to help me, and you were off like a shot—"

"My presence was required here," the boy snapped, his chin lifting slightly in defiance.

"For one who was so concerned about the girl's life and death, you managed to vanish most conveniently."

"How could I be sure *you* didn't kill her?" the boy answered, retreating another step before Sterling's sharp gaze.

"I told you I could be trusted!"

"Ah, well, that settles it then." The boy's eyes darkened dangerously. "I'm sure someone told that girl the same thing right before they murdered her!"

"Aidan!" Van Dyck broke into the exchange with a sharp voice, then turned to face his charge, blocking Sterling's view of the boy. In a lower voice, the gentleman spoke to his assistant. "Will you tell me what happened? And how this man knows you?"

"It's all right, sir," the lad answered, his tone softening in respect. "It has nothing to do with me. But this afternoon I found my friend in an alley. This man stood over her dead body, and I wasn't certain he was not the one responsible for her most undeserved death."

"For your information—" Sterling began, eager to relate how he had spent his afternoon and his last gold piece taking care of the murdered girl's burial. But the gentleman turned toward him with marked reservation in his eyes, and Sterling's urge to defend himself faded. These two, along with the entire ship's crew, would have to learn what sort of man he was. He was an outsider, an Englishman, and they already mistrusted him. Very well. He

wouldn't satisfy them with empty words. He'd prove himself by his deeds, and if they weren't happy with his work, they could doctor themselves.

"I must find Captain Tasman," he said abruptly. He hefted his bag and tugged on the brim of his hat. "I give you good day, sir."

⁂

In the small cabin that would serve as home to himself, Francois Visscher, and Aidan, Schuyler bade the girl sit on a stool while he prepared to rebuke her. "You are entirely too outspoken, Aidan." He forced himself to call her by her familiar name. Since the tavern-going seamen knew her as Irish Annie, they had both agreed that she should be called by her true name. Aidan was a name that could apply to a man or woman, and one they could both use without feeling guilty of a lie.

"Heer Van Dyck," she whispered, "I was upset this afternoon; I am still upset. Orabel was my friend, and she is dead. This afternoon I found her body with that man when I went to say farewell…" Ragged with sorrow, her voice faded away.

"Trust me, child." Schuyler leaned on the edge of the chart table and lowered his hands to his knees. "I do not know him well, but Sterling Thorne has the look of an honest gentleman. He shares his heart freely, and as a doctor he is sworn to do no harm to any living person. I am certain he would not hurt your friend."

Aidan pressed her lips together and looked at the floor, but he could see her eyes fill slowly with tears, like a fountain rising up from her wounded heart.

"Young men do not cry," he whispered, reaching out. He took her chin between his thumb and forefinger, and lifted it slightly, impressed by the way she stubbornly avoided his gaze. Ah, she had spirit! The soul of a great artist dwelt within her, but she would never know it unless she found the key to unlock the prison doors.

"Can I go?" she whispered, each word a splinter of ice.

"Aidan," he answered, releasing her, "it is natural to grieve when someone you love dies. You will be angry, you will

201

disbelieve, you will feel guilty, you may try to bargain with God. Most of all, you will feel sadness and terrible loneliness. But finally you will be able to open your heart to God's grace and accept that life does go on."

Schuyler folded his arms across his chest. His wife's name—Marieke—kept slipping through his thoughts, and he moved toward the small porthole in the cabin to stare out at the wharf and the bustling city beyond. Marieke had been gone nearly ten years, but he had not ceased to miss her. And now he was leaving her resting place, her children, her home.

"*Ja,* life goes on," he murmured, clinging to the memory of his beloved wife's face as he would to a life preserver. "And we must go on with it. So use the emotions you are experiencing, Aidan. Feel them. Understand them. And paint them."

His only answer was a resounding clatter. He turned in time to see Aidan leaving the cabin, her palette lying on the floor, splatters of paint marring the smooth, polished surface of the deck. Sighing in resignation, Schuyler looked about for a rag to clean up the mess.

He could not fault her for her anger. When his wife died, he had behaved in much the same way.

⁂

Trembling with impotent rage and frustration, Aidan stepped around the busy seamen, half-afraid someone would give her a command and expect her to answer it. Shortly before leaving Van Dyck's house she had learned that she would be traveling as a ketelbinkie, a ship's boy. Such young lads were usually placed under the supervision of the cook, and to them fell the mundane chores of stirring pots, running messages to and fro, and all sorts of scrubbing. Abel Tasman, however, Van Dyck assured her, had given permission for Van Dyck's ward to serve as ketelbinkie and unofficial assistant to the cartographer. Though she would still have to obey any and all commands from her superiors—which would be practically every man aboard the ship—officially, she would be Heer Van Dyck's responsibility.

Her stomach growled with sudden hunger, and Aidan hoped that someone would soon blow a whistle or ring a dinner bell. The swollen sun hung low over the western mountains, and she moved to the ship's rail, seized with a sudden nostalgia for all things of the earth and land. How would she feel after seeing nothing but the vast and endless ocean for days? The voyage she'd made from England to Batavia seemed a lifetime ago, and on that ship she'd been so concerned about her mother and dying father that she'd had little time or inclination to study the seamen or the changing geography.

She swallowed hard, wrapping her arms about herself as she thought of her mother. Lili would mourn Orabel's death too. Somehow the news would reach the women at Bram's tavern, and they would huddle together in fear, afraid to show themselves to strangers but having no other choice. For several nights at least, they would concentrate on getting their customers so drunk that it would not be necessary to leave the tavern, but after a while Bram would complain that business suffered when unconscious drunks littered the tables and storeroom. And so Lili's harlots would go out again, a bevy of unemployed seamstresses, knitters, lace workers and laundresses, selling themselves for food to eat.

"If you're Heer Van Dyck's ketelbinkie, shouldn't you be attending to your master?"

The deep voice at Aidan's back startled her, and she whirled around, not certain whether she should salute, bow, or doff her cap to whoever had spoken. She frowned when she saw the doctor standing behind her. He had removed his hat and doublet and now wore his breeches and shirt only, with a pale ribbon holding back his long blond hair. His blue eyes regarded her with frank curiosity and, she thought, a shade of compassion.

"I wanted to be alone," she said, taking pains to lower her voice to what she hoped was a masculine tone. "My master understands."

The doctor nodded and moved to the rail beside her. To her

horror, he leaned forward, elbows on the railing, and showed every sign of lingering.

"You needn't fear me," he said simply. His eyes roved over the rooflines of the city spread on the horizon before them. "I didn't harm your friend, and I wouldn't harm you."

"Is that because of your oath?"

"My what?" He looked at her and blinked in surprise.

"Heer Van Dyck said you took an oath to help people."

"Ah." His gaze moved out into the approaching velvet dusk. "The physician's Hippocratic Oath. Yes, 'tis the most important thing in the world to me." He took a deep breath and adjusted his smile. "Well, *one* of the most important things. I have two brothers, two sisters, and a mother still living, and they are terribly important too. That's why I came to Batavia—I want to establish a place so one of my brothers can join me."

Aidan swallowed, feeling the bitter gall of envy burn the back of her throat. He had *family,* while she only had Lili…

"What is this oath?" she asked, steering the subject away from his loved ones.

He lifted one shoulder in a shrug. "It's fairly complicated," he said, glancing sideways at her. "But basically it is a vow physicians take—to use treatment to help the sick, never to injure or wrong them." His voice softened slightly as he recited what was obviously a well-worn memory: "'I will not give poison to anyone though asked to do so, nor will I suggest such a plan. Similarly I will not give a pessary to a woman to cause abortion. But in purity and in holiness I will guard my life and my art. Into whatever houses I enter, I will do so to help the sick, keeping myself free from all intentional wrongdoing and harm, especially from fornication with woman or man, bond or free. Now if I keep this oath, and break it not, may I enjoy honor in my life and art among all men for all time; but if I transgress and forswear myself, may the opposite befall me.'"

"Your life and art," she repeated, following his gaze toward the

shore. The lights of Batavia were beginning to shine through the thickening gloom, and somewhere among them, Lili was welcoming women in trouble, administering pessaries to women who could not afford to find themselves with child, practicing her own dark art. Perhaps Aidan was wrong to see herself as special. Perhaps even the cutpurses were artists, in their own way.

"Do you, Doctor, see medicine as an art? Like painting?"

He looked at her, and his expression held a hint of embarrassment. "I suppose I do. The practice of medicine gives me great pleasure, and when I do my job well, I know I am fulfilling God's call on my life."

"Oh." She stilled the questions that rose naturally to her mind. In a moment she would be talking about her feelings, and Van Dyck had specifically warned her that men did not discuss their emotions.

She stood still, listening to the bosun's call, the wind humming in the rigging, and the flow of orders through the skipper's speaking trumpet. "Well, Doctor," she said, moving a half-step away from him, "I don't fear you. I don't fear anything aboard this ship."

He lifted a golden eyebrow and looked at her out of the corner of his eye. "Not even the captain's whip? I thought all ship's boys stood in awe of the cat-o'-nine-tails."

"I answer to Heer Van Dyck." She lifted her chin and sneaked a glance at him, and her cheeks burned with humiliation when she saw him smile.

"Tell me your name again," His teeth shone white in the gathering darkness. "I'm afraid I've forgotten it."

"You haven't forgotten it because you haven't asked it," she answered, biting off every word and spitting it at him. "But my name is Aidan O'Connor. And that's Heer O'Connor to you."

"*Heer* O'Connor?" His brows shot up to his hairline. "And why would I use a title reserved for gentlemen when speaking to you?"

"Because I am a great artist; Heer Van Dyck says so." She transferred her gaze from him to the city beyond. "And my people are descended from Irish kings. One day all Batavia will know who I am, so you must call me Heer O'Connor."

"Well, then, let me be the first to acknowledge your greatness, sir." He bent and bowed deeply, doffing an imaginary hat. When he straightened, she thought she detected laughter in his eyes. "I am proud to be the first to be informed of your substantial significance."

Helpless to halt her embarrassment, Aidan stepped away as a sharp whistle blew.

"Time for supper." Sterling turned toward the center of the ship. He glanced back toward her. "Shall we go down and fight for a place at the galley table?"

"I'm not hungry," Aidan lied, backing away further. While he stared at her in confusion, she turned and retreated into the gathering shadows. She'd rather go to bed without dinner than face him in the bold lantern light.

⚜

"Forgive me, God, for not trusting you."

Kneeling in the small church off Broad Street, Lili clasped her hands, ready to lay down arms in the bitter battle her life had become. She had endured too much, witnessed too many painful scenes, and Aidan's departure had broken her heart. All day she had floundered in an agonizing maelstrom of emotion, at once angry, hurt, depressed, and sorrowful. These were the same emotions she had felt after Cory died—perhaps she had never escaped the raw and primitive grief that overwhelmed and overtook her so many years ago.

In the daily work of providing for Aidan and the others, she had established a mindless routine that helped camouflage the deep despair of her loneliness. And perhaps, she could admit now, she had been happy to flout society's morals because in doing so she was thumbing her nose in the face of God, who had allowed Cory to die.

But Lili was tired of rebellion and blame. She could not fight against the Almighty, and Aidan was now beyond her reach, beyond her help. Only a loving God could bring her home; and only a forgiving God could untangle the mess Lili had made of her life.

Choking back the sob that rose in her throat, she looked up at the gold-painted cross hanging above the simple altar. "Ah, no, I didn't give you a chance," she murmured. "I didn't give you much of anything in those days, Lord. Sure, and didn't I want to make my own way? But I can't do it any more. And since the thought of going to sea got into Aidan's wee head, I know I've got to come to you."

Guilt swept over her in waves, and she clutched the back of the pew before her. "I'll listen to you again, Lord, haven't I said so? I'll clean up the girls and see about finding them decent work. And far be it from me to be telling you how to run things, but I'll be wanting to know if you could bring Aidan back safe. 'Tis a terrible thing to love a child and lose her…but you'd be knowing all about that, wouldn't you?"

Lili closed her eyes, waiting. Silence sifted down, as thick and lovely as an Irish snowfall, and she relaxed in the knowledge that the God of her youth would not forget her. A thrill shivered through her senses, and she smiled.

Going back, Lili picked up the strings of time and hummed a hymn from her childhood, then began to sing. The sound of her voice filled the small chapel, and her heart expanded as she lifted the long-forgotten words to heaven:

> Jesus, the very thought of thee with sweetness fills
>   my breast:
>
> But sweeter far thy face to see, and in thy presence
>   rest.
>
> O Hope of every contrite heart, O Joy of all the
>   meek,
>
> To those who ask, how kind Thou art! How good to
>   those who seek!

But what to those who find? Ah! This nor tongue
  nor pen can show:
The love of Jesus, what it is none but his loved ones
  know.

Darkness rose in the church, first filling the pews, then shadowing the altar, then creeping imperceptibly up the walls as night swallowed the building. But Lili sang on, ignoring the darkness, as her heart at last warmed with the holy light she had abandoned so long ago.

Nineteen

꘡꘡꘡

For four days Tasman's ships and crew prepared for departure. Along with charts and a few boxes of trinkets the captain thought useful for trading with any uncivilized peoples they might encounter, the loaders brought a prodigious amount of food into the cargo holds. Aidan soon discovered that since the Dutch navy regulated food for its men, the V.O.C. could do no less for any man willing to sail upon its ships. Each vessel was regarded as representative of the Dutch commonwealth, and therefore each ship had to offer its men a generous quality of life—which translated into food, and lots of it.

In addition to the regular meals, every crew member of Tasman's expedition was entitled to a weekly stipend of half a pound of cheese, half a pound of butter, and a five-pound loaf of bread. Double rations were allotted to the officers; Aidan soon understood how the others could spot an officer in nothing but his breeches and boots from thirty paces away. She herself had never eaten so well.

The morning and midday meals, served in the galley below decks, would usually consist of bread and a porridge of grits. On Sundays the sailors would feast on smoked ham or mutton or bully beef with peas; on Monday, Tuesday, and Wednesday, smoked and pickled fish with green peas and beans. On Thursday, each man would receive a ration of beef or pork. On Friday and Saturday, the cook's menu would revert to fish and peas.

Fascinated, Aidan watched as the loaders carried the huge

crates and barrels aboard. The ship carried few goods for repair or trading, only supplies for the crew's survival. "And we carry barely enough of that," Van Dyck told her one afternoon as they sat in the cabin and sketched the rigging that appeared through the open doorway.

"I'll never eat my share," she moaned, her stomach already cramping with the thought of so much food. Several of the other seamen had teased her about picking at her food; how could she tell them that one *plate* contained more than she usually ate in a week while working at the tavern? Sailors needed the fuel so they would have the energy to run and lift and climb and carry. But on most days Aidan only had to roll with the waves and learn to hold a pencil steady as she sketched.

Before long they had settled into a workable routine. Each day when she awoke to the clanging of a bell, Aidan would sit up and immediately thrust her frizzed hair into her cap. Once Visscher had left the room (he spent very little time in it, preferring to spend his time in the captain's cabin with the charts), Van Dyck would step outside while she performed her personal ministrations. Then she would go up on deck and watch in amazement at the crew's industrious activity. Aidan had thought Gusta a fastidious cleaner, but the deck-swabbing, brass-polishing crewmen of the *Heemskerk* and *Zeehaen* would have put poor Gusta to shame.

She had been aboard five days when the captain announced that on the morrow, the fourteenth of August, they would set forth on their journey. A cheer rose from the men, and Aidan felt her own heart leap with excitement. Despite her sorrow over losing Orabel and her nervousness over her audacious disguise, something in her yearned to begin this adventure.

Elated with the prospect, she walked back to the cabin to seek out Heer Van Dyck's company. But he wasn't alone. A man in a dark doublet and trousers sat on the bunk across from her master. Aidan backed up, intending to slip out again, but the stranger turned, and Aidan's heart leaped into her throat. *Henrick Van*

Dyck! For an instant he did not recognize her, but then a tiny flicker of shock widened his eyes.

"Sakerloot!" Henrick turned to face his father, the corners of his mouth tight. "What have you done?"

"Nothing untoward, I assure you," Heer Van Dyck answered. He stood over his son, his face a mask of stone. "Aidan is an artist, and I need her to help me complete my map. It cries out for one who can paint flora and fauna, and no one can paint them like Aidan can."

"But this!" Henrick turned toward Aidan again, his face dark with disapproval. "This is wrong! This is against the rules! Surely Tasman would object if he knew he carried an imposter aboard."

"Tasman does not need to know, and you will say nothing to anyone." Van Dyck lifted his hand, gesturing for Aidan to come inside and close the door. When she had done so, he sat on his bunk and looked directly at his son. "Henrick, I cannot expect you to understand, but I pray you will listen and try to comprehend what I am feeling."

"What you are *feeling?*" Disappointment and frustration emanated from Henrick's face, and his voice betrayed the edge of anger. "What you are feeling is lunacy! Dempsey warned me that you had taken leave of your senses, but I did not want to believe him!"

"I am as sane as you are." Van Dyck said, his eyes glittering with restless passion. "And you will listen to me, Henrick, and you will say nothing. This is my wish. As my son, you will obey it."

Henrick did not answer, but his face had gone pale and a drop of sweat ran down his jaw.

"When your mother died," Van Dyck began, lowering his gaze to his hands, "I thought my heart had died as well. We had raised you children, we had made a home, we had found success in the new colony. And when she left me alone, I wondered why God would allow me to go on living."

Aidan sank to a low stool near the door, entranced by his

words. She had never heard her mentor speak of his own past, and her heart squeezed in pity for the pain that marked his face even now. So this sorrow was the root of his suffering, the source of his empathy. What then was the source of his joy?

"Father, you must return home with me." Henrick placed his hand on his father's knee. "This is foolish. Look at you! You are old, you ought to go home where Gusta can take care of you."

"No, son." Heer Van Dyck slowly patted his son's hand. "There is the risk you cannot afford to take, and there is the risk you cannot afford *not* to take. This is my risk. If I am to make something of what's left of my life, I must go on this voyage. God left me here for a reason, and I believe this is it."

"But Father, you don't know what difficulties lie ahead out there in the unknown!" Honest concern and fear laced Henrick's voice. "What if it's true what they say about giant squid and fierce whales? And there are islands inhabited solely by cannibals; I've heard the natives talk about ferocious people who live on the sea islands."

"Henrick—" Van Dyck looked up at his son. "Life is not being sure, not knowing what will come next or how it will come. We guess at everything we do. We take leap after leap in the dark, and that's the joy of living and the beauty of faith. When we grow tired, when we sit still, that's when we begin to die."

He paused for a moment, and when he spoke again his voice was soft and tremulous. "You are young; you are following a young man's dreams. But the old must dream as well! I have not stopped dreaming, Henrick. I dream of stepping on the soil of a land untouched by another European. I dream of meeting people who have not yet heard of the saving grace of God. I want to be an instrument, Henrick. I want to discover the full breadth of God's creation and use my talents to enlighten others! This is my dream, and I will follow it until I draw my dying breath."

Henrick did not answer, but took his father's hand and squeezed it for a long moment. Heer Van Dyck leaned forward and embraced his son, then stood back and nodded in satisfaction.

"Go with my blessing, Henrick, and know that your father loves you well. Thank you for coming to see me off. Thank you for being concerned. But know this: One does not discover new lands without consenting to lose sight of the shore for a very long time."

The older man looked up and gave Aidan a smile. "I'm going out now to watch my last sunset over Batavia for a long while. When you are ready, Henrick, nothing would give me greater pleasure than to share it with you."

Henrick did not answer, and after a poignant pause, Heer Van Dyck moved silently through the doorway and out onto the deck.

Aidan stood from her place, about to follow her teacher, but Henrick's voice stopped her in midstride.

"He's a foolish old man. You know that, don't you?"

She turned slowly to face him. "I don't think he's foolish. And he's not so terribly old. He's young, very young, on the inside."

"And I suppose all that drivel makes perfect sense to you? All that nonsense about losing sight of the shore and such?"

Aidan lifted one shoulder in a shrug. "It makes sense to him. And I have never met a more certain and honorable man." She moved closer and sank to the bunk her master had just vacated. "You won't say anything, will you? I could still be set ashore if anyone found out about my disguise."

"I will say nothing," he said, his voice low and resentful. His eyes ran over her garments, taking in the breeches, the paint-splattered shirt, the braid, and the cap. "Though I cannot agree with what you are doing, this may be God's work. This ship may be the safest place for you now."

Aidan felt her heart leap into her throat. There must be trouble at the wharf—had other girls been found murdered? "What has happened, Henrick?"

"My sister and Dempsey Jasper hate you."

"That's no great revelation." Aidan shrugged dismissively. "Why should that matter?"

Henrick leaned toward her, his eyes cold. "Because Father

respects you. Because he wants to make your name great. Rozamond is afraid of what people will think when your relationship with Father is revealed."

Aidan took a deep, quivering breath to silence the pounding beneath her ribs. "But why would he care so much for me? I am not one of his children!"

Henrick shook his head. "Because he is a foolish old man. Because we were never able to please him. He has been searching for a fellow artist all his life, and I believe he was disappointed when he never found one in his own children." His gaze rested upon Aidan's face for a moment, and in those brown eyes she saw no anger, only sorrow.

"Do you hate me too?" She pressed her hand to her throat. "Have I reason to fear you?"

Setting his jaw, he shook his head, then looked out the porthole. "Not me," he said, resignation heavy in his voice. "But I cannot say what Rozamond and her husband have conspired to do. Dempsey Jasper is careful and cunning, and I fear he has set some dark plan in motion. That is why I say the sea is probably the safest place for you...for some months to come."

Aidan looked away, her mind reeling. Thoughts she dared not form came welling up, an ugly swarm of them. Had Dempsey Jasper anything to do with Orabel's death? The idea seemed far-fetched. Sofie had seen Orabel alive and well the morning of her death. As a gentleman, Dempsey would not be likely to venture to the taverns during daylight hours, and most married men would sooner die than be seen entering an alley with one of Lili's girls. But someone had killed Orabel in the revealing light of day— while she was wearing Aidan's dress. And whoever had killed Orabel in an effort to find Aidan might not hesitate to harm Lili or the other women in exchange for information.

"Have there been any other murders at the wharf?" she asked softly, a score of unasked questions buzzing in her brain. "Other than the girl who died the day we came aboard?"

Annoyance struggled with embarrassment on Henrick's aristocratic face as he looked at Aidan. "How would I know? Such things are not published to law-abiding citizens."

Aidan flinched, hearing the unspoken rebuke in his voice. She was from the underclass; he a gentleman's son. Why should he know or care anything about what happened in her world?

Henrick stood and bowed formally from the waist. "If you will excuse me, I would like a final word alone with my father." His voice resonated through the small cabin and echoed into silence. And then, as he paused by the door, he added one whispered thought: "I wish you well."

Abel Tasman called a meeting that night. The men of the smaller *Zeehaen* crowded aboard the *Heemskerk,* filling the upper deck while Aidan's shipmates hung from the yardarms and peered from hatchways that led below decks. Tasman stood on the high forecastle and looked down at his men...and one woman.

"Most honorable and courageous men," Tasman began, his eagle eye roving over the assorted crew assembled below and around him. "Anthony Van Diemen, governor general of Batavia, commands us to go forth into the unknown to make a complete picture of lands north and west of the continent of Nova Hollandia. Tomorrow at high tide we shall sail first to Mauritius. From that point we will sail eastward at the southern latitude of fifty-two or fifty-four degrees until land is sighted." The corner of his mouth quirked as he glanced at Francois Visscher, who stood next to him. "Though we are not expressly commanded to search for silver and gold, should we find it, we are not to dissuade any man from bringing aboard as much as he can carry."

A great cheer rose from the men, and Aidan clung to a cable as the particularly robust sailor next to her thumped her enthusiastically on the back.

Tasman held up his hand and waited until the cheering died down. When the only sounds were the slapping, sucking noises of

the tide beneath the dock, he pressed his hand to his chest. "Sleep well when your watch is relieved," the captain went on, his gaze sweeping the crowd. "Work hard at your duties. We are well-provisioned and well-commanded. Let me introduce the officers of the command, so that every man, whether he sails aboard the *Heemskerk* or the *Zeehaen,* will know his officers."

Tasman turned behind him to Francois Visscher, and introduced him as first mate of the flagship. In a surge of loyalty, the men of the *Heemskerk,* who had worked under Visscher's strict discipline for the last week, gave a rousing cheer. Next Tasman introduced T'jercksen Holman, skipper of the *Heemskerk,* and Aidan rose on tiptoe to see him. A trim, self-confident presence, the skipper had spent most of the past week in Tasman's cabin, doubtless planning the voyage. Aidan had passed the captain's cabin several times and glanced through the portal, only to see the two men bent over charts spread out on the captain's table.

Next Tasman introduced two men Aidan had not seen before. The first, Gerrit Janszoon, served as skipper of the *Zeehaen.* The skipper was tall, rawboned, and beardless, and looked about with an ingenuously appealing face. A small spattering of light applause sounded among the men, and Aidan marveled that the men of the *Zeehaen* showed so little enthusiasm for their skipper. When the weak applause ceased, Tasman gestured to a man who stood in the shadows of the foremast. The officer stepped forward, moving with nonchalant grace toward the forecastle railing. Towering over Tasman by a full eight inches, he wore no coat or uniform, only dark breeches and a full-cut shirt with the sleeves cut off at the elbow. Something gold winked at his neck, and Aidan lifted her brow, for few of the men could afford the luxury of jewelry.

"May I present Witt Dekker." Tasman extended a hand toward this officer. "First mate aboard the *Zeehaen.*" Aidan immediately lowered her gaze, not wanting to attract this man's attention. Dekker had been a frequent patron of Bram's tavern, and

though it wasn't likely he would recognize her, she could not take a chance now.

Dekker crossed his arms and thrust his jaw forward, his slanting black brows lifting in acknowledgment of the captain's introduction. Aidan found herself surreptitiously studying his face. His profile spoke of power and strength, his lips were firm and sensual. But the set of his chin suggested a stubborn streak, and Aidan did not think she would enjoy sailing under him.

"Finally," Tasman said, gripping the forecastle rail as he leaned forward, "I have procured the services of an excellent English surgeon, who will attend to any man sick or injured aboard either ship." Aidan caught her breath as Sterling Thorne, caught off guard, began to move toward the rungs he must climb in order to reach the forecastle. Tasman waited, an impatient frown on his face, as Thorne climbed the ladder and moved with vigor and grace toward the captain's side.

Tasman's rigid stance softened as he lifted one hand and clapped it to Sterling's shoulder. "You will know how much I value this man when you hear what I am prepared to give him when we return," Tasman announced. "When we have safely returned to Batavia, Sterling Thorne will be honored with my daughter's hand—and you are all invited to the wedding."

On cue, the men responded with more cheering, then someone called for a pint of ale to toast the happy couple. Aidan watched, bemused and bewildered, as Tasman stepped aside, leaving the limelight to Thorne.

The doctor held up his hand for silence, then bowed in the direction of his captain and future father-in-law. "I hope to serve you all to the best of my ability no matter what I am promised upon our return," he said simply. "For I am sworn to aid any man who needs a healing touch, and I promise that my touch shall be as gentle as possible." His eyes twinkled and his mouth twisted in a wry smile. "If not, I have the key to the liquor stores and will make certain you are too insensible to feel your pain."

The assembled crew rocked with laughter, and Sterling paused, smiling indulgently, like a parent amused by the mischief of his children. When the laughter died down, Aidan saw a change come over his features, a somber inward look. "I know that you, like me, must dream of a future life with roots deep in the soil." A touch of sadness lined his faint smile. "I came to the East Indies to make a life for myself, to put down roots so that my younger brother could follow. And if we are successful in this venture, we will find more lands to colonize, more opportunities for men and women to find the freedom for which God designed us."

Aidan glanced at the men around her. She doubted if any of them had longings for roots in the soil. Her experiences in the tavern and aboard ship had taught her that seamen were a breed apart. They walked with the rolling gait of the sea, they climbed rigging as easily as a spider crawled through its web, and they drank like fish in the sea.

But something in the doctor's impassioned speech tugged at their hearts, for they applauded him wildly. Aidan relaxed. It probably wouldn't be wise to talk too much about loving land with men who felt themselves born and bred to the sea, but it was obvious that Sterling Thorne had won the hearts of the men for whom he was responsible.

"He is quite nice, isn't he?" A light, feminine voice spoke near her elbow, and Aidan choked back a frightened cry, nearly convinced that her own shadow had spoken. She turned, looked, and saw a young boy standing beside her, a lad scarcely up to her shoulder, with eyes dark and bright like the stars. No beard yet adorned that cheek, and his voice was still cast in girlish tones.

He looked up at her with an open expression, as if he had found a friend. Aidan swallowed hard, then jerked her head toward the surgeon. "He's all right, I suppose. But I hope I'm never sick enough to need a doctor."

"Me too." The boy thrust his thumbs into the waistband of his breeches, then tilted his head and gave Aidan a quizzical glance.

"Are you aboard the *Heemskerk?* I haven't seen you before."

"Yes," Aidan muttered, hoping his questions would soon stop. "I'm Heer Van Dyck's ketelbinkie."

The boy's brows rose in silent respect. "Good for you. I'm a ketelbinkie aboard the *Zeehaen*. The job's not so bad, but today I worked for the cook and nearly cut off my thumb while I was chopping the heads off pickled herring." He pulled his thumb from his trousers and held it up, a grotesquely swollen digit swathed in white bandaging.

"Goodness!" Aidan gasped in honest admiration. "I hope it's not as bad as it looks!"

"Aye, it is," the boy answered, carefully settling the wounded thumb back into its protected position. "But Witt Dekker brought me over this afternoon, and the doctor stopped the bleeding. I was covered in blood; my shirt was as red as a harlot's lips."

Aidan blinked, uncertain how to answer, but the boy didn't seem to notice her discomfort. "My name's Tiy." He thrust his uninjured hand toward her. "It's nice to meet another ketelbinkie. I figure we ought to stick together. If we're stranded and the food runs out, they always eat the young ones first."

A wave of apprehension swept through her as Aidan extended her hand. This boy was joking—wasn't he?

"I'll swim over and see you sometime when we're at anchor," he offered, stepping away as the men of the *Zeehaen* began to move toward the dock to return to their own ship. "Or you can come see me."

"I—I don't swim," Aidan managed to call.

"That's good." The boy's round face split into a wide grin. "If you can't swim, you won't prolong your drowning when the ship goes down." One of the older men clapped a hand on Tiy's shoulder and shoved him forward.

A sudden chill raced down Aidan's spine. Tiy was only a mischievous scamp, trying to impress her with his bravado. There

wasn't any real danger out on the sea. Hadn't Henrick said that a ship was the safest place for her now?

But try as she might to clear her brain, a host of irritating, niggling shadows of fear remained.

Twenty

꧁꧂

The two ships set sail shortly after sunrise on August 14, 1642. As a flurry of orders flowed through the first mate's speaking trumpet, the hatches were battened, the lines coiled, and the dock workers cast off the mooring hawsers, ropes as thick as Aidan's wrist. She stepped out of the cabin to find a cloud of white canvas sails set and drawing wind over her head. The rope that had held the anchor slithered up, streaming water, and on the soles of her feet Aidan felt the vibration that ran through the keel as the vessel took the wind. The smaller *Zeehaen* had already moved out into the bay, her upper deck crowned by a forest of rigging and sail, through which tiny dark figures hopped and crawled like fleas on a bedsheet.

The bosun of the *Heemskerk* strode back and forth across the deck, barking orders as the lines tightened and sails snapped overhead. The ship moved out into the rising sun, coming to life with a groan as the sails were sheeted home. The *Heemskerk* plunged her bow deep while the lighter *Zeehaen* cut through the water ahead of her, trailing a lacy white wake.

Caught up in the excitement of departure, Aidan leaned on the railing amidships, careful not to place herself in the way of the seamen who scuttled about, each responding immediately to the calls that rang out from the forecastle. To Aidan, it seemed magical, musical: Lines and hawsers sang in the wind, a chorus of timbers creaked with each rise and fall of the sea, faint thumps and murmurs from below decks provided a rhythmic background to the men's work.

She'd seen enough of the ship to have a feel for where things lay. The three-masted *Heemskerk* had three levels—the top deck was pierced by the mainmast in the center of the ship, the foremast at the fore, and the mizzenmast aft. The forecastle contained two small cabins, one of which housed Aidan, the first mate, and Heer Van Dyck; the next-door cabin served as a sick bay and quarters for the doctor. The captain's spacious cabin was situated at the rear of the ship, beneath the quarterdeck.

The holds on the second deck served as storerooms and galley, and in the lowest deck, the orlop, stores of water, food, and gunpowder served as ballast for the ship. A great many large stones rode there as well, Heer Van Dyck told her, to hold the ship aright in case the stores ran empty. This ship, a vessel for exploration, carried only six cannons, all located near portholes on the second deck. Captain Tasman hoped he would have no occasion to use them. Few pirates traveled in these waters, and he hoped to impress any unfamiliar natives with his friendliness, not his firepower.

"You there! Boy!"

Aidan looked up, startled from her reverie, and shaded her eyes. A sailor hung from the rigging a dozen feet above her, one muscled arm wrapped around a yardarm, the other extended to her. "Bring up that rope at your feet and be quick about it!"

Aidan looked down, picked up the coiled rope, and slipped it over her shoulder, praying that Van Dyck's God would give her strength and calm the uneven beating of her heart. She'd never climbed anything higher than a chair in her life, and her arms were as thin as noodles, not at all suited for swinging from rigging like a monkey.

"Are you going to take all day?"

Aidan moved to the railing and clamped her fingers around the netted rigging. Above her men swarmed through the ropes like spiders. She could do this. She could. But when she swung her weight out over the railing, the dark water loomed under her,

and she held to the rigging for dear life. The seaman yelled again, cursing her slowness. Aidan knew if she didn't hurry she'd draw the attention of others. She had managed to lay low during the preparations, but now there was a fresh wind to catch.

"Boy!" the sailor shouted. "Now!"

The bay roiled with choppy waves, and the ship pitched and rolled. Closing her eyes, Aidan willed her arms and legs to carry her weight, then began to reach upward, moving inch by inch, step by step, upon the yielding and insubstantial ladder.

"*Sakerloot,* it took you long enough."

Aidan opened her eyes. She clung to the ropes abreast of the sailor in the rigging, only three feet across from the place where he hung. Gulping, she shrugged the coiled rope from her shoulder, then tossed it to him in a steady, even motion. The toss was poorly aimed, but he plucked it out of the air and immediately threaded the end through a grommet in the canvas and tied an elaborate knot that left her gaping.

Suddenly aware that lingering might only get her into further trouble, Aidan began to shimmy back down. She forced herself to look at the blue sky and the rigging above instead of concentrating on the water below.

Her toes felt the railing and her stomach clenched. She was almost down, but she wasn't at all sure she could make the necessary maneuver that would bring her back to the deck. She froze and looked down at the sea, her heart beating hard enough to be heard a yard away. *Just move your feet and fall,* she told herself sternly. *You will land upon the deck.* But her feet would not move, and her fingers were so tightly clenched around the rigging that she could no longer feel them.

"Help!" she croaked. Out of nowhere, a strong arm seized hers, pulled her from the rigging, and guided her stubborn feet safely to the deck.

"You're a wee bit unsteady on the ropes there, ketelbinkie." The doctor's voice was courteous but patronizing. He lingered, his

hand tight around her arm, until she found her balance and straightened herself.

"Thank you, but I'm all right." She boldly met his gaze, then found herself pitching forward as a particularly high crest set the ship to rocking. A thrill of fear shot through her. If that wave had hit while she was in the rigging, she'd have let go in sheer terror. In blind panic she fell hard against the doctor's chest, then brought her hands up, struggling to push him away as he caught her arms and held her upright.

Aidan stepped back and swallowed hard, her cheeks blazing as if they'd been seared by a torch. Had he noticed anything in that instant when she fell against him?

"It might take a day or two for you to get your sea legs." His voice was softer now, and surprisingly gentle. She looked up, half-afraid to meet his eye, and saw him studying her face with considerable absorption. "Aidan, isn't it?"

She coughed and deepened her voice. "Yes."

"Aidan." He paused, still looking at her with a speculative gaze. "And you are Van Dyck's ketelbinkie, yes? You paint with the cartographer?"

"You know I do." She tossed her braid over her shoulder in a gesture of defiance, then placed her hands on her hips. "If you've no need of me, Doctor, I have work to do."

He lifted both hands in a sign of surrender. "I meant no disrespect. But I am trying to learn the names and positions of over one hundred men—"

"I'll let you get to your work then." She turned away, jumped nimbly over a pile of coiled rope, then put out her hand to steady herself as the ship rolled again. She thought she heard the sound of laughter behind her, but when she turned to look, Sterling Thorne had disappeared among the men roaming the deck.

◦◦◦

According to Schuyler Van Dyck, not one moment of their adventure could be wasted. As soon as Aidan returned from the deck, he

made her sit by the porthole and placed a flat board in her hands. Slipping a sheet of parchment onto the board, he commanded Aidan to look out the window. "We are under way," he said, a tone of reverent awe in his voice, "to discover new lands and new places within our souls. So sketch, my student, and let me see what is opening up inside you now."

"What should I sketch?" Aidan studied the blank page, momentarily stymied. Her mind still reeled with thoughts of her embarrassing encounter with the doctor; sketching and art were the farthest things from her mind.

"You are surrounded by sights and feelings!" Van Dyck walked to the door, threw it open, and gestured to the bustle of activity beyond. "Look at the patterns! Both abstract and real, you are surrounded by them. The rigging-lines shoot in all directions, the sails billow like the bellies of pregnant women, like the pillow you lay your head on at night, like the swell of the sea itself. Look at those men yonder—"

Aidan peered out at the suntanned faces of the seamen she was unsuccessfully trying to emulate.

"Do you see the life in their eyes? The hope of discovery? The desire to master the sea? Live their lives, Aidan. Taste them, devour them, spit them out—and draw them!"

Aidan closed her eyes, trying her best to follow his train of thought. But she didn't want to taste the life of a sailor; she wanted to savor the life of a respectable lady. Schuyler Van Dyck might never understand. He had quite literally been reared with a silver spoon in his mouth; he had never lived in her fallen world. Upstanding men and women did not scurry to the other side of the street when they saw him coming. Their finely dressed children did not taunt him with children's moralistic nursery rhymes.

She breathed deep and felt a stab of memory, a broken remnant from her past life, a shard sharp as glass. When Aidan was sixteen, Lili had scrimped and saved to buy her a new white skirt and cornflower-blue bodice. Aidan had proudly worn her new clothes

to work in the tavern, hoping against hope that Lili's dream might come true and some fine man might look upon her with favor. But not even an hour had passed before a drunken sailor spilled wine over the spotless white skirt, and Aidan fled to the safety of the street where she could cry away from her mother's prying eyes. A rich man's coach had slowly wheeled past, the horses holding a stately walking gait, and the mother inside had pointed to Aidan as if she were an exhibit in the zoo.

"Look there, daughter." The woman's nasal voice cut through the noises of the street. "Look and you will see the truth of the rhyme I taught you." Then, as Aidan listened in disbelief, the woman ordered her coachman to stop. She drew her daughter closer to the window so that the child might see Aidan more clearly.

"How I've splashed and soiled my gown," the woman recited,
"with this gadding through the town.
How bedraggled is my skirt
Traipsing through the by-streets' dirt.
Come girls here, come all I know,
Playmates mine, advise me, show.
How shall I remove the stain
And restore my gown again?
For wherever I may go
People will look at me so
And think, perhaps, such dirt to see
I'm not what I ought to be."

The memory still made Aidan's neck burn with humiliation. She picked up the pencil on her master's table and began to sketch the sea, restless and moving. Life simmered beneath the waves, but above, a host of faraway stars looked down at the sea and smiled smugly, grateful for the unattainable distance between them.

Sterling rubbed at the stubble on his chin as he made his way back to his cabin. He'd embarrassed the ketelbinkie quite thoroughly even before that disastrous wave cast the ship's boy into his arms, but how much of that embarrassment was due to the fear that Sterling might discover Aidan's secret? For Sterling did not need to draw upon his medical expertise to be quite certain—Aidan the ketelbinkie was no boy.

He closed the door to his cabin and took a seat behind his desk, pulling his journal toward him. *The fourteenth of August, in the year of our Lord 1642,* he wrote, pausing to dip his pen into the inkwell. *We are under way and thus far my crew is well—one hundred ten men and—*

He paused and turned his eyes toward the sea. Why had the girl come aboard? The obvious answer was not the correct one, of that he was quite certain. Schuyler Van Dyck did not impress him as being either lecherous or deliberately rebellious. The gentleman was as honorable as any fellow Sterling had ever met. So if the girl was not his lover, who was she? Not his daughter, certainly. Van Dyck was as Dutch as a windmill, and the girl apparently English, even though an Irish brogue colored her speech now and then. Perhaps she was a long-lost relative, a niece or some other gentle lady forced to hide— or, like Sterling, forced to flee an unsuitable and thickheaded suitor.

He chuckled as something clicked in his brain. Of course! Aidan was the wench who had been slugging it out with the old man in the garden! They had been preparing for this little charade even then, and Van Dyck had been trying to teach the girl some manner of self-defense. Sterling's mouth quirked with humor. She would need those self-defense lessons if anyone ever discovered the truth. The ketelbinkie Aidan made a rather spindly-looking boy, but that pale skin, slender form, and those wide green eyes would combine to make a most strikingly beautiful young woman. No wonder the old man had been so keen to know if Sterling had taken a good look at the girl in the garden.

He stretched his legs beneath his desk and stared at his journal. Now that he knew her secret, what was he to do? He couldn't expose her without subjecting her to ridicule, punishment, and certain abandonment once they reached Mauritius. As a physician, he ought to confront her and invite her to take him into her confidence, for women had unique medical problems and he could help if she needed him. On the other hand, perhaps he should play dumb and continue as a silent partner in her masquerade. She undoubtedly had her reasons for joining this expedition, and Heer Van Dyck did not seem the sort to do anything truly foolish.

He tapped the quill of his pen against the page, then abruptly dropped it to the desk. Whatever he decided, he could not write about her in his journal, for all ship's records were the property of the captain and, ultimately, the V.O.C. Tasman could read the log anytime he chose to, and anything Sterling wrote could one day be published throughout the United Provinces.

His eyes drifted to the porthole, through which he could see the gray-blue sea like an enormous sheet of dull-shining metal shading off into a blurred and fragile horizon. Perhaps he should do nothing at present. But if the girl appeared to be in any kind of trouble, he could move quickly to preserve her honor.

He drummed his fingers briefly on the table, relieved to know that she slept next door with Visscher and the old gentleman, and not in a hammock with the scores of crude seamen below. Visscher wouldn't give her a second glance; ketelbinkies were nearly as low as rats on his ladder of significance. And the old man could be trusted, Sterling was certain.

He picked up his pen and dipped it in the inkwell. *One hundred ten men, including one ketelbinkie on each ship,* he finished. *The weather is fine, the winds are strong, and spirits are high. May God have mercy and grant us favor on this journey.*

⚬⚬⚬

Three weeks into the journey, Heer Van Dyck explained to Aidan that Mauritius, their first port of call, was an island colony older

than Batavia. "It may prove a welcome break for us," he said as he stood at the taffrail. His eyes were intent upon the lacy lines of the ship's wake as the narrow waves purled out across the sea. Behind the *Heemskerk,* off the port rail, the smaller *Zeehaen* followed with a most impressive show of canvas, brilliant in the sun, a white flume at her bow giving an impression of great speed.

Aidan lifted her eyes to her mentor's face. Heer Van Dyck was already as tanned as one of the sailors, and when he slept, Aidan could see weblike white markings at the corners of his eyes, the creases of laugh lines the sun never reached. Van Dyck was having the time of his life. Aidan, who as a ketelbinkie had been ordered about, slapped on the back, and "accidentally" tripped twice, was enjoying herself far less than her master.

"There is a funny bird on Mauritius—they call it the dodo." Heer Van Dyck smiled at her. "It doesn't fly, and more's the pity, because the islanders are rapidly killing the beasts off. They say the bird tastes like turkey and is prized on many a dinner table. I hope you shall have an opportunity to sketch one of the birds before we leave. A dodo would be a nice addition to our map."

"I heard Visscher tell one of the men that Captain Tasman plans to completely reoutfit the ships while we are there," Aidan offered. "So we may have time enough to traverse the entire island."

"*Goed,* very good." Van Dyck smiled. "Though I wish Mauritius had more natives. I'm afraid the only people we'll find there are the same sort of folk we knew in Batavia."

Aidan looked away to the southwestern horizon, where Mauritius should appear. She didn't want to meet people like those she had known in Batavia. There were but two classes there, upper and lower, and she didn't feel she belonged to either one.

"Have you completed the oil painting you began the other day?" Van Dyck asked, a hint of rebuke in his voice.

"Almost." Aidan pulled herself away from the railing. "It is nearly done."

"Since the captain has been gracious enough to relieve you of many duties, perhaps you should present the finished canvas to him," Van Dyck suggested as he led the way back to their cabin. "Or perhaps you'd rather give it to the doctor. He has been quite solicitous about your health. The other day he specifically asked whether or not you had experienced any bouts of seasickness."

"He asked about me?" Aidan slowed, her irritation wrestling with anxiety. Did he suspect the truth? Why else would he ask about her?

"He is a concerned physician; he asked about me as well," Van Dyck answered. They reached the cabin, and he swung the door open for her, then caught himself and gave Aidan a knowing grin before preceding her through the low doorway. "Must do something about that old habit," he muttered.

Aidan gave a noncommittal grunt as she followed him in, but her eyes flitted nervously toward the doctor's cabin next door. Perhaps it would be a good idea to tell the physician the truth. But she could say nothing until after they had sailed from Mauritius. If Captain Tasman found out now that he had a woman aboard, he could leave her behind in that Dutch colony with a relatively clear conscience. And while dodo birds might prove to be a tasty treat, she doubted that a book filled with dodo etchings would do anything to enhance her reputation as an artist.

Perhaps she would confide in the doctor. But not until the ships had reached the point of no return.

*

Two days later, Mauritius rose like an emerald from the sea. Surrounded by coral reefs, the island itself consisted of a central plateau ringed by volcanic mountains that rose nearly three thousand feet into the sky. Aidan thought the dark sand of the beach looked like a velvet carpet, and her heart thumped in her chest as she beheld the beauty of the mountains. Batavia was beautiful, too, but she had grown so accustomed to the squalor of the wharf that she neglected to savor the natural splendors around her.

The island's beauty waned, however, as the ship moved southward toward the port. Aidan felt her heart sink as the city appeared before her, patched and faded, its clay walls and thatched roofs rising behind the docks and warehouses. Just like Batavia.

Aidan crossed her arms and gripped them tightly. Even without looking, she knew what she'd find in the heart of Mauritius's port district—the same motley collection of taverns, flophouses, and shops she'd left behind. And there would be procuresses—not Lili, of course, but other women of thirty or thirty-five, unfortunate laundresses and knitters who had fallen on hard times and survived by providing men with the favor of women who had not yet been marked by disease, time, and hopelessness.

Eager to spend the night ashore, the crewmen of the *Heemskerk* hastened to lower and reef the sails. Aidan walked woodenly to her own cabin. She wanted to be off the ship just for a change of scenery, but she dreaded venturing into places she already knew far too well. *At least this time,* she thought, closing the door so she might have a private moment in which to change her paint-stained shirt for one slightly cleaner and more presentable, *I will be visiting the taverns and flophouses as a man, not as a lowly woman.*

Aidan turned toward the wall and lifted her shirt over her head. Suddenly the door burst open.

"Heavens above!" Aidan jerked the shirt close to her chest and cast a dangerous look over her shoulder. A boy's tousled head appeared in the opening.

"Aidan!" Tiy cried, his eyes snapping with joy. "I've come to go with you!"

"Can't a body find a minute's peace?" Aidan felt her cheeks begin to burn. Quickly she thrust her head back into the stained shirt and cast about for an excuse to be rid of the younger ketelbinkie. "Since you are here, Tiy, make yourself useful. Go find my master and ask if I'm free to go."

"*Sakerloot,* you are a grumpy one," Tiy muttered, grumbling as he backed out of the room. "Hurry up, will you? The captain is already loading the barges. If you linger, you'll be stuck here until the next watch is released."

"Just go!" Aidan yelled crossly. When the door closed behind him, she untied her rope belt, tucked in her shirt, then sank onto her bunk and ran her hand over her frizzing hair. Great heaven, what if he had come in a moment later? He would have screeched and run to the captain, sealing her fate with his loose lips and bulging eyes.

But Tiy hadn't seen anything. And that, at least, was a relief and a mercy. She cracked a wry smile. Heer Van Dyck would say that God had looked out for her. Aidan wasn't so sure the Almighty had intervened, but she was grateful nevertheless.

Outside her cabin, the deck fairly rumbled with the thunder of a hundred stomping feet, punctuated by shouts and shrieks. In the midst of such mindless enthusiasm, anyone was liable to come barging through her door.

"Aidan!" She heard the strong voice outside, but this visitor didn't come in. She stepped forward, cautiously, and pulled the door open. The doctor stood outside her cabin, his faded hat on his head, a fresh white shirt tucked into clean black breeches. His golden hair provided a stark contrast to his deeply tanned face and neck, and the way his shoulders strained against the fabric of his shirt made her gulp. Standing there, long, lean, and attractively male, he was quite the most handsome man she had ever seen. She certainly couldn't let *that* thought be noised abroad.

"Are you going ashore?" His gaze rested upon her, remote as the ocean depths, and she wondered why he asked.

"I am." She tightened the rope belt that held her breeches and felt for her dagger, assuring herself that it rested at her back. "Tiy has gone to ask my master for leave to depart."

"Heer Van Dyck left in the first barge and asked me to keep an eye on you," the doctor answered. "I know you young ones

probably have ideas about what you'd like to do ashore, but I thought we could find a quiet place to rest, perhaps to share some conversation."

"I promised to go with Tiy." Aidan ducked through the low cabin doorway, then straightened, fighting to keep her face expressionless when the door closed and hit with a solid whack on her rump.

The doctor's eyes remained serious, but one corner of his mouth curled upward. "I see," he drawled. "Well then, you'd best get aboard. The second barge is about to pull away, and I don't know if the captain will send another boat ashore tonight."

Aidan nodded and dashed for the deck. She spied Tiy near the mizzenmast and waved. "Come! We must hurry!"

Caught up in the euphoria of liberty, they spidered over the netting that served as a ladder, then dropped into the wide barge. The bosun was about to give the order to pull away, but another figure swung out onto the netting and crawled down, landing with a solid thump at the rear of the boat.

"Thank you for waiting, sir," Sterling Thorne called up to the bosun before settling onto a bench.

The bosun gave the order, the oarsmen cast off, and the barge headed out across the wind-whipped waters of the bay.

Twenty-One

~~~~~

Two hours later, Aidan sat on a low stool at the gaming tables, her chin in her hand and her eyes heavy with fatigue. The bosun had given her and Tiy five stuivers each for their work aboard ship, and when Aidan protested that she didn't care to drink the tavern's watered-down ale, Tiy had persuaded her to sacrifice one of her coins at the gaming tables. Now she watched the slick-fingered dealer flash cards to several players while the pile of coins in the center of the table grew taller.

Aidan smiled against her palm. The dealer, a rail-thin Dutchman with a narrow moustache, was cheating his players, but they were too focused upon their own cards to notice. He wore a band of fabric inside the long sleeve of his shirt, and while the players were distracted by exchanging cards and adding to the growing pile of coins, he deftly loaded his hand with high-ranking cards from his sleeve. It was so obvious a trick that Aidan yawned, eager to find a bed and sleep on any surface that did not alternately send the blood rushing to her head and then to her feet.

"Aidan, can I have another coin?" Tiy's bright face dropped into her range of vision. "I've lost all mine, but I can feel my luck about to change. One of the girls over there smiled at me, and if I can just win enough to buy her a drink—" He paused and gave Aidan a knowing wink. "Well, maybe I won't have to spend for the flophouse, you know?"

"You will," Aidan answered. Her gaze roved over the girls who loitered at discreet intervals throughout the room. "If you go up

234

to any of these ladies, you'll lose your stuivers and your hopes too. They will rob you blind, mark my words."

"No!" Tiy looked at her with an incredulous expression. "That sweet thing wouldn't—couldn't—hurt me. I think she really likes me." His narrow chest puffed with pride. "She knows a good lad when she sees one."

"You can have one more stuiver, but no more," Aidan said, fishing another coin from the leather purse at her belt. "A decent bed will cost us two stuivers each, and another stuiver for a wash basin. So with that coin you must win."

"I can win." Tiy flipped the coin against his palm, blew on it for luck, then paused to smile at the harlot leaning against the wall.

"Wait." Aidan grabbed his shirt and pulled him forward to whisper in his ear: "Ask the dealer to deal the next hand with his sleeves rolled up past his elbow. Then at least you'll have a fair chance."

Tiy appeared puzzled for a moment, then the light of comprehension dawned in his eyes. As the dealer called out for new bets, Tiy laid his coin on the table, but stood erect and crossed his arms. "Before you take that," he said, his youthful voice echoing in the room, "I'd like you to deal the next hand with your sleeves rolled up." He gave his fellow players a cocky grin, then winked at the little hussy who smiled at him. "After all, 'tis hot in here, right? And we wouldn't want this fellow to grow too uncomfortable playing the game."

The dealer scowled, then slapped the cards down. "Who do you think you are, lad?" he roared, standing. He spread his hands on the table and leaned forward, bringing his sweaty face within inches of Tiy's. "Are you accusing me of cheating? Why else would you care how I deal?"

"I just want to see your arms, that's all." As unyielding as a rock, Tiy stood his ground. "No one has won a round here in the last hour, and I'll bet these other fellows would like to see your arms too."

The players who were still sober enough to respond lifted their heads like stunned cattle. *"Sakerloot!"* one man bellowed, his face darkening to a particularly violent color of red. "Show us your arms, man!"

"I don't want any trouble." The dealer thrust his arms behind his back, ostensibly to portray himself as a peaceful man, but Aidan knew he was furiously trying to untie the string that held his cheat cards within his sleeve. Without a word, she slipped beneath the table and crawled over the filthy floor, emerging at the dealer's side. Recalling her lessons from Sofie, the Batavian wharf's most accomplished pickpocket, she slid her fingers into the small opening of the man's sleeves and pulled out three high cards.

"Hallo!" She waved the cards over the edge of the table. "Look what I found in his sleeve!"

From his quiet table in the corner of the tavern, Sterling heard the commotion and looked away from his vaguely charming female companion. Aidan knelt on the floor behind a dealer, victoriously waving a handful of cards before a group of enraged players. It didn't require much thought to understand the scene's significance. One of the players was swinging wide with his fist, and if the fellow hadn't been dangerously drunk he would have already inflicted major trauma to the unlucky card dealer.

"Excuse me." Sterling practically pushed the barmaid out of his way. She had been plying him with free drinks all night, but Sterling had steadily poured them out when the girl wasn't looking, probably amazing her with his sturdy English constitution and capacity for liquor.

A full-fledged bar brawl had broken out by the time he reached the table. The tavern owner and the other card dealers fought to defend the hapless one who'd been exposed, and the enraged seamen used their fists and feet to demand justice. Tiy, Sterling noticed, lay flat upon the table, his arms encircling a mountain of stuivers as if he'd discovered the proverbial pot of

gold, but Aidan stood behind the dealer, pinned between the brawlers and a solid wall.

"*Alstublieft,* please stop!" In an effort to free Aidan, Sterling tried to pull the heaviest of the combatants off the dealer, but the mammoth sailor only turned and swung a drunken punch in Sterling's direction. He sidestepped the blow, then shrugged as the fellow landed face down on the floor, effectively knocking himself out. In the midst of the surging chaos, one of the barmaids rushed forward—not to help, but to rifle through the unconscious sailor's pockets. Sterling shook his head, then turned again to Aidan.

Now the fight raged without reason. The odor of sweat and fury filled the air as men mindlessly pounded each other, trying to prove themselves. Torchlit shadows silhouetted the fight on the cracked plaster walls. The sounds of breaking dishes, smashing chairs, and splintering tables only added to the confusion, and blood ran freely. Someone cracked Sterling from behind with a chair. Though the blow nearly knocked him from his feet, when he whirled around he could not pick his assailant out of the confused sea of fighters.

Groaning, he leaned forward, his hands on his knees, trying to bring the room into focus. He had to get Aidan out of here. Once he did that, he could fall in the gutter, it wouldn't matter. But a woman had no business being in a place like this. Schuyler Van Dyck might have given her a few lessons in self-defense, but the young lady had undoubtedly never encountered mayhem like this.

"Aidan!" He lifted his hand to his mouth and called again. "Aidan! Where are you?"

He saw her then—still standing in the corner, still pinned between the wall and the dealer, who looked rather the worse for wear. Sweat and blood soaked the man's moustache and stained his torn shirt.

Sterling lowered his head and prepared to charge.

Ducking and weaving with each blow the card dealer dealt or received, Aidan felt a great exultation fill her chest to bursting. She'd seen a thousand bar fights in her life, but she'd certainly never caused one, and the thrill was nearly too much to bear. As soon as the dealer moved or went down, she planned to wade out into the fight, testing the lessons she'd learned from Heer Van Dyck.

She heard the crack of bone upon bone, saw the dealer's tall form collapse at the knees and twist slightly as he crumpled in a heap on the floor. Aidan moved forward two steps and thrust her fists up, keeping one close to her face, punching the other in the direction of a tall man coming directly toward her—

"Come, Aidan. We've got to get you out of here."

Aidan lowered her fists and focused upon her advancing opponent. This was no enemy. This was Sterling Thorne, and he was coming toward her with a no-nonsense look in his eye.

"I can take care of myself," she protested, bringing her fists up again. "Move out of the way, and I'll show you."

"You'll do nothing of the sort, because I am taking you out of here. It is time all ketelbinkies were in bed." He moved closer, his hand thrust forward, and Aidan's nerves tensed as she read the determination in his eye.

"I'll not go," she repeated, glaring up at him. She lifted her fists menacingly. "I'm not afraid to hit anyone who touches me."

"Hit me then," he said, coming closer, "because we are leaving now."

Real fear gripped her then; her heart began to beat so heavily she could feel each separate thump like a blow to her chest. He *would* take her out. She would be humiliated, and the men would wonder why he insisted upon treating her like a—

Like a woman.

Crimson with resentment and humiliation, she dodged his hand. She'd show him she could be a man. She'd grown up on the

streets of the wharf district, and she could fight and scrap and survive with the strongest of them.

"I'm warning you, Doctor," she growled. He stopped before her, spreading his arms so she could not flee. *The fool. He has just opened himself like a target.* "I can fight, and I *will* fight—"

"Fight then," he said, his eyes bright and bemused. She lifted her fist and plunged it forward, but before she could land a blow upon that chiseled chin, his arms wrapped around her and lifted her from the floor. Slinging her over his shoulder like a sack of potatoes, he headed for the door. Though she howled and pounded upon his back, he didn't seem to feel the blows. He turned and calmly carried her through the melee until they reached the velvet humidity of the night outside.

"If you don't be quiet—" He yelled to make himself heard over her storm of protest. "—you will only draw attention to yourself. And you don't want to make a scene, do you? If you are quiet, those drunken fools from our ship will not remember anything about tonight, not even the fact that a ketelbinkie started a fight and squealed like a woman as *she* was carried from the tavern."

Aidan clamped her hand over her mouth. How had he known? How long had he known? And who did he intend to tell?

Panic swept through her as she hung there in obedient silence. Passersby cast her curious looks, but she lowered her eyes and tried to think.

"I am going to take a room at this inn," the doctor said, speaking more quietly now, "and you will not run away. You will cooperate with whatever I tell you to do. If you do not make trouble, I promise that all will be well and you can return to the ship with me on the morrow." His head twisted toward her. "That is what you want, right? To return to the ship?"

She nodded soberly. "Yes."

"Good." Slowly, he bent and lowered her to the ground, then grasped her arm tightly. They stood outside a small inn, a far more presentable place than the flophouses where most of the seamen

would sleep tonight, if they slept at all. "I've already met the innkeeper and his wife," Dr. Thorne said simply, opening the door and pulling Aidan behind him. One golden brow arched mischievously as he looked at her. "Be on your best behavior, please, and *do* try not to start a fight while we are here."

The innkeeper and his wife were sitting by the fire, and their lined faces lifted in surprise as the doctor pulled Aidan into the large keeping room. *"Goedenavond,"* he told them, bowing slightly. "Forgive the intrusion. I hope you won't mind that I have brought a boy from the ship to share my room. He will be no trouble, I assure you, but he shouldn't be allowed near the others."

"Is he sick?" The mistress's spidery hand flew to the lace at her throat. *"Doctor,* I do not think—"

"He is not contagious; he can't hurt you," the doctor interrupted, smiling at them. "He is sick—" He tapped the side of his head. "—in here."

"Goejehelp!" The mistress looked even more distressed at this news, and Aidan lowered her head to hide her smile. The poor woman probably thought the doctor had brought in a raving lunatic to murder them in their beds and burn down the house.

"He is quite harmless." The doctor gave them an engaging smile. "And he will sleep with his feet tethered to the bed, so you need not fear him wandering in the night. And now I give you a *goede nacht.*"

He turned toward the staircase, pulling Aidan firmly behind him. She followed meekly, but could not resist looking back at the frightened couple. She gave the man a wide smile, then stuck out her tongue and crossed her eyes.

"Sakerloot! May the angels preserve us!" the woman cried, clutching the crucifix that hung around her crepey neck.

The sight of the cross deflated Aidan's defiant mood. As her eyes filled with tears, she lowered her head and followed the doctor up the narrow twisting staircase. The memory of another cross

filled her mind—a golden cross. Even now she could see the face of the girl who had worn it…and who had died alone and unloved.

Aidan leaned against the wall in the hallway as the doctor brought a candle from the hall sconce to light the one in their room. By the flickering light she could see that the chamber had been sparsely furnished with two beds, a trunk, and a single rug upon the wooden floor. The doctor returned the candle to the sconce, then closed the door behind him. With a careful smile and an uplifted brow, he gestured toward the bed in the corner of the room.

"You might as well take that one," he said. "If they hadn't rented the room to me and my 'patient,' they'd have let that bed go to anyone else who wandered in off the street. Take it and be comfortable." Aidan moved toward the corner, still uncertain of his intentions, but she relaxed slightly when the doctor sat on the edge of the other bed and pulled off one boot. Aidan crinkled her nose at the smell of sweaty stockings.

"Let us understand one another," he said, struggling with his other boot as she silently made her way toward the vacant bed. "I know you are a woman; I've known for some time. And I don't plan on tethering you to the bed, unless you plan on inciting another riot tonight."

"I didn't start the trouble at the tavern; the crooked dealer did," she answered, primly lowering herself to the edge of the blanket. She fumbled at her belt and pulled out the short rod dagger that she carried hidden at her back, then flashed the blade toward him. "I sleep with this under my pillow, sir." She glared at him over the tip of the weapon. "If you should touch me in the night, do not be surprised to find this blade between your ribs."

He threw up his hands in mock horror. "I would not think of touching you, milady." A trace of laughter lined his voice. "Upon my word of honor, you shall sleep undisturbed."

Satisfied, she placed the dagger under her pillow, then sniffed

the air appreciatively. The room smelled of straw from the mattresses, the faintly acrid scent of sweat, and something else—probably the chamber pot in the corner. As unpleasant as those odors were, they were far less pungent than those of the straw-strewn floors of Bram's tavern.

The doctor raised an eyebrow in her direction. "I'm sure this is a far cry from what you're accustomed to," he said, unbuttoning his doublet, "but it will have to do. I can't afford to take a room in a gentleman's house."

"A gentleman's house?" Aidan snapped her mouth shut, stunned by his mistaken assumption. Did he think her a lady? Then she bit her lip, considering. He knew she was a woman, and he knew she traveled under Heer Van Dyck's protection and patronage. 'Twas only logical that he should think her of genteel birth.

Fine then. Let him think her grand and accomplished. When they returned to Batavia, perhaps he'd help her find a foothold in society. Then Irish Annie the guttersnipe would vanish forever, while Aidan the artist rose to glorious heights.

"When did you realize that I am not a boy?"

"The first day we sailed." He stood and shrugged out of his doublet and tossed it across the curved trunk. When he had loosened the cuffs of his shirt sleeves, he halted, looking at her. "You ran into me, remember? And though I couldn't believe that any lady would want to go to sea, eventually I came to the conclusion that no boy, no matter how sheltered, could possibly be that…soft. Though I don't fully understand why Heer Van Dyck has taken this dangerous step and brought you aboard—"

"He believes me a great artist." She dropped her shoes to the floor, lifted the linen covering on the bed, and climbed beneath the covers. She would remove nothing else, certainly a lady would not. Perhaps she shouldn't even have taken off her shoes. A genuine, modest lady probably would have kept her shoes on as long as a strange man remained in the room.

"Are you?" The doctor went to his bed and reclined on it,

folding his hands behind his head. "Or have you some other reason for assuming this disguise?"

Aidan lifted her eyes to the ceiling and considered the question. "I am an artist," she answered finally, watching in fascination as a cockroach scurried across the white-painted ceiling. Mauritian cockroaches grew every bit as large as those in Batavia. "But I'm not yet the artist Heer Van Dyck wants me to be. He sees things in me, some great promise, that I don't. Ofttimes he says things I can't believe." She lifted one shoulder and shrugged. "But he is a dear man, and he has taught me a great deal about painting. I may not be great, but I can paint a decent picture, and I am learning. Before I met Heer Van Dyck, I couldn't even afford—" She caught herself and stopped suddenly. The doctor would not understand her poverty. "I couldn't afford to take the time to learn."

"I asked Heer Van Dyck about you." The doctor propped himself up on one elbow and turned slightly to look at her. "He was very careful not to lie. He said you were his ward."

"I suppose I am."

"Where are your parents?"

"Dead."

How many times had she fostered that deception? When Aidan was younger, Lili herself had encouraged her to play the part of an orphan while begging. She didn't feel that she was being disloyal or dishonest. In a way, Lili O'Connor *was* dead, and Lady Lili the procuress lived in her place. The woman who had taught her to be truthful and honest and good expired as soon as the ship anchored at Batavia. The better part of Lili's nature had disappeared, along with Aidan's respect for her.

"I'm very sorry."

Surprised by the compassion in his voice, she looked over at him and saw that he was studying her with unnerving intentness. His smile had vanished, and his eyes seemed shadowed with a dark loss of his own.

"Have you parents?" she asked, overcome with curiosity.

"My father is dead; my mother lives in England," he answered. His gaze settled on his boots, which lay strewn across the floor as if a child had just stepped out of them. "Along with my two brothers and two sisters. There is not enough land to provide an inheritance for all three sons, so one of my brothers will inherit the house and lands while my other brother and I make our way in the world." His voice softened with nostalgia. "My sisters, of course, will marry boys from the village. I had hoped to establish a medical practice in Batavia, so one of my brothers could eventually join me here."

"Are they doctors, like you?" Aidan asked.

Sterling shook his head. "No. Mayfield was apprenticed to a cooper, and Newland has a way with horses like no man I've ever seen. He's a bit slow with people, but seems to speak a horse's language. I've seen him break a yearling with nary a spur or whip."

A flush of embarrassment spread over his face as his gaze returned to hers. "Of course, I suppose your people have little to do with coopers and horses—or even doctors." He stared down and idly traced the pattern of the quilt with his fingertip. "In a bit of romantic fancy I had supposed that perhaps Heer Van Dyck took you to sea in order to escape a particularly amorous suitor. I know now, you see, that I saw you that day in the garden. He was teaching you to defend yourself, and if someone was intent upon forcing his intentions upon you, I could understand why you might want to flee Batavia in disguise."

Aidan closed her eyes against a sudden flood of tears. In spite of her resolve to move forward, her mind returned to the vision of Orabel, pale and bruised, alone in the alley with this doctor. "I can defend myself well enough," she answered, "but others cannot."

His forehead creased in a puzzled frown, then the light of understanding dawned in his eyes. "I had nearly forgotten you were also the boy in that alley," he murmured, looking down at his hand. "How shocked you must have been to come upon me with

that dead girl. She was so lovely, so well-dressed. I assume, of course, that she was your maid."

She wasn't my maid—she was my best friend, Aidan wanted to shout. This man's assumptions were idiotic, but he probably found his fantasies easier to believe than the truth. In any case, if she intended to bury the past and move onward, some relationships should be left behind. Orabel was gone, and Aidan could do nothing about it.

Let him think she stumbled upon him in that alley while looking for her maid. Let him believe Orabel was a lady-in-waiting, and Aidan a lady-in-hiding. He believed a pack of lies, but she'd given up on the truth long ago.

"If you're going to talk all night, please lower your voice," she said, her mood suddenly chilly. She pulled the linen sheet to her chin, hoping he would take the hint. "I, for one, intend to get some sleep."

His hand moved toward the candle, but he paused before blowing it out. "Do you promise you will not sneak out and get into more trouble? I cannot keep track of you in my sleep."

"Do you promise not to reveal my secret?"

His dark eyes flashed a warning, gentle but firm. "As long as your secret keeps you safe, I will keep your secret."

"Then we are agreed." She rolled onto her side, turning her back to him. "Now will you please be quiet so we can sleep?"

The light disappeared in response, and Aidan heard the rustle of blankets and linens as he settled himself in the darkness. But she lay awake for a long time, fascinated by the sound of his deep, regular breathing.

Twenty-Two

The next morning the doctor insisted that they find Heer Van Dyck straightaway. Aidan suspected he was anxious to prove to her guardian that he had not violated the gentleman's confidence. As the city shone in the tangerine tints of the rising sun, they searched the finer inns along the water's edge and finally located Heer Van Dyck in a thatched-roof chapel near the docks.

Aidan recognized the signs of creative rapture as she and Sterling approached. The old gentleman sat on a wooden bench at the back of the makeshift tabernacle, but his wide eyes were fixed upon the ocean, where the sun had painted everything in its path in a wash of shimmering crimson.

"Look at that!" he whispered as they approached. "Feel that, Aidan! Can you see the majesty of the Creator? Can you sense his whimsical mood this morning? He has placed that single streak upon the horizon to delight my soul, to bring his majesties to mind."

"God is definitely playing the jester this morning." Aidan's voice was as dry as the sandy chapel floor. "As he was last night. Heer Van Dyck, our secret is known to our ship's surgeon."

Van Dyck straightened and glanced over his shoulder, then lifted a brow toward the doctor. "*Ja?* Well then." He gave Aidan a satisfied glance. "I have a feeling God approves. The doctor should know the truth. You might need the surgeon at some point, and he will be able to treat you privately. You should not be treated like one of the rabble." Van Dyck returned his gaze to the sun-streaked waters. "*Ja*. God is good. He is wise."

Aidan rolled her eyes, slightly disappointed that Heer Van Dyck wasn't horrified—or at least a little surprised. He took the news as calmly as a man who'd just been to church—which, she realized, he had.

"Well—" Sterling's gazed arched slowly back and forth between Aidan and her teacher. "Now that I have safely delivered you to your guardian, I should report back to the ship. There are several things I must get from the apothecary while we are at Mauritius, and Captain Tasman wants to speak to me this afternoon."

"*Dank u wel,* Dr. Thorne," Van Dyck answered, his eyes intent upon the sky. His hands twitched against the fabric of his trousers, and Aidan knew the old man literally itched to return to his paints and parchments. "Come, Aidan, and sit here. Look at the ocean, at the sky, and tell me how you would paint this."

The doctor hesitated for a moment, his eyes searching Aidan's face, but she merely nodded her thanks and slipped onto the bench beside her mentor, turning her back to the doctor. She watched the surging sea and appreciated the beauty of the water. But her mind's eye focused on the man who was now walking away, taking her most valuable secret with him.

Could she trust Sterling Thorne? Long experience had taught her that she could not trust any man. Heer Van Dyck, however, seemed to think the doctor an exception. Still, she would keep her eyes open and her mind on her work, not risking either her future or her heart to the handsome surgeon.

Shaking her head slightly, she narrowed her eyes and followed her teacher's gaze, committing the beach, the waves, and the shimmering horizon to memory.

❧

Two days passed before Sterling found an opportunity to speak privately with Heer Van Dyck. In the course of those forty-eight hours he had supposed a number of reasons why an elderly aristocrat might wish to take his young female protégée on a dangerous sea voyage, and none of his explanations seemed to fit very well.

But as the ship's doctor and a member of the officers' committee, he felt he was entitled to an explanation—and a reason he should not report this serious infraction to Captain Tasman.

He found the old gentleman standing at the bow of the ship, his eyes fastened to the horizon. The wispy strands of his hair lifted and fell with each breath of the sea breeze. He held a board pressed against his belly as a table of sorts, and with his free hand he sketched the bustling harbor of the Mauritius port.

"Heer Van Dyck," Sterling began, bowing slightly, "I am grateful to find you alone. I believe there is a matter we should discuss."

"Of course." The map-maker gave Sterling a brief smile before returning his gaze to the sea. His pencil moved easily over the parchment as if his hand had a mind of its own. "I wondered when you would approach me. I am only surprised that it took you so long."

A seaman passed behind them at that moment, his whistle cutting through the muffled sounds of the water, and the two men waited silently while the sailor passed. Sterling leaned his arms upon the railing, idly listening as Visscher spouted commands from the forecastle: "Lay aloft, jump to it, trice up, lay out! Sheet home the mainsail, boys, hoist with a will, now hoist away!"

The deck thundered as seamen sprang to obey, and Sterling squinted up at the dark clouds on the southern horizon. It was beginning to rain in soft spatters that caught in his hair and eyelashes, blurring the sky and sea into one gray mass.

"I have a good reason for my subterfuge, Dr. Thorne," Van Dyck said, with marked conviction. "The young woman is virtuous, I can assure you. She is not aboard for my pleasure or any other man's."

"I had surmised that already." Sterling settled his hat more firmly atop his head as the raindrops continued to fall. If the old man could stand here in the wet, so could he. "But I cannot see why you would bring a woman of gentle breeding into such a perilous situation. These men are rough and coarse, and the dangers we face are myriad."

"Even a velvet glove may conceal a fist of iron," Van Dyck answered with a wry smile. "I can assure you, Doctor, that the young lady is quite capable of fending for herself."

Sterling nodded. He'd seen as much in the tavern—and in the inn, when she flashed a dagger before his eyes and promised to use it. "She told me her parents are dead," he said, watching the older man carefully. The cartographer's face remained as impassive as stone. "I am assuming, then, that you are her guardian?"

Van Dyck inclined his head. "In every sense of the word."

"Is she a relative? Your niece, perhaps? Forgive my curiosity, sir, but if I am to keep this secret from Captain Tasman and the other officers, I feel I must understand the reason for it. Unless the young lady was in greater danger in Batavia than here on the open sea, I cannot possibly fathom why you should subject her to this expedition—"

"She *was* in danger," Van Dyck interrupted. His distinguished face became brooding as he stopped sketching and stared into the sea. "She was in great danger of neglecting her gift, which is quite considerable. If I had left her behind, she would have done nothing with it. And the world would have sorrowed, Dr. Thorne, the world would grieve and not know why. She is quite extraordinary, far above the common realm."

Sterling paused, respecting the storm of emotion that crossed the artist's face. "Is she so different from a hundred other young ladies who take art and music lessons?"

"Yes," he said, turning to look at Sterling with an expression of pained tolerance. "How can I explain it?" He looked about the deck for a moment, then pointed to a bucket that collected rainwater on the deck.

"Do you see that bucket of water?" he asked, holding his sketch board close to his chest as he folded his arms. "If you lowered your hand into the bucket and then pulled it out, would anyone ever be able to tell? No. You and I are ordinary, Dr. Thorne; we are conventional mortals. But if young Aidan put her hand

into the bucket and then pulled it out—figuratively speaking, of course, she would leave something behind. Her life would leave a trace in the water. Mark my words—that young woman's life will color the world."

Sterling struggled to comprehend the man's message. "Why is she so different?"

Van Dyck's mouth twisted in bitter amusement. "I think it is because she suffers," he said simply. "She bleeds into the water."

The old man paused a moment, then cleared his throat and turned back to the railing. "She really is unlike any other young woman, but I don't expect you to understand that. All right, then, perhaps you can appreciate this: My protégée is an heiress worth at least twenty thousand of your English pounds. I could not risk leaving her behind." He lifted a bushy brow. "Does that answer satisfy your inordinate curiosity?"

Sterling blinked and retreated a half-step. Aidan, an heiress? By heaven, no heiress he knew would resort to such a drastic action! Then again, he reflected with a rueful smile, he did not know many heiresses. If fortune-hungry suitors were relentlessly pursuing Aidan in Batavia, perhaps this was not such an extreme plan. After all, her faithful maid had been murdered in the street and the girl had no parents or brothers to protect her.

"Do you not think," he said, lowering his voice as he edged closer to the rail, "that Captain Tasman would understand your motivation in this case? Surely he would forgive your action and allow the girl to abandon her disguise."

"Captain Tasman," Van Dyck said, grinning, "knows his seamen better than you, Doctor. An unattached woman on this ship, particularly one as lovely as my ward, could no more return to Batavia with her virtue intact than a lawyer could feel compassion gratis." His lips twisted into a cynical smile. "And if you know men like I do, Doctor, you'll understand why the disguise is necessary. Keep her secret, I beg you. Her life and honor depend on it."

Sterling nodded slowly. "All right, Heer Van Dyck," he said, returning to the rail as the older man regarded him with a level gaze. "You have my word on it."

❦

Captain Tasman spent nearly a full month on Mauritius refitting his ships, restocking fresh water and supplies, and ordering his men to do a thorough scraping of the ships' hulls. And as she did odd jobs for the seamen, Aidan learned a great deal about sailors' superstitions. Part of the hull scraping, she learned, was necessary to rid the ship of barnacles, weeds, and remoras, small fish only seven or eight inches long. The stubborn sucker-fish attached themselves to any flat surface and could only be dislodged with great effort. Despite the fish's small size, the seamen believed remoras capable of dramatically impeding a ship's progress.

When she was not coiling rope or mending canvas below deck, Aidan spent her time sketching ashore. She discovered many strange and new sights in this part of the world, including the infamous dodo bird. 'Twas a pity, she thought as she sketched a hen atop a nest of eggs, that the animals were too slow-witted to escape those who sought to snare them.

One morning, on a quest for some new adventure, Aidan accompanied the doctor into town for another of his visits to the apothecary's shop. Not finding anything unique upon the streets of Mauritius, she implored the doctor to walk with her along the beach in an uninhabited part of the island. He agreed, a bemused look on his face, as she led him out of town, past the ramshackle houses and thatched huts that reminded her too much of dreary Batavia.

Quick-moving shadows of clouds skimmed over the barren beach, while the distant mountains provided a scalloped border to the western horizon. Aidan felt a beauty in the desolate spot, a quiet solitude unknown along the crowded wharf. The great blue bowl of sky stretched above her, and slanted sunlight shimmered off the glowing foliage that grew beyond the beach, marked by a

line so dramatic she could almost believe God had set the boundaries of sea, sand, and forest with his finger.

She left the doctor on the shore and walked down to the water's edge. Slipping out of her soft shoes and stockings, she stepped into the sand, feeling her weight sink as the beach shifted to accommodate her presence.

Closing her eyes, she lifted her face to the sun, relishing its warm caress on her face. Her skin was probably as tanned as a native's, and she'd undoubtedly have to take six months of milk baths to restore it to a ladylike shade of white. But she could not rise to nobility overnight. It would take time for her engravings to be published, discovered, and appreciated. And during that time she would continue to learn and work with Heer Van Dyck. One day—she exhaled happily at the prospect—Gusta would be forced to admit that Aidan had indeed made a lady of herself.

But until then, there was time for *living*. She opened one eye and squinted at the rolling, crashing waves. She had never visited the beach of Batavia, had never felt free to wander the island. But Heer Van Dyck would encourage her to swim if he were here; he'd tell her to *devour* the sea, to taste it and spit it out and sketch it.

"Feel like a swim?" She tilted her head mischievously toward the doctor. Shock flickered over his face like summer lightning, then he grinned at her.

"Surely you jest," he called, resting his hands on his hips. "The water is much colder here than in Batavia."

She did not listen, but tiptoed into the water, feeling its icy touch through the fabric of her breeches.

"You aren't, ah…" Sterling's voice faltered. "Aidan, you can't do this."

"Why not?" she called over her shoulder. Her clothes would soon be sticky with salt and seawater, but later, back on the ship, she could rinse them out in a rain barrel. Right now she wanted the water to tingle her skin and her face; she wanted to feel the waves lift her from her feet. With her shirt sleeves flapping about

her arms, she ran further into the water, then squealed in glee and retreated from a crashing breaker.

"Come on, Aidan," the doctor called, an imploring note in his voice. "You forget yourself!"

"Perhaps you ought to forget *your*self," she called back, gauging the next breaking wave. If she waited until it broke, she could run full bore in the surf and reach the place where the waves rocked in a gentle rhythm. Laughing in sheer delight, she ran in, splashing wildly, until the cold water rose up to her rib cage, pressing the breath from her lungs, enlivening every sinew and particle of her flesh.

"Aidan! Come out!" the doctor called, moving toward her. "You do know how to swim, don't you?"

"It's all right." Aidan turned and lifted a wet arm to wave in reassurance. Her soaked shirt was like a second skin; she felt like one of the legendary kelpies her mother had described in nighttime stories. As a creature partly of the sea, partly of the land, she could live forever in the water.

"Aidan!" The doctor's voice had a sharp edge now. "Come out! I am losing patience!"

"It's all right, I can touch the sand," Aidan yelled, standing erect to demonstrate. "It's right—oh!" A wave caught her off guard, lifting her from the sandy bottom, breaking over her head and arms, then carrying her forward in its curling momentum. Aidan thrilled to the power of the surge, feeling herself borne up and away, but when she sought the surface, she panicked when she could not find it. She opened her eyes, felt the sting of the salty water, and reached out to grasp nothing but a watery expanse.

Blood pounded thickly in her ears as she fumbled to find her footing. How foolish she was, so intent upon devouring the sea that she had allowed it to devour her! She listened, straining to hear some sound that would set the world aright again, but she could hear nothing but the muffled sounds of the sea and her own frantic heartbeat.

Her lungs began to burn. If she opened her mouth to scream, water would rush in, and until she felt either the emptiness of air or the solidity of the bottom, she was helpless.

So this is how drowning feels. Aidan stopped thrashing and closed her eyes, hoping that in surrender God might have mercy and take her quickly. She would have to open her mouth and breathe in water. It could not be avoided; her chest would cave in if she did not fill it with *something*—

An iron vise gripped her arm, pulling her upward with surprising force. Aidan opened her mouth and gulped wonderful, sweet air as sheets of water streamed from her shirt and her hair. An arm braced her shoulders now, probably an angel's. He'd come to escort her into the presence of the Heavenly Judge…

"You are a wondrous fool, girl." Relief and ridicule mingled in the voice that addressed her, and Aidan opened her eyes to see Dr. Thorne, not Gabriel, standing before her. Like her, he was drenched, too, his doublet, breeches, and shirt stained dark by the seawater.

Despite the cold, Aidan felt heat stealing into her face. "Thank you," she whispered, her teeth chattering as he held her upright. They were beyond the breakers, standing in chest-deep water. "I—I don't understand what happened."

"Undertow," he answered, his brow still creased with worry. "It catches you and pulls you under. I didn't think you'd know how to escape it."

"I never knew such a thing existed," she answered, suddenly grateful for the warmth of his hands on her shoulders. "I have never swum in the sea. I only knew I had to try it once."

The smile he gave her was utterly without humor. "And now that you have tried it, will you come away? You should not have gone into the water. Do you obey every inclination that fills your imagination?"

"Not usually." She stared up into his face. He had just risked his life to save her. And here they were, safely out of the treacherous

current, yet his hands still remained on her shoulders, warming her through the light fabric of her shirt.

Was the yearning that showed in his face as apparent on her own?

"Are you hurt?" His gaze slid from her eyes to her neck. "Sometimes a person can be scraped against the bottom—"

"This person," she whispered, lightly placing her fingertips upon the soaked fabric of his doublet, "is fine." A gentle rounded wave pushed forward and lifted them, as one, for a dizzying moment, and Sterling brought her close, holding her safe until the wave dropped them back to the sandy bottom.

His nearness made her senses spin. She'd been around men all her life—drunks, lechers, pickpockets that put Lili's girls to shame, egregious con men and card sharks, but never a man like this. His strength wrapped around her like a warm blanket, and suddenly Aidan wished she *was* a kelpie, that she could pull him under the water to live with her forever in the sea.

The dull rumble of thunder broke into her thoughts. "Rain," Sterling said, loosening his grip slightly as he glanced out toward the sea. She looked and saw sullen masses of clouds on the horizon, briefly veined with lightning, bringing in an afternoon storm.

She pressed her hands to his chest, reluctant to have the moment end. "You know how to swim," she said matter-of-factly, desperate to continue the conversation. "How did you learn?"

"My brothers and I swam in a lake near our farm." Gently, he took her hands in his own and led her through the water. "And now we must get ashore, and you must dry off." A reluctant grin tugged at his mouth. "Though I know you fancy yourself invincible, I am of the opinion that a cool wind and wet clothing bring on the ague, and I'd hate to see you get sick."

He released her hands as they passed the breakers and stumbled up onto the sand, but she pulled at his wet sleeves, unwilling to let the magic moment pass. He had accused her of obeying her

slightest inclinations, and a particularly strong one now gripped her imagination.

"Doctor," she said, digging her heels into the sand.

"Yes?" He bent to pick up his cloak from where he'd dropped it on the beach, then looked at her with patient amusement. "Are you cold? Here, let me put this around you."

Expertly, he snapped the sand from his cloak, then unfurled the garment around her shoulders, tying it below her quivering chin. Aidan studied his face as he worked; then, without thinking, she laced her hands behind his neck and searched his warm eyes. They stood together for a long moment, breathing each other's breath, then Aidan closed her eyes as Sterling Thorne gently bent his head and kissed her. His tender lips were warm and salty, and his mouth moved across hers with a hunger that belied his outward calm. For a long moment they stood there, two souls joined by the sea, then his lips left hers and moved across her cheek. He pressed her head to his shoulder, his fingers entwined among the loose hair above her braid.

"Forgive me," he said, his voice trembling. He would not look at her, but placed his hands on her shoulders and gently pushed her away. "You are a fine lady, and I have forgotten myself." He looked past her toward the looming clouds in the distance. "Please, let us forget this ever happened. This will be a long voyage, and I am betrothed to another woman."

She listened with rising dismay, then turned away and staggered up the beach. She had seen enough of the real world to know how men acted when they desired a woman. The men she knew from Bram's tavern would not have hesitated to take her body, heart, and soul in the instant she put her arms around them, yet she had never offered herself to anyone else. She was fool enough to yearn for *this* man, and he did not want her. He could make all the excuses in the world about treating her like a lady, but the fact was he didn't want her.

The rejection stung Aidan's soul, and she shivered, suddenly

chilled as the sun disappeared behind the encroaching clouds. The heavy sand pulled at her knees and ankles, slowing her down. But she could not delay, for Sterling Thorne's faint shadow stretched behind her.

"Do not fear my attentions, Doctor," she snapped, not looking back over her shoulder. "I doubt that I will have cause to be in your company again. 'Tis certain I will not choose it."

Humiliation coursed through her, and she tugged at the string of his cloak, loosening it until it fell from her shoulders. Without its weight, she moved more quickly. As she hurried away, she pulled her heavy braid over her shoulder and squeezed it, hard. She'd like to squeeze Sterling Thorne's heart right now. But she'd get more seawater from her clothes and hair than she could get blood from his heart.

Twenty-Three

On October 8, 1642, the *Heemskerk* and the *Zeehaen* sailed from Mauritius, heading for the fifty-second parallel. Adhering to Van Diemen's plan, Tasman intended to sail south until he reached fifty-two or fifty-four degrees south latitude, searching for the rumored southern continent. The ships encountered masses of seaweed and drifting logs, a certain sign of land, but a cold and dense fog soon convinced Tasman to change course. After checking the position of the southern constellations, Tasman ordered his pilot, Visscher, to plot an eastern course on the fortieth parallel. He returned to his cabin in morose silence.

For three weeks Aidan had sat in her own cabin and struggled to paint several insect specimens Heer Van Dyck had collected upon Mauritius. He was eager for her to perfect her watercolor techniques, for he was firm in his belief that they would soon discover an important unexplored continent. His own map lay spread on the table, with penciled grid lines marking latitude and longitude, awaiting only the actual coordinates of the unsighted land. But day after day passed with only bitterly cold winds, obscuring fog, and temperamental storms to mark their advance.

On November 24, after weeks of difficult sailing along the fortieth parallel, a lookout in the crow's nest cried out, "Land ho!" Aidan, along with every man aboard the two ships, spilled out to the deck, straining to see through the turbid mist that brooded over the waters like a vengeful spirit. The land rising in the distance appeared to be another mountainous island, of definite

shape and a goodly size. Heer Van Dyck assured her it was uncharted. This was no unknown continent, but it was a sizeable piece of property, and now a Dutch possession.

The old gentleman fairly glowed with the prospect of exploration and darted back into the cabin to prepare his supplies. "Hurry, Aidan," he called through the doorway. "Make yourself ready! Captain Tasman will want to send a party ashore!"

But Abel Tasman was not as intrepid as Heer Van Dyck imagined. Aidan watched as the captain stood on deck and surveyed his discovery. He stood motionless, one arm crossed defensively across his chest, the other holding his finger to his lips, restraining the order to lower the barges for a landing party. The weather had worsened since they moved closer to shore, and the heavy clouds overhead now churned in the pulsing breaths of the wind.

Aidan moved to the rail, shivering as a tremor of fear and anticipation shot through her. The cold wind needled her flesh through her stockings and stirred the fog over the water.

This was the moment she had waited for. If she were to rise in the world, she'd have to do the work she'd been gifted to do. But how could she step out into this hostile environment? She had dreamed of exploring a quiet, sunny beach where friendly natives waved welcomes and roasted wild boars in honor of their arrival— not this alien stillness.

The densely forested mountains of the unknown island could be hiding a great many *unfriendly* natives. Aidan scanned the shore as the ships turned and sailed slowly down the coast. Ostensibly searching for a safe harbor, each man aboard the two ships also searched for any sign of life.

"There!" One sailor gestured to a group of trees near a shallow stretch of beach. "Look, Captain! See the marks on the trunk of that tree!"

"How high up would you say those marks are?" Tasman pulled his spyglass from his pocket, pressed it to his eye, and squinted toward the shoreline. "Six, eight feet?"

"At least twice the height of a man, Captain," Visscher answered. His seamed face lengthened in a scowl as he pointed to another clearing. "Look at that palm. There are notches at least five feet apart. Such markings could only have been made by a race of giants."

"Or a band of monkeys," Aidan murmured to herself. She didn't believe in giants, but she'd heard that the natives near Batavia could shimmy up tall coconut palms with remarkable ease. What was to prevent these island dwellers from doing the same thing?

"I see a gathering of shells on the shore here," Tasman remarked, still scanning the beach with his spyglass. He turned and snapped an order to the coxswain at the wheel. "Bring us into this harbor, sir, and drop anchor. I will dispatch a patrol to make a brief survey."

Heer Van Dyck stepped out of his cabin with his sketch board under his arm. "And who will the captain be sending ashore, sir?" he asked.

Tasman's expression was tight with strain, but he managed a brief smile. "The doctor, of course. Holman and Visscher, and four of the stoutest men we have." He turned and nodded to Visscher. "Send them fully armed, with muskets loaded. And make sure each man carries a blade."

As if in response to the command, the wild wind hooted through the rigging. Tasman paused to scan the swirling sky, then amended his orders. "But we will do nothing for the present, gentlemen, except batten down the hatches and reef the sails. I fear we are about to endure a storm unlike any we have yet experienced." His mouth quirked in a faint smile as he looked at Van Dyck. "On your map, sir, mark this as Storm Bay."

"And the island?" Heer Van Dyck asked, bowing slightly as the rain began to splatter on the deck.

Tasman hesitated for only a moment. "In honor of our governor general at Batavia, call it Van Diemen's Land."

For days continuous rain and wind pounded and imprisoned the crew. How cruel, Aidan thought, for God to bring Heer Van Dyck within a few feet of his dreams and then hold the unknown land at arm's length. But the map-maker worked as best he could, rolling with the steadily pitching ship as he consulted with Visscher about the island's probable length and breadth as well as its exact longitude and latitude. When the rain eased somewhat, he risked his health going out to the ship's master and asking for a reading of the harbor's depth. This he dutifully noted on his chart, wheezing and coughing as he fretted over the vast empty space that still existed between Batavia and the charted coast of South America.

Finally, on December first, the rains eased. Tasman's heavily armed shore party climbed into a barge and began rowing toward land. The men of the *Heemskerk* and *Zeehaen* watched from the decks and portholes, each man's heart thumping in anxiety and anticipation. During the nights, some had reported hearing the sound of drums from the island, and one or two seamen even claimed to have seen the ruddy light of a fire. Aidan wondered how could anyone build a fire in the midst of a drenching storm, but she kept silent and lingered inside her cabin doorway, out of the way. Soon, if the island was safe, she'd be traversing it on foot, collecting the flowers and specimens she would need to complete her book. And then she would sketch and paint her way to a new identity; she would return to Batavia and begin a new life.

Now, overcome by curiosity, Aidan slipped out of her cabin and climbed the ladder to the high forecastle deck, where Heer Van Dyck watched with Captain Tasman. As she inched closer to the rail, she noticed that a deathly stillness had fallen over the group. Dr. Thorne had been one of those chosen to go ashore, and she could see his blond hair spilling out from beneath his hat as the barge moved slowly through the waves. Now they were nearing the breakers, and the sight of the crashing surf made her cheeks burn with the memory of their last encounter.

Since that day on Mauritius he'd kept a polite distance between them, never speaking more than a casual word to her, treating her with no more familiarity than any other seaman. But sometimes, as she ate in the galley or worked in her tiny cabin, she looked up and found his gaze upon her. He was always quick to avert his eyes and move on, but the realization that he watched made her feel a bit uncomfortable…and more than a little pleased.

There was no sound save that of the wind and the waves as the barge neared the shoreline. Aidan held her breath as one of the officers leaped out to guide the boat through the breakers, then a riotous clamor of noise erupted from the jungle that bordered the beach. High shrieking sounds pierced the heavy silence, accompanied by the babble of confused voices and screams unlike anything Aidan had ever heard. The men in the boat froze in their positions, and the officer in the surf stumbled to his knees in confusion.

The forest seemed alive with menace, and judging from the sound of things, the natives weren't happy with the Dutchmen's approach. Panic welled up in Aidan's throat, and she clutched the railing, searching the trees for the telltale gleam of weapons.

"Get out of there!" Aidan whispered under her breath, her eyes fastened on Sterling's broad form. "For heaven's sake, row for your lives! They are waiting for you!"

As if he had heard her whispered plea, the lead man—she thought it was Holman, skipper of the *Heemskerk,* lunged back into the barge. The oars flashed like the wings of a dragonfly as the boat retreated; within the space of a few moments the men were scrambling up the netting, nervously looking over their shoulders toward the shore.

"*Sakerloot,* what a noise!"

"Did you ever hear the like? It curdled my blood!"

"*Goejehelp!* We must be away from this place!"

Dr. Thorne came aboard quietly, with a relieved expression on his face. "I'm only glad no one was hurt," he called up to the captain as he passed. "'Tis obvious they had set an ambush. I

would imagine that our presence in the harbor spooked them as much as they disturbed us."

The sight of smoke rising from the treetops convinced the captain that a landing should be attempted elsewhere. At the moment, he urgently needed fresh water, not an armed confrontation with savages. He'd been commissioned to find new lands, gold, and silver, not native peoples. The Dutch had dealings with more than enough tribes already.

"Let us move away from here," Tasman called, his voice ringing out over the now quiet sea. "Helmsman! Signal the *Zeehaen,* and indicate that we will move north in search of an uninhabited shore where we can refill the water casks."

The helmsman ran to obey, and Aidan turned to Heer Van Dyck, who had watched the entire episode with an agonized expression on his distinguished face. "I had hoped they would be friendly," he said sadly. "I had such high hopes."

He had left his walking stick in the cabin, so Aidan gave him her arm and led him back to their quarters.

❧

Quieter water and calmer weather allowed the two ships to anchor at a smaller, uninhabited island near "Van Diemen's Land" and finally put ashore for supplies. When Sterling Thorne pointed out that no Dutchman had actually set foot on Van Diemen's Land to officially claim it, Tasman considered his options. Rather than send another attention-attracting barge filled with seamen, he decided to send the ship's carpenter overboard. The poor man, encumbered by a burden on his back and so frightened he could barely swim, bobbed between the ship and shore for what seemed an eternity, then scrambled to the beach and hastily erected a wooden marker emblazoned with the arms of the House of Orange. With Dutch possession thus officially established, the hapless man dove back into the surf and swam like a fiend to rejoin his comrades.

By December 4, Tasman had navigated three-quarters of the

island and convinced himself of its size and breadth. With bad weather looming in the north, he decided to quit Van Diemen's Land and continue on his eastward tack.

Aidan knew Heer Van Dyck was bitterly disappointed that he was not able to explore the newly discovered land, but the elder gentleman shouldered his disappointment with a touching attempt at indifference. He pretended not to mind that one-quarter of Van Diemen's Land remained uncharted. After the episode at Storm Bay, a measure of light dimmed in his eyes, and for the first time since she'd known him she felt his spirits begin to flag.

She knew he strongly disagreed with Tasman's decision to quit the island before completely circumnavigating it. "He is a sailor, though, not a cartographer," he explained to her in the privacy of their cabin, "so I must be patient and excuse him." His lids drooped over the crescents of flesh beneath his eyes, and the hands upon his knees trembled. "But as an explorer, I would have thought the desire to know would have held him to his task. If a thing is only half done, it is not done at all, no?"

Aidan spoke in soothing tones, urging him to bed, to rest. During the journey she had come to play the part of confidante, daughter, and apprentice to her mentor. Apart from her, the old gentleman had no one in whom he could confide. His status as a gentleman automatically set him apart from the rough seamen, and his aspect as an artist effectively separated him even from the other officers.

Aidan alone understood. Like him, she was an outcast, but life on the fringe of shipboard society did not bother her. Occasionally she looked toward the *Zeehaen* for a glance of Tiy, thinking that it might be fun to play a hand or two of cards with the other ketelbinkie, but more often her eyes and ears were attuned for the sight and sound of Dr. Sterling Thorne. He had begun to call at their cabin before settling into his own cabin at night, for Heer Van Dyck's failing health had also attracted the doctor's attention. The old gentleman had developed a cough that would probably

not become serious, the doctor told Aidan, unless he allowed himself to dwell in a state of melancholy. He would have to lift his spirits, and the sooner the better.

On December 13, blessedly few days after their last sight of land, the lookout again gave a cry. The captain immediately stepped out of his cabin and was rapidly flanked by his officers. Aidan and Heer Van Dyck joined the crowd at the railing for a look at the majestic land that rose like a treasure from the sea.

A mountain range topped by pure white clouds towered on the horizon. The image struck Aidan with breathtaking intensity, and for the first time in weeks she felt an irresistible urge to paint.

"Surely this vast elevated land is the edge of the fabled continent," Tasman called, too overcome by the grandeur of the scene even to reach for his spyglass. Absently he gestured toward the coxswain at the helm. "Take her northward along the shore, sir, until we find a suitable harbor. God did not will that we explore that miserable land we found earlier. This must be the haven we seek."

For the next four days the two ships slowly followed the shoreline of the promising land, and on the evening of December 17 Tasman gave the order to drop anchor. Convinced that he had found the uncharted continent he set out to discover, the sight of inland fires and smoke did not deter him. "God brought us here without losing the life of a single man," he told the crew of the *Heemskerk* as they gathered on the deck at sunset. The officers of the *Zeehaen* had arrived by barge a few moments earlier. "Tomorrow morning we shall disembark and send a party ashore. We will not go bearing arms this time—no muskets, no swords, no weapons of any kind. The natives here will see our peaceable intentions, and God will honor us."

"Captain." Francois Visscher stepped forward and smiled briefly, the white of his teeth flickering in the torchlight. "If I might urge caution, would it not be wise to aim our cannon toward land in case of an attack? These natives, no matter what

sort they are, have never seen a cannon. They cannot know that we have aimed a weapon toward them, but our men will have the security of knowing we stand at their backs, ready to defend them."

"God will know too." Tasman pressed his hand to his chest. "And he will know the true intentions of our hearts. No, we will proceed as I have said." He paused, hearing the murmur of discontent that rippled through the crowd, then lifted one shoulder in a shrug. "I cannot, however, send a man ashore without his dagger, for men are armed with a blade even in church. No visible weapons, then, though each man may carry his blade hidden behind his back or in his boot. But no muskets, no swords, no torches, and—" He looked pointedly at Visscher. "—no cannon. How can we be sure the Spanish have not found this place? We do not know these people; we do not know what they have seen."

Visscher responded with a stiff salute, then stepped back into his place.

"One more question."

Aidan jerked her head around as Dr. Thorne stepped forward, his countenance shining with resolve. The men shifted their positions to see him, respect and admiration on their faces. He'd set at least a half-dozen broken bones and applied poultices to two dozen bruises, so they had come to trust him completely.

"*Who* will go ashore?" he asked, his eyes snapping with curiosity. "I'm sure those who are going would like to spend the night with such knowledge before they depart in the morning."

Tasman pressed his lips together, considering the question, then nodded.

"A good point," he said. He gestured toward Gerrit Janszoon, skipper of the *Zeehaen,* who had come aboard for this meeting. "The *Zeehaen* will send her own barge, and Gerrit can make his own choice of men. As for us of the *Heemskerk,* you, doctor, shall surely be needed. Francois Visscher shall go, of course. We must send the chaplain to consecrate the shore, a carpenter, a pair of rowers—"

266

"Captain Tasman."

Aidan's heart froze in her throat when she realized that Heer Van Dyck had spoken.

"Please, sir." The old gentleman stepped forward and gave the captain a gallant smile. "It would be a very great honor for me to venture aboard with your men. It is a story I would rejoice to tell my grandchildren when we return home. And," he inclined his head toward Aidan, "my young apprentice would like to search for unusual flora and fauna. The V.O.C. would be very pleased if we were to bring back a pictorial record."

Tasman's gaze seemed distracted for a moment, then he shook his head. "You may go, Heer Van Dyck," he said, frowning. "But not the ketelbinkie. A boy that scrawny can serve no practical purpose and is only likely to get in the way."

"Pray reconsider, Captain." Aidan flinched as a heavy voice broke into the conversation. Glancing behind her, she saw that the first mate of the *Zeehaen*, Witt Dekker, had stepped forward. With a thin smile on his lips, the *Zeehaen*'s first mate gestured toward Aidan. "Captain Tasman, the ketelbinkie would undoubtedly be of service to the old man. What's the harm in letting him go ashore?"

Anxiety shot through her at the thought that Dekker had even noticed her existence, but the *Zeehaen*'s first mate barely glanced at her as he made his suggestion.

Tasman frowned for an instant, then nodded impatiently. "Very well, with the cartographer and his boy, the barge is filled. Once these seven are safely ashore, the boat may return for another party."

"*Dank u wel, mijn vriend,*" Heer Van Dyck answered, bowing again. Aidan watched, amazed, as the entire gathering silently watched him return to his cabin, almost as if they stood in awe of this regal man. Would she ever command that kind of respect as a great lady? Perhaps. If she was successful in this venture.

Tasman tweaked the end of his moustache, gave the foreign

shore a last appraising look, then nodded with an abrupt jerk of his head. "Sleep well," he called, as a dull rumble echoed from the mountains in the distance. The meeting ended, and the men retreated to either their posts or their hammocks.

Aidan paused at the threshold of the cabin and studied the dark horizon. Stars gleamed like crystal diamonds in the cloudless black canopy. Why, then, did she hear thunder?

She shivered as the truth slammed into her—the rumbling sound was not thunder, but the rapid, staccato sounds of drums. For no reason she could name, the sound raised the hairs on the back of her neck.

Her master's insistent voice urged her forward. "Aidan! Get you to bed! We begin our work tomorrow!"

She stepped into the cabin and saw that the fire of passion burned again in Heer Van Dyck's eye.

"Help me pack my little bag, will you?" he called, rocking on his hips as he looked around the cabin. "Where are my pencils? And the board with my Not paper?"

"Here, sir." Aidan batted away the recurrent gnat of worry and stooped to help her master.

❧

"Sakerloot, Aidan! Rise and look!"

Startled by the urgent tone of her master's voice, Aidan rose from her bunk and padded in her bare feet to the porthole. What she saw in the water froze her blood.

Sometime during the night, while the winds blew and the drums pounded, native warriors had entered their boats and pushed off from shore. Pods of natives rode the waves now, only a few yards away from the *Heemskerk* and *Zeehaen,* awaiting the strange visitors who had arrived with the evening tide.

"They are expecting us!" Heer Van Dyck cried, reaching for his sketch board even as he stared out the window. Aidan placed a pencil in his fumbling fingers, then sat back and watched in fascination as he began to sketch the long, narrow wooden boats each

filled with a dozen warriors with shaved heads, wearing grass skirts and animal skins. Ten native boats bobbed in the waters between the Dutch ships and the shore. Aidan made a quick count: The Dutch were already outnumbered by at least ten men.

"Will the captain still want us to go ashore?" she asked, searching anxiously for the meaning behind this strange welcoming committee.

"Of course." Van Dyck tossed one half-finished sketch aside and slid another parchment onto his board. "Look, my dear, at the one lifting his hand to us! Surely such men are hospitable."

"I hope so." She opened the door and looked out. Abel Tasman and Francois Visscher were already on the deck; in fact Aidan was certain Visscher had spent the night watching the dark shoreline. Both men wore looks of weary resignation.

"I think we'd better go out, sir," she called to Heer Van Dyck. "The captain is speaking to Visscher now."

By the time Aidan and Van Dyck reached the knot of officers, Tasman was reporting that Janszoon of the *Zeehaen* had decided not to send his contingent ashore until after the *Heemskerk*'s men had made a safe landing.

"Someone has to make the first approach." Tasman tightened his arms across his chest. "And so we shall do it. Heer Van Dyck, I am honored that you and your ward are present to record this moment in images. Now, where is my confounded son-in-law? Oh, here he is."

Aidan turned, startled to see Dr. Thorne standing behind her. He gave the captain a sharp salute, then bowed slightly to Heer Van Dyck. "I trust you are well, my friend," he said, smoothing the points of his doublet, "and I hope you are up for a grand adventure." He looked around the deck and smiled. "Does anyone here have a knack for languages? We shall have to attempt to speak to these folk in the boats."

"Aidan is as good as anyone aboard ship," Heer Van Dyck suggested, prodding Aidan forward. She felt the back of her neck begin

to burn as a dozen pairs of eyes fell upon her. "My ward speaks English, a bit of Dutch, as well as a smattering of Irish Gaelic."

"What a clever boy." Tasman's tone was dry. "Well then, shall we send you off? I can think of nothing to be gained by waiting, and we need a full day to gather supplies. By the well-fed look of these heathens, I'd say there is fresh food and water aplenty upon yonder shores."

"Let us not wait a moment longer," Heer Van Dyck agreed, moving with stiff dignity toward the rope netting that dangled over the side of the ship. Aidan followed, gathering up Heer Van Dyck's bag of art supplies and her own slippery courage. She peered over the railing at the barge riding the crystal blue water below. The two oarsmen were already in place—one frowned at the natives, the other grinned like this was the lark of a lifetime.

Gently rebuffing her helping hand, Heer Van Dyck moved slowly over the rail, clinging to the ropes as he gingerly made his way down. Aidan followed, careful not to step on the elderly man's fingers, and finally dropped to his side in the front of the boat. Dr. Thorne entered next, then came the ship's carpenter with the necessary coat of arms, and Francois Visscher. Finally, Jan, the chaplain, stood on deck, recited a prayer for the safety of those involved in the journey, and climbed into the barge as well.

Abel Tasman lifted his hand in a stiff salute as the oarsmen braced their oars against the *Heemskerk*'s hull and pushed toward the shore. Gripping the side of the barge with one hand and the bench with the other, Aidan gritted her teeth and prayed that her master had not made the most foolish mistake of his life.

~~~

Like moths to light, the native boats drew near the Dutch barge. Jabbering in a tongue only they could understand, the warriors called to each other in high, excited voices while the Dutch explorers nodded with careful, pleasing smiles on their faces.

"Just keep calm and keep your expression friendly," Visscher advised in a low voice as the barge rowed smoothly through the

quiet waters of the bay. "Keep your hands on the side of the boat—they must see that we carry no weapons."

Aidan was only too happy to obey. Twisting, she placed both hands on the rim of the barge, gripping it so tightly that her knuckles went white. She smiled and nodded and smiled again at the natives in a canoe that raced alongside. The tallest warrior, who was as bald as an egg and about as expressive, pointed at her, then at the *Heemskerk* in the bay.

Aidan nodded at him and smiled.

"Skipper, look over here," Dr. Thorne called from the other side of the boat, his tone as casual as if he were discussing the weather. "I do believe this fellow intends to ram us."

Visscher's head jerked around, and every occupant in the barge turned to look. One heavily loaded canoe came on with great speed, its sharp prow pointed directly toward the barge's midsection.

"Oarsmen, reverse!" Visscher hissed, his round face going pale. "Full reverse, now!"

The order came too late. The canoe rammed the Dutchmen's boat, cutting the slower vessel nearly in half. Aidan threw up her hand as the water rose to meet her. Visions of drowning, of cannibals, of bloody heathen sacrifices flashed through her imagination. Then gray water engulfed her, and the world disappeared.

Sterling Thorne

*It is easier to sail many thousand miles through cold and storm
and cannibals, in a government ship,
with five hundred men and boys to assist one,
than it is to explore the private sea,
the Atlantic and Pacific Ocean of one's being alone...*

Henry David Thoreau, *Walden*

Twenty-Four

~~~~~~

In an instinctive grasp for stability, Sterling clutched the edges of the barge as the canoe cracked the boards like an eggshell. The chaplain and carpenter, who sat in front of the boat, pitched forward into the surging sea, and several of the natives jumped in after them.

Aidan, who sat just in front of Sterling, turned slightly, her eyes wide with fear. Just as she opened her mouth to scream, onrushing water filled the broken vessel and tipped the stern into the ocean. Sterling felt himself sliding backward. The last thing he saw before he went into the sea was the terrified look on Aidan O'Connor's face.

The salt water stung his eyes, blurring his vision, but still he searched for any sign of movement. *It may be hopeless,* he thought, *but as long as God gives me breath, I will not lose her.*

Silvery bubbles shot out of his doublet and rushed past his face, then his vision cleared. Muffled sounds reached his ears—frenzied shouting, crashing, pounding from the surface above. He cast to the left and right, then caught a glimpse of white. There! Just a few feet away. If he could only get to her—

His air was almost gone, but Sterling was determined not to give up. At last his hand grabbed onto her shirt and held tight. She resisted in an initial impulse of panic, then he felt her submit. With Aidan in tow, he broke the surface and turned her to face him as she drank in deep gulps of air.

"Breathe deeply," he said firmly, holding her securely about

the waist. "When I count three, you must take the deepest breath you can. We have to go under the water again."

She stubbornly shook her head, and he pressed his forehead to hers, mindful of the sounds of fighting around them. "It is the only way," he whispered, his voice taut with urgency. "If you want to live, breathe. One, two, three!"

He gave her no opportunity to argue, but pulled her under, then pushed away from the fighting, toward the shore and a quiet little cove he'd noticed from the ship. If they could escape notice for the next few moments, they could hide in the undergrowth until evening, then swim back out to the *Heemskerk*.

He swam until he felt his own lungs tingle, and knew that Aidan needed air. Quickly he brought her up again, grimacing as she yelped in terror when their heads broke the surface.

"Quiet, I tell you," he said, shaking the water from his own eyes. He could touch the bottom here, and quickly found his footing. He turned to see how far they stood from the *Heemskerk,* then jerked back in surprise when Aidan released a blood-curdling scream.

A dripping savage, bedecked with seaweed, had surfaced not two feet in front of her. The warrior lifted a stout wooden club and shouted something Sterling couldn't understand. Aidan fainted dead away in the water, collapsing against the native's bare chest.

Sterling instinctively reached for her, then pulled back. The warrior was gazing at Aidan with a mixture of reverence and fear. If Sterling attacked, the native would undoubtedly crush his head without a moment's hesitation, and Aidan might well be drowned in the rescue attempt. But something in the warrior's eyes told Sterling that if he withdrew, Aidan might not be harmed.

Torn between responsibility and rationality, Sterling hesitated, then dove underwater and swam in a diagonal line toward the shore. The natives would probably assume he had fled to the ship. If all went well they wouldn't find him…and they wouldn't harm Aidan until he could get to her.

Standing amidships aboard the *Zeehaen* with Snuggerheid at his side, Witt Dekker saw the attack and leaned forward, his heart pounding in anticipation. What luck! He had not had a chance to question the ketelbinkie about that day in the alley, but he had decided that it didn't matter anyway. The first chance he got, he intended to get the boy and the old man alone on the island and quietly kill them there. Now it appeared that these natives might effectively do his work for him.

"Sakerloot!" Gerrit Janszoon muttered, his hand moving swiftly to the sword at his belt. "What can we do, Dekker?"

"Nothing," Witt answered. He sidestepped the dog as his eyes searched the churning water. The barge bearing the cartographer, his ketelbinkie, and the doctor had gone down. But when the doctor resurfaced with the ketelbinkie in tow, Witt Dekker saw something else—something he couldn't believe he had overlooked.

Heer Van Dyck's ketelbinkie was no boy.

The realization hit him with the force of a physical blow. He punched Janszoon with his elbow. "The cartographer's assistant—do you know his name?"

Janszoon stared at him as if he'd gone mad. "What?"

"The ketelbinkie's name!" Witt demanded.

"Something Irish, I think. Erin—no, Aidan. What difference does it make?"

"No difference," Dekker muttered. But it did make a difference—all the difference in the world. How could he have missed the truth? The girl he had sought—Aidan O'Connor—had been on board the *Heemskerk* all along. Practically under his nose, enjoying the protection of the old man and, evidently, the doctor as well.

Witt suppressed a smile and turned back to view the carnage. The natives swam like fish, and two of them had already stumbled from the waves to the shore, dragging a bewildered captive onto the sand. With merciless efficiency they lifted their clubs, beating

the man senseless, while their comrades pulled another stunned Dutchman from the surf.

Dekker looked to the *Heemskerk*—Tasman stood on the deck, his hands on the railing, his mouth closed. The man was either in shock or quite willing to let his men perish.

"This might be a good time to take action, Tasman," Witt drawled under his breath. "None of your men will survive unless you do *something.*"

Almost as if Tasman had heard Witt's mocking suggestion, a cannon unexpectedly thundered from the other ship. The *Zeehaen* resonated like a sounding-box to the crash of the *Heemskerk*'s sixteen-pounders, and the mountains echoed the sound—a curious dead thump, as low as thunder but surely more menacing to the natives' ears. Tasman had undoubtedly hoped to frighten the natives away, but the struggles in the water grew more frenzied and agitated as the fearful savages attacked the invaders.

Witt leaned forward, bending to tweak Snuggerheid's ear as yet another Dutchman was fished from the sea and pulled onto the beach. He resisted the urge to cheer. A sure bounty awaited him in Batavia—a rich reward for the deaths of the girl and the old man. And he hadn't had to lift a finger.

One particularly burly savage dragged a fourth man onto the beach. Witt squinted through his spyglass and smiled to himself when he recognized the tall, bearded figure of Schuyler Van Dyck. That noble forehead was already cracked, his elegant beard and face marked with trails of blood. Now, where was the girl? He couldn't see her on the beach. Maybe she had already drowned by the time the doctor got to her.

"Look there!" He felt a tug at his sleeve, and lowered his spyglass.

"Where?"

"A survivor." Janszoon pointed to the water near the *Heemskerk*. A dark head bobbed through the gentle waves, and a dozen hands reached out from the railing.

Irritation raked up Dekker's spine, and he jerked the spyglass up to his eye. "Can you tell who it is?"

Water streamed off the portly figure that struggled up the netting. The survivor had lost his hat, but wore an officer's dark coat. "Visscher." Dekker sighed and lowered the glass in relief. "How fortunate that the *Heemskerk* will not lose her pilot and first mate."

"But what of the others?" Janszoon's eyes swept the troubled waters. Nothing much remained of the barge—only a few broken pieces of wood floating forlornly over the breakers. A hat bobbed gently upon the tide, tossed from wave to wave as it steadily approached the shore.

"Time will tell if any survived," Witt answered, glancing across to the *Heemskerk*. "But I do not think Tasman will want to remain in this inhospitable place for very long."

Four hours after the attack, Sterling crawled steadily through the undergrowth toward Van Dyck's body. The old gentleman had not stirred since the natives brought him ashore, but Sterling felt a physician's obligation to make certain nothing could be done for his patient.

He'd been playing cat and mouse all afternoon. After the massacre in the water, the natives had returned to shore. The majority had left the beach, probably to return to their village, but a half-dozen lookouts remained, and Sterling doubted they would relax their vigilance until the two Dutch ships had departed from the harbor. And so he had crept through the brush all afternoon, trying to examine the bodies of men for whom he felt an acute responsibility, but for whom nothing could be done. The natives patrolled the beach in a random pattern, and Sterling had to wait until they had moved on before he could advance and inspect his fallen comrades.

Cautiously, lest any sound or movement attract the natives' attention, Sterling furtively crept through the thinning brush,

then darted forward to the beach. When he ripped open Van Dyck's doublet and pressed his cheek to the man's cold, wet chest, his ear confirmed what his eye had already told him: the gentleman was undoubtedly dead, apparently killed by one crushing blow to the head. One arm lay at an unnatural angle, doubtless ripped from its socket in the frenzy of destruction, and one of the artist's hands was missing—Sterling didn't even want to suppose why.

Van Dyck, then, was the fourth murdered man. Also dead were the rowers, the carpenter, and the chaplain, each of whom Sterling had found, examined, and quietly moved to a less exposed location. Still missing were Van Dyck's ward and Visscher, the first mate, though Sterling hoped the seaman had the good sense to swim back to the ship. The officer would most certainly be among the dead if the natives had found him. They had not hesitated to kill the men…he could only hope they would be less brutal with Aidan, who in a wet shirt and breeches was obviously female.

Sterling lifted Van Dyck's arms and crossed them in a dignified posture of rest. He did not have time to bury any of the bodies, but since their souls had long since flown to their eternal resting places, proper burial was certainly not a priority at the moment. Only Aidan mattered now—and her speedy return to the *Heemskerk*. Sterling wasn't certain how long Tasman would remain in these waters, or what he might do in reprisal for the attack. Indeed, Sterling would not be surprised if the cannons began to fire again to avenge the lost Dutchmen. The warning shot Tasman discharged during the attack had only agitated the incensed savages. What might they do to Aidan if Tasman began to bombard this beach with cannon fire?

Crouching low in shadows, Sterling turned from the water and studied the winding wisps of smoke that rose from a stand of trees beyond the beach. If Aidan was alive, she must be there. He closed his eyes and prayed for darkness to descend.

He never intended to sleep, but anxiety and exhaustion had drained his strength, and he fell into a shallow doze. When he abruptly awoke, the sunset had spread itself like a peacock's tail, luminous and brilliant, across the western horizon. In a flurry of panic he looked toward the sea—the two ships still rode the tide like silent sentinels, their sails reefed and anchors set, waiting for—what? He fervently hoped they were waiting for him and Aidan.

Sterling licked his lips, tasting dried salt, sand, and the coppery tang of blood. Thirst burned his throat, but he could not take precious time to search for fresh water. If God was merciful, he could locate Van Dyck's heiress and escort her back to the ship within an hour or two, then they could eat and drink their fill.

He stepped out from behind the leafy screen that had sheltered him and took his bearings. The ships filled the horizon at his left hand, the distant sound of drums came from the forest at his right. The native lookouts had moved closer together in a show of solidarity, and now sat as motionless as statues in the center of the beach, their eyes intent upon the dark blue bay.

Sterling moved carefully behind them, prowling like an alley cat, watching his shadow lengthen and finally disappear. He smiled in quiet relief when the rising moonlight revealed a worn footpath through the brush. Moving with the same silent tread he had used to evade his siblings in their games of hide-and-seek, Sterling followed the trail, fretting lest a single footfall snap a twig or rustle a leaf and expose his presence.

He wasn't certain how long he walked—the interval felt like an eternity—but at length he reached a village of thatched huts. A series of black stone boulders had been set up as some sort of totem or monument, and Sterling moved silently up the rock formation and flattened himself against the rock at the top, studying the village from this elevated vantage point. A dozen large huts encircled a roaring fire, and over two hundred people danced,

sang, and chanted around the huge fire pit. Sterling could see no sign of Aidan in the surging crowd.

He climbed down from the rocks and raced in a low crouch to a dark and quiet spot between two of the huts. Some sort of cage, probably an animal trap, had been stashed there, and Sterling coiled into the flickering shadows behind it and peered out between the bamboo bars.

In the center of the village, a nearly naked warrior threw a bough on the fire, sending an eruption of sparks into the velvet sky. Huge tongues of flame leaped into the air, followed by a boiling cloud of dust and ash. Then Sterling saw Aidan, her pale complexion stark against the fire-tinted darkness.

Still clad in her white shirt and breeches, the heiress sat in a bamboo chair, her bare feet tied together at the ankles, her wrists bound in her lap. Her long braid had been loosened, and waves of red hair spilled over her shoulders in a coppery tide, fluttering in the heat and motion of the dancers. A wreath of spotless white flowers hung about her neck; others spilled from her lap onto the hard-packed earth at her feet. Her complexion had gone pale under her tan—pale as the flower petals that brushed her throat. But beneath that copper crown, her green eyes blazed like emeralds.

Sterling felt a reluctant grin tug at the corners of his mouth. These were fiercely savage people, but they still had sense enough to recognize a beautiful woman when they saw one. And, thank God, apparently they had not harmed her.

Judging by the dancers' enthusiasm, this celebration—or whatever it was—had just begun. After eating, drinking, and making merry, the natives would certainly tire and fall asleep. Then, perhaps, he could free the girl.

He settled back, trying to make himself as comfortable as possible. "In purity and in holiness I will guard my life and my art," he murmured. "Into whatsoever houses I enter, I will do so to help the sick, keeping myself free from all intentional wrongdoing and harm, especially from fornication with woman or man, bond or free..."

Aidan wasn't exactly sick, but she certainly needed help, and long ago Sterling had sworn never to withhold assistance when it was within his power to give it. "Yet for her," he whispered, entranced by the resolute and fearless expression on her face, "I would offer aid and support even if I had not sworn to do so."

The memory of another promise—his betrothal—passed through him like an unwelcome chill, and the thought of substituting Lina Tasman's lukewarm indifference for Aidan's fiery passions made his throat ache with regret.

Sighing heavily, he rested his head on his crossed arms and tried to ignore the heavenly scent of roasting meat. His stomach churned, but he willed it to remain silent with the same strength of purpose that made him suppress his longings for the girl who now needed him. Later there would be time enough to eat and time enough for regrets—as long as a company of warring Dutchmen did not burst in upon this scene and disturb the tenuous peace.

Holy God, he prayed, closing his eyes to block the unearthly scene before him, *give me wisdom. And prevent Abel Tasman from doing anything we would all regret.*

Aidan nibbled at the foods the natives held to her lips, drank gratefully from the gourd they offered, and generally tried to appear pleasant though not altogether approving. She had fought and struggled and thrashed between the two brawny natives who brought her to the village, but they proceeded straightaway to tie her to this chair, then grinned at her weakness. She tried her bonds and found them tight. She pleaded with the women who adorned her with flowers, but in response to her entreaties they smiled and patted her bound hands as if she were a child who ought to know better than to protest.

To protest what?

She had been watching them for at least an hour, but she still could not understand the purpose for this gathering. The natives

seemed to be elated at their victory over the strangers who had invaded their waters, yet Aidan hoped with all her heart that they had not succeeded in chasing the Dutch ships from the harbor.

A tall, cocky warrior with a broad face and thighs like tree trunks came toward her, then tilted his head and regarded her with a sly smile before moving on to join his companions by the fire. Aidan's mouth twisted in exasperation—clearly she was a focus of attention, but she wasn't certain whether they envisioned her as an object of worship, a defeated foe, or the featured course of their next meal. Stunned by the brutality of her comrades' murders on the beach, she was now perplexed by the natives' generosity. Little children, naked and dark in the moonlight, tottered up to deposit bananas and other small fruit in her lap, while the men danced in strange circular patterns around the fire as if to show off their skill and prowess.

The part of her brain not immediately occupied with survival speculated about the fate of her companions. For all his bravado, Heer Van Dyck was an old man and in no condition to fend off a savage attack. And the doctor—he must have survived. She had a fleeting memory of him pushing her toward the shore, then one of the savages had surfaced from nowhere. Lightheaded and gasping for breath, she felt the world spin around her and later awakened on the beach, surrounded by broad-faced, squatting natives.

But what had happened to Sterling? He knew how to swim, so surely he had gone back to the ship. Perhaps he would convince Captain Tasman to organize a search party, and soon he and the others would burst into this gathering with swords and muskets ready to free her.

No.

Some ruthless inner voice scathingly reminded her that Tasman would not risk a barge to save the life of a mere ketelbinkie, especially an orphan for whom he might now be responsible. And if the doctor revealed that Heer Van Dyck's ketelbinkie was a woman, the captain might be so angry at her deception that he would not risk the life of even a single crewman. After all, the

mere signs of hostile natives on the island he called Van Diemen's Land had been enough to deter him from going ashore.

She could no longer deny the truth. In all likelihood, her fate rested entirely in her own hands. If her mentor was dead, she was alone, abandoned, already forgotten. Heer Van Dyck always said that God wanted to work in her life, but she could see no signs of God in this place.

The sound of food being scraped from a bowl brought Aidan back to the present, and she stiffened. The tenor of the celebration had changed. The natives' revelry seemed to be winding down. Just like a typical night in Bram's tavern, the feasting had stopped, the noise diminished, and men and women had begun to slink away in pairs. Only a few men now remained huddled in conversation around the fire, and soon those would grow weary and fall asleep, just like the sailors who drank too much of Bram's ale and passed out before the fireplace.

But what did they intend to do with her?

The answer was not long in coming. The hum of the men's conversation died down and ceased for an instant, then the group cheered with sudden delight, as if some great debate had been decided. One warrior, the tall, broad brute who had smiled at Aidan earlier, stood from the circle. A swath of shiny black hair flowed from the top of his head like a crest, and his powerful, well-muscled body moved with easy grace as he came toward her with a sharpened stone in his hand.

Aidan clenched her fists as he hesitated a few feet away from her chair. He swallowed nervously, and she watched in horrified fascination as his Adam's apple bobbed in his throat. His dark eyes probed at her face and form, and Aidan knew this was no cannibal come to claim his dinner. This was a suitor coming to claim his prize. She had seen that look in the eyes of a hundred hungry males, and hard experience had taught her that such men were not easily dissuaded.

Where was Lili when Aidan needed her? It was time to bring

out the old story about the white streak in Aidan's hair, time to dissuade, to defend, to discourage this man like the others.

The savage had made up his mind. He came forward, his eyes raking her with a fiercely possessive look, the sharpened stone extended.

"Faith, sir, you don't want me," she whispered, pulling use-lessly at her bonds as he sauntered forward. She gulped as he sliced the bonds at her wrists with one smooth stroke. Keeping his eyes upon her, he made a low sound in his throat and moved to cut the vines holding her ankles to the chair.

Aidan closed her eyes, then felt the pressure of her fetters ease and opened them again. The warrior's solid frame blocked her path, and she looked past him, searching for an escape route. She had not fought off a hundred lecherous drunks to have a heathen savage forcefully take her maidenhood in the middle of a jungle. Nor had she worked like a ship's slave and donned an unnatural disguise to end her life in anonymity.

Fight! something inside her urged. *Do something!*

But what could she do? Thousands of miles from civilization, without a friend or a farthing, here she did not have even the most basic structures of society to uphold her rights and freedom.

Snorting slightly, the savage warrior stooped before her and threw his arms about her waist. "No!" Aidan protested as he lifted her. She struck at his shoulder in protest, drawing laughter from the other men at the fire. Anger replaced the fear she had known earlier. This was a man like any other, and if he had wanted to harm her, he would have done so long ago.

"Listen, I warn you!" She bristled with indignation as he carried her away from the fire. "As soon as you put me down, I'm running away!" Her abductor paid her no attention, so Aidan turned her face toward the other grinning fools by the fire. Pointing toward the shore, she yelled, "The Dutch will come for me, do you understand? They will come! And they will not be happy about this!"

The warrior snorted and bent his knees, and Aidan suddenly

found herself inside a small straw hut that sat a distance away from the others. The man released her, dropping her more like a sack of potatoes than a prized bride, and Aidan cried out as she landed on the packed earthen floor.

"You stinking savage!" she cried, seething with anger and humiliation. The man before her only smiled and muttered something unintelligible, then knelt at her feet and took the sharpened stone from his belt.

Aidan froze, not certain what he intended. The stone was razor sharp; she had seen evidence of that when he cut the vines at her wrist. Did he intend to kill her if she didn't submit? Was this some sort of threat?

Slowly, almost reverently, the man lifted the stone and placed it over his chest, cutting a three-inch slash in the flesh of his breast. As the blood quickened and began to flow, he smeared his fingertips in the dark liquid, then reached toward her.

Horror snaked down Aidan's backbone and coiled in her belly as the warrior leaned closer. She scrambled backward until her head hit the thatched wall, then dug her fingers into the sandy floor and held her breath as his hand slipped into the collar of her shirt. He paused, found her collarbone, and smeared his blood on her flesh.

Aidan didn't have to know the language to understand the significance of the gesture. Marked with his blood, she now belonged to this behemoth.

Apparently satisfied with this ritual, the native squatted back upon his haunches and began to slice a thick yellow fruit he pulled from a basket. He cut off a section, licked it with a smile, then offered it to Aidan.

She shook her head, pressing her lips together as a cold sweat prickled under her arms. The truth crashed into her consciousness like surf hurling against a rocky cliff. No one was coming for her; no one cared. She was alone with this murdering savage, and for all she knew he himself had killed Heer Van Dyck, the one man in the world who had believed in her.

The native tossed the fruit back into the basket, then rose to his hands and knees and loomed over her, his dark eyes narrowing speculatively.

Closing her eyes, Aidan felt a shiver start from somewhere at the base of her spine, then a sharp and sudden sound brought her eyes wide open.

"You will stop right there, sir, or die."

The native groaned in surprise and reared up, astonishment marking his broad face. Before the man could stand, Sterling brought his foot firmly in contact with the man's solar plexus, sending the brute sprawling back upon the sandy floor. He lay there, gasping for breath as his hand rubbed at his breastbone. Sterling hovered over him, wanting to make certain his adversary would not rise until they could be away.

"Where did you learn that?" Aidan's tone held respect and a trace of grudging admiration.

"Montpellier—the school of medicine," Sterling answered. He pulled a sodden handkerchief from his belt, then stuffed it into the man's mouth. "I knew the blow would work in theory, but had yet to see it actually performed. A wonderful thing to know, really— one blow to the solar plexus will leave a man gasping for the space of several minutes."

Aidan scrambled to her feet. "Shouldn't you hit him again? So he will gasp for more minutes?"

"I'm a doctor; I can't *hurt* him." Kneeling by the struggling man's side, Sterling pinched the man's nostrils and held his mouth shut.

"Won't that kill him?"

"No." After a moment of frenzied effort, the man's eyes fluttered shut, and Sterling immediately released him. "When a person cannot breathe, he falls unconscious before he dies. He will wake soon, and by then we will be gone." He paused for a moment and looked up at Aidan. The hut was lit only by moonlight

that streamed in from a ventilation shaft in the domed roof, but still the sight of her stole his breath away. If they weren't on the run for their lives, he might be tempted to forget more than one vow.

"Hurry," he said, turning from the sight of her as he extended his hand. "We must get away from here before he wakes and rouses the others."

She took his hand, and he pulled her through the narrow passage in which he had hidden, then darted down the long trail to the beach. She followed quietly, undoubtedly grateful to be away from the fate she had nearly suffered, and spoke only when he led her into a sheltered glen not far from the beach.

She fell to the ground, breathless from her ordeal and their headlong rush. "I'm exhausted," she said, her voice breaking. "And I need some water."

"There's no time for that now." Sterling parted the palm fronds that screened them from view and looked out across the silvery beach. Two ships still rode the horizon, two blessed shadows backlit by the moon. But Tasman certainly would not tarry much longer. The savages could mount an attack with the next sunrise, and flaming arrows could do a great deal of damage even to large ships.

"We have to swim out to the *Heemskerk* before dawn," he said, turning to face Aidan.

"Swim?" Even in the dim moonlight he could read the alarm in her eyes. "I can't swim! Even if I could float a wee bit, there's no way I could float all the way to the ship!"

"There's no other way."

"Yes, there is; I've thought it all out." She rose to her knees and eagerly reached for his hand. "We could steal one of their boats and paddle out before sunrise."

Sterling shook his head. "They have lookouts posted on the beach, and I am certain their boats are guarded. I spent all afternoon watching them. They may be ignorant, but they are not

foolish. And in case you haven't noticed, they aren't extremely fond of men. They allowed you to live only because you are a woman."

Her lips thinned with irritation as she pulled her hand from his. "*Live?* You call that living? I would rather have died. If you hadn't come along when you did—"

"Believe me, you would *not* rather be dead," he answered in a clipped, tense voice that forbade any argument. "So you might try being grateful for the fact that you are spared and safe. I watched you for some time. I would not have let anyone hurt you."

He heard her breath quicken, and she looked away. "I am grateful, of course." She glanced around, faltering in her attempt to apologize. "Well then. Suppose we light a fire on the beach. Someone aboard the *Heemskerk* would see it and come to rescue us."

"I hate to tell you this, my dear," Sterling said, "but Captain Tasman has no great need for either of us. He is fond of me, perhaps, as his physician and future son-in-law, but would he risk more men to pull me off this hostile shore? I doubt it. He is already sensitive about an earlier expedition where he lost a goodly number of men; he will not want to risk more." He shrugged. "The fire would attract the natives, as well, and 'tis likely we'd be dead before our companions ever reached us. No. It is a good idea, but our people won't come to us. We have to go to them."

She fell silent for a long moment, her long hair hiding her face, then she pushed her hair aside and looked at him. "So what do you propose to do?"

"I propose," he said slowly, formulating the idea even as he spoke, "to build us a raft—something small, anything that will float. Perhaps we can find a bit of wreckage from the barge. We'll put it in the water, hold to it tightly, and kick our way out to the ships before sunrise. We'll call out and be brought aboard, then the captain will be free to leave these waters with a clear conscience."

"What about the others?" Her voice was troubled now. "Heer Van Dyck, and Visscher, and the chaplain—"

"Four are dead, including the old gentleman." He gentled his tone. "I am truly sorry about the cartographer. I appreciated him very much."

Aidan clamped her jaw tight and stared straight ahead.

Sterling stood and brushed the dirt from his damp breeches. He couldn't do anything about her grief. He could only give his life, if necessary, to see that she got to safety.

He crouched by her side and gave her a careful smile. "Wait here, ketelbinkie, until I return. And trust me to have you home before sunrise."

Twenty-Five

~~~

Frozen into blankness, Aidan struggled to breathe. Her mind froze with the chilling reality. Heer Van Dyck—her teacher, her mentor, her friend—was gone. Orabel was gone. Like her father, who had carried her away from her tidy English existence, they had come into her life and passed out again, leaving her lonely and bereft.

She hugged her knees to her chest and turned her face toward the sea as a sense of loss welled in her chest. What would it have mattered if she had been abandoned in this uncharted wilderness? Her life, too, was nothing but a mist; surely she mattered less to the world than a man like Schuyler Van Dyck.

She closed her eyes as her mind turned to the last night they had shared aboard ship. "Do not fret so," he had told her, watching as she frowned at the oil painting of a sea gull she had been working on all day. Something was missing from the bird's aspect, but she could not discern whether it was the spot of light in his eye, the tilt of his head, or the elevation of his wing.

Finally she had thrown her brush across the cabin, spattering a trail of white paint across Heer Van Dyck's map. Carefully he picked up a rag and wiped it off, his gentle voice snapping through her conscience like a whip. "The strength lies in the strain, Aidan. God does not give us overcoming life overnight; he gives us life as we overcome. You must learn to master the gift within you; do not let it master you."

"I'm *trying*," she cried, dismayed at the whining note in her

voice. "But you make it look so easy. Your pictures are so peaceful, you never have to blot or erase a sketch, you always seem to know what you're doing."

"Ah, my dear, you have found the key." His gentle eyes crinkled when he smiled. "To know what you are doing, you must first know who you are. And it is far easier to sail through a thousand miles of sea and storms than to explore the private realm of one's inner heart. Look inside, my dear, and discover who God meant you to be. When you discover *that*, your work will reflect the truth."

She stared at him, dumbfounded and more confused than ever, but he placed the paintbrush back in her hand and urged her to continue. "This shows great promise," he had said, thrusting his hands behind his back as he studied her poor little painting. "Great promise, indeed. You are very nearly there, Aidan."

Very nearly where? she had wanted to shout. She had come such a long way since beginning her work with Heer Van Dyck; she could paint and sketch and see the world with more clarity than she ever dreamed possible. He had opened her eyes to technique, to creativity, and to the possibility that God had gifted her out of love. But she had not attained the level of maturity he desired for her, and now he was gone.

She was still mourning his loss when Sterling returned, his arms burdened with vines and broken wood. "I could use your help," he said, spilling the materials at her feet. "Time is short, for unless I'm mistaken, Tasman will sail away at first light."

"What's to stop him from leaving us now?" she answered dully. A sourness rose in the pit of her stomach. "It is all for nothing. It is no use. We are doomed to fail."

"Believe *that* and you will never be what Heer Van Dyck intended you to be." The doctor grinned at her as he knotted a length of vine.

"Heer Van Dyck?" She stiffened at the challenge in his voice. "What would you know about his intentions for me?"

"I know that he considered you a great talent," the doctor answered, slipping a noose around the boards at his feet. "He once told me that the world would grieve if you did not succeed. He believed in you enough to risk your life and his honor by bringing you on this expedition."

Mercifully, the moonlit shadows hid her embarrassment. She was neither a talent nor a lady, and now that Heer Van Dyck was dead, she would never be either. He would not finish his map. She would not draw the flora and fauna to adorn it, and no one would ever sponsor her so she could complete her book of engravings.

"Heer Van Dyck was a sentimental fool." The words hurt her throat, as though she'd swallowed some sharp object. "He thought a great many things."

"He thought you a great lady—far above the common realm, I think he said."

Aidan lowered her head as blood began to pound in her temples. Had the old gentleman really said such a thing? Knowing where she had come from, how could he?

But he was faultlessly honest, she remembered. He could not even bring himself to lie when he brought her aboard the *Heemskerk*. Yet if he had told the doctor she was a great lady...

"Why are you telling me this?" she asked suddenly, searching the shadows for the doctor's face.

"Because I want you to live." His voice, soft and vibrant, seemed to fill the hollow where they crouched. "Because I see that you are sorrowing, and sorrow will do you no good now. Mourn if you must, but wait until we are aboard the ship and away from this place. Then you can reveal yourself to the captain and know that you are safe. And you can be the great lady you truly are."

"What?" Startled at the sound of her own cry, Aidan glanced up, half-expecting the forest beyond to erupt with blood-thirsty savages. When none appeared, she lowered her voice and leaned closer to hiss in Sterling's ear. "Why would I want to reveal myself? I have just resisted one savage, why would I want to resist the

advances of a hundred men until we return to Batavia? Are you insane? I cannot think of a more lunatic idea!"

"You won't have to fight off the other men."

"And who will stop them?"

"I will." His voice was a salt-encrusted croak, rusty with weariness, but still a tremor of emotion ran through it. "Marry me, and I will protect you. No man would dare dishonor another man's wife."

Aidan looked up, shocked beyond words at his proposal. But her heart betrayed her—it leaped at his words like a child promised her one desire.

∾∾

Sterling heard her quick intake of breath and silently cursed his own clumsiness. He ought to have prepared her for this. A lady ought to be gently wooed and won, but he had no time for such civilities. Indeed, he could scarcely believe his own brashness, but when confronted with her beauty, her sorrow, and her passion all in the space of an hour, heaven itself could not have stopped the words from his lips.

"Marry you?" Her words were quick and cutting. "Heavens above, how could I? You are promised to another."

"Well, I—" He paused, his mind sputtering as he fumbled with the boards and vines. He could think of no honorable way to dispute *that* objection. In truth, every man aboard both ships knew he was betrothed to Lina Tasman. He could not marry Aidan without incurring the disapproval of his captain and most of his companions—excepting, of course, those who would applaud him for recognizing a bit of delectable female flesh when he saw it.

"Forget my honor," he snapped, furiously lashing the boards together with the raw vine. "Better to let my honor be tarnished than to let yours be violated by the likes of those men aboard yonder ships! Let them think me a worthless cheat and a scoundrel."

"You may be both, for all I know, but what would they think of me?" Every curve of her body spoke defiance; doubtless he had offended her modesty and virtue. "They would say I tempted you, that I came aboard to catch a handsome husband and did not hesitate to take another woman's betrothed. Well, sir, that is not true. And just as I would have fought off that savage, I would fight you, too, if you—"

"Be assured, my lady—" He stopped, forcing himself to calm down. By heaven, why did this girl arouse such strong passions within him? He was only trying to help, to save her from an impossible situation, and yet she looked at him as though he wanted to use her like some cheap hussy.

He reached out and took her arm with gentle authority. "Listen, lady, and hear me well. I am only attempting to keep you from certain disgrace and hardship. You are a lady, and I respect you. You need not fear me."

She looked up, her eyes like green ice, and Sterling suddenly realized that color had begun to bleed back into the air. The heavy darkness had thinned, and as he glanced over his shoulder he could see a definite brightening in the east.

An oddly primitive warning sounded in his brain. The sun would soon rise, even now the seamen were awake and slogging down their morning cups of coffee. In a matter of moments, the ships might bloom with sail.

"We should go now," he said, gesturing abruptly toward the beach. "There is no time to waste." He dropped the boards, then reached for her hand and pulled her to her feet. "This is the plan," he said slowly, his voice urgent and low. "We will walk as quickly as we can into the water. As soon as it is over our heads, you must lean forward upon these boards and kick with all your strength. The planks will float, and the vines will hold them together. But don't look back, don't argue with me, and don't worry."

Her face clouded with uneasiness, but she bent down to grasp one end of the wooden planks, then looked up and nodded.

"Let's go," Sterling said, lifting the other end of the boards. "The sun is rising."

⚜

Aidan pushed herself forward, struggling to match her stride to Sterling's longer steps, the wooden planks heavy and cumbersome in her hands. There were three planks, three thin pieces of wood which would keep her afloat, preserving her life, lifting her to freedom…and who knew what else. For she had not had an opportunity to rebraid her hair. Dressed like this, with her hair curling and her long shirt wet and dirty, few men would look at her and not see a woman.

The sharp shells on the edge of the beach sliced her bare feet, but Sterling's cry urged her forward. They pressed through the breakers, resisting the snarling waves that pushed them back toward the island, and soon the water had risen to Aidan's chest. "Now," Sterling said, spreading the entwined planks upon the water. He turned and spanned her waist with his hands, then lifted her up until she fell forward. The planks formed a raft beneath her, and held firm. In an instant Sterling sprawled by her side, his broad form warming hers, his left hand firmly over her right, holding her tight even as his strong kick propelled them toward the waiting ships.

"Keep kicking, Aidan," he shouted, glancing over his shoulder. "Don't quit!"

Following his glance, she looked toward the shore, then let out a tiny whine of mounting dread. A dozen natives had turned over a canoe and were steering it into the waves while at least two dozen others ran down the beach. Aidan had been so intent upon kicking that she hadn't heard anything above the crash of the water and her own frantic breaths. Now the air filled with warbling war cries. Her heart leaped to her throat, and when she looked back again, she saw the man who had claimed her as his own riding at the front of the advancing canoe. The cut on his chest gleamed red in the early morning sunlight.

"Don't look, kick!" Sterling commanded.

Gulping down her fear, Aidan commanded her legs to work harder than they ever had in her life.

⚬⚬⚬

"Ahoy, *Heemskerk!*" Sterling called, churning the water with his kick. "Man overboard!" His pulse quickened at the steadily increasing whoops of the natives, and through the roaring din he breathed two words: "God, help!" Summoning a deep breath, he called again: "*Heemskerk!* Captain Tasman! Ahoy!"

A score of tanned faces appeared at the ship's railing, then a long arm pointed down toward them. The lookout's voice seemed to rise an octave as he sounded the alarm. "Captain! It's the doctor and the boy! And the savages in full chase, sir!"

Sterling felt Aidan shift beside him and knew she was looking over his shoulder at the approaching enemy. *God, don't bring us this far and fail us now.*

Sterling felt a hot surge of joy when a bundle of netting appeared at the railing and fell, unfurling over the side and smacking the water with a solidly reassuring sound. He guided their makeshift raft toward the rope ladder, then kicked with the last reserves of his energy.

"Here," he said, reaching out for the netting as they drew near. "Aidan, let go of the plank. Take the rope."

She stopped kicking and sagged in relief against the planks as momentum carried them forward. Sterling thrust out his hand, bringing them to a halt half an instant before Aidan's head would have bumped into the ship.

"Come on, ketelbinkie," he said, speaking in as reasonable a tone as he could manage. "Let go of the boards. Here is the rigging, we have only to climb up."

But Aidan's fingers remained splayed over the edges of the first plank. "I—I can't."

"Come, love." Hooking his right arm through the rope ladder, Sterling slipped his left arm around her shoulders, then

tenderly pried her rigid fingers from the board. "We're almost home."

Alerted by the noise, the men of the *Zeehaen* lined her deck, adding to the confusion and noise with shouting and threats of their own. Sterling silently urged Aidan to respond, knowing that soon Tasman might unleash the cannons.

Finger by finger, Aidan relaxed, then allowed him to guide her to the rope ladder. Oblivious to the cries and shouts from the *Zeehaen* and the railing above, Sterling braced his weight on the lower rungs of netting and concentrated on her movements. She had just shifted her weight to the rigging when a strong hand reached out from the murky depths and nearly pulled Sterling from his perch.

Shock jolted through him as he whirled and looked down into the sea. The huge warrior was treading water there, one hand stretched toward the rope webbing, his dark eyes intent upon Aidan. She screamed, but couldn't seem to move.

As Sterling tensed for battle, the warrior touched the wound on his chest, then pointed to Aidan, a proprietary gleam in his eye. No one needed to interpret the unintelligible words spilling from his lips. Clearly he consider the lady his property.

"No, she's not yours!" Sterling swung his body over Aidan's to shield her from the savage. Mimicking the man's gesture, he touched his own chest, then wound his hand in Aidan's hair, tilted her head back and kissed her full on the lips.

An appreciative chorus of *oohs* and *ahhs* rose from the canoe and the Dutch ships alike. Though Sterling couldn't see what was happening behind his back, he knew his actions would leave no room for misunderstanding. Let the world see and know that the woman Aidan O'Connor had his heart, and if any man would fight him for her, Sterling was willing.

A youthful voice broke the silence and echoed across the water. "*Sakerloot!* Captain, come quick! The doctor's kissing the ketelbinkie—and she's a *girl!*"

Aidan did not fully understand everything that transpired in that moment. She only knew that when her life stood in dire jeopardy, Sterling's body wrapped around her like a shield and his lips claimed hers. Suddenly nothing else mattered. She knew she was safe. Protected. And cherished.

She leaned back against the security of his strong frame, feeling the rise of the netting as her weight pulled it away from the ship. Sterling had broken off the kiss, but her face still gravitated toward his, like a flower seeking the sun. Her eyes flew open in time to see Sterling lift his fist and brandish it toward the warrior. A musket thundered from the deck, a warning shot that cracked the prow of the canoe, and the warrior in the water slipped away like a cur when someone throws a stone at it. The other warriors, daunted by the *Heemskerk's* size and the unknown power of the musket, sat motionless in their boats, unwilling to fight.

"Quickly, darling, before he changes his mind," Sterling murmured. In a surge of adrenaline she climbed the rope, cheered on by shouts of applause, astonishment, and approval from her shipmates.

From the deck of the *Zeehaen*, Witt Dekker stared at the drama unfolding aboard the *Heemskerk*...then managed a choking laugh at the thought of his own stupidity. He had been as blind as the others, but now all the pieces fell into place.

Clearly, Dempsey Jasper's missing guttersnipe had given Sweet Kate the golden dress, and in exchange the harlot had provided the trickster with breeches and a sailor's shirt and cap. And the boy's fragile features—where had he seen them before? At the tavern, surely, if the girl and Kate were friends. Something about the ketelbinkie's nose reminded him of Lady Lili, but that coppery hair could belong to no one but Irish Annie.

He rubbed a hand over his mouth, marveling at the simple genius of the girl's plan. Who had envisioned such a masquerade?

And why had she followed the old man on this dangerous voyage? Unless she was more intuitive than Dempsey Jasper believed, she could not know that Van Dyck's son-in-law had put her in danger.

So if the girl wasn't hiding from Dempsey Jasper, she had to be bent on performing her harlot's trade at sea. The supposedly noble and honorable Van Dyck was apparently so enamored of this vixen that he had planned to keep his little hussy by his side throughout the entire expedition!

Witt felt a slow smile of admiration creep across his face. The old man had not looked like a lecher, but the cloak of gentility could cover all sorts of dark and unexpected sins. *This* one would surprise even Dempsey Jasper.

Dekker lifted his spyglass and saw the girl moving through the crowd of men on the upper deck, the doctor at her side. Of course. Now that her rich patron was dead, the flaming-haired harlot had thrown herself into the arms of the next man to cross her path. Sterling Thorne.

"Well, Dr. Thorne," Dekker whispered, lowering the spyglass, "I hope you're prepared to guard your little titmouse. For she will not return to Batavia."

Dekker followed her movements until that coppery head disappeared inside a cabin. He had been hired to kill an old man and a girl called Aidan. Now half his work was already done. He could snuff out the wench's life whenever he chose, and in the meantime, he might find the game...interesting. She was a mouse, alert and skittish, and she had every reason to be. She did not know that the cat had already sighted his quarry.

Dekker smiled as he turned toward his cabin. A sea journey of some months was a long time to pass without a woman's company. At least now he knew where he could find a very pleasing one at a moment's notice.

Twenty-Six

꧁꧂

The ends of Abel Tasman's moustache were bristling with indignation when Sterling and Aidan walked into his cabin. They'd been aboard half an hour, scarcely enough time to change into dry clothes and quench their raging thirsts, but immediately after commanding the ships to make sail and head out on a northeasterly course, the captain convened a meeting of the officers' committee.

Sterling stiffened as he recognized the tribunal-like quality of the assembly before him: Visscher and Holman of the *Heemskerk*, Janszoon and Dekker of the *Zeehaen*. Heer Van Dyck, who often sat in on officers' meetings in his role as cartographer, was unfortunately gone forever, and the old man's beneficent presence would be sorely missed.

This *should* have been a meeting to assess the events of what Tasman had aptly named Assassin's Bay, but the captain's eyes conveyed little but the dark fury within him. Sterling knew Abel Tasman was less concerned with his doctor's safe return than with his daughter's open humiliation.

"Would you care, *Doctor*," Tasman said now, rapping his knuckles firmly on the table before him, "to explain the events of the last twenty-four hours? We sent you ashore with six men, and you have returned with one woman—a wench with whom you actively engage in an indecent public expression of the basest carnality."

"Hold now, Captain," Holman interrupted, his own eyes frank and admiring as he looked at Aidan. "I'd hardly call one kiss an indecent expression of carnality."

"This man—" Tasman's finger shook as he pointed at Sterling. "—is betrothed to my sweet daughter, who waits for him in Batavia."

"I beg your pardon, Captain." Sterling lifted his chin and met Tasman's furious gaze. "If you will allow me to speak freely, I would have you know that your daughter was less than pleased with our betrothal. I found her delightful, perfectly pleasing, but before we sailed, she told me that though she would marry me in order to please you, her heart belonged to another." He lifted one shoulder in a shrug. "I had thought perhaps God might soften her heart toward me during our voyage. But as we left it, sir, she does not hold me in any special regard. She loves someone else—"

"She is a dutiful and obedient girl," Tasman interrupted, a thunderous scowl darkening his brow. "She will wed whomever I choose for her."

"That may be," Sterling answered, turning his gaze to the other gentlemen, "but sirs, the matter of my betrothal has nothing to do with what transpired on yonder island. As you saw, the natives attacked. Fortunately—" He inclined his head toward Visscher. "—this officer was able to swim to safety. But the old gentleman, the rowers, and the chaplain could not swim or were overpowered by the savages. After I escaped, I examined each of their bodies to make certain there was nothing I could do for them."

"But what of this girl?" Dekker posed the question, his eyes gleaming like volcanic rock as his gaze raked Aidan's face and form.

"Why was she spared?" Holman asked.

Sterling lifted his shoulder. "Apparently they did not see a woman as a threat. I believe they saw her—" He turned to Aidan, his eyes caressing her softness. "—as a treasure."

"But how did they know," Holman insisted, "that she was a woman? We have watched over this ketelbinkie for months, and yet we never knew."

"May I remind you, skipper," Sterling paused and delicately cleared his throat, "the young lady wore no doublet or coat, only

303

a shirt. And when the boat sank, she was thoroughly wet." He lifted a brow, not wanting to explain the obvious. From the sudden rise of color in Tasman's face, Sterling knew the facts had been received and correctly interpreted.

"This does not explain how a woman got aboard my ship in the first place," Tasman growled. He looked at Aidan with a cold and piercing eye. "If you are to blame for this, Doctor, you ought to be hung from the yardarm for the entire company to witness your treachery. I expressly forbade any women on this voyage—"

"Captain, the fault was not Dr. Thorne's." Silent until this moment, Aidan's quiet and feminine voice, uncloaked now, broke the stillness. She returned the captain's stare, her eyes sharp and assessing. "If the truth be told, the idea belonged to Heer Van Dyck. He wanted to create a truly memorable map, and so he dared to bring me aboard for the sake of the art." Her eyes filled with tears at the mention of her mentor, but she managed a tremulous smile. "He disobeyed your order, but I'll not allow you to blacken his name. He was a gentleman in every sense of the word, and totally protective of me. He never intended that I should be exposed, or that my presence should cause strife upon your ship."

"Van Dyck was a perfectly capable map-maker," Visscher protested, leaning forward with one hand upon his knee. "Why would he need an unskilled woman's help?"

"I once asked him the same thing." Sterling stopped the pilot with a stern glance. "And he said that the older he grew, the more clearly he realized his shortcomings. In truth, sirs, he assured me that Aidan—" He paused, glancing sharply at Aidan. She had once told him her full name, but she might not want him to share it here.

"O'Connor," she said proudly, drawing herself up to her full height. "My name is Aidan O'Connor."

"Your name might be Mary Queen of Scots, for all I care." Tasman slapped his hand upon the table. He narrowed his eye as

he stared at Sterling. "So you discussed this with the cartographer before yesterday. You obviously knew a woman was aboard my ship."

Sterling's face burned under the accusation. It was too late to backtrack; he had slipped and revealed another secret. Well, truth was better revealed than hidden.

"Yes, sir, I knew." He lightly touched his forehead in a mock salute. "But she kept out of the way, worked only with her master, and distracted no man from his job."

"Not even you?" This quip came from Dekker, who leaned his cheek on his hand, his dark eyes snapping with insolence.

"I did not shirk any of my duties," Sterling answered quietly. He could not say she had never distracted him; indeed, she had occupied his thoughts and dreams for many a day and night.

Tasman shifted his gaze to his officers. "Well, sirs, I have an unattached woman upon my ship, something I have expressly forbidden. Any other contraband would be tossed over the railing. What on earth am I to do with her?"

Dekker opened his mouth and lifted a hand as if he would speak again, but Sterling was quicker.

"Excuse me, Captain," he said, stepping forward and nodding formally, "but if you'll give me a moment alone with the lady, I believe I will be able to provide an answer."

Tasman's nostrils flared with fury as his eyes met Sterling's, but when none of the other officers supplied a suggestion, he lifted his bantam frame from the chair and thrust his hands behind his back. "Ten minutes," he said, moving stiffly toward the door. "We will leave you alone for ten minutes, and then you will provide a satisfactory solution, or I *will* hang you from the yardarm."

"Captain?"

Tasman paused before the door, his back to Sterling. He did not turn his head. "Yes?"

"I am, of course, assuming that you no longer consider me fit to become your son-in-law."

When Tasman answered, his quiet voice held an undertone of deathly cold contempt: "Dr. Thorne, I would sooner burn in the fires of torment than allow you to stand for one moment in my sweet daughter's presence."

Sterling exhaled slowly as the other men filed out. Dekker paused and lifted a questioning brow in Sterling's direction, but Sterling ignored him. He concentrated instead upon Aidan, who had paled and swayed slightly at the captain's stern response.

"He hates you now, you know," she whispered as the door closed. "The captain despises you on my account."

He gave her a lopsided smile. "He will not always hate me. As soon as we have returned and the V.O.C. makes heroes of us, all will be forgiven."

"Still, 'tis dangerous to be disliked by the captain," she continued absently. "I, for one, would not want to be in your shoes."

"I was hoping you would." Sterling reached out and gently grasped her shoulders, turning her to face him. "There are only two possible solutions to this conundrum. I know seamen, and I know how they think. The captain could decide to maroon you on the next friendly island we discover—"

A tremor passed over her face, and a sudden spasm knit her brows. "Surely the next option is more pleasant!"

"I would hope so." He softened his voice and his grasp on her shoulders. "If you would not care to be marooned, perhaps you would prefer becoming my wife. If you live in my cabin, you will be safely out of the sailors' way. The men may be rough and coarse by nature, but they will respect a man's wife…especially if she is a lady."

He closed his eyes, unwilling to face any signs of despair or reluctance in her eyes. "It is the only way, Aidan." His voice echoed with entreaty. "Marry me, and you shall live."

❧❧❧

Caught off guard by the sudden vibrancy of his voice, Aidan stood stock-still. The tiny cabin whirled around her. Marry him? It was

the second time he had proposed such an arrangement, and there was no more love in his voice or words this time than there had been at the first. He could not love her. Until a moment ago he had been unhappily in love with Lina Tasman, the captain's "perfectly delightful daughter" who loved someone else. Sterling wanted to marry Lina; for Aidan he felt only obligation. He had brought her back aboard ship as a result of his sworn oath never to do harm, and so he had decided to do the chivalrous thing and propose marriage.

Marry him? Oh, how she would love to, if she could have his heart as well as his protection. She had never met a man like Sterling Thorne, one who was brave and passionate and strong and capable, but he did not even know what she truly was. He imagined her some exalted and extraordinary lady; how would he react if—when—he learned she was nothing but a Batavian barmaid?

He could not love her. He had only kissed her in order to save her from that determined savage. If Lina Tasman had been hanging on that rigging, he would have bestowed that kiss with true fervency. He had acted bravely, but acts of desperation could not be a solid foundation for a marriage.

"Aidan?" She looked up, and found his eyes searching her face. His voice was soft with disbelief and hurt; he had interpreted her silence as refusal. "Would you truly rather be marooned or harassed rather than live with me?"

"No." She lifted her hand and placed it gently upon his chest. "I will marry you, Doctor, but in name only." She steeled herself against the thought of his seeking out Lina Tasman again, but he seemed confident that he could convince Abel Tasman to forgive all this. "When we return to Batavia you may have the marriage annulled. You will be free to go—I will *want* you to go where you like and do what you will."

⌒⌒⌒

Her words, once she got them out, struck Sterling's heart like the sharp and sudden blow of a thrown dagger. She cared nothing for

him—that much was evident in the patronizing way she now patted his chest, like a great lady showing affection for a beloved servant or pet. She appreciated his gallantry, his courage, and perhaps even his devotion, but as soon as he was no longer needed, he would be free to go. Her voice had emphasized the word—she *wanted* him to go.

Sterling dropped his hands from her shoulders and stepped back, feeling a rush of heat burn the back of his neck. She was a descendant of Irish kings, fine and well-bred, but there had been fire in her kiss and passion in her heart when her lips lifted to meet his. Perhaps she was not completely out of reach. If he was any kind of man, he could make her care.

"So you will wed me in name only." His voice sounded thick and unnatural in his own ears. "But you will have to share my cabin. For your own safety—there is no other way I can protect you."

Her long lashes shuttered her eyes as she looked down. "I know."

He cleared his throat, pretending not to be affected by her words. "I will find the captain and make the arrangements," he said, his heart thumping erratically in his chest. "You'd best fetch your things from the cabin you shared with Heer Van Dyck. Francois Visscher will no doubt appreciate being rid of your paints and papers."

"I'll go now." She turned and opened the door, and Sterling caught it behind her, watching her slim form move through the doorway and across the deck. A score of entranced men stopped their work to watch her walk, a slender vixen in a flowing shirt and baggy breeches, a tide of red curls tumbling down over her back.

Sterling shook his head and stepped out of the cabin. He had to find Tasman and make one final arrangement before a wedding could take place.

❧

Sterling found the captain standing at the taffrail with Francois Visscher. Gerrit Janszoon and Witt Dekker had just climbed into

the barge that would row them back to the *Zeehaen,* and Dekker's brow lifted in another unspoken question when Sterling appeared at the railing.

Ignoring the men in the barge, Sterling waited until the rowers moved the boat out of hearing distance before he addressed the captain.

"Captain Tasman?"

Tasman turned, his brilliant brown eyes fixed upon Sterling. "You have an answer for my predicament, Doctor?"

"Yes. The young lady has agreed to become my wife." Sterling forced a smile, for surely a bridegroom ought to appear happy. "We would be pleased if you would perform the ceremony at once."

"Indeed I shall." Tasman's brow wrinkled with contemptuous thoughts, even as his lips curled in a knowing smile. "Better late than never, eh, Doctor? Perhaps I should be grateful that you will not wed my daughter—"

Frowning, Sterling interrupted. "I will have you know, sir, that I have not behaved improperly toward the lady, and her own conduct has been quite above reproach." He paused. "I *was* betrothed to your daughter."

"That did not stop you from kissing the wench before every man on these two ships." Tasman spoke softly, but the venom was clear. "Did you take one moment to think of my daughter, sir, when you drew that false ketelbinkie into your arms? My daughter will undoubtedly meet these ships at the port. She will be there, dressed in her finest gown, awaiting your return, and you will step forward with another woman upon your arm!"

Sterling flinched but did not retreat. "I assure you, sir, that I never meant to hurt Lina. I would do anything to spare her pain, but at the time I could think of no other way to save the map-maker's ward. Even now I can think of only one way to keep her from becoming a hindrance upon your ship, so I am prepared to take her as my wife and my responsibility."

"There is another way." Tasman tilted his head slightly, then jerked his chin toward the retreating barge. "Another officer has considered my daughter's feelings and honor. In an effort to spare Lina from the shame of a broken betrothal, Witt Dekker has volunteered to marry the map-maker's wench."

Sterling felt an icy finger touch his spine.

"That," he spoke slowly, searching for words, "would not be a good idea."

"Why not?" The angry color was fading from Tasman's face, but his eyes were still narrow and bright with fury. "Does the woman mean so much to you?"

Disconcerted, Sterling crossed his arms and pointedly looked away. "We are a good match, I think. She is English, as am I. We have endured a recent trial together. She has agreed to marry me, not Dekker. She does not know that officer, and I cannot believe she would want to marry him."

Tasman did not reply, but slowly pursed his lips in a thoughtful expression. Standing erect, he thrust his hands behind his back and stepped so close that his breath brushed the hair falling upon Sterling's shoulder. "At least be honest with me, sir." His eyes snapped with malice. "If you want the cartographer's assistant instead of my daughter, you shall have the woman you choose. But know this—if she causes one moment's trouble aboard either of my ships, I shall set you both ashore at the first possible opportunity. Do you understand?"

Sterling found a perverse pleasure in the captain's challenge, and he smiled. "I will marry her now, sir. And you need not worry about anything. She is a lady and quite capable of handling herself."

Tasman nodded abruptly. "Bring her to my cabin with a witness," he called over his shoulder. "I shall take care of this irregularity immediately."

❧

Sterling paused a moment after rapping on the door, then closed his eyes in relief when a voice bade him enter.

He stooped to enter the small cabin, then relaxed when he saw T'jercksen Holman at his desk, a quill in his hand. The skipper lifted a brow as Sterling entered.

"Come in search of other adventures, Doctor?" Holman asked, a trace of amusement in his voice. "I'm afraid you'll find nothing here. I am a family man, I have simple tastes. There's not a single woman to be found hiding among my trunks."

"I do not seek adventures, sir; I've had my fill of those today." Sterling clasped his hands at his waist, feeling at once foolish and presumptuous.

Holman shifted in his chair, then folded his hands. "Then why are you here?"

Sterling drew a deep breath. "The captain has agreed to marry me to the lady. We are to be wed at once, in the captain's cabin. I am to bring a witness, and I thought of you."

Holman smiled, a quick curve of thin, dry lips. "I am honored." He reached for his hat. "And I would not want to keep an anxious bridegroom waiting."

"There is one more thing." Sterling bit his lip as Holman froze at his desk. "My bride, sir—the lady has nothing to wear but the boy's clothes she brought aboard. And since she will henceforth be living among us as a woman, I thought it only right that she have a woman's gown, particularly for the wedding."

Holman gave a brief croaking chuckle. "Do you not find her attractive in breeches?"

"Of course, sir." Sterling looked down at his hands and grinned. "But so does every other man aboard." His smile faded. "And I know that you bought silk gowns for your wife and daughter while we were anchored at Mauritius."

Holman frowned, his eyes level under drawn brows. "Why should I deprive my family in order to please a red-haired wench who has the bad sense to turn up where she ought not be?"

Sterling looked the skipper directly in the eye. "I would not deprive your family, sir, but I believe you would seek the best for

your bride, were your wife in Aidan's place and you in mine. You are an honorable man and a gentle soul; you would not suffer a woman to be wed in a man's clothes when she could be outfitted like the gentle lady she is." He drew a deep breath. "I would be happy to reimburse you for the expense once we reach Batavia— as soon as I receive my wages."

"You certainly shall, for there is a limit to my generosity," Holman answered, standing. He moved to his bunk, then knelt and pulled out the trunk that rested beneath his bed. He lifted the lid, then shifted several dark-colored doublets and breeches until he uncovered two bright piles of silk, one green, one brown. "My wife and daughter will not be deprived, no matter how fervently I wish you well," he said, slowly pulling the fragile fabrics from his trunk. "When we return to Batavia, you will pay me three hundred guilders."

"Three hundred!" Sterling protested, his mind reeling. He remembered inquiring on his mother's behalf in a dressmaker's shop in Batavia. The most ornate ball gown in the shop sold for ninety-five guilders. Three hundred was outright robbery, but Sterling had no other choice. Van Dyck had said that Aidan was an heiress, and a lady of quality could not be married in men's rags—even if she was marrying a virtual pauper.

"Three hundred guilders…each," Holman answered, standing. He thrust the bundles of silk into Sterling's arms, then gave him a broad smile. "Now—shall we attend your wedding?"

⟢⟡⟣

Aidan paused beside the table in Van Dyck's cabin and ran her hand over the unfinished map. "Farewell, master," she whispered, feeling the fine quality of the vellum beneath her palm. Her eyes filled with moisture, and her voice went suddenly husky. "I shall miss you very much."

She had already tossed her paints, pens, pencils, and brushes into a crate, but she could not bring herself to touch her master's map. It was a mocking shadow of all he had dreamed for himself

and for her, hopes that now seemed lifeless and void. Six years before, she had gone to sea and found herself acting out of survival instincts. Now, as then, she would have to abandon her dreams of a new life. And now, as then, she found herself paired with someone who might bring about her downfall. Lili had led Aidan into the seedy wharf district of Batavia, and Sterling Thorne could lead her into an emotional dominion more treacherous than any Batavian alley.

The door creaked in protest as someone pulled it open. Aidan shrank back in reflex as Francois Visscher entered the room, his arms filled with two gleaming bundles of fabric. "These," he said, tossing his burdens on her narrow bunk, "are for you, a gift from the doctor. And this—" He gestured at the art supplies still scattered around the cabin. "—must be gone at once. I tolerated the old gentleman because Tasman told me I had to. But you I will not accept." He finished with a flourish, thrusting his hands to his wide hips, his face settling in a marble effigy of contempt.

"I am sorry, sir," Aidan said, cautiously moving about to gather the remaining canvases that littered the cabin. "I will clean up and be gone in a moment. If you will excuse me—"

"A wench," he interrupted, forcing the words through clenched teeth. "A useless woman! The old man must have been senile! What did he see in you, the dreams of his lost youth or his lost art? I would not have slept in this room a single night if I had known what you were. Shame on you, girl, you should have known better! What did you hope to gain by playing on his sympathies, his money or his favor? You are a disgrace to all women, a blot upon the face of seagoing men."

Against her will, rage rose in Aidan's soul. This man had insulted her master and his art, and she had never met a finer, more eminently Christian man than Heer Van Dyck.

"I am not a disgrace." She dropped a sheaf of papers into the crate and stepped forward, not willing to let herself be put down by this brute. She lifted her chin and met his angry gaze head-on.

"Heer Van Dyck said I am an artist…and one day you will know that I am."

Flushing to the roots of his hair, Visscher stepped back. "I don't care what you are," he said, his voice taut with anger, "but when I return, you had best be gone from this cabin. And take all that foolishness with you."

"Get out and your wish will be granted." Aidan jerked her head toward the door.

She was surprised when he obeyed, and in the resulting glow of pleasure she gathered up the rest of the art supplies, found her missing box of paints, and stuffed her discarded wet clothes into the crate. She paused at the table with Van Dyck's map, then hastily rolled it up into a tube. She wasn't worthy to complete it, but she would not leave it here for Visscher and his ilk to deface with their messy renderings.

She was on her way out the door with the crate when she noticed the two bundles Visscher had dropped onto the bunk. For her, he had said, from the doctor. A gift.

She lowered her crate to the bunk, then picked up the green silk. A sweet floral fragrance clung to the fabric, and fine twine, like that from a dressmaker's shop, held it together. Curious, Aidan slipped the loop free and gasped in amazement as she unfolded an elegant shirt, underbodice, sleeves, and skirt.

These were the components of a fine lady's gown! Where in the world had Sterling procured them? She ran her fingers over the rich emerald silk of the skirt, bodice, and sleeves, and smiled as a wave of nostalgia swept over her. She had dreamed of wearing a dress like this…but her dreams had never included a husband generous enough to provide it.

A wedding gift. The man never ceased to surprise her.

Aidan held the skirt up to her waist, and sighed in pleasure as the soft fabric rubbed against the rough texture of her man's shirt.

Was there anything Sterling Thorne could not do?

Twenty-Seven

~~~~~

Sterling jiggled his leg nervously as he and Holman waited for Aidan in Tasman's cabin. The captain sat behind his desk, his brows drawn downward in a frown, his pen driving furiously across the page of his log as he pretended to ignore the men waiting in his cabin.

Silence filled the air like a heavy mist. In an effort to avoid Holman's gaze, Sterling shifted his eyes to the wide windows over the stern. Through the open space he could see the *Zeehaen* following in the *Heemskerk's* wake, the smaller vessel rising rhythmically on each strong swell of the sea.

He frowned at the thought of Witt Dekker aboard that ship. The man had offered to marry Aidan himself, and Sterling knew Dekker well enough to know that he did not value the young woman's talent, her soul, or her heart. Most likely he saw her as a means to curry Captain Tasman's favor or a pretty prize to enjoy in the privacy of his cabin.

A soft knocking sound came from the door, and Holman stepped forward to open it. Aidan stood in the open doorway, but Sterling blinked in surprise, for this lady and the ketelbinkie were as different as lace and oilcloth. She wore one of the dresses he had purchased from Holman, and no apparel had ever suited a woman more perfectly. The dark green silk accented her emerald eyes, and her skin, bronzed from the sun, glowed against the dark fabric.

Sterling quickly averted his eyes as Aidan entered. Any sign of obvious attraction to his bride might prove perilous. Apparently

she intended to cast him away as soon as they reached Batavia, and Tasman still resented the fact that Sterling could not ignore the vibrant creature who had been thrust into his arms.

Holman cleared his throat and squared his shoulders. "In the absence of the chaplain, Captain Tasman has asked me to perform the ceremony," he said. Holman pointedly ignored the fact that ages-old tradition gave the *captain* the honor of performing marriages at sea.

Sterling's eyes drifted to Tasman, who scowled darkly. This was one wedding that clearly would not be approved by the ship's captain.

"Being the skipper of the ship, I have the authority." Holman turned and lifted a brow toward Aidan. "I trust you do not object, my dear?"

Sterling thought he would burst with impatience as Holman observed useless civilities. Tasman's frown seemed to grow deeper and more ominous by the moment. "It matters not, just commence," Sterling said, locking his hands before him.

Holman shrugged and pulled his prayer book from his doublet. He opened to a marked page, then lifted his gaze and stared pointedly at Sterling. "I believe, Doctor, that it is customary to hold your bride's hand, not your own."

"Oh." Flustered, Sterling reached out for Aidan's hand. As Holman began reading the prayer that opened the wedding ritual, Sterling could not help but notice how small and delicate Aidan's hand was. Were these the fingers that would astound the world with their skill? They hardly seemed strong enough to wield a paintbrush, let alone open doors and carve out a name for immortality.

"We Dutch believe," Holman was saying now, his eyes drifting from the prayer book to Aidan's flushed face, "that together with the procreation of children and the avoidance of fornication, there is a third reason for the institution of marriage—companionship. God specifically made woman to be a helpmate for man. Just as a

head cannot survive without a body, a groom cannot survive without a bride. Like Ruth and Boaz, you should cleave to each other and never be separated. Marriage is companionship in care and in joy, in bustle and in rest, in loss and in gain, in recreation and in work, in risk and in fortune."

Sterling stole a quick glance at his bride. He wondered if Holman guessed she had insisted upon a marriage in name only. Would he urge them to cleave to each other if he knew Aidan planned to annul this action as soon as the voyage ended? Perhaps the skipper was speaking from his knowledge of the obvious facts. They scarcely knew each other; therefore he urged them to become friends and companions.

"At the core of your marriage should be affection, tenderhearted sentiment, and love," Holman droned on. Like little chips of quartz, his eyes glittered shrewdly above the prayer book. *He is doing this on purpose,* Sterling thought. *Deliberately making me squirm. He's enjoying it!*

"A man and his wife must be tied to one another through a very dear and affectionate marriage-love. Through the kindling of affection in all friendship and dearness, you should warm each other's hearts with conjugal feeling and love."

"Yes, yes, get on with it," Sterling interrupted, feeling Tasman's burning gaze upon the back of his neck. "We promise to be friendly companions."

"But, my friend, there is much more to a happy marriage." Holman lowered the book, and Sterling sighed in frustration. Holman was a man of the sea, but his first allegiance fell to hearth and home. The officer could talk about his family for hours. And now he had a captive audience to listen to his sermonizing about the joys and responsibilities of married life.

"Hearts as well as souls and bodies must be united in the union of marriage, for fidelity in affection ensures purity in the married home. The true test of your love is that you take pleasure in no one's company more than that of your spouse."

"That is very wise, sir," Aidan spoke up. A rosy flush spread over her cheeks—a blush that Sterling, in spite of himself, found utterly charming. "But I am sure the captain would prefer that we be married quickly as well as thoroughly."

"Er...yes." Holman glanced over Sterling's shoulder, nodded to acknowledge Tasman, then lifted the prayer book again. "Will you, Sterling Thorne, have this woman to be your wedded wife, to live together after God's ordinance in the holy estate of matrimony? Will you love her, comfort her, honor and keep her in sickness and in health, and, forsaking all others, keep you only unto her so long as you both shall live?"

Sterling ripped out the words impatiently. "I will!"

Holman then turned toward Aidan. "Will you, Aidan O'Connor, have this man to be your wedded husband, to live together after God's ordinance in the holy estate of matrimony? Will you obey him, and serve him, love, honor, and keep him in sickness and in health, and, forsaking all others, keep you only unto him so long as you both shall live?"

"Yes." Aidan's answer was so soft Sterling strained to hear it.

"Then—" Holman paused, running his finger down the pages of the prayer book. "Hmm," he muttered, "there's no one to give the bride away, no ring, no chaplain to pray—oh!" He brightened and smiled. "Here we are. Let us pray."

Sterling bowed his head, but peered through his lashes at his bride. Her light breathing fluttered a wayward curl at her cheek, and for a dizzying moment he wondered how it would feel to lose himself in that fiery riot, to hold her in love and not in panic, to know that she came to his arms willingly and not out of necessity.

"Send thy blessing upon these thy servants," Holman intoned, still reading from his prayer book, "this man and this woman, whom we bless in thy name; that, as Isaac and Rebecca lived faithfully together, so these persons may surely perform and keep the vow and covenant betwixt them made, and may ever remain in

perfect love and peace together, and live according to thy laws; through Jesus Christ our Lord. Amen."

A strange glint of wonder flashed in Holman's eyes as he closed his prayer book and smiled at Sterling. "You may now salute your bride, Doctor."

Sterling turned, drawn more by the force of the skipper's suggestion than by any desire to kiss Aidan in the face of Tasman's burning disapproval, but she quickly stepped toward the door. "I'm certain the captain has important things to do," she said, fumbling awkwardly with her skirt as it snagged on a corner of a trunk. Sterling bent to help her free it and caught a glimpse of a shapely ankle—an ankle he'd seen a hundred times when she wore a boy's breeches. Yet the sight had never stirred him as it did at this moment. Some intense attraction flared through his being, and he kept his eyes lowered lest she see what he was feeling.

"I shall retire to my—to the doctor's cabin," Aidan finished, moving through the doorway. "Perhaps I may be of service there."

Holman bowed slightly and gave her a rare smile. "You have made a lovely bride, Mejoffer."

Sterling puzzled over the word until he realized that the skipper had just referred to her using the Dutch address for a married woman. He flinched, abruptly realizing that the skipper spoke of *his* wife.

"I'd better go see if she needs help," he said to no one in particular. He smiled his thanks at Holman, then nodded carefully at Tasman before moving toward the door.

"She will need it," Tasman called from behind his desk. "There is a most violently ill fellow waiting in your cabin. I myself sent him to see you not half an hour ago and gave him leave to spend the night in your care."

⌘

Aidan had made up her mind to be as pleasant as possible, but her nose curled in disgust when she entered the tiny cabin that served as the doctor's home and hospital. Here the air was thick with the

earthy odors of the human body: stale sweat, grimed skin, the tang of urine and the sickly sweet scent of vomit. A flour-faced seaman, his shirt splotched with rum and spewed food, lay upon the low bunk beneath the porthole. Visscher had tossed the crate with her belongings upon the other bunk, which was still strewn with blankets and the doctor's discarded wet clothing.

Straightening in the cramped space, Aidan braced herself against a beam in the sloping ceiling. The seaman on the cot opened one eye, then grinned appreciatively. "I'd heard there was a woman on board," he said, displaying an astounding assortment of blackened and yellow teeth, "but I never thought she'd be visiting me."

"The doctor will be visiting you," Aidan replied, heaving the crate aside in order to find a place to sit. A moment later the door opened again and Sterling entered, his eyes moving first to her, then to the drunk. As she expected, the drunk won his attention. "Hobart, isn't it?" he asked, crossing the cabin in three long strides. "Haven't I warned you not to drink your entire ration at one time?"

With nowhere else to sit, Sterling knelt on the floor and pressed his fingers to the man's neck. "Your blood is moving steadily," he announced. As the drunk shook his head in denial, Sterling lifted the flesh above and below the man's bloodshot eyes, then began to rummage in a small case stashed under the bunk.

Aidan leaned back upon the cluttered cot, fascinated in spite of herself. She might as well have left the room; Sterling seemed entirely concentrated on his patient. He treated the drunk with a wise mix of patience and firmness, for a sailor who drank his entire ration of rum in one hour did not exactly deserve sympathy.

"Hmm," Sterling murmured, prodding the man's swollen stomach. "Is this tender?"

"*Ja, ja!*" the sailor groaned, clutching his gut. "And that's not all that hurts. I've pains in my loins, stomach, and bowels, sir, and ofttimes my arms and legs swell up like a dead fish."

"How are your teeth?" Sterling asked, ignoring the obvious.

"Looser than wet string," the patient complained. He squinted one eye suspiciously as Sterling rummaged in his bag, then gasped as Sterling pulled out a sharp knife. "*Sakerloot,* Doctor, you aren't going to cut me!"

"Not tonight," Sterling answered, calmly pulling a shriveled lemon from the same bag. He cut several slivers from the rind, mixed them in a mug with water, then gave it to the bedridden sailor. "Drink it. You're suffering from a touch of the scurvy, my friend, and it's because you've been avoiding the peas and fruit. You must eat what's set before you, or these pains will get worse."

Trembling in fear, sickness, and something else—a touch of reverence, Aidan supposed—the wizened sailor rose up on one elbow to guzzle down the concoction Sterling offered. She tilted her head, watching. There was something remarkable in the image of Sterling on his knees, lifting a cup to the older, weaker man. Scarcely aware of what she was doing, she fumbled in her crate and found a sketch board, parchment, and a pencil.

And while Sterling tended his malodorous patient and listened to his myriad complaints, Aidan sketched her husband.

The shades of night had begun to fall by the time the old sailor gave up his struggle and fell asleep. Sterling carefully replaced his medical implements in his bag, almost afraid to glance toward the bunk where his bride lay sleeping. Unwilling to discuss their peculiar situation and tend to a very loud, very smelly patient at the same time, he had largely ignored her all afternoon. But he had heard every sigh, every crackle of her paper, every scratch of her pencil as she sketched. She had fallen asleep right before the old man, for he heard her soft, regular breathing even above the pull of the sea and the angry flap of canvas in the wind.

Content to know the old sailor would sleep peacefully through the night, Sterling lowered himself to the floor and braced his back against the sloping wall. Aidan lay curled up on his bunk, her

legs folded under the shimmering silken skirt, her hands pressed together and tucked beneath her chin. Her hair swirled like a molten river across his pillow, and copper ringlets curled on her forehead and on the exposed flesh of her throat. The soft pink light of sunset shimmered over her delicate face like beams of golden radiance, and soft color lined the sweetly curled lips that had voiced a promise to be his wife.

By heaven, she is beautiful.

He didn't know how long he sat there, but the sound of movement outside brought him out of his reverie. A whistle blew, signaling the change of the watch, and Sterling knew if he didn't get some sleep, he'd be fit for nothing on the morrow.

He stretched out his legs, then bent one knee and rested his arm upon it, his mouth twisting in a wry smile. If Tasman had seen fit to invite this patient to lodge himself in the doctor's cabin on Sterling's wedding night, it was a certain bet that a steady stream of patients would find themselves assigned to sick bay in the days to come.

Sterling exhaled heavily, then pushed himself up off the floor. He stepped out of his boots to muffle his steps, then lifted Aidan's heavy crate from the end of his bunk. It would fit nicely beneath his own bed, once he cleared out a space for it. Tugging gently, so he wouldn't disturb her, he removed his damp clothes from the bed, then found a dry blanket in his own trunk.

He moved to the head of the bunk, about to drape the blanket over Aidan's shoulders, but saw her sketch board by her side. He picked it up, then lifted it to the fading beam of sunlight that shot through the porthole.

What he saw astonished him.

She had drawn him and the old sailor. The likeness was apparent enough, but Sterling knew in a heartbeat that he could never be the man she had depicted. He recognized his own body, his frame, his hands. But a radiance glowed about this doctor's face. The eyes brimmed with compassion, as if the Blessed Lord himself

were offering a cup of water to a sick and enfeebled prisoner. The seaman was clearly recognizable—she had caught his teeth, the crepey age lines around his eyes, and the wispy long braid his vanity would not allow him to cut.

"By heaven above," he whispered, sinking to the foot of the bed, the picture in his hands. He felt shocked by a sudden elusive thought he could not quite fathom, then awareness hit him like a punch in the stomach. Van Dyck was right. She was extraordinary, more exceptional than Sterling had dreamed.

What had the old gentleman said? *Her life will color the world.* Sterling held the picture in his hand, staring at it until the last trace of light vanished. Then he quietly stood and covered his bride with the blanket, bracing his shoulders to accept the responsibility of the rare treasure God had placed into his care.

Standing at the bow of the *Zeehaen,* Witt Dekker stared at the *Heemskerk* and watched darkness overtake the larger ship. No light shone in either of the forecastle cabins, so the doctor was either asleep, out of his chamber attending to some emergency, or enjoying his first night as a husband.

Witt closed his fist deliberately around the golden cross at his neck. He had tried to get the girl. The captain would have given her to Dekker in a heartbeat, but by some stroke of luck or cunning, Sterling Thorne had won the prize. And in those first few minutes aboard the flagship, Dekker discovered that the dangerous night had worked some magic in the valiant doctor's soul, for he was obviously smitten with the wench. A man did not give up a captain's daughter for a tavern maid unless he knew the hussy was rich…or was so infatuated he couldn't think clearly.

For now, Aidan O'Connor was married to the doctor and safely tucked away aboard the *Heemskerk.* Still, they would cover many miles before returning to Batavia. Van Dyck was dead, which meant the girl was an heiress already—but only if she lived to claim her inheritance.

As officers, Dekker and Janszoon often visited the *Heemskerk*. It would be an easy matter to call upon the doctor one dark night and find that he had been summoned away by one of the other officers. With one careless slip, the lady could find herself overboard while the ships plowed through the sea. It was virtually impossible to find a lost soul in the heavy darkness of black waters.

Dekker smiled. Tasman might even be relieved to find the hussy gone. He'd been mad as a viper ever since he discovered he'd been tricked by that fool Schuyler Van Dyck.

Humming contentedly, Dekker thrust his hands behind his back and watched the full moon rise across an inky sky.

Twenty-Eight

On the fourth of January, 1643, Tasman's expedition reached the extreme tip of the island north of Assassin's Bay. Tasman called the point Cape Maria Van Diemen, then convened a meeting of his officers. Their exploration of the rocky coastline had been conducted in a hasty and superficial manner, due in part to the hostile reception at Assassin's Bay and the captain's urgent need to re-provision his ships with fresh water and fruit. Janszoon and Dekker hoped to send another landing party ashore in search of gold and other riches, but after the unpleasantness of Assassin's Bay, Tasman was eager to leave that particular land formation behind.

As ship's doctor, Sterling had been invited to attend the officers' meeting, and he shared Tasman's plans with Aidan before venturing down to the hold to tend a man with bloody flux. Thankful that at least *that* sailor had not attempted to move into their cabin, Aidan leaned against the open door and watched her husband move confidently down the companionway.

Sighing, Aidan closed the door behind her, then sat on the bunk. Tasman's plan to move ahead suited her, for nothing in her training or her dreams had prepared her for the strange life she now led. Wearing women's garb—either the green silk, the brown silk, or a combination of both—she tried to be a dutiful doctor's wife, though she had no idea how to play that particular role. She was kind to the patients who regularly appeared in their cabin, and she stayed out of Sterling's way as he applied various treatments. But mainly she painted. Watching the sea through the

porthole, she painted waves and stars and celestial beings riding the winds and swells so high they looked like rolling hills.

Occasionally she painted the sunburned faces of the seamen who came to the cabin requesting Sterling's attention. Most of these "illnesses" were innocent enough—a stomachache that disappeared after a few soft words from Aidan, or a splinter which she promptly pulled out with a sewing needle. She suspected that the long weeks at sea had made even the most independent sailors hungry for the sight of a woman.

She handled the seamen easily, for they were not unlike the thirsty, attention-starved men who loitered at Bram's tavern on hot, humid afternoons. She had been terrified that one of them might note her resemblance to Irish Annie from the Broad Street Tavern, but if any did, no man dared mention it. None dared behave improperly in her presence, for Sterling had earned a reputation for strength and courage at Assassin's Bay.

Yes, she could handle the seamen. But she had no idea how to handle the man with whom she now shared her life. They had been married for over two weeks, and Sterling had not once reached out to touch her. He spoke cordially to her, treated her with respect and deference, and slept either in the second bunk or, if a patient slept in the cabin with them, on the floor. But he did not look at her with the same intensity that had marked his face back at Assassin's Bay.

Aidan smiled ruefully. Perhaps it was her fault, after all. If she had not been insistent upon a marriage in name only, and if Tasman did not send a steady stream of sick sailors for the doctor's personal attention, then perhaps he would seek her softness just as the other seamen did.

No.

She deliberately closed the door on those fantasies, forcing herself to remember her plans. Her future, if she wanted to paint, depended upon a clean escape from this sham of a marriage. She was almost surprised to realize that painting was a part of her now;

she could no more leave it behind than she could decide not to breathe. In the days after Van Dyck's death she had little to do but paint and think, and she had discovered that her paintbrush expressed her thoughts far more eloquently than her tongue. She painted the vast loneliness of the sea, the misty-eyed yearning of a seaman for his sweet wife at home, the ponderous wonder of a whale brushing the boards of a ship as he idly scratched his back on his jaunt through the deep.

She pushed aside the usual artistic conventions Van Dyck had explained—how great Dutch artists represented time with a clock, diligence with a distaff, the brevity of life with a candlesnuffer or skull—and she painted what her heart dictated, not caring what anyone else might think. No one would see these practice paintings, in any case.

Yes, she told herself, she would paint. She would become the artist Van Dyck had wanted her to be. She had lost her mentor, but surely she would discover another, and then she would find respectability among the clean and tidy houses west of Batavia's Market Street. Later, after she had established herself and published her first book of engravings, she would marry a respectable gentleman and rear a half-dozen respectable children. She only wished it could be as Mejoffer Thorne.

But Sterling Thorne did not want an artist-wife; he wanted the sea captain's daughter. This marriage would have to be annulled—a process easily enough accomplished as long as the relationship had not been consummated. A host of seamen aboard the *Heemskerk* could testify that the doctor had never treated her as a true wife.

Why should he? He loved Lina Tasman, and as soon as they returned to Batavia, he would fly away to resume his courtship of the captain's virtuous daughter. Without disgrace or shame, he would swear to a magistrate that he had married Aidan O'Connor only to preserve her honor, and the good people of Batavia would applaud his nobility and courage.

"He may be courageous and noble," Aidan murmured to herself, "but the man is also a slob, even worse than Lili." She picked up a discarded stocking he had casually tossed on the floor and, without thinking, fingered the soft wool. Then she came to her senses, tossed it into his trunk, and slammed the lid.

She had no intention of permitting herself to fall under the spell of a handsome man, and she could not afford to be distracted from her dreams by silly romantic notions. She was meant to be an artist, not a doctor's wife. As long as he did not reach for her—or she for him—her future was safe and secure.

Two weeks after the expedition left Cape Van Diemen without further exploration, the lookout sighted land like "a woman's two breasts" in the distance. The *Heemskerk* and the *Zeehaen* cautiously approached the shoreline, the memory of Assassin's Bay haunting every sailor. The natives who spilled from the forests behind these shores, however, wore broad smiles of goodwill and joviality. Before agreeing to send a landing party ashore, Tasman ordered his ships to wait at anchor for two days to make certain the natives held no hostile intentions. By the second day he could scarcely restrain his men from jumping overboard and attempting to swim ashore. Tempted by the aromas of roasting meat and the sight of smiling women, his men lined the railing and stared at the shore with eyes wide with longing.

Obviously fascinated by the huge winged ships that anchored in their waters, the natives of these islands prepared a feast on the shore. From the deck Aidan could see smiling faces, meat roasting on an open fire, and bright blossoms adorning the necks of women, men, and children alike. The sight of the scantily clad, raven-haired women was enough to drive the sailors into a near frenzy, and at last Tasman relented and gave the order for a shore party to disembark.

The natives met this shore party with celebration and open friendliness. They freely offered water, food, and hospitality, the

openness of which scandalized the prudish Dutch. As she waited on deck for the barge that would take her and Sterling ashore, Aidan overheard one of the rowers talking about the native women. "They demonstrate not the slightest hesitation in removing all their clothing," he said in amazement. "And the most audacious among them actually *touched* our sailors, inviting them to—"

Aidan moved out of earshot to spare both herself and the talkative sailor from complete embarrassment. Sterling had gone back to the cabin to compose a list of useful herbs and supplies he might find on the island, and when he finally arrived, they boarded the last barge and pushed off for shore.

Her heart thrilled when the barge touched the sandy bottom of the bay and Sterling lifted her out of the boat. Aidan was wearing her breeches instead of a cumbersome silk skirt, and a group of native women immediately splashed toward her through the shallow tidewater, giggling as they reached out to touch her red hair, her face, her fluttering shirt.

"I'm very glad you wore trousers, my dear," Sterling said as he lowered her to the sand. He took her hand, protectively leading her away from the horde of curious women. "I'm afraid they would have dived under your skirt in search of your legs if they were not readily apparent."

The welcoming committee followed them up the beach. Apparently satisfied that Aidan was female, the sociable women next turned their attention to Sterling. Aidan stood, mystified, as one particularly lovely girl came forward and shyly pressed her hands to Sterling's lips, then her own.

Aidan frowned. It was a primitive gesture, but effective, and its meaning—as well as the girl's dark beauty—were not lost upon Sterling. Aidan could see a flush of dusky red advancing up his throat as he fumbled for words. "I, er, uh, you see—"

The girl laughed and stepped closer, *too* close, and an unexpected flash of jealousy sprang up in Aidan's heart, stinging like nettles. "No," she said, firmly wedging herself between the

forward beauty and her husband. Recalling the gestures of the natives at Assassin's Bay, she placed her hand on her heart, then pressed her hand to Sterling's chest. "Mine," she said simply, shrugging at the other women in the circle. She looked the brazen beauty in the eye and repeated herself so there would be no mistake. "Mine."

The girl rolled her eyes and pressed her lips together, then retreated to a chorus of giggles from the others. Another girl, still young and flat-chested, stepped out from the others and shyly took Aidan's hand.

"I suggest we go with her," Aidan said, pulling Sterling along. "I'm not leaving you alone with these—" She bit her lip, choking on the word she'd been about to say. She'd dealt with wanton temptresses at the wharf, but she couldn't imagine trying to compete with an Eve in this Garden of Eden.

The child led them past the fire pits laden with roasting pig, fresh fruit, and cauldrons of bubbling stew, pausing only long enough to allow Sterling and Aidan to fill wooden bowls with a sample of each fragrant dish. The atmosphere here was heavy and sweet with the breath of flowers, the sharp tang of herbs, and the fresh scent of rain.

After they had filled their bowls, the little girl motioned to them again, and Sterling followed her dutifully. Aidan's heart raced when she saw where the child had led them. A row of thatched huts sat apart from the feast—simple, primitive buildings much like those of the natives on Batavia. These people appreciated aesthetics, however, for wreaths of flowers adorned each doorway.

The girl led them to one of the huts, then stood beside the entrance. She pointed at Aidan, then at the door. *"Wa-go,"* she said simply, smiling. When Aidan shook her head, not understanding, the girl pointed to Sterling and Aidan, then to the hut again. *"Wa-go,"* she repeated, her brows lifting. She looked away toward the feast, where couples who had finished eating now stood with their

arms around each other and their minds clearly on something other than food.

Suddenly Aidan understood. *"Wa-go,"* she repeated with a smile.

The girl lowered her head in a stately salute, then pulled the circlet of flowers from above the door and held the wreath aloft. When Aidan lowered her head, the child slipped the garland around her neck and smiled sweetly. *"Ta-gush-ra-nay,"* she finished. She paused and grinned at Sterling.

"I think she likes you," Aidan chuckled, breathing in the sweet scent of the flowers.

"I think she is a forward little imp." His hand pressed against the small of Aidan's back. "But she obviously wants us to go inside. Shall we obey before she calls attention to us?"

"Good idea." Aidan smiled at the girl one last time, then pushed aside the woven mat that covered the low opening and crouched to enter.

This hut bore little resemblance to the starkness of her abductor's hovel on Assassin's Bay. Tightly woven grass mats covered the floor, and overflowing baskets of flowers sweetened the air. A lustrous stream of moonlight poured from a vent in the center of the roof, lighting every recess in a soft silvery glow.

"Well." Aidan stood in the center of the hut, then slowly sank to the mat and rested her dinner bowl upon her crossed legs. "I suppose we might as well sleep here tonight. There seems to be no trouble afoot, and I don't believe the captain will send a barge back to the ship."

"Are you certain?" Sterling stood above her, hesitation evident in his features. "If you'd feel safer in our cabin, I could ask one of the men to row us back. I wouldn't blame you for feeling nervous after what happened in Assassin's Bay."

Aidan smiled at the intense expression on his face. Always the doctor, he was thinking of her mental and physical welfare. "I'm not nervous," she answered. "These people are friendly, we could

not ask for better hosts." She lifted her brow. "Though they could be a little more reserved."

"I rather liked their…friendliness." Balancing his bowl upon his palm, Sterling casually sank to the mat beside her, and Aidan's heart jolted as his arm brushed hers. This was not what she had planned. He could have sat across the room or across from her, where they might regard each other as two equals, as two friends, but he had chosen to sit next to her, so close that she could feel his breathing.

She stared down at the floor and nibbled at a piece of meat from her bowl, confused by the curious quivering in her stomach, a sensation that left her feeling like a breathless, giddy girl of sixteen. Despite the native girl's shy smile and none-too-subtle innuendoes, this should be a night like all the others. They ought to just whisper their goodnights and turn their backs on one another, struggling to sleep as well as they might. This night was different only because they were away from their cramped quarters and free from the stench of illness. For once they were alone, away from sick sailors. But that was no reason to forget all the things that kept them apart.

As if he'd read her mind, Sterling suddenly asked, "Where is Captain Tasman?"

"Far away, I expect. He would certainly be upset—" She lowered her eyes, terribly conscious of his scrutiny. "—to find us here, like this."

"I'm sure you're right." He spoke in a voice husky with contentment…probably due, Aidan supposed, to the delicious meat in his bowl.

"These people are too forward," Aidan said. "Those women are worse than—well, I've heard stories about women who live down at the waterfront. There are procuresses less forward than that girl who came up to you—"

His eyes gleamed with an odd light when she looked up at him. "I don't want to talk about the riffraff down at the docks." He set aside his bowl as if he had suddenly lost his appetite. "I want to know if you meant it."

"If I meant *what?*"

"You said I was yours." His voice was velvet edged with steel, and Aidan knew she could not lie to him. She gripped her arms, feeling an unwelcome surge of excitement at the question.

"Of course you are mine." She smiled, taking pains to keep her voice light. "Until we return to Batavia and a judge can undo all the skipper did, we are lawfully wed. Later, of course, I will be safe and you will be free to return to Captain Tasman's house and beg his forgiveness."

"I don't want his forgiveness." Her pulse skittered alarmingly when he stretched out and reclined beside her, propping his head on his hand.

"But you said—"

"I never wanted his daughter. I could never want her—" His hand reached through the growing darkness and touched her arm, sending a brief shiver rippling through along her flesh. "—the way I want you."

Aidan's blood surged hot. She felt her heart beginning to melt, and her eyes lowered to meet his gaze. "Sterling," she whispered, "I don't want you to think you must—"

"I don't want to think anything, if thinking means I must analyze the feelings that have drawn me to you. You are my wife, Aidan, and I am glad of it." His extraordinary eyes blazed as he looked up at her. "I don't want to hear another word about undoing what Tasman did. I want you to remain my wife. Not in name only, but in truth. Forever and always."

"Sterling—" She halted as a wave of emotions rose and crested inside her, then broke into a flood of tears. How could she speak the things she felt? She was an artist, not a poet, and yet she wanted to tell him that in her heart he had sown hope where there had been none, that his care had caused a rare and tender feeling to blossom in her soul.

"Darling," he whispered, gently reaching up to wipe the tears from her cheeks. His hand fell to her neck, and he pulled her

toward him. She pressed her hand against his chest, trying to think of all the reasons she should not allow herself to be close to him, but her reasons and excuses had flown away. She was his wife. He was her husband. And she knew, despite all her protestations, that she did not want this marriage annulled. She wanted to be his forever.

"Is something wrong?" he asked, his breath warm and moist against her face. "I did not mean to make you cry."

"Nothing is wrong," she answered, relaxing into his cushioning embrace. Their eyes locked as their breathing came in unison, and then Aidan willingly lost herself in his arms.

Twenty-Nine

❧❧❧

Dawn had spread a gray light over the bridal bower when Aidan awoke to the soft chirping of tropical birds. Her eyes flew open and memories came flooding back; then she felt the solid presence of Sterling's body behind her. She smiled and brought his hand to her lips, blushing as she remembered the hunger in his kiss and the gentleness in his touch.

Aidan clung to the strong arm that encircled her waist, her mind curling around sweet memories of giving and receiving and loving. Sterling Thorne, the man who legally possessed her body and will, now owned her heart and mind.

Let the morrow come, she thought. *Whether we live here, in Batavia, or in England, nothing matters except that we are together.*

It was not like this for everyone, she realized. Not for Lili's women. Sometimes men paid for pleasure without spending a whit of care or concern upon the women their money provided. Yet Sterling had been careful with her, gentle, tender—he had treated her like a lady.

She wanted to keep the memory of last night pure and unsullied, but other images enveloped her—dark and shadowy recollections of a troubled night in her childhood. She had been fourteen and recently arrived from England. Searching for Lili, she had walked into the tavern's darkened storage room and lifted the lamp to discover her mother with a strange man.

She had backed out of the room, fighting down the bile that rose in her throat. The man was not married to her mother; he was

not even a friend. And her mother—how could a God-fearing woman do such things?

Aidan had run through the narrow streets until she thought her lungs would burst, then reluctantly returned to the tavern. She had nowhere else to go. Her mother had changed in the months since Da's death. Aidan had heard her weeping at night, beating her breast and railing against a God who would take a good and decent man out of the world and leave his wife and child defenseless.

Aidan felt surprising calm when she confronted her mother the next day. She had expected Lili to be embarrassed and remorseful, but her mother's eyes were flat and her voice sharp as she told Aidan that she had no other choice. If men wanted to pay for fleshly conversation, that was their business. Since God had taken Lili's husband, the Almighty shouldn't mind if she took what had rightfully belonged to Cory O'Connor and used it to eke out a living.

Aidan listened, shuddering in revulsion. "How can this 'fleshly conversation' be good if there is no joy in it?" she whispered, anger filling her voice. "Look at you, Mother—so angry, so hard, so bitter! If this is what I have to look forward to—"

"No, Aidan, this life is not for you!" Lili whirled to glare at her. "This is not love! This is not marriage! You, my precious lass, will find a man who loves you, someone who will take you away from this place!" She slipped an arm around Aidan's stiff shoulders, and her rusty voice softened. "What you saw is but the physical *act* of love, not the thing itself," she said. "It is like the grass growing next to the beach. In its proper place, 'tis a thing of beauty, and it brings forth life. But if you took a clod of grass and brought it into the tavern, it would no longer be beautiful."

"It would be *dirt*," Aidan snapped, knowing her words had the power to wound. "And those who took it from its rightful and proper place would be *dirty*, they'd be *stained*."

Lili's eyes went suddenly blank as windowpanes, as though the soul they mirrored had abruptly vanished. After a while she

whispered, "Well, naturally, I was wanting to explain these things to you." Her voice seemed as dead as her eyes. "You grow up, lass, and then you'll see. You love a man and lose him and see how you feel about love after that. Maybe then you'll feel a wee bit of pity for your tired old mother."

The memory closed around Aidan now and filled her with a longing to turn back. *Yes, Mother, I've found a man and I've loved him, and I am beginning to understand. For I feel so alive in his embrace, I can imagine I would feel dead inside if I were to lose him. I am not a tavern maid in his arms, I am Aidan, his wife, his love, his lady—*

The thought arrested her, and she shivered. Why did Sterling love her? *Because he thought her a lady.* What would he think of her if he knew the truth? This marriage was based upon a misconception, and his love would fade like a vapor if he knew who she really was. Sterling treated her like a gentlewoman because he believed her to be one. If he had known her true origins, he would never have behaved so sweetly; indeed, he would never have married her. What did he say only moments before taking her into his arms? *I don't want to talk about the riffraff down at the docks.*

Riffraff. That's what she was. If he knew the truth, he would hate her for entering his life, for touching him, for…loving him.

Feeling suddenly trapped by his heavy arm, she lifted it from her waist and dropped it to his side, then sat up. The movement woke him, and she heard him stir beside her. But she kept her back turned as she struggled to master her emotions.

"Good morning, love." His voice, heavy with sleep and contentment, sent a shiver of awareness down her spine.

"Sterling," she whispered, not turning around, "I must know something."

"What?" The playfulness vanished from his voice, but his hand touched her back, a steady, reassuring pressure.

"I am your wife—but no longer in name only."

"True enough." A gentle softness filled his voice, and he sat up

and reached for her. She placed her hand on his chest and pushed him away, not able to look into his eyes…yet.

"Sterling, if you want an annulment when we return to Batavia, you can no longer say our marriage was unconsummated. You'd have to lie to the magistrate."

"I told you last night," he said with quiet emphasis, "I do not want any other woman. I have no regrets. I married you willingly, and I meant every word I have ever uttered in your presence."

"Truly?" She lifted her gaze then, and a new and unexpected warmth surged through her when his blue eyes darkened with emotion.

"Truly." He reached out and ran a finger along her jaw. "But perhaps I have spoken out of turn. I would regret last night only if *you* wanted to end our marriage."

Aidan took a deep breath as a dozen different emotions collided in her heart. "You thought I want an annulment? I don't! Well, I did, but only because I thought you were in love with Lina Tasman. And I know you took that oath to help people. It would be like you to marry me in order to help me, but you don't know the person you've married—"

She stopped abruptly. She was about to reveal too much. "Sterling," she whispered, taking his hand between both of her own, "my past is not without stain or blame. I would spare you any association with it; indeed, I have cut myself off from it. A doctor should be respectable, and so should his wife, and for that reason alone you might do yourself a disservice if you remain married to me."

"There is nothing in your past, Aidan, that would make me disavow you." He placed his hand upon her shoulder, and she wondered if he could feel the rushing of her pulse beneath the skin. He was saying the right things, things she wanted to hear, but still he had no idea of the truth. And if she told him, what would he do? Turn away in disgust probably. Or wonder aloud how he had managed to snag Batavia's rubbish into his arms.

"You think me an artist, a boy in disguise, but you do not know me."

"I think you are extraordinary, exceptional, and the gentle mistress of my heart." Suddenly she was in his arms, his hands warm against her skin, his lips whispering into her hair. "I have thought of nothing but you since the day I saw you brawling in that bar. I loved you then, foolish girl, and I will cherish you until the day I die. So speak no more of the past or your disguise, and trust me to take care of your tomorrows."

His light touch unfurled streamers of sensation Aidan had never known, and she could only nod in agreement as his hands spanned her waist, drawing her to him.

Contented, happy, and feeling more victorious than was quite proper, Sterling adjusted the collar of his shirt and stepped out of the bridal hut, making his way along the flower-strewn path back to the beach. The wind was sweet, the air pungent with the scent of brine, the sky a faultless wide curve of blue from horizon to horizon.

Debris from the feast covered the beach—broken bamboo poles, discarded animal bones and fruit rinds, half a dozen jugs from which all the rum had been drunk in an orgy of excess. Here and there Sterling caught sight of a sailor snoring under a palmetto bush, but he shrugged and kept walking. These fools would wake scratching insect bites and squinting through throbbing headaches, and they'd undoubtedly be lining up at his cabin door later in the day. But nothing could spoil his euphoric mood.

He had married a woman who loved him. Was there any feeling more powerful? Last night she had abandoned the last of her pretenses, and they had embraced as husband and wife. And this morning, frightened and still insecure, she had sought reassurance again. He hoped he had put the last of her fears to rest.

He smiled as he walked over the beach. Secrets of her past still troubled her, she said. Some skeleton in the family closet, no

doubt, perhaps the reason both her parents were dead and she the sole family heiress. Perhaps her father had been a pirate or a tax collector—chuckling, Sterling shook his head. He had far too active an imagination. She probably had a mad uncle locked away in an asylum somewhere in Europe, or perhaps she was the child of her father's mistress.

It didn't matter. He looked up at the sky, where faint wisps of clouds were blowing in from the east. Lovely. Everything was lovely. This was another Eden, and he had discovered and loved the woman God created especially for him. He had felt her uniqueness as he held her in his arms; his heart had swelled nearly to bursting when she murmured his name just before falling asleep. "Sterling," she had said. Not "Dr. Thorne." For the first time he could recall, she had called him by his familiar name, and he had thought he might burst from the sudden swell of happiness that flooded his soul.

He pulled on the edges of his doublet, enjoying this sense of peace and satisfaction. He had won the only woman to ever pique his curiosity as well as catch his eye.

"Dr. Thorne!" Visscher came jogging over from a huddle of men near the water, and for once, the sight of the taciturn officer did not wipe the smile from Sterling's face. The barge lay on the shore, two oarsmen standing by the bow, while a third man lay stretched across one of the benches, his face as pale as candle wax. "This man is ill, sir," Visscher said, falling into step beside Sterling. "He's been vomiting blood since eating that roasted pig last night."

Sterling stopped and rubbed a hand over his stubbled face, scrubbing roughly to wipe off his ridiculous grin. He hated to leave Aidan, but if he left her sleeping here while he attended to this man, he could return soon. The thought of another private rendezvous in the little hut spurred him forward.

"How much of the pig did he eat?"

"The whole thing," Visscher answered with a grim smile.

Sterling climbed into the boat and looked down at the man's wan face. The old sailor was covered in sand, and beads of sweat clung trembling to the gray stubble of his beard. His wide gray eyes darted nervously from the doctor to the first mate.

Sterling ruefully shook his head. Patting the sick man's hand, he glanced back toward the beach and the huts where his bride lay sleeping…perhaps dreaming.

"We'll have you fixed up in no time, man." He nodded for the oarsmen to commence rowing. "But let's hurry and take care of you, shall we?"

Wrapped in Sterling's cloak, Aidan sat up, dazed and deliriously happy. Her first night with her husband had been *nothing* like the tavern girls had said it would be. He had been gentle and kind, compassionate, even *reverent* as he claimed her as his wife.

She turned her back to the mat-covered doorway and hugged her knees. If only she could wish the world away for a few more hours! Sterling had said he ought to check the ship; there were bound to be a few upset stomachs and accidents in the night before. The men of the *Heemskerk* and *Zeehaen* had not experienced generosity like this in several months. Without a doubt a number of them would have overindulged in spirits, food, and native friendliness.

"Many a seaman who would not lose his footing in the rigging in the midst of a gale," Sterling had said, "will find himself unable to stand upon the solid shore after a night of merrymaking."

"What about you?" she murmured in return. "We made a bit merry ourselves last night."

"Indeed we did." He paused to brush a gentle kiss across her forehead. "But you, my lady, are the only wine these lips will ever seek."

He kissed her again, boldly but briefly, and when he rose and stood beside the door she felt a sudden chill at the loss of his warmth.

Aidan smiled as she remembered the look of love in his eyes. She ought to get up and search for some breakfast, perhaps comb her hair and wash her face, but she couldn't bear the thought of leaving this private place where love had touched her for the first time.

Sighing, she lay down and spread his cloak over her. The scent of the wool reminded her of Sterling—robust and clean, tinged faintly with the odor of medicinal herbs. The fragrance mingled with the fresh aroma of the grass sleeping mat, the woven walls of the thatched hut. She would never again smell hay or grass or clover without remembering this place, without thinking of Sterling and the truth that he loved her.

Sterling still does not know about the tavern and Irish Annie, a cynical inner voice reminded her. But if he did not want an annulment in order to marry Lina Tasman, Aidan had already won half the battle. She would just have to guard her secret. After they returned to Batavia, she would keep him away from the wharf and any other place where she might be recognized. Perhaps she'd convince him that they should return to England where his family lived…and where no rumors of Aidan's past could follow.

The first few days after their arrival back in port would be risky, but if Aidan went directly from the ship to a respectable inn, she could avoid anyone from the Broad Street Tavern. Sterling did not frequent the taverns or the wharf district, thank the good Lord, and of all the people at the wharf, only Lili and Orabel had known that Aidan planned to go to sea.

Heer Van Dyck's children knew her as Aidan O'Connor, of course, but they would likely be so distraught over their father's death that Aidan would be the last of their concerns. Before they could spread rumors, Aidan would make certain she and Sterling were booked on a ship bound for England.

Her dreams were coming true in ways she would never have believed possible. Respectability would be hers, for what woman was more respected than a doctor's wife? And Sterling would not

make demands upon her; he wanted her to paint. As his wife she would have the time and the means to pursue her art. She closed her eyes, envisioning a tidy white house with an artist's studio where she painted all day and enjoyed life with her husband.

Soon, very soon, her dark days at the wharf and her trying experiences aboard the *Heemskerk* would merely be a distant memory, never to be dredged up again. She settled contentedly under the fabric of Sterling's cloak and inhaled deeply. Some memories, however, were worth revisiting again and again and again…

She heard the soft sound of the flap at the door and closed her eyes, pretending to sleep. He had returned much sooner than she'd hoped, so perhaps no one needed him…except her.

He did not speak, but she heard the heavy sound of his breathing. She lowered her head, covering her smile with his cloak. He was playing with her, teasing her, and she would let him enjoy his little game. She heard the rustle of fabric, then a soft creaking sound as he dropped to the mat beside her.

Aidan caught her breath as his hand fell upon her head and tentatively stroked her hair. "So beautiful," he whispered hoarsely, his hand moving between her hair and the skin of her neck. "So lovely."

Aidan froze. The voice was not Sterling's, nor was this his touch. This hand was too heavy, the voice too harsh. She choked back a scream. No doubt this was a drunken sailor who had wandered in from outside, and Lili had always said a wise girl could talk a man out of almost anything if she kept cool and did not panic.

"I think," she began, her voice a tremulous whisper, "that you are in the wrong hut."

The hand that had been tracing the length of her bare arm suddenly lifted, a grown man's weight pressed upon her, his power holding her helpless as his lips moved closer to her ear. She crinkled her nose at the overpowering smell of alcohol and the musty odor of wet dog.

"You are mine now, lady," the stranger whispered. Aidan opened her eyes and looked over her shoulder, her heart accelerating in terror when she recognized Witt Dekker's slanting black brows and catlike eyes.

Forgetting Lili's lessons, Aidan opened her mouth and screamed. Almost immediately Dekker's hand clapped across her mouth, cutting off the sound. He held her face in an iron grip, his fingers bruising her jaw and cheek. His body lay over hers, pinning her beneath his weight as he whispered drunken threats in her ear.

Aidan's eyes burned with tears of anger and frustration as she struggled to free herself. Had she spent years dodging drunks in Bram's tavern only to fall victim to a slobbering sot thousands of miles from Batavia? No! And yet there was nothing she could do. She had dropped her guard for one man and another had walked into his place.

Tears slid hot and wet from the corners of her eyes, and her jaw ached from the rough way he gripped her. She lifted one arm to try and push him away, but she could not reach him, and her struggles only seemed to make him tighten his grip.

"I have waited patiently," he muttered, his breath hot and putrid against the side of her face, "and the time has come for me to sample the favors of the famous Irish Annie. I hope you said a sweet farewell to your husband, for you will not see him again. I will be quick, you see, and when I am done I shall twist your neck just so—" He pulled slightly on her head for effect, and a blinding pain shot from her neck to her toes. "And you will be dead."

Aidan choked on a deep sob and closed her eyes against the sight of him. Then suddenly, against the blackness, a bright light crossed the backs of her eyelids.

"Release my wife!"

The voice was Sterling's, and the bitter hatred in it was unmistakable.

She felt Dekker's weight lift from her, and she silently moved her jaw to make certain it was not broken. She turned to look;

Sterling stood tense as a bowstring in the doorway, his dagger drawn and ready, his face dead white and sheened with a cold sweat.

Dekker jumped up, shaking his head. "Sorry, doctor. I was— I was meaning to get my way ashore—"

Gasping for breath, Aidan shook her head in disbelief as the first mate addressed her husband. The officer staggered like a drunken fool, but he hadn't seemed one-fourth as inebriated when he muttered threats in her ear.

"What are you doing here?" Sterling ground the words out between his teeth. Dekker bobbed his head like a cringing slave and staggered his way toward the doorway.

Aidan swallowed hard, trying to dislodge the knot of despair in her throat. Witt wasn't as drunk as he pretended. He had meant what he said, and he had recognized her as one of Bram's tavern maids. If Sterling pushed too hard now, Dekker might reveal her secret.

"What are you doing here?" Sterling repeated, his chest heaving with mounting rage. Killing anger burned in his eyes, and he would not hesitate to use the knife on Dekker unless—

"Let him go, Sterling," she moaned. Pulling the edges of his cloak around her throat to shield her bruised neck from his sight, she pushed down her fear and despair. "He is drunk; let him go."

"He was sober enough to find his way here."

"He doesn't know…what he is doing." Aidan lowered her gaze. She would never be able to look Sterling in the eye and lie. "He—I don't think he would have hurt me. Let him go in peace."

Sterling lifted a fist to his hip, still unconvinced. From the corner of her eye Aidan saw Dekker turn toward her, an expression of cunning appreciation upon his face. The instant Sterling transferred his gaze from Aidan to Dekker, however, the sly look vanished, replaced by the slack-mouthed gape of a drunken fool too inebriated to know his own name.

Sterling stepped forward, grabbed the officer by the front of his shirt, then forcibly lifted him from the floor before dragging him toward the entryway. With a strangely detached curiosity Aidan noted that the hut no longer had a door—in his haste to reach her, Sterling had ripped the fragile woven curtain away.

He pushed Dekker out the door with a warning and a shout of frustration, then came to kneel beside her, pulling her into his arms. "I heard you scream," he said simply. "I'm so sorry, Aidan. I left you unprotected, and I swore I never would. I never will again."

Surrendering her guard and her will for the moment, Aidan curled into the safety of his embrace and wept like the little girl she could never be again.

⁂

Nestled against Sterling's chest, Aidan slept. As he caressed her hair and the soft places of her skin which were already blue-black from the force of that villain's grasp, Sterling cursed himself for the hundredth time. Why had he left her alone and exposed? He had assumed that since these natives were friendly, Aidan was safe. But he had forgotten about the vices and sinful inclinations of his own companions. If he had tarried on the boat for the next barge, and if he had not heard that one brief scream…

He shuddered and pressed a protective hand to the top of her head. He had been married for only one month, but even before this romantic interlude he could not imagine life without her. She brought light to his life, gentleness to his medical practice, a sweetness to his days. In her generosity she had insisted that Dekker was drunk and meant her no harm, but what would a sheltered lady know of drunks—or of men, for that matter?

But Sterling knew. He knew that drunks often knew very well what they were doing, and Dekker wasn't so drunk that he couldn't find his way into the hut where Aidan lay asleep and unguarded. Sterling also knew that pleasure-deprived men often committed acts they later regretted…or should regret, if they retained their God-given consciences.

Drunk or not, Witt Dekker acted out of clear intention, Sterling believed. He would let Aidan think Dekker's attack was an accident so she would not spend the remainder of the journey afraid and locked in her cabin. But Sterling would never allow Witt Dekker to be alone with his wife again.

Thirty

꧁

A fter spending nearly two weeks in the paradise Tasman called "the Friendly Islands," the Dutch ships loaded fresh stores of water and fruit, then weighed anchor and departed. On the sixth of February the lookouts sighted another uncharted archipelago, but the physical geography of these islands was anything but friendly. The islands lay within a lacework of shallows and dangerous coral reefs, and only careful, skillful sailing prevented them from wrecking in the labyrinth of treacherous shoals.

Tension tightened every sailor's face as the officers navigated the dangerous waters. Aidan, too, felt the anxiety, but shipwreck was the least of her concerns. Her greatest fear was that Witt Dekker might tell Sterling of her past. She walked a tightrope of sorts—at the moment, perilous sailing kept Dekker occupied aboard the *Zeehaen,* but if the situation grew desperate enough to warrant a meeting of the officers' committee, Tasman could send for Dekker and Janszoon.

So she prayed every night that the situation might remain as it was—risky enough to keep Dekker busy, but not so risky or so carefree that he would be summoned aboard the *Heemskerk.* She was not certain if God would answer her prayers—she had not offered enough in the years since her father's death to even deserve his notice. But Sterling, like Heer Van Dyck, prayed every night before bed, before every meal, and immediately upon rising every morning. He seemed to walk with God, to possess a steady and confident peace that she sorely lacked.

And so Aidan began to emulate him. She knew God existed—
she had known that since her childhood—but she couldn't say
that she'd ever really *talked* to him. And so, while Sterling knelt by
his bunk and prayed, she did the same, tenting her fingers and
politely asking God to keep an ocean's distance between her
beloved husband and Witt Dekker.

As the ships moved cautiously through the hazardous shallows
and shoals and Witt Dekker remained aboard the *Zeehaen,* she
began to relax. Perhaps God had indeed heard and answered her
prayers.

With a delicious freedom she had never known, she painted
every day. She lacked the cartography skills necessary to finish
Heer Van Dyck's map, and though she still mourned her mentor,
his death had released her from her obligation to paint watercolor
flowers and insects and trees. She packed away his charts and
straight edges, then used his canvases and brushes and oils to create the pictures that bloomed in her imagination.

Up till now, she had painted only the things she could see in
the natural world. But Heer Van Dyck had taught her to look
inside herself, to examine the personalities and creatures that
populated her imagination. She sketched everything that moved
aboard ship, using common objects and faces as the basis for her
fanciful imaginings, then created colors brighter and images more
flamboyant than any she had ever seen in Heer Van Dyck's art
collection.

Instead of her tutor's reproving eye over her shoulder, she now
enjoyed the supportive presence of her husband. Sterling knew
little about painting, but he knew enough to praise Aidan's
efforts, even those she wanted to toss into the sea. On days when
her brush could not capture the emotions and images in her
mind's eye, he would take it from her hand, kiss her paint-stained
fingertips, and remind her that things would look better on the
morrow.

Their cabin was no longer the casual drop-in quarters for

every man with an ache or pain. Sterling had ordered all but his sickest patients to remain in their hammocks, suspended even in the galley if need be. His bride, he insisted, deserved better than a crowded cabin reeking of sickness and flatulent seamen.

With every day that passed, Aidan felt herself growing into the role of Mistress Thorne. It was easy to believe she could be genteel when Sterling sat at her feet and rested his head in her lap while she painted. His gentility and love had begun to refine her in a way that all Gusta's lessons and harping could not. He praised her, and she responded by rising to the level of his expectation. He demanded that the seamen respect her, and she walked among them with her chin held high and her gaze uplifted.

Most of all, Sterling loved her, and Aidan's heart leaped each time he called her name. She was Mistress Thorne—Mejoffer Thorne to the Dutch—and the name lent her a respectability and dignity she could not have earned in a dozen years of painting.

Her gratitude spilled out in an overflowing love for her husband. His voice filled her days, dreams of him filled her nights, and if she awakened in the dark she found comfort, security, and freedom in his arms. *Let the officers argue, let the men grumble about all the gold they haven't found,* she told herself one February afternoon as the ship steamed toward the western sea. *It matters not. I have Sterling, and he is happy with me. In that lies my respectability.*

Thirty-One

To Aidan's dismay, once the two ships cleared the treacherous shoals, Tasman summoned the officers of the *Zeehaen* to the *Heemskerk* for a consultation. She sat in the cabin, worried and unable to paint, as Sterling was called away to participate in the meeting. Her fears did not abate until he returned two hours later with nothing more serious than expedition matters on his mind.

"What did you talk about?" she asked, sinking beside him on his narrow bunk. She pressed her hand to his wrist and felt for the steady beat of a calm heart. If Dekker had told him anything, Sterling would not be so composed. He'd be furious with Dekker—or with her, depending upon which one he believed to be a liar. When she could not refute Dekker's story, he'd abandon her, leaving her without hope or help.

"The captain wanted to gather our opinions about the future," Sterling answered, giving her a wicked grin. His pulse beat steadily as he pulled off his boot and dropped it. "Should he sail west and south of the known coastline of New Guinea or travel back to Batavia along the route he already knows?"

"And?" Aidan released his wrist and folded her hands demurely, like a schoolgirl. "What did the others say?"

"Well—" Sterling let the other boot fall. "Dekker and Visscher are still eager to find gold. They voted for sailing southwest into the unknown. But Holman always thinks of his family, and he was quick to mention the possibility that we'd be blown against a shore from which it might be difficult to retreat."

Aidan fidgeted impatiently, eager to hear the entire story. "How did Janszoon vote?"

Sterling shrugged. "He would have sailed east from the Friendly Islands; he's still bent upon finding a route to Chile. But Tasman has given up on that; he thinks only of returning home. Holman is of like mind." He chuckled. "So am I."

"Are you in such a hurry then?" She pressed her hand to her throat in mock horror. "Am I such a trial that you cannot bear to be cooped up in this wee cabin with me for as long as it takes to explore the wide world?"

"I am in no hurry at all." He pulled her into his arms, then leaned back and kicked at the bar on the door until it fell into its supports, effectively closing the way to any who would interrupt.

Aidan pressed her hands to his chest and smiled into his startlingly blue eyes. "So, Doctor, what did Captain Tasman decide? Are we to venture into the unknown or take the safe way home?"

"We're going home, my love," he whispered. He cupped her face between his hands, and Aidan felt her heart skip a beat as his kiss sang through her veins.

"Wherever you are," she whispered, "is home enough for me."

The crews of the *Heemskerk* and *Zeehaen* had made up their minds to go home, but for the next two weeks overcast skies and gloomy weather made it impossible for Tasman to determine his position. He needed a clear sight of the stars or the sun to judge his latitude, and the ceiling of oppressive low clouds made navigation difficult. Pytheas of Massalia, an ancient sailor who journeyed upon the seas in 333 B.C., had reported that beyond Britain there was neither earth, air, or sea, but a mixture of all three—something like the element that held the universe together. "It has the consistency of jellyfish," Tasman recalled Pytheas writing, "and renders navigation impossible." Modern navigation had proven Pytheas wrong, of course, but Tasman could easily understand why the ancient mariner had felt he sailed in a sluggish and soupy sea.

Afraid they might sail unaware into deadly shallows and break apart upon razor-sharp shoals, Tasman ordered the sails reefed on both ships. The furled sails fluttered wildly in the occasional winds, rattling against the spars with a chattering noise that set the men's teeth on edge. Oppressed by the gloom, men walked the decks like phantoms, appearing out of the murk with an abruptness that startled one another.

For the remainder of February and most of March they drifted in the thick haze, saying little, watching the food and water rations gradually disappear. But as the days of March ticked off on the captain's calendar, the wind freshened. On April 1, the rising breeze tore great windows in the fog, and gazing over to port Tasman caught a sudden vision of land crouching on the horizon.

"Meester Visscher," Tasman called to his pilot, "take us closer. Unless I miss my guess, that is Cape Santa Maria, and we are on our way home."

The tensions of the past few weeks vanished as the men on deck erupted in cheering, and Tasman stood silently, accepting their thanks and congratulations...for accidentally stumbling upon an already charted passage. This was no great discovery; they would find no gold as they sailed home along this coastline. But after the tension and oppression of the silent sea, Tasman no longer cared.

～❧～

The coxswain of the *Zeehaen* turned the ship to follow the *Heemskerk*'s lead, and Witt Dekker peered through his spyglass at the land mass appearing off the port bow. This was New Guinea, without a doubt; these shores had been charted for years. This, then, was the beginning of the end of their expedition, and Tasman had not accomplished a single one of his goals. He had not found a route to Chile or the fabled Southern continent. More important, he had discovered neither gold nor silver, only mountainous lands, treacherous harbors, and tribes of nearly naked savages, half of whom would kill an intruder before welcoming him.

Time was running out. They had been instructed to sail along the northern coast of New Guinea, searching for a passage south to Cape Keerweer, but if no passage existed, they'd likely reach Batavia before the end of summer. Tasman would have to stand before the officers of the V.O.C and explain his empty hands and empty cargo holds.

Dekker leaned back upon the foremast and scratched at his stiff beard, his eyes roving over the busy decks of the *Zeehaen's* sister ship. As first mate, Dekker would not have to cringe before the officers of the V.O.C., but he'd face his own peers—the sailors who loitered at the taverns of the wharf district when not at sea. They would expect him to come back a rich man, and he would have nothing but a few tall tales to account for this journey.

The dog at Dekker's feet lifted his head with a sudden low woof, his ears pricked to attention.

"Excuse me, sir."

Dekker glanced down, annoyed at the youthful voice that interrupted his thoughts. The cook's ketelbinkie stood there, the accident-prone Tiy. The boy had just returned from the *Heemskerk,* where the doctor had to bandage yet another of his fingers. The youth was as clumsy as an ox and about as bright.

"What do you want?"

"The doctor sent this for you," the boy said, holding up a small pouch. "I told him one of our officers was complaining of aching teeth, and he said you should mix this with your pottage or drink it down with water." The boy handed over the bag and clasped his hands behind his back. "I believe it's lemon rind, sir."

Witt sniffed the pouch and shrugged. "So it would seem."

The boy bobbed his head and was about to leave, but Witt reached out and caught his shoulder. "Ketelbinkie—did you see the doctor's wife while you were aboard the *Heemskerk?*"

The lad's mouth curved into an unconscious smile. "*Ja,* sir, I did."

Witt dipped his head slightly. "Is the lady well?"

A worried, thoughtful expression flitted across the boy's face, and Witt reached out to pat him reassuringly on the shoulder. "Do not worry on her account, my lad. She and I are old friends. I knew her in Batavia."

"Oh." The boy's features relaxed. "She is well, sir, and painting so much that there is little room to move in the doctor's cabin. But her pictures are marvelous! I am certain she will be a rich and famous artist when we return. She is a very great lady."

"Her—a great lady?" Dekker scoffed. "Have you forgotten that a few weeks ago she was a ketelbinkie like you?"

The boy stiffened in dignified outrage. "She wore a disguise, sir." He glanced quickly left and right, then leaned forward and lowered his voice. "The doctor explained it to me. His wife is descended from an Irish king and had to masquerade as a boy to escape some bit of trouble in her family's past. But after they return to Batavia, the doctor and his wife are planning to sail to Europe, where she can sell her art."

Dekker rubbed his hand over his mouth, hiding his smile of amusement. What sort of story had the wench fed her doting husband? Irish Annie, a princess? This was too rich, too ridiculous to be believed!

"Thank you, boy." Witt turned toward the railing and lifted his spyglass, searching the *Heemskerk* for any sign of that Titian-haired royalty. "I cannot wait to congratulate the lady on her bright future."

⚬⚬⚬

One week later, Dekker was on deck when a sudden, cold, lucid thought struck him: He was approaching his problem from the wrong direction. With the old man and the girl dead, he stood to receive ten thousand pounds, payable as soon as he returned to Batavia. But the remaining ten thousand pounds of the girl's inheritance would undoubtedly find its way into Dempsey Jasper's purse. Why should that scoundrel profit? He had done nothing, while Dekker had been scorned by the wench, insulted

by her husband, and kept from sleep by fretful thoughts of how and when he would kill her. Most trying of all, ever since he'd seen her kissing Sterling Thorne, Dekker had burned for her with an obsessive attraction he could not afford to indulge.

So why not let the vixen live? She was still in disguise, that much was evident from the ketelbinkie's story. She had found happiness and love with her pious doctor husband, who believed her a well-bred lady. Ha! If he knew the truth, he'd run from her like a chicken from a dog. For Sterling Thorne was every inch an English gentleman, priding himself on his godliness, his sobriety, his proper and courtly behavior. If he knew he had taken a harlot to his bed...

Witt doubled over with laughter. No wonder the good doctor eagerly volunteered to wed the wench! She had not only sold him a cock-and-bull story about her origins; undoubtedly she'd given him many happy nights as well.

"It is so simple," he whispered, inhaling deeply to catch his breath. "How blind I have been! How irresistibly delicious the answer is!"

Dekker threw back his head and exhaled a long sign of contentment. He would spare Aidan O'Connor's life. She would inherit twenty thousand pounds soon after they arrived and the old man's estate was settled. Witt could take his ten thousand pounds from her and demand another thousand pounds per month for the rest of his life. Why kill a charmed goose when one could collect the golden eggs? If she truly was as talented as everyone said, he could grow rich along with her.

And he would follow her. To England, to Ireland, wherever she went. He was a man of the sea, accustomed to travel, without a home of his own. But her money could buy him a nice slice of life in any port town, and if she truly loved her noble husband, she'd pay anything for Witt Dekker's silence.

Witt rubbed his nose and leaned against the rail, suddenly eager to return to Batavia. Ten thousand pounds could buy a lot of pleasure in that port.

In the midst of sketching a caterpillar she'd seen on the Friendly Islands, Aidan heard voices on the sea. She leaned toward the porthole, cautiously peeking to see which of the *Zeehaen's* seamen was coming aboard. She had been delighted to see Tiy recently, though the lad had come with another nasty cut on his finger. She had listened to him prattle for several minutes while Sterling stitched up the cut, then lost herself in her painting and nearly forgot the boy was there.

The barge was too close to the ship for her to get a good look, so she put down her sketch board and pencil and thrust her head through the porthole. The vessel rode the crystal clear water below, and a shirtless seaman lay across one of the benches. Even from this distance she could see that one of his arms lay bent at an unnatural angle. His face was as pale as paper, his long hair wet with sweat.

"Sterling," she called, pulling her head back into the cabin. "The *Zeehaen* has sent a barge, and there's a wounded man aboard. He doesn't look good."

"What is it, a cut?" Sterling moved to the porthole and rested his hand upon her shoulder with easy familiarity.

"A broken arm, I think." Aidan picked up her sketch board again. "He's still in the boat, but his mates have come aboard."

A sharp knock interrupted her, and Sterling pushed the door open. Aidan felt a cold hand pass down her spine when she saw Witt Dekker standing outside.

"We need a doctor," he said simply, nodding to Sterling. "There's an injured man—"

"How dare you show yourself in front of my wife?" Sterling demanded, a thread of warning in his voice. "It's bad enough we must meet. I had hoped to spare her the sight of your face for the remainder of the voyage."

A grimace of pain crossed Dekker's face, as if someone had unexpectedly slapped him. "I beg your pardon, Doctor," he said,

removing his hat, "but necessity compels me to seek you. And while I am here," his eyes shifted to Aidan, and he bowed slightly, "I thought to take this opportunity to humbly beg your wife's forgiveness and pardon. I am not certain what happened so many days ago at the Friendly Islands, but I know I behaved abominably."

Aidan cut a glance from Dekker to her husband. Sterling blinked, but his features had hardened in a stare of disapproval. "Unless my wife wishes to see you—"

Dekker laughed gently and held up his hand. "Doctor, I'm afraid our meeting is unavoidable. And lately my conscience has been troubled. I know you have borne me ill will ever since that disgraceful day, and I have come to apologize. I was out of my mind with fever and I had drunk too much." He lowered his head in an attitude of shame. "I know it is not a worthy excuse, but it is a reason. And though I do not fully recall what happened, I know that I vexed you, sir, and I am certain I frightened your gentle wife. And for that—" His gaze caught and held Aidan's. "—I most sincerely do apologize and beg your forgiveness. I would not harm such a gentle lady for all the world's treasures."

Sterling did not answer, but looked toward Aidan, awaiting her response. Flustered, she dropped her pencil and reached for it on the floor, grateful for an opportunity to shield her face from both men's prying eyes. What did they want of her? Sterling, she knew, would welcome Dekker or cast him off, depending upon her wishes, but could she afford to be hostile toward a man who knew her secret past? And why had he threatened to kill her? She had done him no harm, she could not even recall *meeting* Dekker at the tavern.

She straightened in her chair and slowly lifted her gaze to Dekker's. His dark brown eyes were soft and dreamy, as cloudy as a March sky, with no sign of malice or hostility. Sterling would honor her wishes, but Aidan knew he would be pleased if she could forgive, for peacemaking was part of his nature.

Perhaps she *had* heard the rum talking that horrible day.

"You are forgiven, sir," she said.

"Ah." Dekker thumped his hat against his breast in gratitude. "Thank you, Mejoffer. I was beginning to fear that of all the men aboard this ship, I alone would feel your rancor. All the other men speak of your kindness, and I feared I would never know your smile—"

"Didn't you come on behalf of an injured man?" Sterling interrupted pointedly.

"He remains in the barge." Dekker gestured toward the starboard rail. His lips curved in an expression that hardly deserved to be called a smile. "I will let you precede me, Doctor, for two of us will upset the boat, and you are the one with the expertise in these matters."

Sterling stepped through the doorway, then hesitated. He glanced back at Aidan, who sat stock-still in her chair, and gave her a fleeting smile. "I'll return in a moment," he said, his gaze shifting back to Dekker. "I will not be long."

"Of course not." Dekker airily waved him away. "And I have other business on board."

Aidan picked up her sketch board and pencil again, sighing in relief when she heard the heavy clump of footsteps moving away. The first mate's apology might have been sincere, but she would never feel at ease around him. She moved her pencil over the paper in a downward slant, then nearly jumped out of her skin when Dekker's voice sliced through her thoughts.

"My dear Mejoffer—"

Aidan felt a lurch in her stomach, the scratch of fear upon her spine as Dekker stepped into the cabin and closed the door.

"What do you want?" She clutched her sketch board to her chest. "Get out now, before I scream through the porthole. A score of men are working right outside this window—"

"I would not harm a hair on your pretty head," Dekker answered, settling himself comfortably upon Sterling's bunk. "I have come here today to discuss business. And because I am certain your husband means to come back quickly, I will be brief."

"What business could I possibly have with you?" Aidan spoke calmly, but with the eerie sense of detachment that comes with an awareness of impending disaster. This man could not possibly bring good news.

Placing his two forefingers together, Dekker pressed them against his lips, his eyes twinkling like dark stars as he studied her.

"You should know, *Mejoffer,*" he said, folding his hands together in a comfortable gesture, "that the old gentleman, Heer Van Dyck, rewrote his will before departing Batavia. Upon his death, which unfortunately has come, you will receive an amount of several thousand English pounds. Upon your return to Batavia, you will be a prosperous heiress—but perhaps you already knew this."

Aidan stared at him, feeling as though he had punched her in the stomach. Heer Van Dyck left her money? Why? He had already given her so much—his time, his thoughts, the benefit of his experience. His estate belonged to his children; it was inconceivable that he should leave such a sum to her.

"Why—who—how would you know that?"

Dekker shrugged. "Before we departed, a gentleman called Dempsey Jasper offered me five thousand pounds to kill you. It seems that Van Dyck's children—"

"They want what is rightfully theirs," Aidan stammered in bewilderment. "And I don't blame them. I never asked Heer Van Dyck for money."

"The children want you to go away," Dekker countered softly, mockingly. "They do not want it known that their father consorted with a barmaid. They are far more concerned with their reputations than with the money—that is why, I suppose, I was to be so well paid for killing you. Though, of course, Dempsey agreed to double the amount should the old man die too." A cold smile twisted Dekker's face. "So I suppose they are not entirely unconcerned with their own inheritance."

"By heaven, no—" Shock blocked the words in Aidan's throat.

Dempsey Jasper wanted both her and her master dead? Could he possibly hate that much? He had always been the picture of a perfect gentleman, the dutiful son-in-law.

Then another thought careened through her brain. Appearances were not what they seemed. Witt Dekker was lounging across from her now like a perfect gentleman, but his hands had once twisted her neck while he threatened to kill her.

"You really did mean it, didn't you?" she whispered. "Back there on the island—you really would have killed me."

"But of course." His thin mouth curled in a one-sided smile. "And I would have escaped scot-free, too, if that lovesick husband of yours hadn't been so besotted that he couldn't stay away an hour." He must have seen the rising terror in her eyes, for he held out his hand in a gesture meant to be reassuring. "But as I just told you, I wouldn't harm a hair on your head for all the treasure in the world. I have had time to reconsider, and I hear that your art—" His eyes flickered over the paintings and sketches scattered about the cabin. "—holds great promise. There is a handsome profit in art, particularly in the Dutch ports." Dekker's gaze fell upon one of Aidan's favorite paintings, a watercolor of Sterling standing by the rail at sunset, and his voice softened: "The Dutch are such fools for art."

"I scarcely believe you care so much for art," Aidan spat out.

"Well there is money to be made in it," he said, tilting his head to examine another piece. "And therefore I care a great deal. Enough to offer you a proposition that will enable you to remain happily married and paint for as long as you like."

With effort, Aidan looked up at him. "What sort of proposition?"

"A simple one." He gave her a narrow glance, then smiled. "You will collect your inheritance when you return to Batavia, and you will give me the ten thousand pounds I would have earned by killing you. That is only fair, my dear Aidan."

She flinched at his familiarity. "And then?"

He shrugged. "Then you shall go your way with your husband, but where you go, I shall go." He bent one knee and propped it on the bunk, then smiled broadly. "That's part of a poem, isn't it? Whither thou goest, I shall go?"

"It's from the Bible." Aidan gritted her teeth. "Not that I would expect you to read it."

He laughed as if sincerely amused. "Touché, my dear. In any case, where you go, I will follow, but in the shadows, of course. Your husband need never know I am near. And once a month you shall set aside a thousand pounds for my personal use." His steady gaze bored into her in silent expectation. "Thus shall we be joined till death do us part."

Aidan felt everything go silent within her as his mocking words registered in her brain. She looked down at her hands and clasped them together when she realized they were trembling.

"If I do not agree?" she whispered.

Dekker shrugged. "Then I shall have to tell your husband the truth, at the very least. I shall tell him you were one of the barmaids at the Broad Street Tavern, that your mother is one of the oldest procuresses in the wharf district, and that you yourself were a harlot—"

She lifted her chin and met his icy gaze straight on. "That's a lie!"

His features hardened at her angry retort, and his voice was sharp and cold when he resumed: "It won't matter. I'll give him enough truth to make him run back to England without you. And you know I'm right, or you would not have filled his head with that stuff and nonsense about being descended from Irish royalty."

Aidan brought her hands to her cheeks as color flooded her face. How did this man know so much? He held far too much power over her. He might be bluffing—but he hadn't been pretending when he held her down and promised to break her neck. If Sterling had been only a few moments late, he would have found her lying still and quiet amid the flowers in that hut, just like he found Orabel.

As if he had read her thoughts, Dekker grinned. "You are quite right, lady, to take me seriously. I will tell your husband anything, truth or lie, but if I make up my mind to ruin you, you will be ruined. And if you report this exchange to the authorities in Batavia, I may kill your husband…or even you." He grinned at her, then reached under the kerchief at his neck and pulled forth a gold chain. Perplexed, Aidan watched in silence until he brandished the ornament upon the chain in her direction. A golden cross hung at the end of the chain, an unmistakable Celtic cross that had once been her father's…and Orabel's.

"No!" she moaned. The image of her murdered friend floated across her field of vision. Orabel had been wearing the golden dress Dempsey Jasper had last seen on Aidan, but the cross was missing from the girl's bruised and broken neck.

"Yes, I killed your little friend," Witt said, his features suffused with an expression of remarkable malignity. "She wouldn't tell me where to find you, and at the time I had no idea you had made up your mind to go to sea. But after you revealed yourself at Assassin's Bay, I knew we'd have this meeting." His gaze shifted, and his icy demeanor thawed slightly as his eyes focused on her lips. "You should be nicer to me, Irish Annie. I can be a very patient person…if persuaded by the proper inducements."

Aidan braced her hands on the seat of her chair and looked across at Dekker, whose image had gone slightly blurry. "What is to stop me," she whispered, scarcely able to form the words, "from killing you?"

The devil threw back his head and roared with laughter. "Do you think," he said, struggling to contain himself, "that you could?" He paused, wiping tears of mirth from his eyes with the back of his hand, then gave her a hideous smile. "Be assured, lady, that we are linked in life as well as in death. If, by chance, I come to some untimely end, my last breath will be spent whispering your name. If you do not send my money each month, I will confess to any and all that you and I are linked by love. Every woman

I kiss will know that she could not possibly compare to my lovely Aidan. So—if I die, when I die, the story of our adulterous love will be whispered in every alley and served up with every round of drinks in the taverns. And because I will remain in your shadow, your husband will undoubtedly hear of it."

"Enough!" Aidan couldn't believe that one man could be so ruthless and cruel. But she was trapped, with no way out. She could not expose him without exposing herself, and she could not be rid of him without dealing with his lies as well as her own.

Her lungs tightened as if a gigantic hand had suddenly begun to squeeze her rib cage. For a moment the room whirled madly around her in an explosion of colors and buzzing sounds, then all went black.

She awoke to the sight of Sterling's concerned face above her a moment later, but his presence did nothing to ease her fears. She was lying on his bunk and Witt Dekker was fanning her, the palmetto frond pushing hot air across her face and blowing curls in all directions. She recoiled from him, but now he wore an expression of dutiful, compassionate concern, without a trace of malevolence in his dark eyes.

"Darling, are you all right?" Sterling slipped his hand under her head and held a glass of water to her lips. She pushed the glass away, spilling half of the precious liquid over her bodice and skirt.

Sterling glared up at Dekker. "What happened?"

"I was just describing the poor man's broken arm," Dekker said, his eyes wide pools of innocence. "And suddenly she claps her hands over her ears, tells me, 'Enough,' and faints dead away." He nodded in a generous display of compassion. "Women are a weak sort, Doctor. You can't say much without having them get all queasy on you."

Aidan blinked rapidly, forcing the room into focus. Dekker stood above her on one side, Sterling sat on the other. One man she wanted dead; the other she would give her life to protect.

"Come darling, drink this," Sterling offered again, holding up the glass. Closing her eyes to block Dekker from her sight, Aidan dutifully obeyed.

⁂

An ocean away, Lili halted in midsentence. She had been bent over a book spread on a tavern table, teaching Sofie and Francisca how to read, when for no explainable reason her heart began to burn with the certainty that Aidan was in trouble.

"Almighty God," she whispered, unable to shake the sense that her daughter needed help, "be with her now."

"Are you all right, Lili?" Sofie asked, arching her brows. "You're as pale as milk."

"Pray, ladies," Lili murmured, grasping the back of a chair as she slowly lowered herself into a seat. Her legs felt like water beneath her, and unbidden tears had risen to cloud her sight. "Pray for Aidan. Wherever she is, she needs us now."

The women did not hesitate, but pressed their hands together and began to pray as Lili had taught them. Lili's own heart, however, was too full for words. She lowered her forehead to the table and let her tears water the wooden surface.

God had a son. He would understand her pain.

Thirty-Two

~~~

O n the pretext of giving Sterling room enough to set the
injured man's shattered arm, Aidan left the cabin. Dekker
and his oarsmen had already returned to the *Zeehaen,* so she felt
safe roaming the decks of the *Heemskerk.* She needed time and
space to think, and she needed privacy. As much as she loved
Sterling and wanted to share her life with him, there were some
aspects of her heart she could not let him see.

A pale sun had shone on the water when Aidan first looked out
the porthole and spied the barge, but now an ugly haze veiled the
sky. The rising wind blew past her, lifting her hair off her shoulders,
whipping her skirts tight around her legs. The wind was hot and
humid; in a few moments it would begin to rain. Aidan lifted her
face to the gray sky to welcome whatever weather would come.

She swallowed the lump that had risen in her throat and
braced herself on the railing as she considered the dreadful facts.
Witt Dekker, a distinguished officer with this expedition, had
killed Orabel trying to get to her! And now the past she had
thought she could bury had risen to haunt her footsteps and over-
shadow her happiness.

The ship trembled slightly under Aidan's feet, the boards
brushed by some huge sea creature. Aidan gazed across the dark
surface of the heaving ocean. "Lili, you tried to preserve my
purity," she whispered, seeing her mother's reflection in each little
cat's paw the wind ruffled up, "but you couldn't do enough. The
truth will come out, no matter what. Perhaps Sterling could have

understood if I had been honest from the beginning, but to tell him now, with Dekker breathing threats and lies…"

She gripped the railing. Sterling must never know. He would never understand. His was an honest soul. Like Schuyler Van Dyck, he could no more tell a lie than he could commit wanton murder. She had no choice—she would have to agree to Dekker's plan, pay him whatever he demanded, and pray for deliverance. If God was merciful—if he would forgive her sins and the bitterness of the past years—then perhaps he would rid her of Dekker. The man could be swept overboard in a storm at sea; he could be cracked over the skull in a tavern brawl; an insanely jealous girl-friend could stab him in the heart. But he would need to die quickly, with his mouth closed and his eyes open to see God's justice worked on Aidan's behalf.

"I don't care about the money, God," Aidan whispered as the first drops of rain began to sting her cheeks. "But Sterling must never know what I was. He must always believe me a gentle-woman, for he could not love me otherwise. So if you will kill this vile man for me, I will—"

She would what? What could she give the God who already had everything? She already believed in him, and she had already mended her behavior—she hadn't picked a pocket since deciding to become respectable. The life she lived here, as a woman, was as honest and virtuous as any matron's in Batavia. So what could she promise to seal the deal?

Her mind floated in a sepia haze, then focused on a memory of Heer Van Dyck. One afternoon they had been painting together in his garden, and she had tried to explain why she wanted to leave the tavern and take charge of her own life.

"*Ja,* I see," he had answered, his eyes sparkling. "But you don't understand, my young friend. Take your life into your own hands, and you have only yourself to rely on. Give your life over to God, though, and you have the limitless treasure of his mercy and love at your disposal."

He put down his paintbrush and turned toward her. "All the arts we practice," he said, gesturing toward the canvases they were painting, "are but an apprenticeship. The big art is our life. I wouldn't want to paint that picture alone, so I have placed the brush into the Master's hands."

On that summer day so long ago, Aidan hadn't had the faintest idea what Heer Van Dyck meant. Now his words took on meaning and substance. God had her faith, her good deeds—but what he wanted was her paintbrush. Control. Her *surrender.*

Aidan looked toward the sky, where stark white bones of lightning cracked through the gray skin of the clouds. "All right, God," she said, raising her voice above the howling of the wind. "I yield to you. Take my life, I've made a mess of things, and there is no one else to blame."

There was no answer from the overcast heavens save the rains, which fell like needles against her skin. Aidan lingered a moment more, hoping for some sign that she'd been heard, then slowly turned and sought refuge in the sanctity of Sterling's cabin.

⊷⊷

Four weeks passed without incident. In thoughtful moments, Aidan stared across the sea toward the *Zeehaen.* That sturdy little ship followed the *Heemskerk* like a puppy following its master, and she noticed no signs of distress, no signal that anything untoward had happened within its belly. Once, spying Dekker's broad form on the deck, Aidan retreated into the shadows of the forecastle as if she'd seen a ghost.

One thing was clear: God wasn't going to kill him for her. He would take her father, her best friend, and her mentor, but he wouldn't take her enemy.

"I don't blame you for not wanting that fiend," she muttered. "But you leave me with very hard choices, God."

The sight of Dekker had left her feeling queasy. Pressing her hand to her churning stomach, she paused and looked around the

tiny cabin. Last night she had arranged her sketches into one neat pile, then stacked the painted canvases as carefully as she could. She spent most of her time sketching now, for her paint supply was dwindling and only one blank canvas remained.

Just this morning, Sterling asked why she had reserved that one canvas.

"I'm waiting," she answered.

"For what?"

She had smiled to herself, and for the first time voiced the idea she had not been able to articulate. "For the feeling of almost home. That's when I'll know what to paint."

Aidan shook her head regretfully. After days of praying and wondering what God would have her do, she had awakened to the realization that since the Almighty honored truth, truth was what she should offer her husband. When Sterling had left the cabin this morning, she pulled his battered English New Testament from his trunk and read these profound words: "And ye shall know the truth, and the truth shall make you free."

Today she would tell him about Dekker, about Orabel's death, about her parents, about Lili's desperate bid to survive in Batavia. And she would tell the truth—she had never been a harlot, but she had picked more pockets than she could count, and she had served a term or two in the public workhouse. She had lived and consorted with harlots, beggars, and other ne'er-do-wells, yet she had never considered herself one of them—well, she had never wanted to *remain* one of them.

And if he hated her, she would let him go. With a broken heart, she would take her inheritance from Van Dyck and return to England. Dekker would no longer have power over her. She could slip away, shedding the past in order to find a place where her heart could heal—

No!

Sickness and desolation swept over her at the very thought of living apart from Sterling. Wherever she went, every man would

remind her of him in some way, though no other man could begin to fill his place in her heart.

She pressed her hand to her forehead, feeling a wretchedness of mind she'd never known before. If Sterling could not love her, she would throw herself overboard, leaving him alone with his cherished ideals and false conceptions. Her misery, like a steel weight inside her heart, would pull her to the bottom of the sea. If she were dead, she'd no longer have to worry about Witt Dekker or feel her heart breaking every time she looked at the man she adored.

No, beloved. Think not of death but of life.

The Voice shook her to the core. Heer Van Dyck had occasionally spoken of hearing God's voice, but Aidan had never expected to hear and feel it herself. Hot tears rolled down her face, tears of loss and fear, and it was then that Sterling opened the door.

"Aidan!" His face contorted into an expression of alarm when he saw her tears. "What is wrong? Has anyone—"

"No," she whispered. She clutched her cramping stomach. "But I need to talk to you—oh!"

Without warning, she gagged. Sterling guided her to the chamber pot by the bed, holding her head steady while she vomited. When her empty stomach had heaved its paltry contents into the basin, she stood motionless, gasping for breath, as fresh tears stung her eyes. Now he *knew* something was wrong. She could no longer hide her fears behind a false smile, and she could not postpone this confrontation. Her own body had betrayed her, leaving her soiled and smelly, an object of disgust and revulsion. But no matter. He would undoubtedly feel the same way when he discovered what she had been before Heer Van Dyck pulled her off the street.

"Aidan, darling!" He took her into his arms and pressed her head to his shoulder as she broke down and sobbed. This would be the last time he held her, for even now he was deluded.

"Sterling—"

"There now." He pulled a handkerchief from his pocket and wiped the dampness from her fingers and lips. "Did you eat something distasteful? Was the fish at breakfast undercooked?"

"I didn't eat breakfast." She closed her eyes as his hand pushed her sweat-soaked hair from her forehead. "Sterling, I need to talk to you. About something important."

"All right, but you can talk sitting down." He lowered himself to his bunk, then pulled her into his lap. She allowed herself to remain there, wiping the last tears from her eyes. She needed to have all her wits about her, she wanted to be clear-eyed and strong when she told him the truth.

"Aidan—" His voice was softer now, and thoughtful. "You fainted the other day." His clear blue eyes shone up at her. "How many times in the last week have you vomited?"

She flushed miserably. She had tried to hide her distress from him, but ever since Dekker's visit she hadn't been able to think straight, let alone hold down a decent meal.

"I—I can't remember."

His eyes grew large and liquid, and his hand tightened on her shoulder. "Aidan, my love, I know it's hard to keep track of time aboard a ship, but think—when was the last time you bled?"

Her face burned with sudden humiliation as her mind exploded in sharp awareness. Heaven above, she hadn't even considered the possibility! Lili's girls had explained certain things she could do to avoid an inconvenient or ill-advised pregnancy, but she'd never thought to implement any of those procedures with Sterling.

"Faith, Aidan, I am a physician!" Sterling's eyes were bright with speculation and a muscle quivered at his jaw. "Do not be coy or modest now, but tell me! When was the last time?"

"Four months ago, I think," she whispered. "Before we landed at the Friendly Islands."

For a brief instant his face seemed to open, and Aidan watched

her words take hold. She saw his surprise, a quick flicker of fear, and then joy unlike anything she had ever seen on another human face. Then his arms closed around her.

"Aidan, my love," he whispered reverently, "you are carrying our child."

She sat frozen as Sterling buried his face in her neck. She felt his tears upon her flesh and the subterranean quiver that passed through him. Over his shoulder, she lifted her gaze and stared at a knothole in the wall. Her plan to tell him the truth had just been completely scuttled.

⚜

The late-morning sun was warm, burnishing the objects in the cabin with May's golden glow as it streamed through the porthole. Sterling lay stretched out on the bunk with Aidan crowded in next to him.

After he explained the significance of her physical symptoms, she had worn herself out with weeping and now lay in his arms. She had not spoken or moved in the last hour, and Sterling hoped she slept.

He had been scared silly by the frightened look on her face and terrified by her tears. But this was not sad news—it was wonderful! He had barred the door and lay down to comfort her, and he wouldn't have minded staying in that position throughout the rest of the day and night. Anything to be of service to his wife and child. He didn't mind being Aidan's pillow, and he would talk all night if the sound of his voice comforted her. He would quietly fill her dreams with joyful plans for their child in order to take her mind off the discomforts of early pregnancy.

"Of course, if it's a girl, I won't be disappointed," he said, keeping his voice low. He didn't want to wake her if she dozed, and he wasn't ready to share this news with the entire ship. He knew the first months of a woman's pregnancy were crucial; Aidan had to be protected and sheltered even when the baby had not yet shown itself. And so he would protect his wife, even if it meant holding her on his lap until they reached Batavia.

"I wish you could see what the baby looks like now," he went on, a blush of pleasure rising on his face as he remembered what he had learned in medical school. "'It's a tiny thing, small enough to fit into the palm of your hand, but you'd be able to see all his tiny parts. Fingers, toes, a wee chin, a tiny pert nose—like yours." He gently, tenderly lowered his hand to the gentle swell of her abdomen. "Soon you'll be able to feel the baby moving inside you. They say it feels like a gentle butterfly fluttering, at first."

A breeze gusted in through the porthole, stirring Aidan's hair. "What if it's a lovely red-haired girl?" Sterling propped himself on one elbow and ran his hand over Aidan's gleaming tresses, thick and glossy and full of fire. "I'd like a girl, you know. Or a boy. Or both, if you're thinking of twins. And I'll try to be a good father. Of course, you're so genteel and fine I know you'll be a wonderful mother, but I'm from sturdier stock—I might have to mend my manners a bit. But you won't catch me saying anything that would be bad for the baby to pick up. I promise you that, Aidan. I'd promise you the world, if you wanted it."

Loose curls softened her oval face, coppery in the waning light—except for that one strand of white at her temple. He lightly ran his palm over her hair, but she didn't move. Good. She slept soundly. She needed to rest now, and anyone who tried to disturb her would regret it. With wonder he gazed down at her features, where delicacy combined with strength—the fragility of a lady blended with the fervor of a girl bold enough to follow her dreams.

"We'll stay in Batavia until after the baby is born," he whispered. "No woman should have to endure a sea crossing when she's with child. And then we'll announce the birth in church, and let all the fine citizens of Batavia come to pay their respects."

He grinned, imagining Dr. Lang Carstens bowing before the cradle. That cranky doctor would change his tune when he realized that Sterling Thorne had married into the snobby society he served.

"I suppose there will be a bit of scrapping over who will be the

first to visit our child, him being so highly regarded and all. Governor Van Diemen will visit, of course, because we have him to thank for bringing us together." He chuckled at the thought of the portly governor's part in the baby's conception. "Perhaps we should name the baby—if it's a boy, of course—Anthony, after the governor?" He smiled down at his sleeping bride's face. "What do you think, love? Anthony Thorne? It has a certain noble ring to it, I think. In any case, we'll invite the governor to the christening—"

Aidan stirred. Her long lashes fluttered for a moment, then her eyes opened.

"Did I wake you?" he asked, feeling slightly giddy and very foolish.

Her vivid green eyes had a distant stillness to them. "No." She lifted her hand to touch his face, and he caught her hand and pressed her fingertips to his lips.

"We will be home in Batavia soon, my love," he whispered. "And it's a good thing, for soon we will not both fit on this narrow bunk."

She gave him a wavering smile, then broke into sobs. He drew her close and held her. It would pass, he was sure. Unaccountable mood swings were nothing unusual when women were in the family way.

⁂

The next morning, Aidan lay as still as a log until Sterling had risen, dressed, and gone out on deck. She had insisted that he go to breakfast without her, and he had seemed to understand. What she really wanted was privacy, time to confront her own feelings, to make her own decisions. It was good that she had only one blank canvas left. If she had the luxury of an endless supply, she'd probably surrender to the temptation to paint what she was feeling, creating a succession of storm scenes and blood-red sunsets.

Thoughts of the sun drew her eye to the porthole, and Aidan did a double take when the bright redness of sky and sea caught her eye. "Red sky at morning, sailors take warning," she murmured,

and she drew nearer to the window, expecting to see rough water or angry clouds outside. But nothing seemed amiss, unless trouble stirred beneath the waves.

She smoothed the deep wrinkles from her shirt, then pulled on her stockings and tied on her garters. She wriggled into her bodice, then slipped her skirt over her head. As she struggled to tie the laces at the waistband, she abruptly realized that certain alterations would be necessary if they didn't reach Batavia within a few weeks. The skirt was easily adjustable, but the two bodices were snug and would be gaping within a few weeks. If the winds did not blow them steadily home, she'd be using her needle and thread on more than canvas before long.

She knotted the laces at her waist, then quickly pinned the green silk sleeves to the bodice. Last night she would have enjoyed using those pins upon Sterling's lips—she'd have done anything to stop him from prattling on about his dreams for their child! But what could she say? She couldn't tell him the truth now. His child would be great and noble and esteemed because it sprang from his lineage. How could she tell him that her contributions to the family tree included a procuress and a poor Irish cooper? And while it was well and good that the child's father would be an esteemed doctor, the baby's mother was a one-time pickpocket.

Aidan sank back to the bed, suddenly enervated. She had no choice but to go forward. She couldn't throw herself into the sea; the baby deserved to live. And though she truly believed God wanted her to tell Sterling the truth, the Almighty had unexpectedly brought another powerful force into the situation. If she told Sterling everything and used the baby as her security, after his initial horror and his subsequent disgust, Sterling would insist upon remaining with her for the child's sake. Always dutiful, he would love the baby and despise its mother—and Aidan didn't think she could endure even the shadow of his hatred.

A sudden gust of wind struck the ship, and the cabin heeled sideways, sending her crate sliding to the wall. The seamen outside

her door whooped in excitement, and Aidan braced herself. She could not tell Sterling anything. Witt Dekker, therefore, would be part of her life for weeks—perhaps years—to come. They were not far from Batavia now; and he'd want his money as soon as they landed. He'd follow her, ask about her, and he'd probably offer his congratulations when he learned that she expected a child. If she threatened him in any way he'd do something despicable, perhaps even going so far as to insinuate that the child was not legitimately Sterling's.

She shuddered, thinking of other women at the wharf who had discovered themselves with child. None of them had a husband. In that respect, at least, she was fortunate, for even if Sterling discovered the truth, she'd have a home as long as he loved the child.

The noises outside her cabin changed, and Aidan lifted her head, wondering what had happened. The ship, always alive, now seemed to be stretching and sighing, creaking its timbers and squeaking its stairs. The rising wind began to moan, then burst into a hellish shriek.

Red sky at morning…

The floor slanted again, and Aidan scrambled for the door. Had Sterling managed to come up from below decks? She flung the door open and saw men racing to trim the sails. The low, hazy, mountainous shores of New Guinea passed silently off the port bow, separated from the *Heemskerk* by a hard, metallic sea.

The bosun clanged his bell, the lookouts scrambled down from their masts, and the first mate commanded the watch to man the pumps. The wind hummed through the rigging, strangely flat notes rising and falling as the ship rolled. Masts strained their shrouds and braces first to the port side, then to the starboard.

Aidan braced herself in the doorway as thick, dense raindrops began to splatter at her feet. The sea beyond the rail lunged up in white plumes, and the ship bucked and reared. The gale increased to a torrent, so laden with rain that the sailor at the wheel had to hold his head down and turn his head sideways to breathe.

Aidan lost her balance and fell, hard, to the deck, but she held tight to the doorframe and shielded her eyes from the drenching rain as she searched for Sterling. Meester Holman clung to a mast amidships, bawling orders she could not hear through the storm.

Stunned by the ferocity of the sudden squall, Aidan looked over at the *Zeehaen*. Driving sheets of rain nearly obscured her view, but she could see men on the smaller ship attempting to batten the hatches and secure the sails. A knot of sailors clustered around one of the cannons they'd used the day before for artillery practice, and Aidan guessed they were trying to carry the gun below decks before it broke loose and crashed through the railing.

Off the *Zeehaen*'s port bow a pair of seamen worked to free the fore staysail. Aidan gasped as the small ship pitched forward and a black wave swept aboard. When the ship righted itself and the wave retreated, one of the men who had been standing on the yardarm had vanished, borne away by the devouring wave.

Terror coursed through her, and Aidan scrambled back inside her cabin and slammed the door. Sterling wouldn't want her outside in the rain. Always the doctor, he'd be furious that she'd gotten wet and cold while she looked for him. She wouldn't tell him about the man swept overboard from the *Zeehaen*. There was nothing he could do, though his exaggerated sense of responsibility would probably lead him to blame himself for the accident.

The door opened a moment later, and Sterling rushed into the cabin, his eyes darting wildly about. "My bag, I need my bag," he said, scarcely looking at her.

"Why?" she asked, frightened by the tone of his voice. "Is someone injured?"

He nodded abruptly, then spotted his bag beneath her chair. "Aboard the *Zeehaen*," he said, stooping to retrieve it. "Holman saw the accident through his spyglass. A cannon got away from the men trying to secure it, and I'm afraid the first mate is in a bad way."

"The first mate—" Aidan felt a sudden darkness behind her

eyes, and a chilly dew formed on her skin. "Witt Dekker? He is injured?"

Sterling lifted his bag, stood, and looked around the room as if trying to make sure he'd remembered everything.

"Dekker?" she asked again, feeling bands of tightness in her chest. "Is he hurt?"

"Yes." Sterling looked at her, then leaned forward and gave her a gentle kiss on the cheek. "Poor darling, are you all right? I knew you'd be safe in the cabin, but Dekker needs help. Holman believes the man's leg is shattered, at the very least. If I don't get over there to set it, the carpenter will take it off within the hour." His handsome face went grim. "And I don't think even Dekker could survive a carpenter's amputation."

Aidan gasped as she reached out to clench Sterling's shirt in her hands. By heaven above, was this what God had done to answer her prayers? Dekker might die, he *deserved* to die, but her husband intended to save him!

"Sterling," she cried, spasms of alarm quaking through her body, "you can't go to the *Zeehaen* in this storm! The waves are too high; the barge will be swamped!"

"Darling." His free hand covered hers, and he gave her a confident and tender smile. "Of course I must go. I'm a doctor, and I've sworn to tend the sick and injured, wherever they may be. Besides, the seamen are setting up a guide rope between the two ships. The barge will be made as safe as possible."

"But Witt Dekker—"

"—is a man like any other," Sterling interrupted, "and in need of my help right now." His eyes shown with determination and purpose as he dropped his medicine bag and took her head in his hands, pressing his lips to her forehead. "You ought to lie down, love. It wouldn't be good for you or the baby if you should fall in this storm."

"Sterling, don't go!" The ship shifted as she spoke, and she clung more desperately to him. "Dekker is an evil man! How do

you know God does not intend for him to die? Sterling, he attacked me on that island, don't you remember? And he lies!"

"You forgave him." Sterling's voice was soft as he took her hands and firmly pulled her toward the bunk. He pressed upon her shoulders, forcing her to sit, then took up his bag again. "And though it was difficult, I forgave him too. And now he needs a doctor. He might die if I don't go."

"Sterling, please!" She reached out, but he turned and walked to the door, then turned back and looked at her.

"I hate to leave you like this," he said in a choked voice, "but I must go. And I promise I will return as soon as I can."

"You promised you would never leave me again!"

She closed her eyes and prayed that his conscience would overpower this compulsion to serve, but when she opened her eyes again the door was closed and Sterling was gone. She lay back on the bed, and tears streamed into her hair, over her hand, and onto the pillow.

Her husband was resolved to save the man who would destroy their happiness. And if Witt Dekker thought himself at death's door, he might say anything—truth or lie—to hurt her.

Thirty-Three

~~~~~~~

"Shall I get you a dry shirt, Doctor?" Gerrit Janszoon's face was somber and dark in the torchlight.

"That would be nice, thank you." Sterling sipped on the mug of broth the cook had provided. He'd been aboard the *Zeehaen* for nearly twelve hours, and he now believed Witt Dekker would live, though the leg was unsalvageable. Even under the best conditions Sterling would have been unable to save the leg and the patient too. The bosun and coxswain had forced Dekker to drink whiskey until he passed out. The carpenter then handed over his saw, and Sterling performed the neatest amputation he could, under the circumstances. The arteries were cauterized with a red-hot iron, the torn flesh mended with a needle and thread, and fine English leeches applied to the cut edges to lessen the swelling.

"*Ja,* you did good, Doctor," the carpenter was saying now, his only remaining front tooth gleaming in the dim light of the hold. "I don't expect that I could have done better myself. I would not have thought to sear those wiggly worms under the skin—"

"Blood vessels," Sterling corrected him absently. "And yes, you might have thought of it...if you wanted to prevent him from bleeding to death."

Janszoon returned with a dry shirt, which Sterling took with an appreciative smile. "By the way, Skipper," he said, shrugging out of his own soaked shirt, "is there any way we might flash a signal to the *Heemskerk?* My wife was quite worried about my passage during the storm." He caught the knowing look that passed

between the skipper and the carpenter and hastened to correct the impression that he was a henpecked husband. "Women worry, you know. Especially when they are in a delicate condition."

Janszoon's brow lifted in surprise. "Really now! That's quite a secret you've been hiding. We'll lift a glass in your honor, Doctor, as soon as we find another jug. I think we poured everything available on this deck down Dekker's gullet."

"I'll appreciate the thought." Sterling fumbled to find the buttons on his shirt. "But as the storm's stopped, I'll be leaving you gentlemen. As you might suspect, I've reason to be getting back to the *Heemskerk* as soon as the oarsmen are ready."

"I'll order up two men for you directly," Janszoon said, winking broadly at Sterling. "And give our regards to Captain Tasman—"

A low groan from the patient interrupted him. Sterling forgot about his shirt as he leaned over Dekker's perspiring body. He lifted the man's eyelid, then frowned. Dekker's pupils were fixed and dilated—not a good sign—and his body simmered with impending fever.

"When the cannon struck Dekker," he said, searching for a pulse in his patient's neck, "did he hit his head on the deck?"

"No sir," the bosun answered, fidgeting in the doorway. "He smacked it on the mizzenmast."

Sterling opened his mouth to ask why in the world they hadn't shared that bit of information, then thought better of it. No sense in upbraiding them for ignorance. He bent to examine his patient again. He'd spent all his time worrying about Dekker's leg, when the blow to the head might be a far more serious injury.

"Cancel that order for the barge, Skipper," Sterling told Tasman, his eyes focused on Dekker. "I may be here a while."

Janszoon nodded soberly, then gestured toward the doorway. The bosun and carpenter exited immediately, and Sterling smiled grimly as he watched them go. No one wanted to linger around a dying man.

~<a~⋆~a~

Sterling sat in a chair beside his patient and watched death bear down with a slow and steady deliberation. He could do nothing to stop it. Time passed, and though he knew the sun was rising and setting on the deck above him, he was trapped in the endless night of the lower deck, where the sick and dying were shunted aside.

He dozed when his patient slept, fretted when Dekker writhed in agony. Though Sterling blew white hellebore, pepper, and castery into his patient's nostrils—the commonly prescribed cure for apoplexy—Dekker ranted and raved throughout his final hours. The storm outside had abated, yet another storm raged in the man's soul, and Sterling was powerless to subdue or temper it. Indeed, Dekker seemed unaware of anyone else in the room.

Once when Sterling approached with a drink intended to calm the man's nerves and ease his pain, Dekker struck out as if fighting an invisible enemy, sending both the cup and its liquid flying across the room. Another time Sterling thought to ask for the man's little dog, thinking that the animal might snap Dekker out of his delirium, but Snuggerheid was nowhere to be found. A mournful seaman finally reported that the dog must have been lost in the storm after Dekker fell.

Sterling had seen unpleasant deaths, but none as desperate as this one. Dekker called for his missing leg; he screamed for someone to stop the burning; he cursed his mother, his father, and someone called Dempsey. Sterling stiffened, his temper soaring, when Dekker invoked Aidan's name and called her the vilest names imaginable, but then he forced himself to remember that Dekker was lost in the ravings of madness. This was death, and this was how unredeemed, guilt-stricken men often died. Sterling let Dekker rave and storm, grateful that at least the man's end would come quickly. A sputtering candle did not last long.

Finally, after many hours, Dekker grew quiet. Sterling pulled his stool nearer to the man's bunk and held a looking glass to the

man's nostrils to check for signs of breath. The glass misted slightly; the man still lived.

He was about to remove the mirror when Dekker's hand rose and gripped Sterling's wrist. His eyes, so fevered and wild only a few moments before, opened and stared at Sterling with complete lucidity.

"Doctor," he said simply, his face devoid of any emotion.

"Yes, Mr. Dekker," Sterling answered, allowing the man to hold his arm. "Do not be afraid. I am with you."

"I am dying?"

Sterling nodded slowly, feeling the stir of compassion within him. "Yes, you are. I am sorry."

"You won't be." Dekker shifted his eyes, then released Sterling's arm. His hand moved, spiderlike, toward the kerchief at his neck.

"Do you want me to remove it?" Sterling set the looking glass aside. "Is it too tight?"

"The cross," Dekker said, his eyes like obsidian as he looked at Sterling again. "Give it to your wife. Ask her…what it means."

"What the cross means, Mr. Dekker," Sterling whispered, "is that you can have eternal life and peace through Jesus Christ our Lord. It is not too late. If you would confess your sins and beg forgiveness, Christ is always willing to forgive. The things that trouble your soul will be washed away in the flood of God's mercy and love."

Silence. Sterling leaned forward and looked more closely at his patient.

"Mr. Dekker?"

The man's eyes had gone wide and blank. Witt Dekker was dead.

Sterling stroked his fingertips over the officer's eyes, not bothering to hold the glass to his nostrils again. He knew the narrow, pinched face of death; he'd seen it a dozen times.

Impulsively he pressed his fingers under the kerchief at

Dekker's neck and felt a thin gold chain. Pulling it from beneath the kerchief and the man's shirt, Sterling found a handsome gold cross at the end of the chain.

Odd that a reprobate like Witt Dekker would wear a symbol of Christ. Odder still that he should refer to Aidan when he mentioned it.

Sterling flipped the cross over on his palm, and his mind went numb with shock when he read the inscription: *My love is yours forever, Aidan.*

◆

Sterling climbed the companionway ladder in a daze, his thoughts traveling in a hundred different directions. The golden cross hung now about his own neck, and his mind reeled with unanswered questions. Why would Witt Dekker wear a cross inscribed with Aidan's name? How had he received it? Was it something he meant to give her or something she had given him? Had he stolen or bought it from Aidan—and had it been given to her by another man?

Ask her what it means, Dekker had said, and Sterling fully intended to. There had to be a reasonable response, an answer that would put the pieces of the puzzle into their proper places.

"I'll have that barge now, Skipper," Sterling called to Janszoon as he walked out into the bright sunlight on the deck. He ran his hand over the three-day growth of beard on his face. Aidan wouldn't appreciate his scruffy appearance. "If you'd call the oarsmen for me—"

Janszoon turned and laughed. "*Goejehelp* you, Doctor, you have been too long below deck! Look up, we are home!"

Sterling straightened, surprised and more confused than ever. A coastline stretched along the port bow, and a harbor loomed in the distance. The *Heemskerk* sailed ahead of them, her sails already lowering.

"Batavia?" Sterling asked, dumbfounded.

"*Ja,* Doctor." Janszoon grinned, then turned toward his cabin.

"Wait but a moment," he called over his shoulder, "and we'll drop anchor, then you can take the first barge going ashore."

"But I don't want to go ashore!" Sterling lengthened his stride to keep up with the skipper. "I want to go to the *Heemskerk*. My wife waits aboard that ship."

"Doctor." The skipper paused in the doorway of his cabin, a look of pained tolerance crossing his face. "We have two barges aboard this vessel. Do you think I can tell this land-hungry crew that one of the boats must take you to the *Heemskerk* before it can carry them ashore to wives and sweethearts?" He frowned and folded his arms. "I think not. I would have a mutiny on my hands."

"But, Skipper—"

Janszoon disappeared into his cabin, and the resolute slam of the door made it clear that the discussion had ended. Sterling went to the rail, watching as the outskirts of Batavia, the pride of the Netherlands, slid slowly by. This colony and her people had not welcomed him on his first arrival, but this time things would be different. His wife was a gentlewoman and an heiress, and their child would be born here. He lifted his face to the caressing breeze and the warmth of the sun, enjoying the idea of his own neat little house in the fine part of town.

"Excuseert u mij." He put out a hand to stop a passing seaman. "What day is it, sir? I've been below for so long I lost all track of time."

"May fourteenth," the man answered, grinning as he heaved his gunnysack onto his shoulder. "And a fine day for coming home, heh, Doctor?"

"Yes, it is." Sterling planted his hands on the railing and breathed deeply. It was a fine day for making a new start and—he frowned suddenly, remembering the golden cross hanging above his heart—for settling unfinished business.

Thirty-Four

꒰ꙭ꒱

After promising one of the oarsman that he would name his child after him, four hours later Sterling climbed the rigging and boarded the *Heemskerk*. The flagship had reached port at least two hours before the *Zeehaen,* and the vessel had a desolate, almost ghostly feel as he hurried over the deck. Poor Aidan might be frightened in this solitude, and he couldn't forget that she hadn't wanted him to go to the *Zeehaen.*

He hurdled several coils of rope and piles of canvas, then burst into their cabin. "Aidan?"

Her paintings rested in a neat stack upon the bunk, and a sheaf of parchments lay next to the paintings, alongside the crate with her brushes, palette, and paint boxes. Her brown silk skirt and bodice lay neatly folded at the edge of her crate, and her men's clothes lay under the brown silk.

His eyes fell upon one painting he'd never seen before. It was the large canvas she'd been saving for home—the one she said she'd paint when they neared Batavia. He lifted it and sat down on the bunk, his eyes blurring with hot tears as he studied the picture.

"Oh, Aidan," he murmured, caught up in the dark hues, the restless and haunting images on the canvas. "I wanted your home-coming to be happy."

The painting was fresh, for the back of the canvas still felt damp from the oils. The dominant figure, shining against the background of night sky and sea, was a man in iridescent robes whose starlit hands appeared to create three creatures on a beam

of light traversing the sky. The first creature was a mist-colored caterpillar munching on a leaf that dangled from a beam of starlight. The second was a silvery chrysalis, and the third, a vibrant butterfly that seemed to unfurl his lustrous wings before Sterling's eyes. It was a painting of life and renewal and hope, but the eyes of the Creator were dark with sadness, as if he regretted working his magic at all.

Sterling pressed his lips together as the painting's message struck his heart with the force of a physical blow. Aidan saw the beauty in her life, in their love, and yet she was sorry for it. Why? Did her sadness have anything to do with Witt Dekker?

"Mondejuu!"

Sterling whirled around, surprised by an unfamiliar voice. A stout, bearded man in a heavily ornamented doublet stood behind him, his eyes intent upon the painting, his mouth gaping in admiration. He murmured something in Dutch that Sterling could not understand.

"I'm sorry." Sterling frowned in confusion. "But I am Sterling Thorne, the ship's doctor. I don't believe we've had the pleasure of meeting."

The gentleman snapped to attention and answered in clipped English. "Of course, Dr. Thorne; I have heard nothing but good about you." His round eyes darted again to the painting in Sterling's hand. "But I had no idea you were an artist!"

"I'm not. My wife painted this." Sterling lifted the painting, then carefully lowered it back to the chair where he'd found it. "And if you'll excuse me, sir, I'd like to find her."

"Your wife?" The man's nose quivered for a moment, then he swelled his chest and abruptly inclined his head. "Allow me to introduce myself—I am Anthony Van Diemen, governor general of the Colony. Let me be the first to welcome you home, Doctor, and to congratulate you on your choice of a talented wife. I have never seen anything like that picture. Though I expected great things when I asked Heer Van Dyck to accompany this expedition,

I never dreamed that treasures like this would result." His fat finger pointed toward the metamorphosis painting. "That work is quite exceptional."

"My *wife* is exceptional." Sterling shifted and glanced toward the door, eager to be rid of his pompous visitor.

"Could I interest you in selling one or two of her works?" The governor's eye wandered greedily toward the stack of canvases on the bunk. "I would love to look through this treasure trove before her work reaches the gallery."

"I think she would be very pleased," Sterling muttered, sidling toward the doorway. "But if you'll excuse me, sir, I'll leave you to look through them at your leisure. I really am late, and I must find her."

Without waiting for a response, Sterling rushed out, his eyes searching every exposed deck, the rigging, the piles of canvas where she might be hiding in some sort of teasing game. "Aidan!"

"Ahoy, Doctor," came a voice cracked with age and disuse. "Are you looking for your wife?" One of the seamen, a grizzled veteran, grinned down at him from the rigging.

"Have you seen her?" Sterling called. "Is she below in the galley?"

"The lady went ashore in the first boat," the sailor answered. "Meester Holman escorted her. He was very eager to see his family."

Sterling's mind reeled. Aidan left the ship! But where would she go? Where did she live? He suddenly realized that he knew very little about the woman who bore his name and carried his child.

He dashed forward and sprinted across the deck. The barge that had brought him from the *Zeehaen* was now halfway across the bay, nearly to the docks.

"Won't be another barge for a while," the old sailor called from his perch. "So you might as well sit and wait. Those of us who are left are in no hurry."

Biting back his impatience, Sterling settled himself atop a mountain of coiled rope and stared at the dock, willing a boat to come back for him.

The first stars had appeared in the vault of the heavens by the time Sterling reached Schuyler Van Dyck's house. An elderly woman with red-rimmed eyes opened the door to his knock, but when Sterling inquired about Aidan, she forcibly slammed the door without a word of explanation.

"Wait," he shouted, pounding on the door. "I must know what has happened to her! She is my wife!"

"That wench will not be allowed over the threshold of this house again," the old crone rasped through the keyhole. "And you dishonor my master's memory by speaking her name. Now be gone!"

He backed away, stunned by such a reception. Had Aidan endured the same disdain today? If she was not welcomed here, where would she go? And why had she gone off without him? She had been unhappy when he left to tend Dekker, but surely her anger had faded by now.

He paused, remembering the brooding emotion evident in her last painting. Perhaps her anger hadn't faded. Or perhaps she thought he honestly intended to abandon her. The idea made no sense, but sometimes Aidan brooded about things that mystified him.

He walked to the street and sat on a carriage block, twisting his hat in his hands as he considered her options. She might have gone to an inn; an unescorted lady could take a room with no questions asked if she had a good reputation in the town. The bulge of impending birth had not yet begun to show beneath her gown, so no one would think ill of her for traveling alone...yet.

He forced a smile. Perhaps this was some sort of game, something they would laugh about in years to come. "But darling, I thought you'd know I'd go to such-and-such a place," she'd say, and he'd smile and kiss her forehead, amazed at how ignorant and foolish he had been in their early days.

But at this moment, he could not find any humor in the

situation. His labors aboard the *Zeehaen* had left him exhausted, hungry, worried, and badgered by a series of questions revolving around a golden cross...

A coach and four approached from the center of town, and Sterling stood, noting that the black plumes of mourning adorned the horses' heads. He stepped back from the carriage block so the occupant of the coach could alight. A young woman, soberly dressed in a mourning veil and black gown, exited, then nodded to her husband. The second man, however, halted upon the carriage block and stared curiously at Sterling.

"I know you," he murmured, removing his crepe-rimmed hat.

The first man, his arm linked through the young woman's, paused on the cobblestone path. "Henrick, Gusta is waiting for us."

"I'll be along in a moment," the second man answered. He waited until the couple had entered the house, then he lifted a finger and pointed to Sterling. "You were the doctor aboard the *Heemskerk,* my father's ship. I spoke to you briefly before the ship sailed."

"Yes." Sterling bowed formally. "Let me be among the first to convey my condolences. Your father was an exceptional man, and a gentleman in every sense of the word."

The young man nodded, his eyes glistening with unshed tears. "Thank you, sir." His brows lifted. "I don't mean to inconvenience you, but sometime I would like to hear exactly what happened to my father. Captain Tasman came by earlier this afternoon to bring the sad news, but my sister and I still have many questions."

"Tasman came here?" Sterling felt a curious, tingling shock. "Did he, by chance, mention what happened to Aidan, your father's protégée? She seems to have disappeared from the ship."

"The captain did not mention her." Henrick leaned heavily upon his cane. "But I would imagine she has returned to the gutters where Father dug her up." An icy expression settled on his face. "If you have the bad taste to seek that sort of entertainment,

Doctor, I would imagine that you could find any number of women like her on the corner near the Broad Street Tavern. The procuress there has a stable of women who will do most anything for a coin or two, and I've heard that my father's little protégée, as you called her, is the procuress's own daughter."

A sudden surge of rage caught Sterling unaware, like a bolt of white-hot lightning that struck his chest and belly. He stared at the man in astonishment, his fury almost choking him. Then he reined in his emotions. Young Van Dyck had just suffered a serious blow. Perhaps he wasn't thinking clearly. Certainly he was misinformed.

Numb with shock, Sterling stiffly thanked Henrick Van Dyck for his help and walked slowly down the street.

Thirty-Five

Sterling wandered the streets, stumbling through alleys, over cobblestone paths and dusty trails. He begged the innkeepers to search their guest registers, but no one had seen a young woman who called herself Aidan Thorne or Aidan O'Connor. Sterling's panic began to rise. His steps led him back toward the wharf, toward the docks, the taverns, and the flophouses. He didn't think he'd find Aidan in such miserable conditions, but she had come ashore in a barge crowded with seamen, and one of the men from the *Heemskerk* might know where she had gone.

After the clean scents of the sea, the odors of the crowded wharf seemed to close in on him like a vile mist, and the cheerful vulgarity of the crowds near the dock irritated him beyond measure. He paused before the threshold of the Broad Street Tavern. The name of the place registered in his frenzied brain, so he pushed his way through the crowd to the bar. A tall, broad-shouldered man stood there, one hand on the spout of a cask, the other holding a pewter mug.

The barkeep caught Sterling's eye and dipped his chin in a slight nod. "What will you have?" he asked, filling the mug. "Rum, ale, wine, or whiskey?"

"Nothing for me." Sterling turned to search the room. The place teemed with loud women and tipsy seamen, and a cloud of tobacco smoke hovered over everything.

"You can't stand at my bar for nothing." The bartender's fist

rapped the bar near Sterling's elbow. "So I'll ask you again—what will you have?"

Sterling glanced over his shoulder. The man's face had darkened menacingly. "Pour me a pint of ale then." Sterling fished a coin from his purse, dropped it on the counter, then turned back to the room. "And leave me alone for a while."

"Suit yourself." A moment later the promised pint slid over the polished mahogany counter. Sterling ignored it, his eyes flitting instead over the crowd that swayed and stirred to the boisterous music. He thought he recognized a couple of seamen, but they were happily engaged with the tavern maids: each had an arm already entwined about a slender waist.

Sterling clenched his fist against the rising tide of frustration and despair that rose within him. Confound the woman! Where had she gone, and why hadn't she left word or sent a message to him? This was no accident and no game. The Aidan he knew and loved wouldn't want him to worry. She had either come to great harm, or she had not forgiven him for leaving the ship to tend Witt Dekker.

The memory of her face loomed before him as if a curtain had been ripped aside. "Sterling, please," she had begged him, her eyes filling with tears. At the time he had thought her passion and unreasonableness merely harmless symptoms of her pregnancy. But what if his leaving had caused her to doubt his love? Did she think he would always place his patients before her? She knew he lived for her and the coming baby—or did she?

He turned and scrubbed his hand through his hair, as if it might stimulate his brain to more effective thought. He wrapped his hand around the pewter mug and squeezed it hard, searching for a reason, a clue, some insight that might lead him to where Aidan was.

The bartender came forward and glared down his prominent nose. "What's that you're wearing?" he asked, his voice as flat and rough as sandpaper.

"What?"

"Around your neck," the bartender growled. His huge hand reached forward and tugged on the gold chain until the cross clinked against the polished bar.

"It's a cross," Sterling answered dully. "Lots of people wear them."

"Not like this," the man responded. He leaned closer, and Sterling flinched at the sour smell of the man's breath. "This is Aidan's cross—her daddy gave it to her." The glitter in the man's half-closed eyes was both possessive and accusing. "So tell me how you came by it."

Sterling stared in silence for a moment, then the man's words registered. He knew Aidan! And he knew this cross had been hers!

"Where is she?" Sterling demanded, stiffening. His own hand reached out and closed around the bartender's wrist. "If you've seen her, you must tell me now."

More surprised than frightened, the bartender blinked. "Why do you want to know?" His eyes narrowed again in suspicion. "And who are you? Aidan's got herself in a bad way, and she's with Lili now."

"Lady Lili—the procuress?" Sterling's stomach churned. The procuress would know how to take care of an unwanted baby, and if Aidan was 'in a bad way'…

Accepting this knowledge as a sort of password, the bartender nodded. "*Ja,* though Lili's not procuring any more, if you take my meaning. But I still let her and the girls live in my spare room, and they still serve food and drink here."

"Aidan!" Sterling gritted his teeth. "Where is the girl?"

Exasperation flitted across the tavern owner's features. "I was getting to that." He frowned as if Sterling had greatly offended him. "Some old fellow took Aidan away, but she's back, and not at all happy. Lili's with her now."

"Where?" Sterling's grip on the man's wrist tightened with a force that surprised them both.

"The back room," the man answered, jerking his chin over his shoulder. "You'll have to go out the building and through the alley, but that's where I let the girls sleep—"

Sterling didn't wait to hear the rest.

❦

"It's over, Mama." Aidan lay upon one of the straw-stuffed mattresses. Her hair fell in a tangled tide around her shoulders, and what had once been a fine emerald gown was splotched with mud, tears, and a lifetime of regrets.

"How do you know, lass?" Lili brought the oil lamp closer. The room was empty but for them; the other girls wouldn't return until nearly sunrise, when the last drunks were swept out of the tavern.

Lili's face shone like gold in the flickering light, peaceful and smooth with the secrets of wisdom. Aidan wondered how she could ever have thought her mother unattractive. This face was loving, this dingy and foul room the one place she would always be welcomed with no reservations.

Lili had greeted her with tears and embraces, and though there were no strings attached to her welcome, there were questions to be answered. Aidan had spent the afternoon telling her mother about her marriage, her husband, and the coming baby. After hearing the entire story, Lili had promptly shooed the other girls out of the room, then found a basin and towel for Aidan to wash her face and dry her tears. Now in the silence and the lamplight, Aidan thought she might once again find a measure of peace.

"How do I know it's over?" She took a deep breath and gave her mother a sad smile. "Sterling went to Witt Dekker, and he didn't come back even after the storm stopped. Dekker swore to destroy me, Mama, and I know he told Sterling everything. He was evil. I waited for three days, and Sterling never came back. I knew he'd have to come to the cabin to fetch his wages once we anchored, so I left the ship before the *Zeehaen* even came into port. I knew he wouldn't want to see me…and he might not even want the baby."

Lili blew her nose, then looked at her daughter, her gaze as dark and tender as the sea at sunrise. "He might have a change of heart," she whispered, reaching out to smooth a wayward curl from Aidan's forehead. "People can change, you know. You ought to talk to him. I could look around and see if anyone has seen him."

"No, Mama." Aidan dropped her lashes quickly to hide the hurt in her eyes. She could never explain that Sterling would be horrified and humiliated by the thought that a procuress was asking for him. He'd be even more humiliated if the word got around that Irish Annie carried his child.

Voices sounded outside the door, a pair of men arguing, and Aidan closed her eyes and wished for sleep. She'd like to sleep for a month at least, and wake again on the sea, where for a while she had been happy and content. She'd left her paintings and sketches aboard the ship, not daring to bring even one sketch from that world to this one. 'Twas bad enough she was forced to return with her memories…and a true tragedy that the babe within her womb would be born in this sordid place and not the paradise where he had been conceived in love.

The arguing outside grew louder, and Aidan realized that someone had opened the door. "Go away, there's no one here for you," Lili called in her most commanding voice. Aidan heard the rustle of her skirts as she moved toward the door.

"I'm searching for Lady Lili."

Aidan's heart contracted at the sound of Sterling's voice. She cringed beneath the thin blanket that covered her, hoping he would go away and forget he had ever found this place—how *had* he found this place? Why had he come? To berate her? Accuse her?

"If it's a procuress you fancy, you'll have to go elsewhere. But if it's Lili you seek, you're in luck. I'm Lili."

Heaven above, was her mother going to *speak* to him?

"I'm Sterling Thorne, and I'm searching for a woman called Aidan. The tavern owner said I might find her with you."

"How do you come to be wearing Aidan's gold cross?"

Beneath the blanket, Aidan pressed her hand over her mouth. By heaven, Witt Dekker *had* told him the truth! He must have explained how he murdered Orabel, or perhaps he told Sterling that Aidan herself had given the cross to him.

"Please." Sterling's voice was lower now, and frankly pleading. "Aidan is my wife. She carries my child. And though I don't know who you are or what you intend to do, if you lay one hand upon her or harm the baby, I'll—I'll not be responsible for my actions."

Aidan heard her mother's cackling laugh as the door creaked. "Come in, Dr. Thorne," Lili said, her voice surprisingly pleasant. "It's a pleasure to meet you at last. I'm Lili O'Connor, your mother-in-law."

Aidan closed her eyes and groaned. For a moment, hearing the desperation and resolve in Sterling's voice, she hoped he had come to find her. That hope withered with Lili's announcement.

Slowly she sat up, letting the blanket fall to her lap, looking across the empty space toward the door where Sterling stood. The blood had faded from his strong face, leaving him ghostly in the shadows, but the sight of him was powerful enough to steal her breath away.

"Aidan." He took a step toward her, then stopped, and she thought she saw a flicker of anxiety in the depths of his soft blue eyes. "I'm not sure what's happening here, but first, I have to know—you haven't done anything foolish, have you? The baby is all right?"

So that was it. He came, not out of concern for her, but out of fear that she'd found someone to rid her of the child.

"The baby is fine," she answered, her hand automatically going to the slightly rounded bulge under her skirt. She swung her legs to the floor, then straightened, assuming the most dignified position she could manage on the low bed.

She took a deep breath and tried not to look at him. Better to get the truth out in the open, tell him everything. Then, at least,

when he left, he'd understand the confusion in which he'd been entangled. *The truth shall set you free.*

Sterling gave her a lopsided smile. "I came back to the *Heemskerk* as quickly as I could," he said simply, his eyes wide with pain and unspoken questions. "You were gone."

"Dekker?" she asked, lifting her brow.

"Dekker is dead." Sterling looked pointedly around, then glanced at Lili.

"Go ahead, sit," she said, waving him toward a three-legged stool near Aidan's pallet. "Make yourself comfortable, talk things over with Aidan. And don't mind me, I'll just, er—"

"Doesn't Bram need you?" Aidan suggested.

"Yes, that's right, he does." Lili picked up her shawl from the table. "I'll just go and check on things at the gaming tables." She paused and flashed a wide smile at Sterling. "So nice to meet you, Doctor."

Sterling nodded in response, then sighed in relief when she had gone. As the door closed, he sank to the stool and leaned toward Aidan. "Aidan, what were you thinking? I have been frantic half the day and all night, fearing that you had come to harm. I've been everywhere searching for you."

"Sterling—" She reached out, about to take his hand, then decided that touching him was a bad idea. She drew her hand back and crossed her arms as tight as a gate. "You don't have to pretend." She let her eyes drift to her own golden cross around his neck. "I know Dekker told you…things. He was an evil man, and he swore that he would tell you the truth and a pack of lies if I did not pay him ten thousand pounds when we arrived in Batavia and a thousand pounds per month for the rest of his life." She laughed hoarsely. "I suppose I don't need to pay him now, but the truth is out."

"No, the truth is yet to be discovered." Sterling's eyes flashed toward her and she could see no lingering gleam of affection in his gaze. "Yes, Dekker gave me the cross, and he bid me ask you about

it. But when I couldn't find you, I was told to search for you here. And now I find that the tavern keeper is your friend, and the procuress claims to be your mother."

"She is," Aidan sighed. "Or rather, she was—she's not procuring any more. And yes, Bram helped Lili raise me after my father died. And Orabel, the girl you found murdered, was my best friend." She clenched her jaw to stifle the sob in her throat and struggled to maintain her composure. "I am no fine lady, Sterling, no matter how hard Van Dyck tried to paint me as one. I am an heiress only because he was generous. He called me a great artist, he said I would be special." Her voice broke miserably. "For a little while, I believed him."

Her heart constricted so tightly that Aidan could barely draw breath to speak, but she forced the words out: "I loved you; I wanted to be the wife you needed. I didn't even know about the inheritance until Dekker demanded that I give him half. My father always said we were descended from Irish kings, but that was a very, very long time ago."

Sterling did not answer, and Aidan could not look up at him. He might be feeling any number of things—horror, revulsion, anger, even pity—but she could not bear to see any of those things in his eyes.

"There is one other thing I would have you know." She lifted her hand in a flash of defensive spirit. "I am not one of the tavern girls. Lili was quite strict with me as I grew up here. I have done many things of which I am ashamed, but never did I give myself to a man…the way I gave myself to you."

She paused, awaiting his response. There was nothing else to say.

"Aidan," he whispered, with a coolness marred only by the thickness in his voice, "I love you. This is a surprise, yes, but why does it matter? I have always loved the things that are different about you, though you can't seem to love those things yourself."

She did look up then, and saw that his eyes glowed with the clear, deep blue that burns in the heart of a candle flame. "I can

tell you that I love you until the ocean runs dry, but you won't believe me…until you learn to love yourself as God created you. Why can't you accept who you are?"

"What?" She choked on her words. "I know who I am! And I am not proud of the things I've done! Half the men in yonder tavern know me as Irish Annie, and I will not have you take me into your arms, knowing you will resent her for the rest of your life—"

"Aidan, darling." In one movement he left the stool and sank to the floor in front of her. She lifted her hand, prepared to push him away, but he drew her into his arms. She twisted in his embrace, seeking to free herself, but he was always more powerful than she. He gently rocked her back and forth, whispering small comforting sounds into her hair.

"Go away," she cried, her face buried in his shoulder. "You don't want me. You want a fine lady, someone you can be proud of."

"I'm proud of *you.*" His hand ran over her hair, smoothing the tangles. "Don't you know how I adore you? I am in awe of you, Aidan, and the past doesn't matter."

"It does!" She tilted her head back to look into his eyes. "Everything matters to the people here. You cannot be respectable unless your father and grandfather were received by the governor, you cannot be good unless your family owns a thousand acres in Europe."

"None of that matters to me." His gaze clung to hers, watching her reaction to his words. "Aidan, you've spent all your time trying to be something you are not. Be true to the gifts God has given you. Van Dyck was right; you are an artist. Your sin has not been wrong *doing,* but wrong *being.* You've tried to be what everyone else expects, you've tried to do everything apart from the one who created you."

"Not any longer." She lowered her head, resting her cheek upon Sterling's chest, just above his heart. "I surrendered my life to God weeks ago," she murmured. "And even though I thought

you didn't want me anymore, I didn't get mad at God again. I just came...home."

"Home?" She heard the smile in his voice. "Home is where we are, Aidan, where we are together."

Silence, as thick as wool, wrapped itself around them as she sat in his embrace. A group of seamen walked by outside, their laughter filtering through the wooden door.

"What would you have me do?" she finally whispered, scarcely daring to hope for Sterling's response.

His hand was gentle as he caught her chin and lifted her face to his. "You are my wife and my love," he said, his blue eyes gleaming in the lamplight. "I want you to come with me, to make a home with me, to be the mother to our child. Take my name, take my life, take all that I have. And never doubt me again, Aidan. I am a man of honor, and I do not give my love so lightly that I could take it back again."

Hope flooded Aidan's soul, and she slipped her arms around his neck. "Every time I closed my eyes, I saw your face," she whispered. "'Tis a picture my heart could not erase, no matter how hard I tried."

A tremor caught in her throat as a tender smile came to life on his lips. He loved her—for herself, as she was, with no deception between them. And when they kissed, it seemed to Aidan that she had finally come home.

Thirty-Six

❧❧❧

Aidan twirled slowly in front of the large looking glass in her bed-chamber, admiring for the twentieth time the burgundy satin gown Sterling had ordered for the governor's reception. Though privately dissatisfied with the results of the latest Tasman expedition, Governor General Anthony Van Diemen had announced a grand reception to honor the sea captain and the only truly noteworthy accomplishment of the voyage—the discovery of the revolutionary young artist, Aidan O'Connor Thorne.

Sterling stepped into the room and caught her hand, pressing it to his lips. "Are you ready, darling?"

"Yes." She picked up the small cape that fitted over the gown, a delicate creation of sheer silk. Falling from her neck to just below her elbows, a cape was the most elegant way to modestly conceal a blossoming pregnancy.

Sterling led her out of the small house they rented, then presented her to the uniformed coachman who helped her into the open buggy. The coachman smiled at her, touched the brim of his cap, then nodded respectfully to the doctor. "The governor sends his regards," he said with a bow. Then he took his place at the rear of the carriage and whistled to the groom, who cracked the whip and sent the horses trotting off toward the governor's mansion.

Aidan breathed in the fresh air of the open road and smiled in delight. Beside the road, green-white ripples of surf glistened in the sun, and the cloudless sky glared hot and blue overhead. It was a perfect June evening—a good day to leave behind her painting

and enjoy her husband's company. Though their honeymoon aboard the *Heemskerk* had certainly been enjoyable, Aidan knew it would never compare to the simple bliss of having her loving husband alone in her own house.

With easy familiarity, she rested her hand on Sterling's knee and leaned against him. "Will they all be there, do you think?" she asked. "Tasman, Visscher, Holman, and the other officers?"

"All of them," Sterling answered. "Even Lina Tasman and Jan Van Oorschot, the man to whom she is newly betrothed." He took Aidan's hand and pressed it to his lips. "They would not dare risk offending the governor by their absence. Everyone who is anyone in Batavia will be there to see your paintings and offer their congratulations to Governor Van Diemen's latest discovery."

Aidan felt a warm glow flow through her. In the month since the expedition's return to Batavia, she had been lauded and praised. Governor Van Diemen had proclaimed her a genius, a beauty, and a genuine lady, and her brilliant doctor husband suddenly found himself with more patients than he could handle. Strangely enough, none of the society matrons who invited her to tea seemed to know anything about her former life. Even Van Dyck's children and housekeeper, who certainly knew of Aidan's unsavory past, had not dared to say anything against the governor's favorite artist.

The carriage slowed to a halt on the pebbled drive, and the footman sprang to open the door. "Just be yourself, love," Sterling whispered, squeezing her arm before slipping out of the carriage.

Aidan followed, then stood on the carriage block for a moment as the footman fumbled with the elaborate train of her skirt. The governor's mansion sat only a few yards from the beach, and lovely yellow-and-white-striped tents had been set up on the lawn. The guests mingled over the grass and under the shady tents, but more than a few turned as Aidan waited on the carriage block. Standing there, like a statue, Aidan felt the pressure of a hundred pairs of eyes upon her—and the heaviness of public expectation.

She was Aidan O'Connor Thorne, the artist who might make Batavia famous. She was also the wife of Sterling Thorne, the legendary doctor who had proved his mettle and skill on the Tasman expedition. In a moment, she and Sterling would be mingling among the respectable gentlefolk. Together they'd murmur polite greetings and flowery insincere phrases of introduction to people who might go home and criticize everything from her hair to her shoes. Some of them were kind, like Heer Van Dyck and Governor Van Diemen, but others were as lost and unsatisfied as she'd been while she lived at the wharf.

Why had she ever yearned to be accepted by these people? They were respectable, but they weren't happy. Happiness was found in love, and in the peace of understanding God's plan for one's life.

Sterling extended his hand and she took it, then stepped carefully from the carriage block. Below the noise of the party she could hear the steady push-pull of the sea, the ceaseless rhythm of life, like the beating of the tiny heart beneath her breasts. Elemental sounds, arising from things that truly mattered: God's creation, life, and love.

"Sterling," she whispered as he turned her to face the crowd. She looked out upon the sea of faces—some expectant, some petulant, all curious.

"Yes, love?"

She looked into his beloved face, seeing nothing else.

"Would you care for a stroll along the beach?"

His tight expression relaxed into a smile, and his blue eyes blazed into hers, shooting sparks in all directions. "Would you?"

"Yes." She squeezed his hand, remembering that long ago afternoon when she'd walked away from him on the sand, wanting to wring the blood from his heart. They'd both come a long way since that day.

His golden brow arched in surprise. "Right now?"

"Now."

Before the eyes of the startled company, Aidan dropped his hand, picked up her skirts, and moved toward the beach, skimming over the sand as lightly as a bird. Sterling's laughter rang out behind her, and she dashed away, caught up in this spontaneous game of tag.

He chased her into the streaming sea foam before she turned to face him. "Sterling," she called, shivering as cold water seeped into the seam of her slippers, "I love you!"

"And I love you, Mejoffer Thorne." He smiled and pulled her close.

Aidan twined her arms about her husband's neck, then turned to see a crowd of curious guests watching from a discreet distance. She closed her eyes, wishing them away, as Sterling's hands slipped under her arms and wrapped around her waist. A delightful shiver spread over her as she remembered another time she had danced on the beach. In starlit dreams she had danced in a burgundy satin dress like this one, her partner conjured by girlish fantasies and longings.

How much more wonderful to dance with the man God had brought into her life! Sterling was more than she could ever have imagined, more than she had dared to hope she might deserve.

Ja, Heer Van Dyck would say. *God is good.*

"Wife," he said, laughing as the surf splashed over their feet, "I will enjoy watching you explain this to the governor!"

"I can't explain in words," she said, "but tomorrow I shall paint you by the seashore. I will gild God's glorious sunrise behind you with the rosy hope of tomorrow, and paint the bright light of love in your eyes." Standing on tiptoe, she brushed her lips against his, tasting sea salt in his kiss. "That is explanation enough."

"So it is." As the waves broke behind him and a gull pinwheeled overhead, he kissed her again, then lifted her into the cradle of his arms and carried her up the beach.

Epilogue

D o all your stories end with a kiss?"
      The question caught me off guard, and I felt myself blushing as I looked down at the red plastic tablecloth in an effort to avoid Taylor Morgan's brilliant blue eyes. "Well, of course, they should," I answered, shrugging. "I mean, isn't life all about finding the right person and living happily ever after?"

"Maybe." Taylor picked up his glass and swirled the ice cubes thoughtfully. "But I thought one point of this research was to find out what the future might hold for your life. After all, if you are one of Cahira's descendants, are we to assume that you're going to fight for right, then marry some handsome bloke and end your story with a kiss?"

"The world pretty much belongs to men *and* women now." I avoided the bright power of his gaze as I folded my hands on the tablecloth. "And I already told you—I'm the storyteller, nothing more."

Having finally run out of words, I looked around the restaurant. It was nearly ten o'clock, and we'd been sitting at the table for nine hours—long enough to order a half dozen soft drinks, two separate meals, and two banana splits. Professor Howard had slipped away hours ago for his dentist appointment, but I barely noticed when he left. I was too caught up in the story of Aidan O'Connor...and, I confess, a little caught up in Taylor Morgan too. He listened intently to the entire story, laughing in all the right places and frowning in the rough spots.

"There's just one thing that bothers me," he said now, setting his glass down on the table. "Cahira's descendants were supposed to fight for right, correct? Well, Aidan didn't fight. So how does she fit into Cahira's prophecy?"

I lifted my finger and wagged it at him, schoolteacher style. "She *did* fight—against the system—but there's more." I flipped to the last page of my notebook. "Remember Lili? And the twenty thousand pounds? Well, since homeless women in those days were often forced into prostitution, Aidan and her mother set about setting things right. With the money Aidan inherited, Lili founded a school for girls and destitute women. The curriculum was designed to teach the values, morals, and principles all young women needed in order to become godly wives and mothers. The school quickly filled its vacant beds with girls on scholarship, but due to the institution's association with the esteemed Aidan O'Connor Thorne, the most elegant matrons of Batavian society also vied with one another to see who could most generously support the Schuyler Van Dyck School for Young Ladies."

"Oh, that's rich!" Taylor laughed. "I'll bet the Van Dyck children were thrilled to have their names on a school run by a former procuress."

"Well, probably not," I admitted. "But Dempsey and Rozamond Jasper scandalized Batavian society by divorcing in 1645—an extremely unpopular recourse in those days. Dempsey immediately married an English heiress and returned to Europe; Rozamond was forced to live in her brother's household for the rest of her days. And though Henrick Van Dyck remained in Batavia, little else is recorded about him. Apparently he lived and died quietly, without doing anything noteworthy or making trouble for the governor's favorite new artist."

"What about Aidan?" Taylor asked. "Did she stay in Batavia?"

"For a while," I answered. "For three years after the Tasman expedition Sterling and Aidan lived in Batavia, where they had two children, a boy and a girl. They returned to England in 1646,

and Aidan's paintings were acclaimed throughout Europe for their emotion and distinctive style. While all the Dutch masters were painting realistic morality plays, Aidan delved into fantasy and the art of imagination. Most people didn't understand her, but they couldn't deny her talent."

Taylor smiled thoughtfully. "And Abel Tasman—let me guess. Tasmania?"

"Yeah." I grinned. "The place he called 'Van Diemen's Land' is present-day Tasmania. Assassin's Bay is part of modern New Zealand, and his 'Friendly Islands' are the islands of the Tongan archipelago. Abel Tasman continued in the service of the V.O.C., but in 1649 he was convicted of mistreating two sailors, suspended, and stripped of his rank. Though he was reinstated at the end of 1650, his reputation suffered severely. In 1653 he was suspended again after a duel with a Frenchman—"

"Lively fellow," Taylor interrupted.

"Very," I answered. "There's some evidence that he 'went native' after the duel. But he came to his senses, established himself as a wealthy landowner in the richest, snobbiest part of the colony, and died in 1659 at the age of fifty-six."

"So." Taylor folded his arms on the table and leaned toward me. "What's next? After you write this story, that is?"

"Well, there's always Flanna O'Connor." I closed my notebook and tapped it against the table. "She was the Civil War heroine. She entered a man's world, too, but for completely different reasons than Aidan."

Taylor held up his hand in self-defense. "I'd like to hear the story," he said," but I think my legs have fallen asleep."

"Mine too," I admitted with a laugh. I was still a little stunned that he'd sat through the entire tale.

The waitress—a different woman now—came over and stood with her hands on her hips. "'Bout time you two are done," she said, teasing as she took our empty glasses away. "I was thinking we were going to have to stay open all night just for you."

She slipped the check on the table, and Taylor and I went through the usual motions of grabbing for it. I caught it, but he took it from me with a no-nonsense look on his face. "I insist," he said. "It's a small price to pay for the best entertainment I've had in many an evening."

We stood and stretched the stiffness from our legs, then Taylor moved toward the cash register while I walked slowly to the door and absently studied a rack of tourist brochures. A flier from the New York Gallery of Fine Art caught my eye, and I pulled it from the rack, then gestured to Taylor when he came my way.

"Look at this," I said, pointing to an insert in the brochure. A colorful sheet of paper announced the display of a collection by the English artist Aidan O'Connor Thorne, including the famous painting "Metamorphosis."

"You're kidding," he said, taking the brochure. His eyes skimmed the flyer, then he looked at me. "Do you want to go? I'm free tomorrow."

"Okay." Taylor Morgan was certainly full of surprises. I thought he'd be sick of me by now.

Taylor read a paragraph aloud: "'No other artist—including Rembrandt and the other Dutch masters—influenced subsequent generations of painters as profoundly as Aidan O'Connor Thorne. Her varied styles and bold experimental techniques were out of keeping for a seventeenth-century woman; modern critics are astounded and baffled at her breadth of work. Some say she painted as if she had lived a dozen lives.'"

Taylor lowered the brochure and looked down at me.

"A dozen lives," I echoed. "A pauper, a pickpocket, a barmaid, a ship's boy, an artist, a lady, a beauty. She was a free spirit, a doctor's wife, a mother, a daughter of the Dutch and Irish and English—"

"A woman of many facets," Taylor murmured.

I walked past him toward the door. I wanted to leave first—no sense in having him think I considered this a date. We had

come separately and we'd leave separately, even though he had paid the check and listened to me ramble for a very long time.

I turned at the door and flashed him a smile of thanks. "Aidan O'Connor wasn't much different from every other woman I know. We all wear a dozen hats."

"What about you, Kathleen?" he called as I pushed the door open and stepped out into the night. "As an heir of Cahira O'Connor, what hats will you be wearing?"

I stared out into the street, unable to think of an answer, and then felt Taylor's hand at my elbow.

"Do you have a dining hat?"

"A *what?*"

He smiled warmly, spontaneously. "A dining hat. I know you eat—we've just had lunch *and* dinner together."

"Oh." I felt heat creeping up my neck. "Of course."

"Then say you'll be my guest for dinner tomorrow, after the art museum. We'll make an afternoon of it and go to dinner in the evening."

I looked away, mentally rehearsing a hundred reasons why I couldn't go. I had to wash my hair. I had to scrub the dog. I needed to finish a book. I didn't want to get involved with anyone right now....

And then I heard myself saying, "That would be nice, Taylor."

He smiled and walked backward for a few steps as he waved good-bye. "Great. I'll see you tomorrow. Shall I meet you at the museum?"

I grimaced when he nearly collided with an elderly woman on the sidewalk. She frowned and sidestepped to avoid him, then continued on her way, muttering about the foolishness of youth.

"Four o'clock?" I suggested.

"Let's make it two." He stopped beside a streetlight and shot me a grin. "Unless you think you'll be tired of my company by dinnertime."

Not hardly, I thought, but I didn't say that to him. "Okay. Two it is. I'll meet you there."

I turned and walked down the sidewalk, knowing without looking that he was still standing beneath that streetlight, waiting to see me safely into a cab.

Fortunately I have a fair amount of pride. I didn't look back for at least half a block, when a taxi finally stopped.

I was right. He stood there watching.

References

Historical information for this book came from the following sources:

Anderson, R. C. *The Rigging of Ships in the Days of the Spritsail Topmast, 1600–1720.* New York: Dover Publications, Inc., 1994.

"Background to Tasman's Two Voyages: 1642 and 1644." Found at Internet website: http://pacific.vita.org/pacific/dutch/tasman.htm.

Fellows, Miranda. *100 Keys to Great Watercolor Painting.* Cincinnati: North Light Books, 1994.

Johnson, Donald S. *Phantom Islands of the Atlantic: The Legends of Seven Lands That Never Were.* New York: Walker and Company, 1994.

Loscutoff, Lynn Leon. *A Traveler's Guide to Painting in Watercolors.* Rockport, Mass.: Quarry Books, 1996.

Novaresio, Paolo. *The Explorers, from the Ancient World to the Present.* New York: Stewart, Tabori & Chang, 1996.

Poortvliet, Rien. *Daily Life in Holland in the Year 1566 And the Story of My Ancestor's Treasure Chest.* New York: Harry N. Abrams, Inc., 1992.

Schama, Simon. *The Embarrassment of Riches: An Interpretation of Dutch Culture in the Golden Age.* New York: Alfred A. Knopf, 1987.

Turner, Don. *Maverick Guide to Bali and Java.* Gretna, La.: Pelican Publishing, 1995.

Whitfield, Peter. *The Charting of the Oceans: Ten Centuries of Maritime Maps.* Rohnert Park, Calif.: Pomegranate Artbooks, 1996.

The Heirs of Cahira O'Connor
Book 3

꧁꧂

The Velvet Shadow

Prologue

꧁꧂

Six months passed before I saw Taylor Morgan again. What had seemed at the outset to be a promising relationship faded like the colors of autumn when the fall semester began. As the oak leaves in Central Park toasted golden brown, Taylor's schedule picked up its pace, and I too stayed busy with schoolwork and my part-time job at the bookstore.

I've never been one to mourn the passing of what could have been a promising relationship. When Jeff Knave broke my heart in the ninth grade, I decided then and there that if a guy couldn't see that I was something special, I'd say good-bye with no regrets. Not that I think I'm more special than anyone else, mind you. But if a thing is not meant to be, I figure it's just not part of God's infinite plan.

So I moved on, and I buried my fascination with Cahira

O'Connor and her descendants with as much determination as I put away my interest in Taylor Morgan. When I had researched Anika of Prague, I'd been giddy with enthusiasm, and I had been thoroughly infatuated with Taylor while I investigated the story of Aidan O'Connor. But since Taylor had drifted away, so had my eagerness for the work of reading, researching, and writing. I hadn't even thought about Cahira O'Connor in several weeks because thinking about her reminded me of *him*...

I was surprised, then, to find Taylor sitting on the steps of my apartment building one afternoon just before Christmas break. He wore a heavy overcoat with the collar turned up against the wind, and for a split second my adrenaline surged at the sight of a stranger at my apartment door. But then those blue eyes flashed in my direction, and my knees turned to water.

"Hello," Taylor said, his voice faintly muffled by the collar and the scarf at his throat. "It's good to see you, Kathleen."

I pressed my lips together and hoped he wouldn't notice that my cheeks were burning. "Taylor? What on earth brings you here?"

He flashed me a brief smile and clapped his gloved hands together. "I just happened to be in the neighborhood."

That was a lie, and we both knew it. Taylor divided his time between his apartment and the college, and both were located on the upper West Side. Taylor wouldn't come to the Village unless he really wanted to see me.

I shifted my grocery bag from one hand to the other, not exactly sure what I should say next. After a brief season of dating last summer, we'd gone our separate ways. So, did friendship require that I invite him in for a cup of coffee, or should I be truthful and tell him that my Chaucer class met in half an hour?

I looked away from those compelling blue eyes and remembered my resolution to forget him. "Taylor, it's good to see you, but—"

He cut me off with an uplifted hand. "Kathleen, I didn't come

here to intrude." His voice deepened in apology. "But I thought you should know about the professor."

"Professor Howard?" I smiled, remembering the soft little man who had first introduced me to the legend of Cahira O'Connor. He'd set me on one of the great quests of my life. "What's the professor up to these days? Did he earn another doctorate?" I pasted on a look of exaggerated astonishment. "No—don't tell me, they've just awarded him the Nobel Prize!"

My voice dripped with sarcasm, and inwardly I cringed. I was behaving like a jilted lover, but Taylor Morgan had never made any promises, never said anything to imply that we were more than just friends. So why was my heart pounding like a kettle-drum?

Taylor stood and jammed his hands into his coat pockets, then lowered his gaze to the sidewalk. "Professor Howard is dead, Kathleen."

A curious, tingling shock numbed my brain. The professor couldn't be dead. I'd had lunch with him just six months ago, and he'd looked fine. And he wasn't old, certainly not more than fifty-five or so. "Dead?" I forced the words through my tight throat.

"He'd been having heart problems." Taylor's square jaw tensed. "I found him in his office this morning. He was sitting there with his head on his desk, and his hand was resting on this." Taylor pulled a manila envelope from the pocket of his overcoat and handed it to me.

I frowned at the sight of my name printed in the professor's neat handwriting. In the center of the envelope, beneath my name, was another: Flanna O'Connor. Cahira's last heir. The one I'd relegated to a mental back burner and hoped to forget.

Caught up in a vague sense of unreality, I looked at Taylor. "What does this mean?"

"I'd like to come in and tell you about it." Taylor glanced down at his shoes again. "It was important to the professor, so I thought you ought to know. If you have a few minutes to spare."

My heart twisted in compassion as I studied his face. Taylor Morgan usually looked like a confident, dashing young intellectual, but the sorrow in his countenance today revealed how much he'd thought of his teacher. And no matter how disappointed I was that Taylor and I had never developed a romantic relationship, he was still a friend.

I made a mental note to borrow notes from the girl who sat next to me in Chaucer class. Being here with Taylor was far more important than studying *The Canterbury Tales.*

"Come on in." I tucked the envelope beneath my arm and climbed the steps. After unlocking the door, I led the way inside and pointed toward the sofa in the living room. "I'll be with you in just a minute," I called, carrying my groceries to the kitchen. "Let me get us something warm to drink, and then you can tell me all about it."

Taylor moved silently past me toward the sofa. And as he passed, I thought I saw a shimmer of wetness on his cheek.

Ten minutes later I had two steaming cups of tea on the coffee table and the professor's envelope in my hands. Barkly, my guardian mastiff, had given the package a perfunctory sniff and then stretched out beside the window, content to watch our guest from a cautious distance.

Taylor sat on the sofa and picked up his mug. He held it with both hands, all signs of false cheer gone from his eyes. He looked like a man who'd just lost his best friend, and I realized I had underestimated the bond between the older man and his protégé.

"I'm very sorry about the professor," I said, sinking into the wing chair facing him. I wanted to reach out and pat his arm but felt too awkward to attempt it. "I know he meant a lot to you."

"He was like a father." Taylor's gaze moved from me to the carpet. "Forgive me if I seem addled. I suppose I'm still in shock. This day has been a nightmare, with the questions and all the arrangements." A muscle clenched along his jaw. "I have to handle everything; Professor Howard had no family. He never married, and his parents are deceased."

"How awful. How did you know what to do?"

"I found an envelope at the front of his filing cabinet, and in it were all his last requests. His library is to be donated to the college, his personal effects are going to Goodwill, and he wanted his body cremated. He wanted no memorial service, no fuss."

I couldn't help frowning. "Sounds awfully Spartan."

"That's what he wanted." Taylor's gaze shifted to the envelope on my lap, and his icy blue eyes seemed to thaw slightly. "Since that package was on his desk, I thought he might want you to have it as soon as possible. It looked to me like he was clutching it when he died."

A tumble of confused thoughts and feelings assailed me as I looked at the wrinkled package. Though the envelope looked new, it had picked up the smell of musty paper and old attics. It bulged at the sides, straining to fit around whatever the professor had slipped inside.

"What do you suppose it is?" I asked, almost afraid to open it. "He wasn't still checking up on Cahira O'Connor for me, was he?"

"He may have been." Taylor stretched one arm along the back of the sofa as he shifted to watch me. "I know he was disappointed when I told him you hadn't mentioned anything about plans to work on Flanna O'Connor's story. I know he was most curious to learn as much as he could…as quickly as he could."

My blood ran thick with guilt. I had not even begun to work on Flanna O'Connor, reasoning that two novel-sized manuscripts on the O'Connor heirs was more than enough research for one lifetime. After all, I had a job, college classes, and a *life*, for heaven's sake. And though the professor had been fascinated by the story of Cahira's deathbed prayer, I didn't really want to believe I was one of her long-lost relatives. The first time I met him, the professor had been quick to point out that all Cahira's noteworthy heirs had red hair with a piebald white streak, just like mine. But surely that was coincidence, the whim of chance, or a one-in-every-two-hundred-years caprice of nature.

"Aren't you going to open it?" Taylor's voice, though quiet, had an ominous quality that lifted the hair on my arms.

"I know what this is about," I said, flipping the envelope. "Professor Howard thought that I was—that I *am*—one of Cahira's descendants. Just because I have red hair with a white streak, he is—*was*—convinced that I'm going to do something of earth-shattering importance with my life. Well, I'm not. I'll be lucky if I get a job at a newspaper. I'm no hero; I'm just me. I told him several times that I was only the writer, the one who could chronicle the stories of Anika and Aidan and—"

"But you stopped before the job was done." His tone rang with a strong suggestion of reproach.

I opened my mouth to give him a sharp answer, then thought better of it. No sense in explaining that I was tired of reading and writing and research. People like Professor Howard and Taylor Morgan never wearied of such things. Taylor would rather spend the evening in a library than at a movie; maybe *that* explained why we never progressed past friendship.

"I'm sorry." I offered the words as a heartfelt and belated apology to Professor Howard. "If I had known he wanted to know— that he only had a few more months…"

"Open it," Taylor urged, his voice flat.

My fingers trembled as I undid the clasp and slid the envelope's contents into my lap. The envelope contained a book, its leather cover brittle and clouded with age, and a single sheet of letterhead stationery from New York University. I recognized Professor Howard's tidy penmanship immediately.

My very dear Miss O'Connor, you may never know how gratified I was to learn of your work on the biographies of Anika of Prague and Aidan O'Connor! Taylor read your first manuscript and sat through what I understand was an invigorating depiction of your second, and he is most complimentary of you and your efforts. Kudos to you, my dear; you have done excellent work.

I also understand that you have taken a sabbatical from your work on the O'Connor descendants. While I can understand your need for a change of pace, I begin to fear for you, Kathleen. With every sunset, we are brought closer to the new millennium, and you must face the dawning of the next century as an heir of Cahira O'Connor. I cannot begin to imagine what wonders and terrors the next century will hold, but I know you will not meet the challenge unprepared. Through your work, I trust you have acquired Anika of Prague's spiritual strength and Aidan O'Connor's creative joy. I pray you will exhibit both of these qualities as you face your future.

There remains only Flanna O'Connor of the nineteenth century. I confess I was afraid you might begin your study of this young woman on a day when I would be unable to aid you, so I have done a bit of research to help you make a good beginning. We are fortunate, you see, for journal keeping was a favorite pastime of women in the Victorian era, and our Flanna was no exception. God has smiled upon us. Enclosed is Flanna's journal, which I discovered in a Boston museum and purchased for your use.

I would not send you into the future unprepared, Miss O'Connor. You are but two-thirds equipped for the task that lies ahead of you. Take then Flanna's journal, and glean from it the lessons you can. And know that I bear every good wish for your happiness and success in your endeavors.

With great affection and every prayer for God's blessing,

Henry Howard

"He bought this…for me?" I dropped the letter on the coffee table and ran my hand over the rough journal, inhaling the scents of age and dust. If the book had come from a museum, the professor must have paid a high price. Astounding, the thought that he'd do something like that for me.

"I believe," Taylor's mouth tipped in a faint smile, "that the professor had begun to think of you as a daughter. He often spoke

of you, and he cherished the few notes you sent him about your research."

The few notes. I cringed, wishing I'd made more of an effort to stay close to the professor. Months ago when we first met, I had thought him an eccentric old man with a naughty penchant for redheads. Later I'd discovered he was a brilliant history professor with more compassion than the rest of my teachers put together.

Once he learned that the heirs of the Irish princess Cahira O'Connor were linked by a common thread, the professor grew terribly concerned for me. On her deathbed, Cahira begged heaven to allow her descendants to fight for right in the world, and thus far each woman who had inherited her red hair and white streak had also been bequeathed an unusual destiny. Anika of Prague, who lived in the fifteenth century, became a knight and fought against spiritual corruption in the Bohemian Hussite wars. Aidan O'Connor disguised herself as a common sailor to flee the corruption of Dutch Batavia's wharf and later became a world-famous artist and philanthropist. And Flanna O'Connor...

My mind darted back to the single bit of information I'd gleaned from the World Wide Web: Flanna O'Connor, a nineteenth-century Charleston woman who disguised herself as a soldier and fought in the Civil War at her brother's side. Commonly known as the Velvet Shadow, she was as well known for her ability to rescue wounded comrades from behind enemy lines as for the singular pale streak which ran through her red hair.

Now I held the Velvet Shadow's diary. I shivered at the thought, then turned the book and rifled through the pages. Line after line of a flowery script filled the yellowed leaves, the ink faded but still legible.

"I don't know how complete the journal is." Taylor tapped his fingers upon his knee in a meditative rhythm. "But surely there's enough material to get you started. And I must say that I agree with Professor Howard in the notion that you've no time to waste. It's nearly Christmas, with the new year not far behind." He leaned

toward me, his eyes soft with compassion and kindness. "What will you do, Kathleen, if you're confronted with some great calamity in the near future?"

"Do you really believe I might be?" I gave him an uncertain smile. My heart warmed to think that Taylor Morgan cared, but I couldn't help feeling a little disconcerted by the knowledge that he feared for my future.

"I don't know what tomorrow holds," Taylor said, rubbing a hand over his face, "and neither did the professor. But he had a great instinct for knowing how people would react in a time of trial, and you must admit that Cahira's heirs rose triumphantly to face their unique challenges." A faint line deepened between his brows as he sorted through his thoughts. "The professor would never claim to be a fortuneteller, but he often said that each age holds its own trials—each decade, for that matter, suffers from its own troubles. The Vietnam War dominated thinking in the seventies, terrorism influenced the eighties, natural disasters made news in the nineties. The coming decade will hold its own tragedies, and how do we know that you will not find yourself involved in something of vital importance? Professor Howard wanted to be sure you'd be prepared for whatever might come your way as an heir of Cahira O'Connor."

I lowered my gaze, then tucked my legs under me, making myself comfortable in the wing chair. While Taylor sipped his tea, I opened the journal's cover and turned a few pages.

The first entry was dated December 24, 1860. A slanting feminine hand had written,

This book is such a lovely gift! Roger Haynes never ceases to surprise me! Tonight I dined with Mr. Haynes and his mother at their fine house in Beacon Hill, and my homesick heart was greatly cheered by their merrymaking and many kindnesses to me. I could almost stop missing Papa, Wesley, and Charleston, but every time the wind blows I find myself

listening for the pounding of waves on the bulkheads, the chattering of palmetto leaves, and Wesley's boisterous laughter. How strange it is to celebrate Christmas so far from home!

Engrossed in spite of myself, I read on.

He had struck a nerve, yet the flame of defiance still burned strong in her eyes. Schuyler waited in silence for her to collect her thoughts, marveling at the persistence of the creative spirit within her. From the looks of her patched skirt and faded bodice he surmised that she had spoken truly when she said she had no money for art supplies. Yet she had found a way to create with a blank building and a chalky island rock.

"There is more to it than you realize," he murmured when she looked up and her gaze met his again. "Art and insight come from the creative Spirit. Almighty God has given you a gift, and I have seen the depth of the gift within you. I would be neglecting my responsibilities to God himself if I did not help you as much as I am able."

The girl met his gaze evenly. "I don't care much about God these days," she answered, "but I know a lot about life. I've lived six years in that tavern, Heer Van Dyck, and I've seen things that would make a gentleman like you shudder. But I want to be an artist. If being a good artist can take me away from the tavern, I'll do anything to learn."